"Joy in the joyous Delphic god…"
— Dante–The Paradiso

"Even thy name is as a god,
Heaven…!"
— Shelley—Ode to Heaven

"And God made the firmament
and divided the waters which were
under the firmament from the
waters which were above the
firmament; and it was so."
— Genesis 1-7

"Sink or swim—
You got fins!"
— Song, the dolphin

PART I: THE PROJECT

CHAPTER ONE
THE DOLPHIN

Dr. Michael Hope sat on the edge of the tank, Aqua-lung on, flippers hanging over the side. He could hear Cloe laughing in the water, waiting for him. He held his face mask, then rolled into the pool. The bubbles sounded instantly and he breathed easily. I could almost live down here now, he thought. Indeed, he had spent so much time under water lately he felt sure it was becoming his second home. He moved effortlessly forward, his legs pumping the flippers rhythmically.

Cloe caught up to him immediately. Hello sweetheart! he thought. He patted the side of her face. He looked at the underwater observation window and saw his colleagues intently watching him. And Cloe. He waved at them. They smiled and waved back.

Are you ready for your session today, Cloe?

Cloe seemed to become more excited than ordinary (if possible! he thought) and shoved her head under his arm.

So now you're a mind reader too.

He noticed as the work progressed that increasingly he would find himself simply admiring Cloe rather than gathering data as his scientific mind told him should. But there was a poetry and a music here that could not be ignored. This creature was more than animal, he often told himself, and much more than a specimen—Cloe was his friend.

Michael reached out and petted the dolphin, feeling again Cloe's soft sensitive skin. What a miracle her skin is! he thought. Smooth, soft, rubbery, it helps her swim faster than she really should—at least according to hydrodynamic theories. It was believed ultra smoothness combined with blubber oiliness cut the resistance of water next to the skin, while extremely powerful and sensitive muscles conformed it exactly to the flow.

Marvelous!

And whenever he touched her like this and felt again the velvetness of her, he could easily understand why they loved so to caress one another as they swam.

Cloe nudged him, scurrying like a kitten, circled him several times, nudged him again, then broke the surface, breaking the water for a dive, then back down to him. I think she's trying to tell me she loves me, he said to himself.

Cloe looked at him, he looked at her. What secrets do these creatures hide, he asked himself again. They want us to understand, almost pleading with us to. Are you really only children? Sea children. They would rather play with a small child than an adult, this is well known.

Powerful yet gentle children: he knew dolphins have more power in proportion to the weight of their muscles than any other animal—truly the princes and princesses of the sea!

But why do you love us so? he mused. There had never been a recorded instance of a dolphin biting a man or woman. Never. Not even while being killed or tormented by a human being. When he thought how a dolphin could easily bite a six foot barracuda in two with those smiling jaws…! It's as though the love you feel for us overrides even the most basic instincts of self defense, he thought.

Dr. Hope petted Cloe's head, then wrapped his arms around her. The dolphin smiled, as always.

Their intelligence, of course, was the essential question. Just what were they capable of?

The dolphin in the maze experiment:

He and Dr. Smith had developed this complex experiment to help the dolphin realize to the fullest its humanoid potential. The dolphin had to swim through an elaborate three-dimensional maze set up in the tank within a certain time to get its fish reward at the end. The maze was changed daily.

Dr. Hope entered the maze, swimming as quickly as he could, then bumped into the clear unbreakable plexiglas, changed direction, going up, then left, then up again…He finally reached the end and swam out the maze. He checked his watch. Two minutes and 35 seconds: a little better than yesterday.

He signaled Cloe. She quickly entered the maze…He watched her swim flawlessly.

When she exited, smiling at him like a school kid at recess, he again checked his watch: One minute, fifty seconds. She got her fish.

She wins every time!

Are ye gods? He wondered: Their timing is far superior to ours. And their compassion perfected—more than mankind could ever achieve, he thought. The ancient Greeks believed they were originally men, errant pirates, whom Dionysus, god of wine, transformed into the playful dolphins, forever penitent of their former lives...

And what is this smile? It seemed as eternally enigmatic as the Mona Lisa's hers.

All right, Cloe, he thought. You win! But what do you want? Only to play, please and...love.

Cloe's flipper came around and slightly knocked him back. She wiggled past him, dove for the bottom, then reappeared before his face mask. Who could keep with you, Cloe? The dolphin is the best swimmer in the world. Cousteau had said dolphins could easily swim circles around his 1200 horse powered boat.

Imagine! Thought Michael. Speed and grace.

They are more efficient and advanced, he thought, than the most sophisticated ships ever built by man. And what's more, he believed...they have souls.

Of course, the project was top secret. Even the slightest leak to the public would undoubtedly cause mass curiosity—something which had to be avoided at any cost. Dr. Hope hurried down the stairs to the basement of the Marine Mammals Laboratory on Key Largo. He was late for the meeting he knew, but as he was the head of Project Love, as it was fondly called, he could allow himself this indiscretion now and then.

He walked smiling into the room. "Excuse me for being late, gentlemen and ladies," he said, "but my session with Cloe went a little longer than expected...She didn't want me to leave." Everyone laughed lightly. They were all familiar with the friendly attributes of dolphins. Some of the women present slightly blushed. Sharon Bentley, chief assistant to Dr. Smith, watched him closely. Dr. Hope was a good looking man, with golden-brown hair parted neatly at the side. There was a boyish innocence in his eyes as he surveyed the room.

"I believe I have great news!" Dr. Hope smiled. "It is the considered opinion of Dr. Smith and myself we now have sufficient anatomical, physiological, medical and…spiritual… data to go ahead with Project Love!"

Applause broke forth through the room. Some of the people whistled, sounding uncannily like dolphin whistles.

"Of course," Dr. Hope said, "I must remind you once more of the absolute necessity for complete and utter secrecy." He said the words with such emphasis that everybody stopped clapping, whistling, and listened attentively once again. There was no one in the room who doubted the importance of his words.

"We've all done very well with this," he said lightly. "Let's not blow it now!" Dr. Hope smiled again.

Everyone laughed, some a little nervously.

"Dr. Smith!" he said, pointing to a white jacked man, "is it indeed your opinion our anatomical and surgical data is now complete?"

Dr. Edward Smith was second in command. He was perhaps the top neurological expert on the Delphinidae in the country as well as a famous physician. The grey-haired elderly doctor would actually lead the surgical team.

He stood up slowly, stepped forward a bit and looked at his colleagues. He said a simple "Yes!" A wave of applause rippled through the room.

After the meeting, Dr. Hope walked back toward Cloe's tank, thinking of his morning session with her. As they neared the culmination of Project Love, he found it increasingly difficult to stay away from the dolphins. They seemed to draw him like a magnet.

He pondered:

Why won't the dolphin bite? The muscles of the dolphin's jaw are extremely strong and they have more teeth in those long mouths of theirs than any other animal. He smiled. They don't even bite the fish they eat, he thought, just hold the fish securely in its jaw, until he swallows it whole.

So…why doesn't the dolphin bite? Is it some kind of unstated but implicitly understood moral code by which they live?

Do dolphins occupy a "real live fantasy realm?"

A heavenly realm?

What do they know we don't? he thought. They are so strong, ten times more power per muscle unit weight than any other animal. And with people so gentle. Their play among themselves can get rough at times, but it is just play and they are very hardy. With people, it's a gentle and very controlled brush of the teeth across a person's skin if pushed, but no more.

Such restraint—surely a sign of moral superiority.

Such strength! He thought a minute. Perhaps their very power lies in their gentleness:

It takes more strength to be kind to one another, he believed, than to kill. It takes…

"The strength of love…!"

"Michael!"

Dr. Hope stopped and turned. Sharon was walking toward him, her hands in the pockets of her white laboratory jacket.

"Yes, Sharon," he said.

"How are you today?" she said when she got to him. She put her hands on his chest.

"Fine, Sharon. How are you?"

"Cloe winked at me this morning!" she said. "I didn't want to tell anybody."

"She's winked at me, too," he said laughing. "I didn't want to tell anyone either!"

They stood in the hall, laughing.

"There's a brilliance in those eyes which is absolutely other-worldly." She looked at him.

"Like yours?"

Sharon blushed. "And her little smile," she said. "She looks like she's in a continual state of ecstasy."

"Floating in the water as though she were on a cloud…"

"Yes," said Sharon, "that's exactly how she looks."

"Dr. Hope!"

Michael and Sharon turned to see Dr. Smith, walking rapidly towards them, "Your work with Cloe has been almost miracu-lous!" he called out.

Dr. Hope smiled. "She is a genius, isn't she."

"Yes," Dr. Smith said. "An absolute genius."

Dr. Edward Smith sat in his cluttered office—thinking about Proj-ect Love. He remembered the first time he had met Dr. Michael Hope, having heard of him from Sharon Bentley, who then worked with Dr. Smith in his own research laboratory.

She had come to work one morning quite agitated. When asked what was wrong, she said, "I met someone last night you ought to meet, Dr. Smith, at a party a girl friend invited me to, a reception given by a Ms. Clair Beatrice, a very sweet and stunningly beautiful young woman, to announce her engagement to Dr. Michael Hope, the eminent marine biologist.

"Now during the party, while I was browsing through Clair's library, I happened upon, hidden back away among some books of dolphins, a diary—Clair's diary...

"I know I shouldn't have, Doctor, but before I knew what I was doing, I was leafing through it. Once I started I couldn't stop. I even jotted down some notes—as I kept looking up to see if Claire had reentered the room:

"Listen to this, Professor Smith! 'Michael took me to his laboratory again to see the dolphins. Oh, he so loves work! But it scares me what he wants to do...'"

Sharon had continued relating what she had read, while Dr. Smith's jaw dropped open. "Then Clair walked in and I quickly slipped her diary back."

"Incredible!" Dr. Smith had finally gasped. "And I thought I was the only one who could do this!

"Sharon, you must introduce me to this Dr. Michael Hope—at the earliest opportunity."

Dr. Smith looked around him in his office. Pictures and photos of dolphins decorated the walls, some peeking at him from behind calendars and memos.

How had these "animals" come to exert such a fascination and attraction over him? He was originally a neurosurgeon, who had specialized in the anatomical basis for intelligence. His long studies and extraordinary mental energy had led him into a whole range of disciplines, everything from marine biology to space engineering, and he had become a "high tech svengali", capable of seemingly performing science magic tricks, in his search for what, exactly, caused intellect.

He was inevitably led to the dolphins, of the order Cetacea, where he soon found a mystery:

Are these smiling creatures our intellectual equals? Not only do dolphins have very highly evolved cerebral cortexes, but their sonar..! We have been looking to the distant stars for signs of extraterrestrial intelligence, minds with capabilities undreamt of by man. Perhaps we should look right in the swimming pool of our own back yard—the oceans of planet Earth!

Dr. Smith knew much about the mind of the dolphin, but so much remained as Cousteau said, "a mystery wrapped in an enigma."

The average size of a bottlenose dolphin's brain is 1700 cubic centimeters as compared to 1450 for humans. Theirs is smaller in cubic centimeters to body weight ratio, but not much, and the similarity between the two minds is truly astonishing.

But there are profound differences as well, he knew. The dolphin's environment lacks the ever present input provided by gravity. This leads to major, and still not understood, contrasts between the mind of the dolphin and the mind of man.

And, their intelligence must be worked out in ways very different from hand manipulators. What is the dolphin analog to the hand and manipulative ability, he had often wondered.

In his previous work, Dr. Smith had graphed dolphin mind maps by inserting electrodes in their pleasure and pain centers, etc. He had successfully taught a dolphin to pull a lever stimulating its pleasure center after only ten tries. Few people he knew (he chuckled) could do better. With monkeys it had taken hundreds of tries.

Meeting Dr. Hope, he had been greatly impressed by this young scientist's dedication and humanitarianism to these "animals" and had become convinced his own research methods were cruel, even barbaric. He would never, he had vowed, insert an electrode in a dolphin again.

Dr. Hope too had been impressed, Dr. Smith remembered. He said he had always wanted to meet the famous Dr. Smith and they both immediately admired each other's talents, and slowly, cautiously, Dr. Hope had begun to tell him his dreams for "Project Love."

Dr. Smith had immediately felt his pulse rise, totally taken by this remarkable man. How like himself when he was young!

"May I join you?" he finally asked.

"Yes, Dr. Smith! We need the best surgeon we can find."

"Another cocktail, Dr. Smith?" Claire had asked. A tear came to his eyes as he remembered Dr. Hope's young bride. How very beautiful, but how frail Claire had seemed. "And you, Sharon?"

Dr. Smith soon abandoned his own research and join Dr. Hope, bringing Sharon Bentley along with him.

He thought again of Sharon. The first time he had seen her she was in a sequined bathing suit astride a killer whale named Namu at Marine World, her luxurious long dark hair hanging seductively over her swim top. He took a fatherly interest in this beautiful young lady who seemed so natural with the animals. She was young enough to be his daughter and when he met her backstage and offered to double her salary working with "Professor Smith," he had sincerely wished he were 20 years younger.

No matter, he sighed. Sharon had proved a most capable assistant, the dolphins seeming to sense a sister in her. And now, he noticed, she and Michael were becoming closer. Good! He thought. Just what Dr. Hope needs now that Clair…

He thought once more of the androgynous, slightly amorphous dolphin. You cannot tell a male from a female without first examining the genital slit, he mused with a wry smile. Myth pictured them as male/female entities. Do the two sexes share each other's thoughts? even emotions? he wondered.

Anatomically, he knew the dolphin's cerebellum, controlling coordination, is considerably larger than man's, enabling them to do feats of athletic prowess infeasible for even our greatest Olympian athletes.

And their cerebrum…Why they have more "silent areas" in their brains than us, for God's sake, he thought. It was believed these "silent areas", areas without direct sensory inputs and out-puts, were where contemplation took place, he knew well. So have these…"animals" passed us on the evolutionary path?

Are dolphins the—missing, missing, link?

Dr. Michael Hope walked alone among the tanks, watching the dolphins through the plexi-walls. They swam up to him, opening their mouths, grinning at him. "Hi Cloe!" he said.

He had always admired and felt comfortable with these ani-mals, even as a boy on his father's trawler, where he had watched them many times swim effortlessly alongside, vying for their favored position at the front prow of the boat. His father had a policy of never hurting a dolphin if at all possible, for he saw in them, as his son later would, their beauty and powerful grace— as they zig-zagged across the front prow of the boat.

As Michael had grown older in his studies of dolphins, he found he most enjoyed being with them alone, apart from the company of others. He seemed to reach a deep rapport with them this way.

He switched on the tank microphones and immediately the familiar but so far undecipherable whistlings were heard.

What is hidden in these "words", he thought. A casual observer would have no idea such communications were continually taking place, as above water the vast majority of dolphin sounds are inaudible to the human ear. Dolphin hearing, he knew, is incredibly superior to human. Even under water, where sound travels four times as efficiently as in air, the human ear would pick out only a few of these strange sounds. Without the hydrophone, these dolphin vocalizations would be lost.

He watched the dolphins play: They held each other with their flippers, as if in an underwater ballet. It was almost too obvious. As Cousteau once said, if dolphins had hands instead of flippers, man might have rivals in the sea.

Rivals? Our betters. The combination of their physical strength and innate intelligence would be irresistible.

What's more, dolphins have more fun than we do, he thought. A lot more fun. And they do not waste time. The only energy they expend in fighting is the absolute necessity of self defense against marauding sharks. Dolphins rarely fight each other, beyond a playful nip—or jousting contest, knights of the sea. They swim through the sea in well-organized yet very free flowing pods—floating societies of friends.

If you capture a dolphin and put another dolphin in with it, the change is immediate and dramatic. They instantly cavort with each other, whether male or female, completely free of sexual overtones. They simply love each other's presence, he thought. Dolphin's sexual lives in the wild might seem loose by our standards of ideal; any mature male can approach any consenting mature female without regard to status, and vice versa, but this seems truly based on their almost unbelievable love for one another.

And dolphin children are given better care than ours, he thought. They will defend their babies with their lives against sharks, and all sharks are terrified of them. Even the sounds they make are enough to terrify them (like Scottish bagpipes, he mused, or even Indian warhoops.)

So…dolphins are friends, lovers, warriors, athletes, parents, without peer.

He felt again as he listened and watched a primordial relationship with the dolphins.

Was I ever a dolphin? he would often wonder.

He began to grow tired from the long day and decided it was time to go home. He grabbed his coat, turned off the hydrophone, waved goodbye to the dolphins, blew a kiss at Cloe, and walked out back to his waiting van.

Tomorrow, he knew, they would be on their research vessel.

As he drove home in the deepening twilight, the red sun shimmering on the horizon, he began thinking of Clair. They had been the social toast of the scientific community, everyone commenting on what a lovely pair they made, he the brilliant young marine biologist, and Clair…A few tears came to his eyes. Beautiful would have been an understatement.

"Why, God…?" he said again. "To take her so young!"

He lay in his bed, looking out the window to golden moon lit surf pounding against ragged rocks. Michael watched a while, becoming almost hypnotized, until finally he drifted into sleep.

Then it happened: Had the dream. He "saw" Cloe.

Among ancient peoples it was considered a good sign to dream about dolphins, and he knew whenever he dreamt of them, swimming, jumping out of water, frolicking, he felt refreshed. But this dream was different…as though he could look inside her head and "see" her mind: a bright, benevolent, shining, smiling light, beaming love.

Michael immediately awoke, staring motionlessly at the surf. "Oh my God," he whispered. Would he tell the others? Could he?

"Dolphins are…'children of light!'…and I've just seen Cloe's soul."

Michael stood on the deck of the *Flying Fish,* looking over the wave tops. The water was swirling, the wind brisk. He was still thinking of the dream.

Cloe's soul!

Would they catch any dolphins for their floating net, he wondered. This was the only way they could do experiments with wild dolphins in the open sea. There! In the distance he saw the galloping herd and the *Flying Fish* quickly entered the pod, where Falco, their chief diver, finally secured one, aiming for the slender junction of the body and flukes with a harpoon of padded tongs which sprang shut when touched.

Dr. Hope quickly got into his mask and fins and jumped over the boat railing to the captured dolphin. He embraced it tenderly, and then it surrendered pitifully.

"Yes, sweetheart," he said, petting it.

Now the others were over the side, putting the buoyed net in the water, and the dolphin was soon swimming around inside.

Immediately a steady string of bubbles emitted from its blow-hole, as it communicated with the others in its pod. Several swam back and around the net, conversely excitedly with their captured comrade, but as in the past, when they realized there was nothing they could do for it, they swam on.

The dolphins they had caught had never tried to jump the net. The only reason Dr. Hope could give for this was they assumed the net, which they analyzed under water with their sonar, extended equally high above, and if they jumped they would get entangled.

The dolphin, a white "common dolphin", soon became partly accustomed to Michael's presence, and they swam around the net to help to get adjusted to it and locate the boundaries.

He petted its head to calm him down, and they swam together in little circles. The dolphin seemed more relaxed now, and to even take comfort in Michael's presence and would not leave his side.

They're so high strung, he thought. He could ram me and kill me in a second of rage at his interment, but he won't. They never do.

The strongest of animals in also the sweetest, he thought. He soon unhooked the net and the freed dolphin soared out.

They quickly took in the dolphin net and sailing at top speed the *Flying Fish* finally caught up to the herd again. They seem to be waiting for me, Michael thought. He watched them from the deck. After all the times he had observed dolphins at sea, he could still hardly believe how fast they could hurtle atop the waves. They effortlessly kept the pace of the *Flying Fish*.

How can they do this? he thought. They can't be swimming this fast, but there they are…flying in and out of the water like finned torpedoes!

He ran down the narrow stairwell to the underwater observation window. They were gamboling around the hull of the ship, undulating like mermaids. He turned on the hydrophones and listened to their high sweet cries. They turned their necks and watched him as their tail flukes propelled them through the water with an undulating, "anguilliform" motion, swaying from side to side as bubbles and water currents soared through: mythological beings in a timeless realm.

Mermaid dolphins! When they swam at high speeds like this, making their almost woman-like cries, he could easily see where the ancient mermaid myths came from.

Their phenomenal speed was still a mystery, making a mockery of the conventional laws of hydrodynamics. Nobody has ever really caught up with them, he thought—swimming at the speed of light!

As night came they turned on their floodlight and watched the dolphins from the observation chamber. Their dance was written in sequins of glowing plankton…sparkling ghost dolphins.

After they returned to shore, Michael went back to the laboratory. He walked around the corner to Cloe's tank. Suddenly his finger-tips were pressed against the side. Song was holding Cloe up at the surface.

"Oh my God!" cried Michel.

He quickly climbed up the steps to the top of the tank, frantically tearing off his clothes. He dove into the water and swam to the dolphins, nudging Cloe with his hands, trying to revive her.

"Cloe! Cloe!" Song cried.

Finally he swam back the side, tears mingling with the water on his face.

"Cloe's dead, Song."

They solemnly buried Cloe at sea, lowering her in the water from the *Flying Fish*. Sharon softly cried, as did a few others.

"I still don't know what it could have been," Dr. Smith said, sadly shaking his head. "Not even a clue."

"Maybe Cloe just wanted her freedom," Dr. Hope said.

"What about Project Love?" asked Dr. Smith.

"Song's ready," said Michael, as he walked off alone toward the stern.

Suddenly, a great gust of wind blew through. It happened so quickly nobody knew something grave had occurred before Dr. Hope was lying on the rolling deck, blood flowing his head.

"Oh my God!" Sharon screamed. "Michael!"

Everyone rushed to the body. Dr. Smith kneeled by his bloody head. "Would somebody get my medical bag over here? Quick! And turn this boat around. He must be gotten to shore! Now!"

The net had come loose in the swirling gust and one of the led weights had knocked Michael with great force to the rolling deck. Dr. Smith bent over him, trying to stop the blood. "He's in critical condition, I'm afraid," he finally said.

"Oh no," someone cried. People sobbed, putting their hands to their faces.

"Please bring him through," Sharon prayed.

The *Flying Fish* churned toward shore.

Michael felt like he was on another planet. Beings of white, misty light were walking towards him as he lay on water. Their heads seemed milky white. They're doctors, he thought.

Now he was on land, lying beside a river. He looked at the river. It was a river of blood, pulsing through like an artery. A golden lion came up and drank the blood, lapping it with its red tongue. Then it turned and walked slowly away.

He saw a deer beside a forest, eating leaves. The little deer seemed very content. His face was full and...gorgeous, as he nibbled at the leaves. Michael reached out his hand to him, and it came over and licked his head.

He sang a song to the deer:

"Oh little deer,

Running through the wood.

Oh little deer,

Being free like you should!"

He patted the deer's face. Then from above he seemed to hear, a high sweet voice. He looked up to where the Milky Way was sparkling across the sky. "We are the Star Dolphins. We are from Shine, third orb 'round Pulse. You have been chosen...Dr. Hope."

Now he was lying on a beach, looking out on a sea of white water. A dolphin swam quickly to shore and beached itself, lying beside Michael. It whistled to him. He looked at it.

It was Cloe!

The waves dashed over the railing as the *Flying Fish* churned through the water. The sun shone down on Dr. Hope's face as he lay on the deck, where the others kneeled and gathered around him.

Dr. Smith's medical bag was by his side as he worked over him. The others seemed dazed as if the accident had happened to each of them personally.

Sea gulls perched on the railing, as if observing.

Sharon couldn't stop crying.

"Will Michael live, doctor?" she kept asking.

"What about Project Love?" she whispered.

Dr. Smith himself felt he was in a dream of some kind, though completely lucid. The feeling of trying to save the life of his young friend was almost more than he, even with all his medical training and expertise, could handle. He almost wished it were someone other than himself working on Michael, and yet he would trust no one else with him.

"I'm not going to let some kid just out of medical school work on him!" he had breathed.

When they finally reached shore, they quickly got him into the back of the van. Dr. Smith's hands were almost covered with blood.

"Which of you has type A blood?"

The van roared to the clinic. "Good."

"He's speaking, Doctor!" Sharon said. Dr. Smith walked back to the table, holding the X-rays.

"Michael." He clutched his hand firmly but gently. "Yes, Michael, what is it?" The others quietly gathered around him.

"What's Michael saying?" someone whispered.

"Can you tell what he's saying?" someone else asked.

Dr. Hope could barely move his lips, but they could see he was trying to form a word. Dr. Smith watched him intently and then leaned his ear over to the man's mouth.

Finally he looked up at the others.

"He's saying one word." Everyone hushed.

"Cloe."

Dr. Smith looked again at the X-rays. His consultation with his colleagues simply reinforced his own prognosis.

Of course they had secret plans for obtaining a human "receptor." The timing was crucial. Dr. Smith had used his considerable connections with emergency room physicians throughout southern Florida, for procuring a patient with a critical head wound, perhaps a young victim of a gang shooting or a derelict with no next of kin, who could be secretly rushed out with a sheet over the face for "highly experimental, super-secret, robot controlled, cranial surgery."

It would have to be someone "brain dead" with the heart still beating, with no real chance of survival. Such a thought would not even have been considered before—or only as so much science fiction…

Now…

"Michael, I don't know much of this you can understand," Dr. Smith said. "I feel obligated to tell you your prognosis does not look promising. An unusually strong wind gust knocked the net down on you, and one of the led weights hit your head. You're on support systems now," he said quietly.

Could he hear him? Dr. Hope's eyelids blinked and then slowly opened.

"Do you understand?"

He looked intently at the man on the table. Dr. Hope ever so slightly nodded his head.

"What is your wish?" It would be an easy matter, in the name of mercy, simply to turn off the support system.

He again leaned over to the man's mouth.

Again he heard one word:

"Song."

Dr. Smith peered intently at the X-rays. It seemed to him enough of Dr. Hope's mind could be saved to allow him to remember his past sufficiently to assimilate new information from Song's. And his motor unconscious sections seemed heal-able—with time.

He looked around at the others. "We've been preparing for this day for three years." He paused. "Shall we proceed?"

"Dr. Smith," one of his assistants asked, "do you feel bad about killing Song?"

"But miss," Dr. Smith said through his teeth, "Song won't…be killed…"

Just put to sleep, he thought.

They all knew dolphins could not take anesthesiology. In order to stay alive in its watery environment, a dolphin must breathe consciously as opposed to the unconscious breathing of humans. Anesthesia "knocks out" the dolphin's conscious mind and thus stops his breathing. After years of trial and error research, and losing some dolphins along the way, an elaborate method was devised: a computerized "breathing machine."

Moving a dolphin was never an easy task. Falco and his assistants went to the pool. They knew Song would be waiting for them—with a smile.

He was frolicking when they got there. He came right to Falco. The old diver put his arms around him and they began putting Song on the padded sling. Even though he offered no resistance, it was a difficult job. "I'm just glad ol' Song's a small dolphin," he said.

This way of transporting a dolphin had been found to be the most successful. The padding was needed so a dolphin removed from the buoyancy of water would not be crushed by its own weight.

They lifted Song on the sling to the wheeled gurney, one man keeping the dolphin constantly covered with water so his body temperature would remain cool.

"I'm gonna miss him."

"So am I."

"Yeah, he was my favorite."

They quickly reached the laboratory. Sharon Bentley met them at the door.

"Hurry!" Sharon said. "Dr. Hope's still alive…but barely."

They wheeled him beside Michael Hope.

Dr. Hope patted Song's head. "We love you, Song.

"If anyone wants to pray, now's the time to do so," he said.

They were silent.

After a moment, Dr. Smith said, "Begin the anesthesia."

"Scalpel," Dr. Smith said.

"Sutures."

The cerebellum of the dolphin is so very important to this operation, he thought, controlling the co-ordination of the… "animal." In dolphins it was considerably larger than man's, giving them extreme co-ordination.

And, of course, the cerebrum, easily the equal of our own. Michael seems to have enough faith even for all of us. If anybody could make it through this, it's him. Dr. Smith had rejected using the remote control robot arms for the operation as originally planned. Perhaps if the patient were anyone other than Michael, but now he felt he needed a "hands on", a more old fashioned and time honored, even almost "country doctor" approach. He had realized the folly of using the robot, which Dr. Smith himself had designed for this specific purpose, when he had begun the final programming.

"What's the equation for 'love,'?" he asked Sharon.

He would, of course, be using only parts of Song's mind, and felt the operation could be done without altering Michael Hope's appearance.

Except maybe his smile! he thought.

Michael awoke slowly.

The first thing he heard was his breathing, very soft but very steady. Then voices, whispering. Human voices, he thought. He felt relieved. Human voices.

Light filtered in through his closed eye lids, pale and soothing. Is it play time? he wondered. He moved the bones in his hands. He noticed the whisperings became louder. Oh joy, he thought, my friends! His eyelids seemed unusually heavy. He felt a spark of concern. Am I all right? Then he remembered.

I'm Dr. Hope. But...

His mind became flooded with feelings of warmth which were conflicted by feelings of fear. But he recognized the voices. His friends. Everything is all right.

He slowly opened his eyes to the light, softly bathing him. People were bent over him. "Hello," he said, looking up at them, seeing them through the blue haze of the light. "What's the... occasion?" He laughed inside.

"Dr. Hope?"

"Yes?"

"How do you feel? Do you know me?"

"Why, Dr. Smith," Michael said. "And how are you?"

I'm a dolphin, he thought. He lightly chuckled to himself. Definitely a dolphin. "Was the operation a...success?" He looked around at his friends.

Wow! Wonderful! he thought. Definitely superior...If they only knew!

He lay in his hospital bed. The air seemed to come in waves around him. Strands of color would appear in these waves and then disappear. The air seemed fluid.

He looked at the bouquet of yellow flowers on the stand across the room. The colors would melt together and then form patterns—Like a Van Gogh painting! he thought.

The sun came in through the window as blinding white light, the delicate curtains fluidly fluttered in the sweet, soft sea breezes. Sharon walked into the room, almost a silhouette in the light. She seemed to glide silently across the floor. She bent over him.

"Good morning," she said. "You're awake now."

Michael nodded his head, gazing into the pink bouquet of her face. She straightened his pillow.

"Did you sleep?"

"All night I, uh, of waves...dreamt in the water," he smiled. "I feel a little seasick."

Sharon smiled. "It's probably just nausea from your medication. You'll get over it soon."

She bustled around the room, straightening little things. Michael watched her every move.

Dr. Smith walked in. He seemed taller than usual, almost menacing. He reached out his hand to take Michael's.

"Good morning…Dr. Hope!" he said.

Michael nodded his head. "Good morning, Dr. Smith. Is everything all right? The lab running smoothly?"

"Yes, Dr. Hope," he said. "You mustn't worry about anything."

Michael looked out the window. He would very much like to take a walk.

The sun was streaking down through the clouds in yellow shinings. He could see the silver ocean in the distance.

"Yes," he said smiling at him. "No worries."

Sharon came in with his dinner.

"Fresh sardines!" she said.

"The dolphin's favorite!"

The others walked in and stood around his bed.

"We're having a surprise party," said Sharon.

"Just for you!" said Dr. Smith.

"Dolphins love surprise parties," Michael said.

They all laughed and talked at once to him.

He looked out the window and saw the sea gleam at him.

"I would very much…to like—take a swim!" he laughed.

In the morning, Michael got out of bed. His balance felt a little shaky as he walked to the window. He looked out over the silver wave tops of the water, watching the sun rise. He put both hands on his head, and stretched his neck a little to one side and then turned and walked out.

Down the hall he saw several of his colleagues walking toward him. All of a sudden they seemed brown and were in the air, dribbling basketballs at him, sneering!

It passed in an instant and Sharon was smiling at him.

"You're up!" she said. "How do you feel?" She put her arm around him, supporting him.

"Good," he said, walking with her.

"Michael," one of the others said, "great to see you up and walking!"

"It's good to be up and walking," he said, leaning on Sharon a little.

"There he is!" Dr. Smith said, walking towards him. "And we were just getting ready to serve you breakfast in bed." He reached out his hand and Michael clasped it.

"Feeling stronger this morning?" he said, looking at him.

"Yes, Edward. I feel good this morning," he said, looking at him.

"You'll be out and about in no time," Dr. Smith said. "As good as new!"

"Better," Michael said, smiling at him.

After two months of observation it was decided by Dr. Smith that Michael Hope could walk about alone.

"Be careful," Sharon said.

He made his way to the beach and walked along the shore. The seagulls sailed just over his head. He looked at them as they flew around him. He softly whistled at them. They seemed almost to light in his hair, as if they were going to build a nest there.

Down the beach a way he saw a little boy playing in the sand. He walked down to him, skipping stones in the water as he went.

"Hi," said the boy. His hands were digging a sand castle.

"I'm a sand castle builder. What are you?"

Michael thought an instant and then said, "I'm a scientist." He kneeled down in the sand by the boy.

"The only thing I don't like about being a sand castle builder," the boy said, "is the waves always come in and tear them down."

Michael shook his head. "You do this for a living?" he asked.

"Yes," the boy said. "It's my job."

"You're a pro, huh?" Michael said.

"Yep," the boy said.

A professional sand castle builder, Michael thought. It guess it would be frustrating.

"Want me to build you one?"

"Well, I'd need a large swimming pool," Michael said. "I have pet dolphins."

"All right," the boy said. "I'll build it first." He started digging in the sand again.

"Rain doesn't help any, either," he said. The two talked of "cabbages and kings" and many things. Finally he finished.

"Well," the boy said, "I have to be going now. I have to see if any others need one built."

He picked up his pail and shovel and walked off down the beach. He looked back at Michael.

"Hope your dolphins like the pool, mister," he called.

"I'm afraid," Michael said, "they might jump back into the ocean."

"Probably where they belong!" he yelled.

Michael watched the boy walk away. He looked again at the sand castle. It was a masterpiece! Tiers and terraces, delicately supported by miniature pillars of sand. Arches and spirals. The dolphin pool in the back yard, filling with water.

"He is a pro!" he said, looking again at the little boy as he ran down the beach.

He stood up and walked out to the waves, the warm light mist caressing him softly. He saw a shell and picked it up. A tern scurried across the sand, leaving little holes behind it. Then Michael turned down the beach. Large rocks jutted up and Michael ran through them. He stopped at one and climbed up it and jumped off into the sand, holding his arms out horizontally beside him.

Maybe I can fly, Michael thought. Like a bird...or an...

He landed in the sand and bent over and picked up a long, bulbous sea weed and tossed it into the waves.

Gulls flew across the sky overhead, crying in the mist-rain.

He saw something in the sand. Michael picked it up. He looked through the hole at the end of it. It was a child's kaleidoscope. He turned the end and looked out toward the ocean, the bright colored patterns whirling by.

Then he remembered the little boy and trotted down the beach to where he was walking with his pail and shovel.

"Hi!" Michael called.

"Oh its you," the boy said. "The scientist with the pet dolphins."

"Is this yours?"

"My kaleidoscope!" the boy said. "I thought I'd never see it again."

The boy looked through it. "It still works! Want me to build you another sandcastle for finding it for me, mister?"

Michael laughed. "I haven't time right now," he said. "Some people are waiting for me. Some people at my laboratory."

"With the pet dolphins?"

"Yes, with the dolphins."

"You shouldn't leave dolphins alone for very long, you know," the boy said, looking through his kaleidoscope. "They get lonely."

Michael laughed again. "Goodbye," he said. He turned and walked away.

"Mister," the boy called out. Michael turned to him.

"I like dolphins," he said.

Down the beach, Michael saw some men fishing from the shore with nets. They were casting them into the sea and pulling them out. They had rubber hip boots on and were walking through the waves with the net.

He watched the fishermen for awhile. "Catching many fish?"

They looked at him, smiling. "A few," one said.

"Mind if I try?"

"Sure," said one of the men, handing him the net.

He cast it into the waves. When he pulled it out, there were several fish in it! leaping about.

"Hey," said the man. "Good catch!"

He handed the net with the fish in it back to the men. "Beginner's luck," he said smiling.

He waved at them and continued walking down the beach. He looked out to sea. "I wonder…"

A small otter scurried across the beach into the waves. Little birds ran along the beach, swooping into the air as Michael neared them. The waves surfed.

Then Michael saw some leaping dolphins! They seemed almost like the corona of the sun as they jumped into the air. They were golden as they flung themselves above the water waves. He had never seen such a beautiful beautiful sight.

He ran through the beach surf, watching them. He fell on his knees, and then got up and ran back the other way. He was ecstatic.

There they are! There they are!

One flipped its tail as it dove in again. They seemed to be performing just for him.

He watched them in the sea. Dolphin bliss. They loved him, he knew. They were acrobats, performing impossible tricks easily. He could almost hear them calling him to come join them.

I want to swim with them!

He had to hold himself back to keep from running headlong out into the waves and never coming back.

Like Ulysses strapped to the mast, he thought.

He remembered a song he once heard on his radio on a rainy night by the sea:

> "A poet of sound lived by the sea,
> And thru the use of magic,
> Transformed his thoughts into melodies,
> As pretty as the pale lilacs.
> And tho he was poor, he had much more
> Than many O many a rich man,
> For he had the sea and a cypress tree
> And the love of a lovely woman.
>
> And she would come to visit him
> At least once of twice weekly,

And she would always stay the day
And they would sing so sweetly.

Now it happened one night when he was alone
His magic was working brightly
He thought he heard way out to sea
The sirens singing lightly.
And tho he was sure his magic pure
He trembled like a blown leaf
For to harmonize with those angel cries,
Was beautiful beyond belief.

Lalalalalalalalalala
He sang as he had never.
Lalalalalalalalalala!
Oh return I might never!

His lady came to visit him
The next sunny morning.
And tho she looked and looked for him,
He had left without warning.

He stood up, watching them. Odysseus, he had read, had heard the mystic song of the leaping dolphins!

Michael walked back toward the lab.

Squeaking, squeaking! was all he could think of as he walked down the street. People would pass by. He would smile at them. Some would nod, some would grin. They clutched their rain coats, he thought. He was enjoying the rain. Hey there, he thought. He got down on one knee and looked up. A girl walked by and stared at him. He gazed into her face.

She bent down to him. "Are you all right?" she asked.

"As you."

"What?"

"If you are," he said. She stood up and he apologized. "You might be late for work."

She regarded him a moment. Then she backed off, turned and walked away. Somebody bumped into him. "Pardon me," a man's voice said.

"Hello," Michael said. The sun broke through the clouds and a shaft of light fell between the two men. The man reached through the light beam and touched Michael on the arm.

"Are you all right?" the man asked.

"As you," said Michael.

"Oh I'm fine," the man said "but I hope I didn't jostle you."

"Oh no," said Michael. He put his arm around the man. "All the best," he said. "Don't slip in the water." The smile. The man noticed it. It seemed filled with sunlight.

"Yes, I'll be careful."

He took Michael's hand and shook it. "Nice meeting you," he said as he walked away. "Uh, what did you say your name was?" he asked, but disappeared into the crowd before Michael could talk.

He started whistling. The clouds swirled over his head. He marched down the street. His heart was swelling with love.

Michael found his way back to the laboratory without any difficulty. Sharon met him at the door.

"You're back! How was your walk?" she smilingly asked.

"It was fine. The sky is beautiful like water. I was in the rain."

He looked at her and she at him. She had always admired Dr. Hope, maybe even loved him and would often watch him when he didn't know.

He smiled at her and could feel warmth in his heart spreading throughout his body.

He reached out his hand and placed it softly on her breast.

"You're very pretty, Sharon."

"Dr. Hope, please," she said, gently removing his hand from her. "Somebody could walk in."

The door opened and Dr. Smith walked in the room. "Well, how's my favorite patient?" he said, smiling at Michael.

"Fine, Edward, and how are you?" Michael said.

"He's back safe and sound, Dr. Smith," said Sharon, slightly lowering her head.

"Now I want to know all about your walk, Michael." He took out a pad and pen. "Did you have fun?"

"All the best," Michael said. "The rain fell down like soft honey."

Dr. Smith looked at Sharon. "You know, Sharon, I think you are right. Our boy is becoming a poet. And a good one. You know," he said again, "I always thought dolphins had to be poets. Well how do you feel? I want to know."

Michael looked at him carefully. I know you do, Dr. Smith, he thought.

"The best!" he said.

Dr. Hope, alone now in the laboratory, slowed the tape of the sweet-sounding audible whistles down to one-quarter speed and listened carefully. What a happy sound! He was beginning to feel dolphins had evolved into a state of almost continual happiness. Happiness seemed to be their predominant emotion. Anything else was off the norm.

He was assimilating more and more, ever so gradually, from Song's mind, he knew.

He listened again to the slowed down tape. It was getting late, and for an instant he nodded asleep. His eyes opened again in a few seconds. Another dream! In the instant he had been asleep he had heard the happy slowed-down whistles saying to him, as joyful as imaginable, as if they came from dolphin paradise:

"Do something! Do something! Do something!"

Michael got up and paced around the room, the whistles in the background.

"Do something!"

He got down on one knee and almost sobbed. He had the key!

Dr. Hope quickly got a portable hydrophone and connected it to the speakers (Squeakers! he thought) on the laboratory walls. He climbed up the wooden steps to the top of the tank and dangled the hydrophone in the water.

The dolphins immediately swam up to it, virtually climbing over each other in their excitement to get to it.

"Hello, Dolly!" he said to the most persistent of the performers.

They made a virtual chorus of Delphinese…swimming and tumbling over each other in such obvious joy and commitment to this object, it was hard not to believe they knew what it was.

Michael almost found himself joining in.

Their twittering patter went on and on, a "joyful noise." Was theirs a—language of love? After some minutes he put the hydrophone away.

Dr. Hope looked again at the dolphins swimming in the tank. Dolly was looking wistfully at him, her friendly, childlike eyes quietly observing him. Then in his mind, he felt drawn into the tank, staring out the plexi-walls at the people coming by.

"My God," he whispered, "we keep you trapped in there, looking at us with the intelligence of genius children."

He felt a wild impulse to shatter those walls. "But what good would that do?

"Someday you will be treated with respect. Some day you will be treated with kindness.

"Someday you'll be treated with love.

"Someday no more prisoner of war dolphins will be taken; the purse seiners and the Marine World boats and the 'research vessels,' will be outlawed and all your brothers and sisters in the sea will swim free of men's nets, never again entangled in their greed.

"Someday...your day is coming."

Michael and Sharon strolled alone along the beach. He seemed even happier today than usual, she noticed. Did something go exceptionally well at the laboratory? she wondered. He walked slightly ahead of her and once again she saw how his walk was somehow different. There was an ease and grace she had never seen before.

He stopped and turned to her and put both hands on her shoulders. "Sharon, do you want to take a dive? I've got two Aqua-lungs in the van."

"Are supposed to?"

"I want to."

"All right, let's go," she said.

They ran back to Michael's van. "Sharon…" he said when they stopped, "I must tell you, I love you." He kissed her on the mouth.

Sharon pushed him gently away, shyly looking at him.

"What about our dive?"

"Yes. Let's go swimming." They put on aqua-gear. Then they walked hand in hand into the surf.

The water swirled all around them, an aqua-blue fluid. Their bubbles danced gracefully. He swam up to her and their face masks touched. She laughed and shook her hair. It trailed out behind her. He took her hand and they swam together. She could feel his strength as he almost towed her behind him. I've never known such a strong swimmer, she thought.

She placed her fingers on his neck. They rose upwards towards the surface and then back down, intertwined their fins and twisted and turned and lay their heads on each other's neck, then swam gracefully side by side.

This is fun, Sharon thought.

On and on through the water they went, making up endless variations to their love dance. He had never known such happiness. He watched her closely and when she could see she was ready, he quickly but carefully rushed her.

Their bathing suits had long ago floated away.

They circled together through the water of love, as the fish swam around them. I am truly in love with you, he thought, truly head over heels over you, girl!

They ran out of the surf in the twilight. They had somewhere in the water lost their tanks, too, but didn't care.

Holding hands they ran to his van and collapsed laughing on the front seats.

"What if the police stop us on the way?" she asked.

"We'll tell them we're dolphins," he smiled.

They drove down the freeway, zigzagging through the cars, laughing.

The major sat in a chair as Dr. Hope and Dr. Smith walked in the room.

"Michael!" Dr. Smith began, his arm around the other man, "this is Major Swinson from National Security. He's very interested in our work with the dolphin's language. He feels it might well prove to be great national defense value. Am I right, Major?" Major Swinson stood. He and Dr. Hope shook.

"Correct, Dr. Smith. We feel you have information that may be valuable indeed to the United States government." He looked intensely at Michael. "Dr. Hope, there have been rumors, perhaps completely wild, that you people down here are on the verge of breaking the language code of the dolphins. You can imagine how seriously we are taking such rumors. Such a breakthrough could put us way in front of the Russians in the ocean warfare category. I must have your data."

I doubt very much you would understand it even if I gave it to you, Michael thought, somewhat sadly. He looked at Dr. Smith and then back at the major.

"Major Swinson," Dr. Hope began, "my research is far from complete and until it is I simply cannot give you the information you request. To do so could disrupt future work. I hope you'll understand."

"Of course I understand, Dr. Hope," Major Swinson said. "But headquarters is firm. If we have to get a subpoena we will! We must have your data and your cooperation."

Michael felt he was being backed into a corner by a shark.

Michael had learned something last night in another "dolphin dream," filtering down from somewhere in Song's mind, he guessed. He was deep in the ocean, swimming without gear. He saw a pod of smiling dolphins and for a moment he could sense a linkup between them: The Dolphin Golden Rule.

He knew of lone dolphins found so desperate for company it was believed they had been banished from their pod, possibly for violating a fundamental law. Since dolphins were such social creatures, banishment was virtual capital punishment, as the outcasts simply could not live without social contact and would usually just die.

What rule had he violated to merit this form of "capital punishment?"

The Dolphin Manifesto: THOU SHALT LOVE ONE ANOTHER.

"Major, I don't believe you should make soldiers out of dolphins. They're much too docile—except with sharks…!"

"Dr. Hope!" the Major countered. "Need I remind you I can get a court order. Do I make myself perfectly clear?"

Michael could see the Major's teeth.

The shark is the one creature the dolphin feels no love for, as it will often attack and kill their young or weak or elderly, all of whom the dolphin will protect. The dolphin will attack the shark if necessary. Using its sonar as a directional device and its great strength, agility, speed and intelligence, it will ram the shark at its weakest points, the liver and gills, with such force as to usually kill it. It was known that if a shark and dolphin fought, the dolphin would virtually always emerge the victor.

Song's mind was on the verge of panic—Shark!

Michael tensed for an instant and then charged, pummeling the man with such a fury of fists the major, even with his military training, had no chance to react.

In moment he was on the floor, blood coming from his head and face.

"My God...Michael!!" Dr. Smith cried out. For a second he looked at the Major lying motionless on the floor, and then at Michael. Then he fell, clutching his chest.

Michael ran from the room. He felt happy now: the threat was gone...

Michael took off his clothes and walked into the warm surf. (First he had wandered about and then he had come here, to his and Sharon's beach.) The moon shone on the waves, like an M.C. Escher lithograph, he thought. They're out there, he thought. He wondered if he could beckon one. He swam easily through the water, enjoying himself thoroughly.

God! he thought to himself. Newton was right. The laws of acceleration and motion can be used for the most efficient movements in water. Do the dolphins consciously or unconsciously know this? Could this knowledge be one of the factors in their incredible speed?

He played around the rocks. Never before had he felt so at ease and at one with the water. The memories of this afternoon in the laboratory had all been pushed far back in the corners of his dolphin-mind; he barely recalled them. Michael floated on his back, and then turned effortlessly and swam strongly against the waves out towards open sea, kicking powerfully and rhythmically, feeling the slightest current in the water. He dove forward into the surf, went underwater, going easily with the fluid forces all around him.

Michael surfaced again and started whistling. He floated in the water for a half hour, whistling as loudly as he could. Then he saw the curved fin. Stars sparkled all around it.

Everyone, he knew, had heard the stories of dolphins rescuing swimmers at sea. They would support the swimmer and forcefully push him toward land. This one came up under his arm, whistling immediately. He seemed to know Michael was not in trouble, and so just felt like playing.

"Do something! Do something!" the dolphin whistled.

Michael now knew the dolphin's whistling completely revolved around action. Cousteau had emphasized how different it was to study dolphins in captivity as opposed to freedom. In captivity, he said, the dolphin would become "deformed." The entire dolphin language hinged on complete freedom, as was theirs in open ocean—a language of motion, expressible only in terms of music, for it talked of social relationships as when people danced. It seemed the dolphins were continually dancing one with the other, hardly stopping except to sleep for four or five minutes every once in a while.

The two soared through the water, Michael and his friend. He twirled in the waves like a magic cowboy, a seaboy.

Seaweeds swept by his face and the brine sang in his ears. He was coming home, back to the Delphic sea.

He swam with the dolphin until he could swim no more.

The legend of the boy and the dolphin: He had seen many paintings on ancient artifacts showing a young boy riding on the back of a dolphin. What freedom he felt here in the surf! The waves bubbled up all around him but so acutely had he become attuned to the water he hardly even took any in his nose. He was taking risks he would never have before, and succeeding easily. His own strength astonished him.

Was the dolphin, somehow, just by being with him, making him stronger?

Finally Michael nuzzled the dolphin and whispered he would like to go back to shore. The dolphin immediately towed him toward land, depositing him by dropping out beneath him in shallow water.

Michael stood up and saw the dolphin's smiling head bobbing above the waves. He waved and then turned and walked toward the beach.

He knew he'd come back. He knew he'd have to.

Michael looked to the beach, where the moon shone white on the sand. He stretched his muscles and shook his head, the water flying from his hair.

He again looked on the white sand and stepped out of the sea.

Sharon had been watching him from the beach. She could see the forms in the moonlight, the man and the dolphin, and she knew it was Michael.

Michael walked toward his clothes. Sharon walked slowly towards him. "I saw you out there," she said. "Are you all right?"

Michael quickly turned his head to her. "Sharon!"

"I heard the noise in the room and found the Major and Dr. Smith on the floor. The doctor told me what happened. He passed out, but he's all right now. The Major, though, is in critical condition." She paused. "I thought you might come here."

Michael sat down in the sand without bothering to put on his clothes. He took her hand and they sat together, heads touching, looking toward the sea, watching the silky smoothness of the sea as the night water rolled, almost glided, into the shore.

"I love you Michael, I hope you know," Sharon cried, burying her face in his shoulder. "No matter what, I love you."

He ran his hands through her hair. "I know," he said. "I love you wonderfully."

They were silent for a while in the quiet and they both heard a soft whistle out to sea.

"They found us," Sharon smiled tearfully.

First they saw the white headlights, then the red one, revolving. "Oh no!" Sharon cried out, "they've come here looking for you!" A spotlight brushed them!

"How did they know to come here?" said Michael.

"Dr. Smith must be with them," said Sharon.

Michael crouched in a shadow, watching the lights.

"Sharon," he finally said, "let's go for the rocks."

"All right," she whispered. They ran for the water, Sharon dropping her clothes as they went, and they were in the waves, swimming for the moon-tinted forms off the beach.

"Stop!" a voice called out through a police bullhorn.

"You must come back to shore at once!"

They swam as hard as they could, and climbed up on the far side on the rock. There they rested, sitting on a ledge, leaning against the rock.

The golden moonlight rolled over the waves. They clutched each other's hands. Again he heard the voice.

"Dr. Michael Hope!" Then, "Michael, this is Dr. Smith…"

He looked at her and then out to sea. "Sharon! Sharon! What should I do?"

She gazed at his face and then out to sea. "Swim," she whispered, holding him tightly. "Swim!"

He took her by the shoulders and looked her full in the face. He laid his finger gently alongside her nose and kissed her mouth.

Then he stood up and dove into the water.

From the gold-bathed rock, Sharon watched Michael Hope in silence. Behind her she could hear the yelling voices.

Out in the ocean Michael was swimming smoothly, easily. He started whistling as he swam. She heard him and smiled. She saw a fin come up under his left arm. Then she saw a fin come under his right.

"Have fun," she said.

CHAPTER TWO
ESCAPE TO BERMUDA

Michael Hope rested on the dolphin.

He wondered where he was. He opened his eyes and looked at the red morning sun, shining through creamy ocean clouds. Then, he supported himself on the dolphin…and saw smiling faces.

"My God!" he said out loud. "I'm the middle of a pod of dolphins!" They were swimming slowly.

The rainbow caravan, he thought, to the pot of gold…

He felt a numb pain in his leg and looked down. Blood was trailing from a long cut into the water. He wasn't sure but guessed it was from the reefs. Michael could see little fishes swimming-swirling beneath him and the dolphins as he looked down into the sea.

Their caravan went on and on through the water. He looked toward a large cumulus cloud near the horizon. Three perfect half-circle rainbows hovered in front of him. He watched them move silently before him like a spirit parade, sparkling, colored, floating arches of glistening light.

Where are we going? he wondered.

The water easily washed over the top of the dolphin's back as its strong muscles cleaved the waves. Seagulls flew over Michael's head, their wings outstretched, calling to one another. One landed on a dolphin's back, perching itself, looking at him, cocking its head to one side. The dolphin carried the bird until it flew away.

Michael laughed a little. "Do you guys get paid for this?"

The dolphins chirped.

They glided over the green, green water.

Suddenly, about twenty yards behind them, he saw the first of a different kind of fin, which he recognized immediately. He looked down at the blood trailing into the water from his leg and then back at the distant fin.

"Sharks!"

At once he sensed a difference in the dolphins. They started clicking loudly, swimming faster. Their main concern seemed to be to get him to safety. He knew of stories where dolphins would actually put themselves in danger to save an injured or weak comrade, even risking the entire herd to do so.

He looked behind him again, noticing several of the rear dolphins had dropped out of sight into the water, turning around, swimming towards the sharks. When dolphins fought sharks, he knew, they fought as a group, whereas sharks, being too stupid to communicate with each other, usually fought alone. The dolphins were, he was sure, devising tactics.

Quickly he saw several more shark fins rise to the surface!

He remembered a story of the early days of Marineland, where dolphins once combined against sharks, and by butting them in the sides and gills, massacred them. He saw the first thrashings in the water. The dolphins were coming up from underneath, ramming the sharks with great force. He saw blood in the water.

Then Michael saw near his bleeding leg a fin coming rapidly toward him! Two of the dolphins swimming next to him turned and confronted the shark. They both attacked at once, ramming it from different sides. The shark sank.

He turned again and watched the fight.

The shark fins are getting smaller and smaller! They're driving the sharks sway!

Soon the shark fins disappeared into the horizon. The warrior dolphins swam back and rejoined the rest of the group. Several had wounds and were bleeding and he wondered how many if any had died.

He clung to his dolphin, the water around him blue and green: the color of the sea. The waves and shallows rocked, the tops white with air. He dipped his cupped hand into the water and let it trickle through his fingers and ran his hand over his face and hair, the salt somehow seeming good.

Then—Michael collapsed on the dolphin's back.

He passed out and woke several more times, how many he could not be sure, feeling like a cowboy in an old western, draped half conscious over a loping horse.

From the sun he guessed he was somewhere off Key Largo in the Straits of Florida, heading for the Bahamas. He remembered vaguely passing by little islands, but the dolphins had kept going—swimming faster.

Michael wondered where they where taking him. Then he realized.

Oh lord, he thought. The Triangle!

Among residents of southern Florida, the Bermuda Triangle was discussed with hushed voices if at all. There was a very real feeling that something was out of the ordinary in those distant mists. Kids would try to get their fishermen fathers to talk about it, but would usually have to pry it from them.

Dr. Hope knew whenever he had to fly to Nassau in the Bahamas on business or vacation, he couldn't help feeling just a little uneasy, almost as if something in the Triangle were waiting for him. Being a scientist, he had tried to disregard the stories of disappearances and unusual sightings as coincidence, or rationally explainable, but could do nothing about the feelings.

He knew was becoming delirious, and knew could not last much longer without water. "Water, water, everywhere"...He leaned over, nuzzled the dolphin's neck, then whispered into its ear. "And not a drop to drink..."

"Please get me to shore," he said.

The dolphin turned its neck toward him and whistled. "I know where I'm going," it seemed to say.

The bright sun shone down on him as he lay on the dolphin, a yellow ball of fire like in one of Van Gogh's paintings. He looked around at the smiling dolphins. They all seemed so unconcerned...but then this was their home.

How he loved them, he thought. They meant more to him than life itself. He would give his life to these creatures, he thought. They were good. They were so good.

Michael looked up at the sun again, the great gleaming ball of yellow light above him. He could almost see the thick layers of paint in Vincent's painting. It even seemed alive to him, reaching out its gold rays of celestial fire, bathing the water in pools of gold and silver in the waves around him.

God is light, Michael thought.

Then he passed out.

Michael slowly awoke. He could feel sand under his fingers. I guess I'm on land, he thought. The sun came forcefully through his closed eyelids. He lifted his hand to shade the sun.

He very slowly opened his eyes and saw heat waves dancing all around his fingertips. He immediately closed them again.

His mouth was parched and his skin felt wrinkled from the length of time he had been in the sea. He was dehydrated and knew he had to find water.

Michael tried to move but was too weak, so he simply lay where he was. Like a beached dolphin, he thought.

He started hallucinating. Or was it real? Perhaps it was only Song's mind revealing itself fully. He couldn't tell for sure any more if his eyes were open or closed. The vision was as bright as the sun:

Love, the vision said, love! Michael leaned up on one elbow straining for the sky. Heaven! Peace! St. John the Divine on the Isle of Patmos. Dolphins were swimming in the sky, circling each other. Come on! they called.

He tried to talk but could not. I must get there, he thought. He heard the dolphin's whistling together. It sounded like the "Ode to Joy" from Beethoven's Ninth Symphony. Oh glory! he thought. He tried to talk again, to yell, or scream, but the words were blocked. He so wanted to talk to the flying dolphins and tell them how happy he was now, how he was being refreshed and rejuvenated inside, but could not "locate" the words to describe his feelings.

All right now, he thought. You know something we don't, right? I know, I know—love one another. Tears were streaming down his face. He buried his face in his hands and laughed.

Love, love, love! How's Sharon? he wondered. Oh he loved her so. Would he ever see her again? The dolphins rose and dove in the air above him. O…you're circling the sun. He thought he saw Jesus and the Virgin Mary. Mary looks like Sharon, he thought. He saw angels riding on the backs of the dolphins, gently nudging them on.

Again he tried talking, singing, but nothing came forth. Then the dolphins whistled louder, a great celestial choir. The "Ode to Joy," his favorite piece of music. Did they know it was favorite music?

The whistling! He tried whistling. He could! Of course, he thought. They want me to whistle! He whistled the "Ode" with the dolphins. He lay on his back on the sand, whistling.

The atmosphere around him took on a luminous quality. The air felt soft. He reached out his hand to touch a dolphin.

Its skin feels smooth.

He wanted to tell them he loved them. He whistled a melody. They looked at him! Then it happened. He broke through. It exceeded his wildest dreams. He could communicate with the dolphins telepathically. All he had to do was think in melody!

Michael slowly got to his feet. He shakily found his balance as he looked ahead up to the sky. He walked towards the water and reached his hands out towards the swirling dolphins.

The dolphins smiled at him.

You're in the kingdom of the sky, calling me to fly to you.

If I only had wings!

The dolphins leaped up around the sun, like a fountain.

Then they seemed to fly around his head, halo-like.

Oh Lord, he thought.

He lifted both of his arms above him—in a sunset/sunrise with the sun overhead. The colors seemed to revolve. He wove his arms over him in little circles.

His legs buckled and he fell to his knees on the sand, the colors before him.

He looked out to sea.

A dolphin jumped into the air, into the sky…

He looked up again.

They danced around the sun!

Michael was lying on his side, curled in a near-fetal position, when he awoke again in the sand. It was early morning and red-sun was shining through cotton ocean clouds.

He stood up. He felt stronger now. Michael looked down at his body and saw he was without clothes. He had forgotten he was without clothes. His body was deeply tan—brown from endless hours in the south Florida sun. Patches of ocean salt and dark sand still clung to him.

Michael gazed far down the beach and saw a small thatched hut. Maybe these people can help me, he thought. He ran down the beach—his swiftness surprised him—and got to the hut and looked in the open window. There was no one home.

Against the wall he saw a pair of sandals and some pants and shirts. He ran around the hut but could see no one. He ran back to the open window and quickly climbed in, grabbing the sandals and some clothes. He found some water and gulped it down, then hurriedly fashioned a knapsack out a pair of pants, filling it with fresh fruit from the table.

Then he climbed out the window and ran back down the beach.

"Please forgive me, friends," he said.

Some distance away, Michael saw a stream flowing into the sea. He ran to it and kneeled down in the water. He drank until his thirst had finally abated, then cupped his hands and poured water over his head. He cleansed his body, and rinsed his clotted cut. Then he lay in the stream, letting the soothing water flow over him.

He noticed a trail alongside the stream. It seemed to lead up the hill to a promontory overlooking the beach. Maybe I can get a view up there, he thought, see where I am. He got up and made his way slowly up the trail to the top of the promontory. It looked over a bay. He looked out on the water. He first he thought it was a reef he saw, with churning water all around it.

Michael cupped his hands over his eyes and looked out. "It's not a reef," he said. He sat down on the grass and then watched. "It's an assembly of dolphins!"

Cousteau had once reported seeing 20,000 dolphins at one time in the Persian Gulf. He said he had never seen anything like it, before or since, in all his years of observation in the sea.

Michael estimated there were twice that number out there, a flurry of dolphins, extending far out to sea, to the horizon and beyond. They were leaping playfully into the air, leaps more fantastic than he had ever witnessed: somersaults and cartwheels, double flips and pirouettes...

He shook his head. "Is this where the dolphins were taking me? A congress of dolphins?" He watched them hours and hours, and hours, it seemed. "They're playing," he finally said. They caressed joyously as they swam together, seeming at times almost to be walking on the water as they frolicked, the sun bouncing white off the wave tops, the careening, living "reef" filling the bay...and beyond. The crescent of foam and flying bodies gleamed in the sun.

It's a love feast, he thought, a collective joy, a bridal shower.

They tirelessly romped and rolled through the water—an apocalyptic sight. The dolphins have amassed for a victory celebration, he thought, good triumphing over evil, light over dark, dolphin over shark! They were easily clearing fifteen feet as they soared and for every one in the air there were twenty in the water, propelling into space like rockets, living missiles, taking off from an underwater, liquid, vapory launching pad and then shooting through the glistening ceiling, playing, tumbling over each other with the abandon of joy, dancing together in a great, mad minuet of love!

The scarlet sun finally began to sink into the flashing, emerald sea. In seconds the dolphins disappeared beneath the water in a bubbling flurry.

Then the water became calm.

Michael walked slowly down the dirt road towards the fishing village. Two little brown-faced children ran up to him, kicking up dust.

"Hullo!" one of them shouted out.

"Hello!" said Michael.

"Where are ya goin', mister?" the other one asked.

"Well," he said, kneeling down to them, "I'm not really sure."

"Y'wanna come see our fort.?" asked the first one.

"Where's your fort?" asked Micheal.

"There," the little boy said, bending his back backwards a little and pointing.

"In the bush?" Michael said.

"Unh humh" the boy said.

"We'll show you!" said the little girl with pig-tails.

Michael stood up and looked down the road to the village. He could see boats in the harbor.

"All right," he said, "let's go see your fort!"

They led him through the bush until they got to the small fort, built in the branches of a sturdy tree.

"You can go up if you want to," the little girl said, pointing to the wooden steps that led up the tree.

Michael smiled at them. He climbed up the tree steps and crawled in through the small doorway and stood up. "I think their father built this," he said. It was cool in here in the shade of the great tree. He looked out the open window and could see the beach. He looked around the fort again and saw two pillows against a wall, then walked over and sat down, leaning against the soft pillows.

The boy and girl waited for a minute and then climbed up the steps.

"Shhh," the girl whispered when they got in.

Michael was lying on the pillows.

"He's sleeping."

When Michael woke, sunlight was streaming through the beach window shining on his face. He looked around and saw a plate of fresh fruit. He guessed the children had brought it for him. Michael immediately ate the fruit, stood up and looked out the open window. The boy and girl were playing on the beach.

He climbed down the wooden steps of the thatched tree house and walked out.

"Good morning," he said to them.

"Good morning!" the little girl said.

"Hi!" said the little boy, putting his hand shyly in front of his face.

"I'm goin' into your village," Michael said. "Wanta come along?"

"Sure!" they said, each one holding his hand.

The walked down the road together, the little boy leading the way and skipping by Michael's side.

A pretty, brown-skin woman approached the little group, adroitly balancing a woven basket on her head. "Hello," she smiled. She stopped and took the basket down, then reached in and took out some candy and handed it to the children.

"Oh boy. Salt water taffy!" the little girl cried.

"Yummy!" said the little boy.

The woman looked at Michael. "You American, senior?"

Michael nodded. She offered him a smoked mackerel from her basket. "You like? You look hungry, senior," she laughed.

"Thank you," said Michael, smiling. "I could use it." He took the offered fish. He looked at her. She was wearing a light flowered dress. She seemed very happy.

"You stay on this island?" she asked.

"I'm looking for a job on a fishing trawler."

"You fish before, yes?" she asked.

"Yes. Many times. My father had his own boat."

"Then I think yes," she said. "You have a place?"

"No," he answered.

Michael felt he was falling in love with her.

Michael leaned on his elbow, looking at the pretty girl lying beside him. She was sleeping, a slight smile on her face. He hardly knew her, yet he was in love. He lightly touched her black hair, shining in sunrays from the window.

Her eyes quickly came open and she sat up, her hand to her mouth. "Oh!" she said. She smiled shyly. "It's only Michael." She stretched out her neck and kissed him lightly on the mouth. "I had very strange dream, last night, Senior Michael," she said, laughing sweetly.

"I dreamt I was making love to handsome fish!"

She took his hand and led him down to the pier to the boats.

"Come on, Michael," she said. "Capt. Jake hire you."

An old black man looked up from mending his net, his face weather beaten and sea-gnarled.

"Hello, Captain," said Marsha. "This American needs a job. He's fished before. You help him, yes?"

"Where you fish?" he asked Michael.

"In the Florida straits," Michael answered.

"O.K." Capt. Jake said, "We sail this afternoon."

Michael took his few things to the small bunkhouse beneath the deck and walked up again. Marsha motioned to him from the dock.

"Come on!" she called, waving her hand toward herself. He smiled and stepped over from the boat.

"Hurry!" she called again, laughing. She started running down the dock toward the beach.

He caught up to her. "We have a little time before you leave." She took his hand and they walked into the palms. They knelt down in the grass. "I love you at first sight, I think. When you come back—you, me, we marry maybe, Michael?"

He kissed her. "Yes," he said. "We marry, Marsha."

She looked pensively down at the grass. "Oh, I want to tell you, Capt. Jake's good man, but he got, how you say...strange beliefs. Don't let them bother you. He means well."

She took both of his hands. "You're beautiful," she said.

He nuzzled her neck. "I love you," he softly whispered in her ear.

Michael leaned on the wooden railing, looking down at the waves. The engine roared steadily in the background. Capt. Jake stood by his side.

"We sail to Bermuda," Capt. Jake said lowly.

Across the triangle, Michael thought.

"We be out two weeks. You keep your share of fish for sale."

"All right," Michael said straightening up.

"But," Capt. Jake said, "you must give part of your fish back t' the sea."

Michael looked at him. "I don't understand," he said.

"The sea witch,' Capt. Jake said. "The Witch of Bermuda! If we feed 'er fish every trip, she no eat us!"

Michael remembered what Marsha had said. Another Bermuda legend, he guessed. Columbus had written of the Sargasso Sea in the diary of his trip across the Atlantic Ocean to "discover" America. His small ship got caught in a great lightning storm and then a doldrums of no wind, almost becoming entangled in the sea weeds of this shallow sea, barely making it through. Other ships, Michael knew, were not so fortunate.

Michael smiled. "I don't believe in witches," he said.

"I've seen 'er!" Capt. Jake said. "So have all my men. She comes down from the sky when the sky turns black, and eats everything. This is why we give 'er fish."

The old captain turned to walk away and looked back at Michael. A sad twinkle came to his eyes.

"Maybe you see 'er too, friend," he said.

Michael looked back out to sea, trying to forget what the old captain had said. He squinted his eyes–Fins in the water..!

"Dolphins!" somebody yelled. A small pod was swimming rapidly towards the boat. They positioned themselves in the wake. Some started rolling in the water, swimming on their backs, caressing one another as they swam, letting the wake pull them along for a joy ride. They smiled up at the sailors. Others, smaller ones, leapt vertically out of the water, falling back in the same position. Still others rolled in the air while leaping, landing on their backs or sides.

Michael watched them happily. He winked at one of them. The dolphin immediately flew into the air, rolling lengthwise as he went, landing back on his stomach.

Then he did it again.

The dolphins soon veered off away from the *Perch*. It's going too slow for them, Michael thought. He watched them swimming rapidly away and felt a great impulse to leap the railing and go with them. He almost began crying, mentally calling out to the dolphins, mimicking in his imagination their sounds, the sounds he knew so well, when again he heard the "The Ode to Joy"—"Keep your hopes up Dr. Hope."

By sunset the *Perch* had reached its fishing ground. Capt. Jake let the boat drift, while the men "shot" the net, laying it in the water. Michael knew from his boyhood days on his father's boat that fish could see the net during the day and would avoid it, but at night they could not. The boat dragged the bag-shaped trawl, called a "drifter," all through the night. The men kept watch, played cards, or like Michael, simply slept.

In the morning they hauled the catch on board. They dumped the fish, still kicking and jumping about, onto the deck, washed them down, throwing every fifth fish back into the sea (to appease the Witch of Bermuda, thought Michael) then sorted them by size and kind, and gutted and iced them. Michael easily took to the work—except the superstition. He had enjoyed fishing as a boy and he was enjoying it again: the smell and feel of the fish, the briny air spraying over the side, the rolling of the deck, all brought back memories of his youth.

His father had been his best friend. "Love everybody, Michael," his father would say as he steered the boat wheel. "Love everybody."

Michael brought himself back, sitting on the deck. He would just fish for the rest of his life, he thought happily. Raise a family on the island with Marsha.

Then suddenly Michael remembered the day in the laboratory and the Major lying bleeding on the floor. It came back in a rush that almost made him faint. He felt little remorse, but the government, he knew, would not understand.

The government, he knew, was looking for him!

Michael was lying asleep when he heard the yelling. The boat was rocking dangerously. He made his way quickly up the stairs. He knew it had to be still day, but the sky was completely dark. Waves were tossing spray over the boat. He hung onto a rope.

"The witch! The Witch of Bermuda!" Capt. Jake cried out.

Michael looked out over the bow of the boat and he too saw the witch—a great water spout coming down from the dark sky, seeming to take on the form of a demi-woman, reaching her whirling arms down towards the *Perch* to take the boat into her great gaping mouth!

Michael did not even hesitate. He grabbed a life vest, put it on, and immediately dove over the side, swimming harder than he had ever swum in his life.

He could hear the men on the boat crying out to the witch, begging her for mercy. A dolphin came up under him! He fell forward onto it, wrapping his arms around it. Quickly they whisked away.

Michael looked behind him. He saw the water spout grab the boat. The men screamed. The boat exploded into the air in a thousand pieces.

The *Perch* vanished without a trace.

Michael was floating on the dolphin when the fishing boat approached. The dolphin submerged, leaving him in the water with his life vest.

"Ahoy there Mate! Y' need some help?" He thought he heard laughter, as the boat neared. "Where'd he come from?!"

"I'm all right," Michael yelled back. He wanted to stay with the dolphin. "Just out for a swim."

"A swim, man! We're a hundred miles from shore."

"He's delirious!"

"Get 'im in!" They dragged him over the side.

"What you doin' way out here, matey?"

"Floatin'."

The skipper laughed. "Hey, you got quite a sense of humor for a man who's almost dead. Why yer lucky…"

"My boat got blown to bits by a waterspout. I'm the only one left alive."

"Whew! Sounds like the witch herself, alright!"

"We saw the dark skies afar off yesterday…Are ya all right, mate?" said the skipper.

"I'm all right," Michael said.

The skipper handed him a whiskey flask. "Here, warm yourself up, matey," he laughed.

"I'm all right," Michael said again, refusing the flask. He looked back out to sea. A "spinner" spiraled through the air…

The next morning, the men hauled in their nets. Suddenly Michael heard a distress whistle. His dolphin had gotten caught in the net! It was still alive, though barely moving.

Michael ran to the skipper, working the wench. "Let the dolphin go!" he said. "He's almost dead."

"The bloody porpoise?" the man sneered. "Why bother. We'll kill it for fish meal." He grinned at his companions. "Get the harpoon, Jimmy!"

Michael could hear the dolphin crying in the water. "No, no!" he said, grabbing the skipper by the collar. "You mustn't kill it!"

The skipper pushed him to the deck. "Try it again, mate, and I'll keelhaul ya!"

Michael sprang for the man from the deck, shoving him in the chest with both hands over the wench. He pushed his head towards the deck.

The skipper screamed out, "My back!"

"You're breaking my heart," Michael breathed.

He stood up, letting the man fall to the floor. He dodged two others rushing for him, grabbed a fish knife, and quickly jumped overboard.

Michael got to the net, cut it and untangled the caught dolphin. The men were cursing in the background.

The dolphin seemed to revive at his touch and swam rapidly away, dragging Michael, his arms around its neck.

"Let's go after him," one of the men said, "kill the bloody loony!"

"Ah—let 'im alone," the skipper said, picking himself up. "An albatross'll pick 'is bones."

He knew at least two dolphins were supporting him in the water. He was too weak to hang on any more. Without their help he would drown. They were holding him up with their snouts.

He knew dolphins would support one another at the surface if hurt or sick or unconscious, or too weak to stay afloat. Without this help they would sink and drown. If they could not surface to breathe, they would suffocate in the water. Just like us humans, he thought. This explained, perhaps, why sick dolphins would often beach themselves, rather then dying at sea.

This also explained to some extent the remarkable degree of interdependence shown in dolphin society. They literally, at times, depended on each other to breathe. Eyeryone was your best friend.

As he turned on his back in the water, held on the surface by the dolphins, he remembered the words of a saint:

"Support the weak," the saint had said.

Michael felt strong arms pulling him in.

"Did you see how those porpoises were holdin' him above water," he heard someone say.

"I hope there's some around when I need 'em," some one else said.

Michael felt fresh, cold water splash in his face. "Are y' alive, mate?"

He nodded his head. They laid him on a rubber mattress. He felt rough hands taking off his clothes, than roll him in a wool blanket. Someone spoon-fed him some hot soup. He gulped at the soup, spilling some on his chin.

"Easy there, mate," a soothing voice said, "you'll be all right, now."

"I wonder how long he was in the water?"

"Hard t' tell."

"He looks pretty sea logged, alright!"

"Ya gotta name there, mate?" some one asked.

Michael tried to speak, but could not.

"Let 'im be. He's too weak to talk now. I better radio into Nassau. Tell 'em what we found!"

Michael's eyes came open, and he tried to stand.

"You just rest easy there, friend," the skipper said, putting his hands on him. "You're gonna be all right."

In the morning, when Michael awoke, feeling very refreshed, he started whistling a sea chantey. The skipper of the *Elegant* walked up to him.

"Good morning, my friend," the skipper said. "Didn't know if you was goin' to make it through the night, and here ya are whistling' a song!"

Michael clutched the man's hand, noting the burliness of him and the thickness of his arms and legs. "My name's Capt. Jones," he said.

"Michael" he nodded. Then added, "Captain…if anyone calls back, will you tell them I got amnesia and can't remember who I am. It's personal…"

The skipper looked at him. "Glad t'…Michael. Are ya all right?"

"I think so."

"How'd ya end up in the drink?"

"Fell overboard off a fishing boat during the storm."

"And they just sailed off and left ya?!"

"Yeah."

"Whew," he whistled. "Well you feel strong enough to work? Could use an extra hand, 'specially one lucky as you."

"Sure I'm all right now."

"Maybe those porpoises of yours'll bring us good luck." He shook his head and laughed. "Ain't never seen nothing like it."

"Skipper! The nets are full of fish. The nets are almost breaking!" a sailor cried out.

"Well haul 'em in!" the skipper yelled.

The men brought the nets in. They were teeming with fish.

The skipper looked at Michael. "Wooeee! I thought you might be good luck. When I saw those porpoises out there holdin' ya up in the water I felt lucky right away."

"Maybe the dolphins herded the fish into your nets," Michael said. He had, of course, heard of dolphins herding fish for people before. In the early '50s in Australia, a dolphin named Old Charley would appear and herd schools of bony herring towards the fisherman. And Jacques Cousteau had televised this occurring today on the east coast of Africa, where the natives call dolphins to herd mullet into their nets, and worship them as gods.

"Nah," the captain said. "Just old-fashioned good luck."

Maybe, Michael thought. From the most ancient times sailors have thought it good luck to their voyage to see dolphins. Maybe it was just good luck.

"All I know is, my friend, you can fish with us any time you like. Never seen such a catch!"

The men pulled in another load of fish. It was teeming.

"Holy mackerel!" the captain yelled. "You did it again, Michael! I'm gonna have to repair all my nets 'cause of you."

Capt. Jones. put his hand on Michael's shoulder. "I think you're about the luckiest fisherman I've ever known," he said, laughing. Then he looked at him carefully in the face. "Where did you come from, my friend?" he said. "Are you a saint?"

Michael laughed. Capt. Jones noticed a light in his eyes. His eyes lowered a bit.

"Well, wherever you came from must be a good place. Men, when we get to Bermuda the drinks are on me. Those rich Americans won't know what hit 'em!"

The approach to Bermuda was always dangerous, even in good weather. Capt. Jones had his weather radio on and his maps in front of him.

"There's a squall comin' in tonight," he said, "but we should be able to reach port before it hits."

Michael and a couple of sailors stood in the pilot house with the captain.

"All this puzzle about the Bermuda Triangle," the captain was saying, "all these disappearances and strange weather...really no puzzle. It's these reefs!

"Look at this map," he said. "See this hook-like string of islands? That's Bermuda, about 19 square miles of land. Now look out here: 230 square miles of reefs around the islands, all of which were once dry land. Imagine the kind of water currents 230 square miles of reef cause. Any skipper knows the weather at sea is related to the currents in the water. When you got great turbulence in the water like around these reefs here, you'll have changeable weather. That's all there is to it." He smiled at the men. "Really no mystery at all. But I've been through these reefs a thousand times and never grounded. And I don't suspect I ever will."

Michael and the men laughed with the captain.

"A piece of cake!" he said, looking ahead over the wheel.

"And then," the captain was saying, putting his arm around Michael, "we find this guy floatin' in the water and he's bein' held at the top by a couple of porpoises! 'scuse me, dolphins. You call 'em dolphins, don't you Michael?" he said, looking at him.

"Porpoises don't have beaks and dolphins do," Michael said.

"Well anyway, they're holdin' him on top of the water so he don't drown. Never seen anything like it!"

"Hey, that is something!" the black bartender said.

"But there's more," said the captain. "Here's the really good part. This guy brings us good luck." He clasped Michael on the back. "You shoulda seen the catches we made after we dragged 'im on board. Best catches I've ever made, man! We're rich tonight. Another round for my men, Sam. And one for yourself."

"Thank you, captain," Sam said, smiling graciously, "but I never drink on shift…"

Captain Jones leaned on his elbow, talking to the bartender.

Michael sipped his wine. He felt a tap on his shoulder. He quickly looked at the reflection in the gold-framed mirror behind the bar.

"Hello, Michael," a familiar voice said.

Michael turned back to his wineglass. "What are you doing here, Dr. Smith?" he said quietly.

"Looking for you, Michael," he said.

Michael remained silent, then said, "How did you find me?"

"The radio report into Nassau. We hoped it might be you. May I sit down?"

"Please do."

"I've rented a villa here. Sharon's there now."

Michael shot a look at him. "Sharon's here in Bermuda?"

"Yes," Dr. Smith nodded his head. "She's really like to see you again, Michael. Why don't you come back with me."

I would love to see Sharon, he thought, but shook his head.

"Not now, Edward."

"I suppose you know the U.S. government's looking for you. Luckily I found you first. Major Swinson recovered, but he's pressing assault charges and National Security has subpoenaed all papers. M.P.s could walk in here at any time."

"I'm not going to worry about it right now, Edward," Michael said. "I'm going to sit here and drink some wine with my good friends. 'Luckily' most of the 'data' is in my head. But I would like to know one thing." He looked intently at Dr. Smith. "Did you tip off the NSC about my research?"

Dr. Smith sat quietly. "…It was for everybody's good, Michael," he finally said. "The country's, mine, your's. Think of the fame, the prestige…"

"I'm thinking of the dolphins!" Michael replied angrily.

"Why don't you come back with me and turn yourself in. If you cooperate fully with the brass and give them all the information they want, I've made a deal so it'll go much easier on you. They might even drop the charges if…"

"I won't give them the information, Edward!" Michael interrupted. "Those people are all maniacs and war mongers. And besides, like I told your major friend, my work is not complete."

Edward stood up. "Here's my address, in case you change your mind." He handed him a slip of paper, then quickly walked away.

Michael turned back to his wine.

"A friend of yours?" the captain asked.

"I knew him in Florida…We worked together on a project."

The doors to the bar swung roughly open. Four Bermudian military police walked in as everyone turned to look.

"Dr. Michael Hope!" the black M.P. captain said loudly.

Capt. Jones looked intently at Michael and then back at the M.P. "Who wants to know," he glared.

"We have a warrant for his arrest." They marched across the room.

He stared at Capt. Jones. "Are you Dr. Michael Hope?"

Michael stood up. "I'm Michael Hope." The captain reached out to cuff him.

"Excuse me, mate," Capt. Jones said, "but nobody takes my friend here anywhere he don't want to go!"

The M.P. captain reached for his gun. Michael's knee flew up and caught his hand, knocking it back into his face, bowling him over a table!

The people started screaming.

Capt. Jones and his men dove for the soldiers and were on them before they could get to their holsters. The fishermen went for their knives!

Michael jumped over the table and grabbed the M.P. captain's pistol. He fired just over a soldier's head.

"The next one's between your eyes!" Michael yelled. Everyone stopped and looked.

He motioned to Capt. Jones. "You and your men take off!"

"What about you, Michael?"

"Don't worry about me. I'll catch up with you. But if you don't see me in fifteen minutes, don't wait, just clear out!"

"All right, if it's what you want."

They ran for the door.

"Captain!" Michael yelled.

The captain looked back from the door.

"Thank you," Michael said.

Capt. Jones smiled. "Any time…Dr. Michael Hope," he said. They turned and ran outside.

Michael motioned to the soldiers. "Slowly unbuckle your gun belts and let them fall to the floor. Now!

"Sam!"

"Uh, yes sir, Mr. Hope."

"You got a room that can be locked from the outside?"

"Uh, yes sir, the cleaning closet."

Michael looked at the soldiers. He motioned with the gun. "After you…gentlemen," he said.

Michael ran down the street until he found a cabby. He had to see Sharon again.

He got to the house and rang the bell. Dr. Smith answered.

"Michael..! You decided to come."

Michael's fist rammed into his nose, knocking the doctor out. He dragged him into the living room and laid him on the couch.

He ran to the stairs. "Sharon!" he called out.

He heard a door open upstairs. "Michael! I'm up here."

Michael dashed up the stairs. They embraced in the room.

"Come back with us, Michael," Sharon cried. "Turn yourself in!" She turned and locked the door and took the skeleton key.

Michael looked at Sharon. A tear came to his eyes.

"You and Dr. Smith. You make a good pair."

Michael suddenly shook his head and ran at the wall across the room, slamming into it!

Sharon screamed. Then he slammed into another wall, leaving a bloodstain. "Michael stop!" she screamed. She was trying to make sense of what was happening. Then she remembered how some dolphins they had caught would not accept captivity and would ram into the tank walls until they finally killed themselves. Michael was committing suicide before her eyes!

"Go!" she cried. She threw the key on the rug. "Just go away!" She collapsed on the bed and started crying.

Michael ran out the door. Sharon sobbed uncontrollably.

Finally, she looked toward the window. "I love you, Michael!" she cried.

He got out of the house as Dr. Smith was coming to.

"Michael!"

He ran down the street under the palms, lighted by the street lights above. A car turned down the deserted street. A cruise car!

Michael ducked behind a shrub, watching the car go slowly by. He watched it turn the corner in the distance. Then he jumped the shrub and ran through the yards.

He breathed heavily as he ran, the wind rising. He was almost stumbling, the street lights gleaming down on his face.

Then he saw the old wooden church.

Michael slowly walked in. There were lit candles on the altar, but nobody was present. Outside he could hear the wind. He walked down the aisle of the pews and fell on his knees before the statue of Mary. He was still bleeding from his nose and ears.

He looked around and on the arching windows saw stain-glass paintings of fish-like creatures.

He looked at them more closely. They were flying smiling dolphins with wings! Michael knew dolphins had been symbols in the early Christian church of the first centuries A.D., symbols of happiness, and love, and devotion—the "sign of the fish."

He swooned and fell to the floor.

Michael felt his spirit leave his body and stand, looking toward the door. He saw Jesus, all in gold, with a golden crown of thorns, walk in the door and down the aisle towards him.

Michael could feel His presence, as if He were nothing but energy: the energy of gold. Michael's mouth came open like a dolphin under water. Agape love. He knew now how dolphins must feel when they look at a man above water. Agape love.

Jesus started talking to him. "The dolphins are anointed creatures. It is evil for men to kill them."

The oiliness of their skins!

"They are anointed creatures," Jesus said again.

Then Jesus vanished.

"Wake up," a small quiet voice was saying. "Oh please wake up, mister!" He felt a hand gently nudging him.

Michael opened his eyes. A young brown-skinned woman was kneeling over him.

"Oh! You're alive!" she said.

Michael smiled up at her. In some ways he felt the same as the day he awoke in the clinic. He was looking at her through clouds, but could see her perfectly clearly. He lifted his hand to her face.

"You," he said slowly, "are going to have my son. I've been looking you for a long long time and now, here...I've finally found you!" The girl blushed.

The two sat talking in the colored light of the stained glass windows:

"I have a little beach cottage on St. George's Island." She smiled at him. "You can come there and rest…"

"We'll get married," Michael said. "Right now!"

She looked at him. "You are serious, aren't you?"

He put his hand to her face, opaque blue sunlight from the flying dolphin shining on her. "Yes! Heather. I am serious. Let's go find the priest. Right now!"

Heather smiled delightedly. "All right, Dr. Michael Hope, my fisherman-scientist." She kissed him and put her arm around his neck. "Come on!" she said, helping him up. "I know where he lives."

They ran down the curving street. The priest was gardening in his yard. "Hello, Father!" Heather called out to the old man in black and white garments kneeling before his orange tulips.

"Well, Heather! You've come to visit us from St. George's I see. How are you today?"

"Excited!" she said. "This is Dr. Michael Hope. He's an American scientist and a fisherman. We want to marry. Will you marry us?"

The Father stood up slowly and looked at Michael. "Marry? And how long have you two known each other?"

"We met this morning in the church," Heather said.

"This morning? Well…"

"Father," Michael said. "Marry us…Please!"

The Father was startled by the intensity of Michael's voice.

"All right, children," he shrugged, brushing dirt off his hands. "God knows what is best."

"I now pronounce you man and wife," the priest intoned. He looked at Michael.

"You may kiss Heather, now," he smiled.

Michael kissed Heather deeply on the mouth. He looked at his new wife.

"Let's go home to St. Georges," Michael said.

"Yes! Let's go home," said Heather.

"We received a radio report late last night," the M.P. captain said, "an S.O.S. from the *Elegant,* the boat Dr. Hope was evidently on. They said they were in the reefs in the squall and were taking on water. The last report said they were going down. We searched this morning and could not find any wreckage, but then that's not unusual around here.

"It seems Dr. Hope is drowned," he said.

Sharon Bentley and Edward Smith boarded the jet to fly back to Miami.

"I don't want to think about it anymore!" Sharon said tersely. "I don't want to answer any questions and don't want to talk to anyone! As far as I'm concerned, we never saw him."

Edward nodded his head. "I agree with you, my dear."

Capt. Jones and his men laughed heartily in the Jamaican cantina. "I think we outfoxed those M.P.s," the captain said, over his rum mug. "They think we're dead and gone. Nobody but me coulda made it through that squall alive!"

"What do you think happened to...Dr. Hope?" one of his men asked.

"Well, we waited almost a half hour for him before we left. I really don't know." He paused. "I'm not very religious, men," he said, "but I said a prayer for Michael Hope this morning. And you know what? A voice kinda said in the back or my mind: 'He'll see you again some day.'

"One thing for sure, men—we can't go back again!"

The two lived a year in Heather's cottage before the child came. Michael grew a short beard and fished on trawlers. They were happy and no one bothered them. They held each other like children all through the nights, as if what they had found could be lost at any time. They took long walks on the beach and swam in the surf and slow danced in the sand under the stars, Michael or Heather humming a tune. He watched her belly grow through the months and knew they would have a healthy son.

When the time arrived for the birth, the doctor came to their home. The doctor and Michael stood in the bedroom, by Heather. The doctor had her wrist in his hand, taking her pulse. He wiped the sweat from her forehead, then looked closely at her eyes. He suddenly looked at Michael and then back at Heather.

"Michael!" he said gruffly, "wait outside."

Michael hesitated for a moment, looking intently at Heather, and then walked out of the room.

Finally, he heard crying and was about to rush in as the doctor walked hurriedly out. His eyes were dilated. "She's having complications! I've never seen this before! Your boy is fine, Michael, but Heather is…dying. I'm…"

Michael rushed for the door.

"She wants you," the doctor said.

He was already in the room, kneeling by her side, crying.

"Heather, Heather. Oh Heather!"

"Remember the day in the church?" she whispered.

"Oh yes, Heather. You were an angel in the clouds."

She tried to talk again, but could not.

He gently grasped her hand.

"What would you name the boy, Heather?" he whispered.

"I think," she said slowly, "I would name him…Heaven."

Michael walked down to the water's edge and into the surf. Heaven was sleeping in his crib at home. He dove into the water, and then emerged, whistling…a lonesome melody…

Finally, something nudged his legs and then a smiling snout emerged in front of him. You've come! Michael thought. He put his hands on the dolphin's back. Hi, my friend, he thought in melody. Maybe you can help me get over Heather, he said to it.

He held onto its fin and the dolphin submerged and they soared easily through the water, bubbles blowing all around them. I loved her so, he said to the dolphin. She was my best friend. I'll never stop loving her. Never. She had my son.

But you know what it's like to lose a loved one, don't you, he said. He had heard their cries, when their hearts were broken. I cried at her burial. But you understand….You're people.

I feel something in my soul, he said, crying out. I dream about her all the time and then I dream about my son and then I dream about you. You always look so wise in your happy way. Do you dream about us? If only we treated you like you treat us. We'd be better for it...He smiled at the dolphin.

Michael took its flipper and they soared through the green-azure water. A sea turtle swam by, flapping its winglike fins. Let's chase him! Michael said. The dolphin took off after the turtle, nudging it with its snout. Michael dove for it and grabbed the back of the shell. The turtle pulled him through the water, while the dolphin swam around them.

He let the turtle go and it propelled away. Then the friend dolphin swam past Michael and Michael grabbed its side and they soared for the surface.

Michael dove into the lagoon again. Now a school of tiny scarlet fish darted past. The dolphin swam by and Michael patted its soft, pink belly. The dolphin looked into Michael's face, smiling joyfully.

You look like Cloe! Michael said.

You look like Song! said the dolphin.

Michael laid his arm on the dolphin's back. What do you know about these waters? he asked. You've seen all there is to see here. Sometimes I wish I were really a dolphin, he said. I think I'd even tolerate the sharks...or kill them, he laughed. They can't be worse then some people I've met.

But how nice it must be to float all the time, to soar effortlessly through the water like an eagle through the sky, to jump fifteen feet into the air and land in a glorious belly flop, to always have friends around.

Why did I have to be a human? They never have any fun. They're too stiff. The dolphin turned its head loosely on its neck.

But you're not.

Michael dove through the glorious waters. Then he climbed up on a rock. The dolphin surfaced in front of him, its mouth open. There was a fish lying on its tongue.

"Been doin' some fishin?" Michael asked.

Out to sea Michael saw an ocean-liner, going slowly by. He waved at it. The ship blew its ocean horn.

Then he was in the water again with the dolphin, careening through the green, bubbling sea.

If I could, he thought, I would live here. I would raise Heaven with the dolphins....

The dolphin zinged by his head and then floated in front of him, smiling in the water.

Heaven! Michael thought.

Michael and the child walked together on the beach. The boy tottered in the sand, his hand loosely in his father's. Heaven was three years old now. He ran up to the water's edge.

"Water!" the boy said, pointing.

"Yes, Heaven, water. Would you like to take a swim?"

Heaven nodded his head excitedly, and the two waded out into the surf. He already could swim, for Michael had taught him before Heaven could even walk.

Michael was sure his DNA structures had been altered by the presence of Song's chromosomes in his mind. How much of this change he had passed on to his son he could not be sure, but he noticed the boy took to water like no other child he had ever seen. It were almost as though the boy needed to be in water. They swam easily through the surf, the man and his boy bobbing in the waves. Heaven laughed with delight.

One day they were in the surf and Heaven noticed something swimming in the waves out to sea.

"Father!" he said pointing. He lifted his son and put him on his shoulder.

"It's a dolphin, Heaven," he said carefully. "A dolphin."

Heaven looked at the dolphin quietly for several moments, and then said, "I want him, Father!"

The dolphin soared towards them, his smiling mouth out of the water.

"Look, Heaven, he's coming to you!"

Heaven giggled with delight. Michael got down on his knees and held his son above the water. Heaven reached his hand out to the dolphin's beak. His index finger touched it just above its mouth. The dolphin turned over on its back, and then swam away, whistling and clicking, seeming to laugh.

Heaven looked at his father, laughing. "He's my friend," he said.

"Yes," Michael said. "He's your friend."

The laughing dolphin swam back to them. Michael carefully let Heaven go and he swam to the dolphin. He petted its side.

"I like dolphins," he said slowly to the merrily giggling dolphin. "I love you, sir dolphin."

The three frolicked in the water—the man, the boy, the dolphin. The dolphin swam tight circles and figure 8s around them. Then it disappeared under the waves.

"Do you want to go with him, Heaven?"

"Yes!" Heaven nodded his head with quick movements.

"Hold your breath, then."

Heaven gasped in air and then went underwater and "Sir dolphin" swam up to them. Heaven's eyes came open. There was another dolphin with it and a little dolphin zinging along! The baby dolphin soared up to Heaven while the other two watched, lovingly smiling. Heaven reached out his hand and the little dolphin brushed it as it swam by. They've brought their baby to meet mine! Michael thought.

Heaven watched beneath the water as the petit dolphin raced around him. He petted him again as he swam near.

Finally they all went for the surface.

"A dolphin family! Heaven," Michael said.

Heaven laughed gloriously as they dashed madly around him, clicking and whistling gaily.

"My friends!" said Heaven, pointing at them. All three put their snouts out of the water and then, almost as if on cue, they did backflips in perfect sync and swam out to sea.

Michael held Heaven between his hands in the water and bubbles bubbled from his mouth as he looked at his boy. He kicked his legs easily and they swam up towards the shining surface. They came streaming out of the water, water streaming off them and Heaven laughed and put his hand on his father's smile.

Then his father submerged again, holding him above the waves.

He came back up. "Take a deep breath, Heaven."

Heaven inhaled, smiling, and then they glided down through the sparkling, glittering ocean. Currents flowed smoothly by Heaven as his father swam through the clean liquid, kicking his legs easily.

They surfaced and Michael floated on his back, holding Heaven on his chest, like a dolphin supporting another. Heaven, like a baby dolphin, smiled a baby dolphin's smile, and they resubmerged beneath the beaming sea.

Finally, Michael swam toward shore with Heaven in his arm. He sat in the sand, the shallow waves gliding by, holding the laughing infant in front of him. He thought he could almost hear him "click" a little.

Michael put him back in the water. Heaven swam slowly with the gentle waves.

"Look, daddy! I'm a dolphin!"

CHAPTER THREE
RETURN

Michael stood on the sand.

The setting sun cascaded gold off his chiseled face as he looked calmly upon the people before him. He turned and walked beside the waves.

"In love," he preached, "there is no yesterday, there is not tomorrow. There is only today. Think of the dolphins! They live in the happiness of every moment." He smiled. "They frolic and care for each other as if the instant were forever."

"I love you, Michael!" a young girl cried out.

"And I love you," he said, looking softly upon her, waving at Heaven in her arms. The little boy waved back.

An old woman reached out to touch Michael's sleeve. At once she felt a peace within her.

"Friends," he said, "find the beauty of love, the truth of love. Do not despair. There is love for the trembling human heart. Watch the dolphins play. They have elegance and mirthful grace in a sea which is also the home of sharks. They do not despair! and neither should we. Good can triumph over evil, and they are the proof. So take heart in their victory and it will be yours.

"The sharks of this world cannot stand before you. You can drive them away with love!"

He walked along the beach. The people followed.

"Happiness is the way." The crowds tried to touch him. "Without it we are lost." He smiled as he looked ahead. "The melody of the heart is joy to which few things compare: like the pomegranates in the trees, a fruit of love beautiful as orchids in the forests. It is as sweet as the sweetest honey, pure as the purest oil, fine as the clearest wine. It is nectar delightful to the taste—a reward most pleasant.

"Search for this joy, my friends, so it does not elude you, for though it is obvious, yet it is hidden, and even the wise easily miss the mark." He walked beside the waves.

"Observe the playful dolphins, swimming in the sea. They share the happiness of heaven. Why can't we?"

He gestured toward the ocean. "They are there, my friends. Take your boats and go find them. Look at the smile of the bottlenose! Watch him frolic in the heights of ecstatic happiness and joy. The dolphins love you, friends. Just for your own sake, with no thought of reward.

"It is plain to see, it is a mystery. It is all over their faces. They are the happiest of creatures…and they want to touch you."

Michael looked toward the waves and the setting sun. A golden dolphin at once leaped into the air. The people gasped and oohed.

He looked back at the people, smiling. "They can hear us," he said.

A little child ran up to Michael and put her arms around his legs. "I love you, Mr. Dolphin," she said. The crowd laughed.

Michael laughed. He knelt down to her. "You love the dolphins, don't you?"

She quickly nodded her head. "Yes," she said. She looked up at him, smiling.

He lifted her up. "Think of the children. They need so much love.

"Oh brothers and sisters," he cried, "feel the spirit! Let it open the path to the ocean of love!"

Somebody pointed out to sea. "Look! Dolphins in the waves."

Michael and the people looked toward the water. There was a small pod of dolphins playing in the distant surf, leaping high into the air.

"Yes!" said Michael, "and they are leaping for joy, just as we should leap for joy. Yes, my dolphin friends, leap for the sky, leap for the clouds, then immerse yourselves again in holy water. Swim gently in the waves amongst the pearls of the coral. Frolic in the seaweeds in the reefs. Chase the little seahorses and gently nudge them.

"Have fun and play. Yes, have fun and play."

Pastor Martin Otis came and sat by Michael on the beach and looked out to sea. The people had dispersed. Michael was twirling a stick in the sand, to the delighted laughing of his son.

"Michael," the big black preacher softly.

"Yes, Martin?"

"I am concerned for you," he said slowly.

Michael looked up at him, his blue eyes shining. "Why, Martin?"

"The crowds...they're too big!"

"These people are my friends, Martin. I cannot forsake them now." Martin looked at him. His eyes seemed white with light. "They are barely floating. They are almost drowning. I must keep them afloat as long as I can."

"All these healings...The rumors are flying."

"I do not heal anybody, Pastor. The dolphins help them to heal themselves."

"Yes, but Michael, the rumors..."

"Are there not twelve hours in the day? Do you not work when there is light?"

"I've read the Bible!"

"So have I, Martin." He reached out to him. "If the people did not need me, they wouldn't come, would they? I want to help them help themselves. And so do the dolphins."

Michael walked with Heaven by the sea. The crowds were present once again.

"We must love another, and nurture the beauty in each of us. Let your light shine as a beacon for the lost. Reach out to a stranded soul. Serve those who cannot serve themselves, and befriend those who have no friends.

"And tell them of the dolphin. Do not be afraid. If they have ears to hear, they will hear gladly. And it they will not, only shake the dust off their heels, for such have thick hearts." He walked through the surf.

"The dolphin has muscles strong enough to walk on water, ears keen enough to hear your thoughts...love pure enough to melt your heart.

"Observe them, my friends, and you witness the spirit, frolicking like a child."

He started singing a song:

"I know there is a place for me
Above this earthly realm—
I know there is a place for me
Where I will someday dwell.

When my Lord comes I know he will
Take me up in his arms
And lay me down beside a spring
Where I will know no harm.

Angels too will comfort me,
And help me find the way,
And God will dwell eternally
And shine as bright as day!"

The officer grinned at the colonel: "We've been receiving interesting reports from Bermuda, of a man, a preacher, who's been attracting large crowds on the beaches over there, preaching love and…dolphins. Seems he thinks dolphins are God's chosen angels. Rumors of miraculous healings are circulating, and some of the people believe he's a prophet or Biblical messenger.

"Here's the punch line. Remember Dr, Michael Hope? We thought he drowned. Seems he's been living as a fisherman on St. George's Island all these years and married a native girl and has a small son. His wife reportedly died in childbirth.

"What would have done with him, Colonel?"

Michael held Heaven in his arms, alone, walking in the surf. He kissed him on the cheek. "See dolphins out there, Heaven?" The boy laughed happily. "You'll swim with them soon now."

Out of the corner of his vision, Michael suddenly saw the helicopter gunship, whirling toward the beach. He spun like a Greek Olympian discus thrower and flung Heaven out into the sea.

"Dive, Heaven!" he yelled. "Dive deep!"

As Heaven cut the water, machine gun bullets splattered the shoreline, knocking Michael into the surf, raising a cloud of sand and spray!

People ran yelling out onto the beach as the helicopter vanished into the distance. They saw Michael in the water, floating in his own blood.

"It's the doctor, the doctor!" they yelled.

"They kill him!"

"Oh no!"

"Wait…! Look!"

"Riptide?"

"No! Dolphins—they carry the doctor out to sea!"

"Look!"

"What is it!?"

"A sign!"

"There…It's Heaven!"

"Now look! He dove under—down into the green light!"

"Where did he go?"

"With his father Michael!"

They all watched in silence.

Heaven surfaced! He was sitting on a dolphin!

"Heaven!"

A young girl swam out. She picked Heaven up and cradled him in her arms. Heaven turned his head and looked back towards the disappearing greenish light. The girl carried him slowly through the wind-swept water. Then Heaven was on the beach, the people around him, some wailing, some laughing:

"They try to kill Dr. Dolphin, but cannot!" one man joyously sang.

"The dolphins come and take him away!" another sang out.

The people danced on the sand with Heaven in the center, whirling dervishly around him.

The colonel read the CIA report of the assassination of Dr. Michael Hope on the beach at Bermuda.

He slowly laid the report down on his desk. Then he stood up and crashed through his ten story window.

The people bowed their heads. Above it was cloudy; rain fell drearily. The boat rocked in the waves.

"Friends," Pastor Otis said, "we are here today to pay tribute to Michael Hope, a shining star, who meant more to us than we can ever say."

"Amen!"

"He taught us a gentle way, the way of the dolphin, those creatures he loved so much."

"Hallelujah!"

"Michael had spiritual strength our mind alone can never fathom. He was with us—yet belonged to another world."

"Amen!"

"Hallelelujah!"

"Michael has returned now to his other home—the spiritual sea!"

"Right, Brother!"

"We have witnessed a miracle—but lost our friend."

Heaven buried his face in the dress of the pastor's wife, crying softly.

"Maybe he come back!" someone yelled. Voices echoed.

The pastor choked up for an instant. The wife lifted the boy in her arms. Pastor Otis continued. "We may never understand what we have witnessed, but we believe Dr. Michael Hope is in peace! And now," he said, "let him be in peace!" He crossed himself. "In the name of the Father, Son, and Holy Ghost—Amen!"

They threw flowered garlands into the sea.

"Amen!"

Heaven started scrambling and crying, trying to get to the water. "Hold him, hold him!" the pastor said, looking at his wife.

If he could have, he would have followed his father in.

The townspeople raised Heaven, and took care of him. The Pastor Otis and his wife became his legal guardians, but he was off visiting others much of the time.

When he turned seven, he started going with the men on their trawling boats. He would be a fisherman, like his father.

Often on the boats he would watch the dolphins play in the bow wave. He would jump up and down and point over the railing, laughing joyously. "Look, dolphins, dolphins!"

"Yes, Heaven." the men would say, "dolphins."

Once he walked into the pilothouse. "Captain, sir," he said.

"Yes, Heaven" the skipper said.

"I just saw my father!"

"Where, Heaven?" the skipper said.

"He was a white ghost and he was riding on the back of a dolphin. He smiled at me and waved his hand. Then the dolphin went underwater and I couldn't see him anymore. Will he come again?" Heaven asked.

"He might, Heaven," the skipper said. "He just might."

One day one of the men walked up to Heaven with a small leather case in his hand. "For you, Heaven. It is many years old." Heaven opened the case.

Inside was a beautiful, rosewood mandolin.

Heaven found a small, secluded beach one day. He walked on the sand near the waves. There, half buried in the sand, lay a large, white beautiful conch shell. He dug it out and held it up to the sun. It sparkled in a pearly rainbow of colors, glinting rays off its smooth, shiny surface.

There was a hole at the end of the shell. First he looked through it. Then he held it up to his mouth and blew through the hole. It made a sound! a soft sweet sound.

He blew through it again, louder. "A dolphin whistle," he laughed.

As he was turning to go home, he looked out on the waves and saw sleek forms under the water. Several dolphins were gliding toward the beach. One turned on its side, its big eye out of the water, looking at Heaven. He softly whistled!

Heaven jumped up and down laughing. He ran out into the waves. Now several dolphins glided up to him, sticking their smiling mouths out of the water, clicking and whistling. One rolled over on its back, its flippers in the air. Heaven petted its belly as it swam by.

Another stopped in front of him, whistling. Heaven hugged it and then got on its back, holding the magic shell tightly in his hand. The dolphin slowly towed him around the water. Heaven laughed and blew the conch.

"I'm the dolphin king!" he sang out.

He went back to the beach the next day. Again he blew his shell. Soon the forms were gliding in the water! He ran out to them again. He recognized some by markings on their fins and scars on their skin.

He started naming them:

"You're Holey-fin," he pointed to one with a hole in its fin. "And you're Ole Nick," he said to one with a nicked snout.

He took rides on several through the day. They all seemed to want to carry them. They chaperoned him through the tide.

When it began to get dark, they took the boy close to land and he walked to shore. "Goodbye," he waved. He blew his dolphin shell and walked towards home.

That night he came back to his dolphin beach. He blew the conch. Soon Heaven heard the dolphins breaching in the water, breathing at the surface. In the stillness of the night, when he couldn't see them very well, he would listen to them: the sound they made as they blew off water and inhaled was somehow very soothing. It was a sound he would always carry with him.

Scott Campbell

In the starlight they swam in the shallow water around him.
He swam with them. He was by now an expert swimmer, and
loved to play with them more than anything.

He would go to the beach now whenever could, and told no one
about it. (This was between him and the dolphins!) He particularly liked to come at night, when the stars sparkled on the waves.

And the dolphins would only come, he noticed, when he blew
his shell...

Heaven would often watch the boats come and go in the harbor. One day a sailboat, a sloop, breezed to the dock.

Heaven ran up to it. "Would you take me for a ride, Mr.?" he
asked.

"Sure. Hop on!"

The sloop was fore-and-aft rigged with one mast and a single
headsail jib. "The wind moves you like an aeroplane," the young
skipper explained.

Heaven nodded. Somehow he knew exactly what the skipper
meant.

"You'll probably have your own someday," the skipper said,
working the ropes in the wind. "You seem to take to it."

They sailed over the calm water.

Heaven looked at the man and smiled. "I love it!"

The people virtually worshipped Heaven as a child-king. No
one ever touched him to punish him, and, they noticed, on one
ever had to. He was always polite.

When he was twelve it was decided he would be married. Since he was a king, they felt he should have a queen. They picked a pretty white girl, also twelve, named Rena, who loved Heaven, for he was very comely: His hair was thick and dark blonde and curly, and he wore it to his shoulders. Rena had hazel hair which curled around her face, like a portrait, and a pug nose. She loved playing pirates. She had a mischievous smile and seemed to understand the boy better than anyone else, even the adults, and the two were always playing together.

On this day, long awaited, they knelt before Pastor Otis, Rena holding a bouquet of spring flowers, Heaven his conch shell.

"Dearly beloved," Pastor Otis intoned, "we have gathered today to unite this young man and young girl in holiest matrimony, with God's blessings."

The people in the garden smiled. Some wept quietly, wiping their eyes with handkerchiefs.

After the ceremony, the newlyweds walked to the harbor to see the gift the people had given him. It was what Heaven wanted more than anything else:

A small two-masted sailing schooner!

With time Heaven gained perfect control of the little square-rigged schooner. Rena, too, soon became an "able-bodied" sailor. Their young friends would often come by to play on the boat and by the time summer came, the *Breeze* had its crew.

The children sailed amongst the reefs, finding little deserted beaches and atolls to go ashore. There they made up games, pretending they were dolphins in a pod. They would create the rules…everyone would become part of the magical body, yet retain his or her own character. The children would choreograph steps and paint their faces and swirl with long ribbons and pieces of yarn. Heaven would often play his mandolin.

At the end of the games they would all come together and jump, reaching their hands toward the sky.

Everyone would win!

At 14, Heaven graduated and the people decided to send him to college so he would educated as his father was. He first considered the University of Bermuda and then Florida, but finally decided on New Orleans. They raised the money from themselves and Rena went too. She was virtually as precocious as Heaven—two child prodigies.

Heaven majored in marine biology, specializing in marine mammals. He also studied computer mathematics, physics, music and ship building. He tended to be shy of people he met in college and spent most of his free time after class in the laboratory, working, he said, "on a secret project." The rest of the time he spent with Rena.

He was always very glad to return to Bermuda.

Although they had been married four years now, they had never made love. For most of their young lives together they were simply too young to know really what to do, so they would often just lie together, side by side, holding each other's hand. Sometimes he would kiss her breasts as she held his head in her arms or lightly touch her between child-soft legs and she would delicately caress him. Usually they would just cuddle together like the children they were.

This night when they had returned from school, they were lying in their bed on board the *Breeze,* letting the gentle rocking soothe them to sleep. But this night Heaven could not sleep. He lit the lamp and got up. Rena woke and sat up in bed, looking at him. He went to his chest and brought out his shell.

"Remember this, love?" he asked showing it to her as it reflected pearly scarlet from the oil lamp.

She nodded her head, looking pensively at it. "You had it at our wedding."

Heaven's face started shining. "Come on!" he said. "We're going swimming."

He led her by the hand down the pier and over the hill to the beach, moonlight lighting the way. When they got to the water, he said, "Listen." He put the shell to his lips and blew.

"Oh, what a pretty sound," she said. He blew on the shell, out towards sea. "It sounds almost like…"

"A dolphin whistle?"

"Yes! Just like a dolphin whistle."

"Look!" He pointed out in the water. In the moonlight Rena saw the fins. She looked back at the shell. "It's wonderful. Do they always come?"

He nodded, smiling.

"But Heaven…why didn't you show me before?"

He reached out his hand to hers. "I was saving it for a special occasion. Come on!"

She took his hand and they ran into the soft waves. The dolphins glided round and between them. Rena laughed, splashing water into the air.

"They feel like wet velvet," she said, petting one.

Heaven kneeled down in the water. "I can't tell you my feelings for them. I don't think I could even find the words, but somewhere, way back…"

He petted Rena's leg and she put her hand on his shoulder. He stood up and lifted her, holding her body in his arms, and carried her to the beach. Behind him, he could hear dolphins breathe and softly whistle. He laid her down on the sand, knelt by her side, and kissed her on the mouth, harder then he ever had before. Startled, her mouth came open and they found each other's tongues. They felt like fire. She put her arms around him. He grabbed her gently but suddenly. The suddenness surprised her, but she did not flinch.

"Oh, love me, Heaven…"

Out in the water, the dolphins whistled and played.

Heaven and Rena sat on large soft pillows leaning against the wall in the living quarters of the *Breeze*. Their friends were dancing around the room to calypso music. Heaven, a golden cup of wine in his hand, laid his other on her belly.

"How much longer now?"

"Anytime," she smiled, a mysterious green light in her eyes.

"Boy or girl?" he asked.

Rena laughed. "A baby dolphin!"

"I wouldn't be surprised," Heaven laughed. "Sometimes I feel like one."

"Sometimes you act like one!" she replied.

He took a drink of wine, then looked seriously at her.

"Rena," he said quietly, "a long time ago I found some papers hidden away—in the old chest—Father's. They had not been disturbed, I don't think. Some of the writing had faded, but I could make most of it out. He was working with some Dr. Smith, trying to communicate with dolphins in the dolphin's own language!

"He had actually completed most of the computer programs for converting English into 'delphinese'! The really odd thing was," he said, taking another sip of wine, "even though I couldn't make out all of his writing—I understood the notes perfectly. They made total sense to me. So I talked my physics prof into helping me on my famous 'secret project' in the lab after classes."

"So that's what it was!" exclaimed Rena.

"I could not tell anyone at the time...not even you. It was so personal, like my father had come back...and I kept having dreams, hearing my father say 'Tell no one!' So I told my prof I was in contact with Dr. John Lilly, the famous dolphin scientist. He was impressed, but I don't think he believed me. When we returned, I got in touch with the college here.

"Anyway (to make a long story short) using father's notes, I was able to finally complete his project!"

He stopped.

"What, Heaven?" Rena asked.

"I'll show you soon. You two will be with me for the final test, succeed or fail," he promised. "I guess you could say...I computerized the conch shell. I completed the fine tuning just last night." He looked around at his friends. "They don't know it yet, but that's the reason for this party."

Heaven paused, putting his hand again on Rena's swollen belly.

"And...her!"

Two days later, Rena had their baby on board the Breeze. They named her Michelle.

After, Heaven sat on the beach under the sparkling stars, with
his mandolin, singing a song:

"A day goes by, a year goes by
But time it can be yours to save.
You plant a flower, the birds soar high,
You live on the crest of a breaking wave.

So you found a girl for goodness sake
And O my what a pair you make,
And you couldn't be happier if you tried.
And on the day she took your hand,
And you took hers to make your stand,
You gazed into her eyes—softly cried.

And a day goes by, a year goes by…

And your love's child begins to grow
Your lover's eyes begin to show
The changes her body and mind are going through.
She takes you gently by the hand,
Her touch asks you to understand
She's played the game of life with you!

And a day goes by, a year goes by…

And she gives forth into the world
Your mind is numb with all the swirl
Of thoughts of love and life's parade.
You sit out under a starry arch
And what was once an uphill march,

Now you know is just a promenade.

And a day goes by, a year goes by
But time it can be yours to save.
You plant a flower, the birds soar high,
You live on the crest of a breaking wave."

Heaven looked up at the starry arch. The mandolin sang in his hands like a happy baby. The waves lapped the shore, singing their ocean song.

He had never seen anything more beautiful than beautiful, little Michelle: innocent as a baby dolphin, he thought, and just as cute…hair like spun gold and eyes of an infant angel.

And Rena? Rena had glowed…

Heaven and Rena held Michelle between them and carefully lowered her in the shallow waves.

She came up laughing.

"She takes after her father," Rena smiled.

Heaven held her in his arms, before his face.

"She loves the water," he beamed.

Rena nodded her head. "She'll be swimming before long."

"Yes," said Heaven. "A mermaid!"

Heaven had designed a papoose-style baby carrier for taking Michelle on short trips underwater. It was made of light-weight aluminum with an unbreakable plexi-glass window, so she could see out, and Heaven or Rena could carry it their backs, using small O2 tanks strapped horizontally on their waists for their own breathing. The "high-tech cradle-board" contained its own O_2 unit on its sides and a pump for discharging CO_2.

He had tried it with many cats, all with success. Rena had been anxious, but Heaven said:

"Think what a thrill it will be for Michelle, riding along underwater, seeing the fish swim by. It's totally safe. I've tested it on a hundred cats, and never lost one. And the emergency buzzer will ring in my ear at the slightest loss of O_2.

"Come on, let's both go down and you can watch Michelle through the window."

"All right," she nodded her head.

They got into their scuba gear on the beach, and then laid Michelle in the softly padded carrier and gently strapped her in.

Heaven turned on the pumps, kissed Michelle (as did Rena) and closed the lid. She lay in there, her eyes open, smiling.

Heaven carefully picked up the carrier and with Rena's help put it on his back, his arms through the straps.

He took Rena's hand and they walked into the waves. They submerged. Rena immediately fell behind Heaven, watching Michelle through the window.

The little girl started smiling and laughing, looking at her mother and the fish as they darted by. She couldn't stop laughing. A young dolphin swam up and smiled in at her.

Finally they surfaced. "Well, did she cry," Heaven asked as they walked to the beach.

Rena, smiling, shook her head. "She loved it!"

They opened the lid. Michelle was still laughing.

Only Rena and Michelle were with Heaven on the deck of the *Breeze* this day, clear and bright. Heaven looked at Rena and smiled at Michelle, smiling in Rena's arms.

"This is it!" he said: "The 'computerized conch.'"

He held it up to the sun—its smooth alloy surface gleamed silvery.

He took the "megaphone", walked to the boat's side, leaned over the wood railing and whispered into the rubber suction cup.

"My dolphin friends—can you hear me?" Out the other end came a strange melodious sound!

He waited several minutes, then whispered the words again:

"My dolphin friends—can you hear me?"

Instantly, several dolphins leaped out of the water, looking up at him, talking rapidly. Rena jumped up and down. Michelle laughed excitedly.

"We love you!" Heaven spoke into the "megaphone."

"And this!" Heaven said, holding up a tiny object. "The 'hearing aide.'"

He placed it in his ear. He heard great cacophony of sounds.

"One at a time! please," he said into the "megaphone."

"Can we help you?" he heard a small voice say.

"My friends," Heaven said, when they were all on board the *Breeze*, "how would you like to go treasure hunting?"

Of course they had all been awaiting his final return from college. Heaven and Rena had both graduated with honors and the "prodigies" had returned to their beloved St. George's Island.

There were whistles.

"Yes, friends, and I believe we will have much luck. We have the help of the dolphins!"

They all knew of course of the sonar abilities of the dolphin, being far superior to those of the most sophisticated American submarine. A submarine's sonar is composed of constant, unvarying sounds, whereas dolphins can vary the frequency and volume of theirs; a subs sonar is unable to differentiate a wooden hull from a metal one, or a whale from another sub, but in total darkness a dolphin can tell one species of fish from another and will always go for the favored one. A dolphin, blindfolded, can easily find an object a little larger than the head of a pin many feet away. A person could throw pennies and dimes into a thick silt and tell the dolphin to retrieve only the dimes, and it would do so.

"I think," Peter Brian said, "we're going to be quite rich."

Everyone laughed. "We must all perfect our scuba-diving technique," Heaven said. "We are going in search of sunken treasure around the Bermuda reefs.

"There is a lot there."

They finally set sail into the waters off St. George's for the large cave rock Heaven had found earlier in his search for a base of operations. It had an underwater entrance into a protected grotto. The *Breeze* soon reached the rock and they set anchor.

The friends swam into the hidden grotto with their supplies in water-tight containers. Heaven carried Michelle in her "cradle board."

By nightfall they had set up camp. Someone got some wood they had brought and built a fire. The cave soon became warm, the flames dancing relaxedly on the rock walls. They all sat around the fire. Heaven played his mandolin. Everyone listened enraptured, for he had now attained complete mastery over the delicate instrument, given him so long ago on the fishing boat.

The sound had only deepened and mellowed with age.

Early in the morning, after quietly rekindling the camp fire as the rest slept, Heaven stood in scuba gear by the pool in the grotto which led down into the sea. He put the rubber cup of the "computerized conch" to his lips:

"My friends," he whispered, "will you please come in."

Within minutes the water started bubbling and three bottle-nose dolphins appeared at the surface, their mouths open, their eyes shining brightly. They looked ghostly white in the flickering firelight of the cave: To Heaven they seemed an ancient and wise extraterrestrial race, come down to earth to light the way for troubled mankind—suspended together at the surface as a tightly knit group tied together by invisible strings of E.S.P. Their heads were above the water and they shined in the light, moving with such delicate ease in the medium, they looked almost like fountains.

He sat down on the edge of the grotto.

He listened to his "hearing aide":

"Do you believe in us?" a voice asked

"Yes I do," Heaven said immediately.

He remembered reading in college the words of Dr. John Lilly, famous dolphin researcher: "If one works with a bottlenose dolphin day in and day out for many hours, days and weeks, one is struck with the fact that one's current basic assumptions and even one's current basic expectations determine within certain limits the results obtained with a particular animal at a particular time."

In other words, he had told himself, it is important to "believe" in the dolphin's abilities!

"Yes I do," Heaven said again.

They rolled in the water delightedly.

"Will you lead me to the treasure?"

"Which one?"

He listened while the dolphins had a "conversation." Seismic research done with dolphins had shown when dolphins are together there are long silences in the vocalizations of different dolphins. They do not, in other words, all vocalize at once, but rather seem to be listening to each other in turns.

This was, he knew now, indeed the case.

"Can we trust him?" one asked another.

Pause. "I believe so. He was chosen."

"Remember his father's legend, the man who would not betray us."

"Yes. The dolphin-man. His story is taught to our young."

"Their evil ones tried to kill him, the ones who would corrupt our brothers and sisters and use them in their plots."

(Tried? thought Heaven.)

"Yes. Take advantage of our love for them and turn it to death."

"The dolphin-man would have died protecting us."

(Would have died?)

"But his spirit lives again—thanks to the Star Dolphins!"

So, Heaven thought, I did see my father's ghost on the dolphin! And who are the Star Dolphins? he wondered.

They talked on and on, now discussing ethics, now discussing morality, now philosophy.

"What would you do with these riches, friend Heaven," one of them finally asked him.

"Would you use them to help?"

"I swear on the blood of my father I would!"

They talked among themselves a little longer (they almost seemed to love to converse for its own sake, Heaven noticed, wishing to examine every subtle nuance of every subject which crossed their convoluted minds, like esoteric sages) then nodded their heads "Yes!" excitedly.

Heaven smiled and quickly got on the back of a dolphin.

Down through the azure waters they dove as many-colored fish darted to and fro around them. Heaven smiled behind his facemask. It was like riding on a "sea-train" with an all around view. To be more correct, an undersea plane, for the dolphins use their fins like the manes of an airplane, to literally "fly" through the water. They soared over a coral crusted cliff.

In minutes they were approaching the floor of the reef. Thousands of fishes, it seemed, whisked and flew about: Butterfly fish, yellow with long snouts swam lazily by; orange Garibaldis chased one another; blue Blacksmith fish floated by in schools; little orange Clownfish hovered in the tentacles of the poisonous anemone which were their homes; a couple of small tiger sharks approached but quickly darted away. A rockfish sulked.

And then Heaven saw, through the crystal clear waters, there in the deep blue distance...the sunken ship. He quickly swam for it and up onto the deck. He looked around the ancient vessel. Was it an old Spanish galleon, possibly a treasure ship, taking gold back from Peru when it ran aground on the reefs? A timber of a mast, broken off about half way, stuck eerily up like an abandoned sunken Christmas tree.

He peered around. A dolphin was standing over something on the deck, "standing"on its tail. Heaven shone his flashlight.

Could it be…?

A treasure chest, Heaven thought, looking at what almost seemed a replica of the chest his father left when he died, the one in which Heaven now kept his magic conch, the computerized version, the hearing aide, and his father's papers. But what's this chest doing up here on the deck. Ah, he thought, perhaps some nobleman was desperately trying to get his new-found riches into one of the life boats as the ship was going down, but was forced to leave it behind. But wait, it would have washed overboard. Yet here it was. Who…what..?

He looked at the dolphins, smiling, it seemed, almost mischievously. Might they know what's in it if they scanned it closely with their sonar? he wondered. He took out his knife and slowly pried open the chest. There was a golden glitter!

Heaven gazed at the revealed treasure, than at the dolphins and then back. He could hardly believe it. It seemed the dolphins had led him to the most fabulous treasure in the sea! Here were gold doubloons by the hundred's! Here a gold-covered flint-lock pistol! There a sword with a silver handle!

Dolphins are better than Superman and X-ray vision! he thought. Heaven laughed inside.

He swam down amongst the coral again, almost needing to shade his eyes. Everywhere were scattered gold coins! as if someone had flung them over the coral-bed. He picked one up and brushed it off. On the front was a boy riding a dolphin!

The colors of the coral pulsated in every rainbow hue, iridescent in the muted light. The magic of the water seemed everywhere. Delicate sea fans waved placidly; green and red and blue sponges, soft to the touch, nestled; a school of blue and yellow fish floated by. The coral sparkled like jewels in the most fabulous treasure of all: the divine sea. Pink parrotfish swam around a ruby-red bed of coral; trigger fish, sapphire-blue, darted in and out of the crevices.

The coral, he knew, could be a hazard to treasure hunting, as it is very sharp and often covers all trace of treasure with a sparkling blanket of limestone. Often it must be chipped away to get to the treasure below, a sad job indeed, Heaven thought, for the beauty it reveals is in its way worth more than any gold doubloons—Coral is living ancient sculpture, he thought.

He searched among the treasure again. His eyes immediately saw a solid gold ring. He looked closely. On it was a smiling dolphin with a curly tail! He showed it to the dolphins. They seemed to laugh as if to say, "We knew it was there all along."

There! A...winged salamander with ruby scales. Legend, he had read, accorded salamanders the ability to live in fire. It was a marvelous good luck charm. There! A lacy necklace made of gold chains. And there! A four-inch long gold manicure set topped with the bust and head of a beautiful woman.

What these ancient Spaniards did with gold! thought Heaven.

And this. His hand moved slowly: An emerald studded golden cross.

Heaven knew he was looking at a million dollars worth of treasure almost within arm's reach. Most treasure hunters search many years to make one such find. He had found his first in a matter of days. And, of course, it was because of the dolphins.

As he thought about the potential of this...he began to experience nitrogen narcosis ("rapture of the depths")...feeling "drunk", intoxicated. His mind was weaving.

He quickly put some pieces he had gathered in his belt pack, signaled thumbs up to the dolphins, and started swimming toward the rock. He climbed slowly out of the grotto. Rena ran to meet him. He put his arm around her and handed her the treasure. "They're for you," he said, taking off his face mask.

She looked at him, then carefully took the glittering objects and held them in her open hand. They sparkled in the firelight, the dolphin ring smiling with what seemed an almost internal shine.

She grasped the pieces to her breast. "Oh, Heaven…!" Then she kissed him on the cheek.

The others ran up, stopping just short of him, almost at attention. Rena showed them the pieces. Everybody oohed and aahed. Heaven smiled, his face shining in the flickering light.

"This—is just a drop in the bucket!"

They all swam down to the treasure. Heaven led the way. Rena carried Michelle in her "papoose-carrier."

When they reached the sunken ship, they first laid out a "grid" of white cord and then began meticulously picking up coins and other silver and gold wonders, treasures beyond their wildest wishes. They "collected" through the day, trying not to disturb the beauty of the coral.

That night the young friends laughed and danced. The dolphins joined the cry from the grotto. Everybody sang songs as they cleaned and examined the many pieces of treasure they had found, in this, just the first day. They knew now they were quite rich.

"How shall we use our new-found wealth?" Heaven asked the group.

Nobody said anything, except young Peter, who yelled out, "Not an all expense trip to Miami, I hope!" Everyone rocked with laughter.

"Nope, Peter," Heaven laughed. "I suggest building a new ship, a three-masted schooner, this time fore and aft rigged with an engine and all the comforts of home—something to fly around the world in!"

Everyone applauded and whistled.

"And I suggest naming it... *The Dolphin!*"

Everyone went wild.

They decided to build their own ship, Heaven having taken a course in ship building in college. They sold as much of their treasure as they needed to finance their new project. The engine was made to order, the finest of its kind, and specialists were brought in when needed. The dolphins helped, too.

They found a secluded beach and set to work, first covering the ground with pilings. Then they laid the keelblocks in a perfectly straight line, and day by day the vessel went up. Heaven knew a number of trapezoids adjoining each other approaches a curvilinear figure—the ships hull—and by applying calculus the exact area could be found.

The construction proceeded slowly but steadily: First the keels went up, bar keels, curved. Then the stem and the stern posts. Next the frames, the beams, the stringers and the decks, the pillars for supporting the decks, the double bottoms for taking on water ballast, the shell plating, the bulkheads, the foredeck and the steering gear, the bridge and the living quarters in the forecastle, the quarterdeck and the hatches, and finally the derricks and the masts. The sails were fore-and-aft rigged, parallel to the line of the keel, curved to approach the shape of an airplane wing.

As Heaven watched through the months the construction of the ship, he noticed at times he would feel like Noah: often he felt a need to escape to sea.

Finally the ship was completed! In a great ceremony they christened it *The Dolphin*. Heaven blew his conch shell.

They were ready to fly!

The Dolphin rolled easily through the waves. Heaven and Rena stood at the foredeck.

"It's beautiful!" said Heaven.

"It sails through the water like it was alive," Rena agreed.

Heaven looked at her. His eyes sparkled.

"It is alive," he said.

They were out only a short time before dolphins approached, riding the bow like surfers on an endless wave.

"I wonder if the dolphins can read," Rena laughed, "the name of our ship."

Suddenly Heaven grabbed his "megaphone" and "hearing aide" and ran for the railing. He spoke into the "computerized conch" and listened to the response. Then he quickly got his "dolphin harness" and ran for the railing again. He looked back at Rena, who was watching him intently.

"I'm goin' surfin'!" he smiled.

Heaven jumped up on to *The Dolphin's* railing, and then made a perfect swan dive. Rena gasped. The dolphins veered to make room for him as if they were performing in a Marineland water show, and Heaven dove deeply beneath them.

Under the cascading dolphins, as they adroitly swam around, under and above him, Heaven looked up and shot for the surface, wrapping his arms around a galloping dolphin! He rapidly put the padded harness around it, then mounted the dolphin like a "seahorse," soaring in and out of the wake, like he had seen the ghost of his father do so long ago.

Then...he stood up on its back, holding the harness like a lariat on a bucking bronco. "Yee-ha!" he heard someone yell from the deck. He had seen stunts before where dolphins towed a man around a pool. This, he felt was an improvement, riding the dolphin like a combination bare-back cowboy and surfer. He dropped one hand from the harness and held it straight up in the air, then looked forward into the sun and shook his long, thick, shoulder-length hair. The spray kissed his face in rainbow sparkles. Everybody on *The Dolphin* was jumping up and down, almost doing somersaults over the railing. Only Rena remained perfectly still, her hands folded in front of her mouth as she silently watched him.

Heaven got down on one knee on the dolphin's back and undid the harness, then dove sharply and deeply as again the dolphins veered around him. He waited until he saw the stern of the ship, quickly swam for the rope ladder, and bounded up to the deck!

Everybody ran to meet him. Rena fell into his arms.

"Wow, mon!" said Johnny, the dreadlocked black first mate.

"Better than giant worm riding on Dune!" exclaimed Peter.

"I'm just glad you're still alive," Rena breathed.

"What was it like!" asked another.

"Beautiful!" said Heaven, catching his breath. "But...I don't think I ever want t' do it again!"

They had only been out a few days when Johnny spotted the purse seiner. Heaven looked through his binoculars. "They've got dolphins in the net, alright! Lots of 'em…" he said angrily.

The purse seiner is the mortal enemy of the dolphin. It is far different from a trawler which can do no real harm to dolphins, aside from occasionally catching one in their drift nets. The purse seiner goes out of its way to find dolphins, herds of them, and then encircle them in a mile-long net. The purse seiner has been called a dolphin killer, plain and simple.

Heaven had studied this dilemma in college: For some reason, tuna like to swim under floating objects. Being virtually the fastest fish in the seas, reaching 40 mph, they love to swim under dolphin herds, which spend much of their time on the surface, swimming at high speed. Once this bond is established, the tuna will follow the dolphins wherever they go.

The purse seiner knows this and looks for dolphins as signs of large schools of tuna below. When they spot them, high-speed skiffs are launched from the boat to encircle the floating dolphins, trapping the tuna. And the dolphins. Many dolphins, especially the stronger males, will leap the nets and escape, but many others get entangled in the seine nets as they are being drawn. Others go into a state called "passive behavior" and sink to the bottom. Still others panic and become helpless, most especially pregnant females and mothers with new babies. These are all termed "accidental deaths."

Laws protecting the dolphins have been passed, but are not uniformly enforced and still allow several thousand to be killed each year. "Back-down" procedures have been developed which allow the dolphins to spill out the nets, but are not 100% effective nor are they always used. One lax skipper can wipe-out an entire herd. "Dolphin safe" labels do not always guarantee what

they advertise. U.S. laws, of course, do not apply to foreign seiners.

"Peter!" Heaven yelled into the intercom, "start the
engine!"

"Aye, aye, sir!"

"What we goin' t' do, Heaven sir?" asked dreadlock Johnny,
his long "dreadlocks" of black curly hair hanging down.

"Save the dolphins," Heaven said quietly.

The Dolphin approached the seiner. Heaven took the bull
horn and the binoculars.

"Release the net and free all dolphins!"

An answer came back. "You nuts? We got a whole school of
tuna down there! Who are you?"

"You can read the name of the vessel yourself," Heaven
answered. "Are you the captain?" he said, focusing on the man.
"Release all dolphins! Immediately!"

"I am. And if I don't?"

"We'll ram you!"

"Are you nuts!? You'll sink the goddamned boat!"

"That's the idea, captain. You got two minutes to release all
dolphins."

By this time they had reached the trapped victims. Heaven
looked down into the net. He turned abruptly and looked away.

"They're drowning!" he said.

It was one thing, Heaven now knew, to read about dolphins
trapped in purse seine nets. It was quite another to actually see
them go through the final stages of an agonizing death. The air
was filled with their anguished cries.

He looked back at the grotesque scene. "We'll cut the damn
thing ourselves."

The dolphins were struggling to escape.

Heaven procured a grappling hook and carefully lowered it over the side, catching the net. He secured it.

"Full speed astern, Peter!"

The Dolphin began pulling the net apart, taking it around back toward the seiner. The dolphins started spilling out into the water, leaping away, crying out for missing loved ones, Heaven noticed.

"What the hell ya doin'!" Heaven could see the skipper jumping up and down in the pilot house.

"Rena," Heaven said, "take Michelle below and strap her into her bed." She immediately did.

"Peter, full speed ahead." *The Dolphin* headed for the seiner. "I want them to remember this and pass it onto their friends," Heaven said to his mates.

In minutes Rena's voice came over the intercom. "All secure."

"Everyone one hold on!" Heaven yelled. He looked back at the dolphins. They were swimming clear.

"Ramming speed!!"

Wam! There was a great noise and impact as the smiling head and snout of the metal dolphin at the front of the ship rammed the purse seiner!

"Yer sinkin' us, for God's sake!" the skipper yelled.

"Use your skiffs!" Heaven said.

"Full speed astern, Peter!

"Pass the message on to your friends," Heaven yelled into the bullhorn: "Don't—kill—dolphins!"

"Who d' you think y'are?" the captain yelled. "God?"

From the wheel house, Heaven and his friends viewed the scene of the listing purse seiner, passing the binoculars one to another. Johnny laughed as he watched lifejacketed men leap off into the swirling sea, a dark laugh that seemed to convey feelings they all had—anger and sadness and a sense of vengeance.

Rena stood quietly by Heaven's side. "We can't just leave them," she said, Michelle in her arms again. "A storm's coming. They might drown."

Heaven was silent as he looked through binoculars. Dark clouds were rapidly approaching, the wind rising.

"Maybe the dolphins save 'em," Johnny laughed.

Heaven but the binocs down. "Rena's right. We'll have to bring them in."

"How about using the seine net?" Peter smirked.

They all giggled.

"Lower the life boats," Heaven said.

The purse seine skipper was floating in the water, waiting to be picked up by a skiff, when suddenly he saw the young man in a wet suit riding a dolphin toward him!

Capt. Jones had ordered every one into the skiffs first, living by a strict code of the captain being the last to leave a sinking ship, when he fell overboard as the boat lurched.

Now, Capt. Herbert Jones remembered the last time he had seen someone on a dolphin—years ago, picking up Dr. Michael Hope not many leagues from these very same waters!

The "dolphin-man" approached and reached out his arm and yelled, "Get on!" shouting over the rising wind and waves, and the old captain swung up behind him. An eerie shaft of golden sun ripped through the gathering, dark wool clouds, encircling them in a tropical aureola-borealis of shimmering light.

On board *The Dolphin,* the fishermen shivered in the wind. Heaven's mates held rifles on them.

He felt a little like Capt. Nemo.

"You can sleep under canvas on the deck until we drop you off in Jamaica," he ordered.

"Captain, come with me!" The two went below.

"Don't—kill—dolphins! Captain," Heaven roared, as they entered his quarters.

"I am truly sorry, sir," said Capt. Jones. "It won't happen again."

He looked closely at Heaven. "May I say, sir, you remind me very much of a man I met many years ago, right in these waters. I was on a small trawler at the time, a boat I captained named the *Elegant,* and we pulled a man in who was bein' held afloat by porpoises…uh, dolphins, I should say sir. This man was very nearly drowned, but we pulled 'im through and took 'im on to Bermuda."

Heaven looked quickly at the captain, his hair and beard white, but his muscles still bulky and firm.

"What might yer name be, captain?" the old sailor asked.

"I'm Capt. Hope."

"My lord!" Capt. Jones ejaculated. "This man was named Dr. Michael Hope, sir! if I recall."

Heaven sat, almost fell, into his chair, gazing at the skipper.

"He was my…father!" Heaven said breathlessly. "Are you… Capt. Jones?"

"I am indeed, sir!"

"Father mentioned you in his papers…"

"Well, well! If it ain't a small ocean after all, just like they say." He reached out his hand. "I am mighty proud to meet the son of Dr. Michael Hope, and a fine strappin' young man you be, too, sir!"

Heaven could hardly speak. Finally he said, "We'll put your men ashore in Jamaica. However, I would be pleased if you would sail with us awhile…Capt. Jones."

"I am at yer service, Capt. Hope. Yes, sir! Yes indeedy!" He laughed heartily. "Starkist will never know what hit 'em!" he winked, his old eyes sparkling.

They sailed to Jamaica, where they put most of the fishermen off on a remote, isolated beach, Capt. Jones and a few of his men staying aboard *The Dolphin.* They sailed westerly.

Finally, they reached the Gulf of Mexico, were about to turn south, when Capt. Jones said, "If you sail west by southwest, you'll soon reach a tiny islet that ain't on every chart. Just too dinky, I reckon." Then, appearing like a speck out of the mists was a minuscule island with miniature beaches!

"I can't believe it!" Heaven said. "You're right Capt. Jones. There! It's sure not on this chart…Just like Pitcairn's Island!" He scanned with binoculars. "Or maybe Gilligan's!" he laughed. "I think we're home….Let's lower the boats!"

On the beach, Heaven took Rena by the hand, and waving at the others, walked with her out of sight. They reached a small cove.

"Rena," he said, "I'm going under. If I'm not back in five minutes—come looking for me."

"Five minutes? But Heaven…"

"Trust me, "he said as he undressed. "I believe the human body hides a kind of 'mechanism,' inherited from the distant past. When this mechanism is finally rediscovered, humans will be ale to go underwater at great depths and stay for long periods of time…without air tanks. Like dolphins," he smiled. He paused. "I think I've found the mechanism."

118

Rena clutched him.

"I think the mechanism is...the heart! Most people concentrate on their lungs, when the idea is really to get more oxygen into the blood. Besides, too much air in your lungs could give you the bends in deep dives. Dolphins don't get the bends because they store oxygen in their blood."

He looked at her. "You have to open your heart. Like the dolphin." He kissed her.

He checked his watch with her's. "Trust me," he said again.

He walked into the waves, and started swimming lazily. Then with a great gasp he surface dived, kicking straight up and submerged. Under the water, Heaven swam easily and slowly. The seconds went by. He felt good. He looked at his watch: One minute...One minute thirty seconds...Two minutes. Great. Two minutes 50 seconds, the critical period. He felt relaxed. Three minutes...

On the beach Rena anxiously waited, checking her watch every few seconds. Four minutes. She clasped her hands in front of her and started nervously jumping up and down, looking at the water. Four minutes and 30 seconds...Five minutes!

She gulped some air and ran full speed out into the water. She went under, looking for him. Then Rena felt a tap on her shoulder! She turned around. It was Heaven! His cheeks were puffed out. He took her hand. They swam together.

Heaven checked his watch. Seven minutes and five seconds!

A slight smile came to his lips.

Heaven rocketed up out of the water, shaking sparkling droplets from his hair. His mouth opened and he gasped for air.

Then he submerged again, his arms coming straight up, his hands touching over his head. He treaded easily now. Rena was in front of him, her legs and arms moving smoothly, her hair flowing with the currents. He closed his eyes, feeling perfectly in tune with the water, as though he had lived in here always, as though this were his only home…

Now Heaven entered a deep trance, a feeling of total remoteness—delphic other worldliness: He "saw" Rena! Minute clicks, millions per second it seemed, flew out toward her—virtually laying a texture over her. He saw her shape, her size…He even "saw" her softness.

Heaven opened his eyes. The image was exactly right!! He closed his eyes. There she was again!

A fish swam between them—Heaven "saw" the fish, following in perfectly as it swam lazily by.

He knew it now. He was echolocating—had even somehow developed frequency modulation sonar—just like a dolphin…!

Heaven rushed up, coming out of the water with every ounce of strength in his lithe body. He cleared the sparkling, diamond white surface, arched and dove back in, "saw" a tiny fish and chased it with his eyes closed, caught it in his mouth and then swallowed it whole! He reached the bottom of the cove and did a handstand on two rocks…now swirled and somersaulted through the seaweeds.

A shark swam towards him, took one look, and quickly turned and swam away. Good! Heaven thought.

Now he swam over the coral again, "surveying" his domain, then ascended up to the surface and swam easily, lazily toward shore. Heaven walked out of the easy waves and onto the beach, looking behind as Rena emerged. He collapsed onto the sand.

Rena walked up and knelt down by him. He put his hand on her hair, his eyes sparkling as he gazed up at her, the sun a luminescent rainbow halo around her head.

"It's over," Heaven said.

CHAPTER FOUR
HEAVEN

Their first houses went up in trees. They made the floors of myrtle, the walls of juniper, painting them mosaic with stainglass windows. The tree houses opened to the sea and they could sit and watch the dolphins playing on the waves.

On their day their homes were complete, they gathered round.

"Love reigns," Heaven cried out. "Love reigns over us!"

The thunderclouds above roared and gushed out their water. Everyone looked up. Flocks of winged little children, many colored talking parrots, soared free through the trees...

Heaven ran for the water and jumped into the waves. He submerged. He did not come up for seven minutes. When he surfaced he was smiling—with a fish in his mouth. Everyone ran out to him, laughing. They played and splashed in the water.

Heaven touched Rena on the hip. She swam down with him, her lithe body soaring through the sea. Their fingers entwined underwater. He surfaced, holding her in his arms.

Suddenly a brilliant white light soared by under water, like a comet out to sea! Then it reappeared. Then it disappeared...

Heaven swam through the depths, going a hundred feet down, echolocating intently. All at once the beam flew up to him and stopped! It was a being of light...with sparkling flippers! Or were they wings? It hovered in front of Heaven like a fluttering hummingbird, its flipper wings a blur, robes of light flowing with the currents.

The being looked at him, smiling, a warmth so strong Heaven almost faded from consciousness. Then it reached out, the shining sleeves of the glowing robe hanging loosely down, and touched Heaven on the face with ribbons of light.

It shimmered in the currents before him. Its face shone, long, flowing hair hanging down like seaweed...

Eyelids blinked. "Flippers" fluttered...

The light caressed Heaven's shoulders, a look of blissful wonderment over its face as it gazed at Heaven with rainbow eyes, eyes which seemed to gaze from its heart and soul.

Then he faded into the distance...!

Heaven's mouth came open and he gulped some water. He swam quickly for the surface, almost choking. He floated still on the top, looking up at the clouds in the blue sky.

Heaven had just seen his father!

Heaven went immediately to his tree house. He sat in his chair, staring vacantly out to sea.

Rena knelt beside him. "Are you all right?"

Heaven looked at her, gazing in her face, then fell onto the floor, rolling with her on the Indian rug, the one with winged dolphins woven among silver stars. He lay on his back, Rena on top, laughing.

"Do you believe in angels, Rena?"

"Yes."

"Dolphins are angels...Sea angels."

They made love in bed in the night. He suckled her breasts like a baby.

Slowly the "Utopia" began to take shape. Learning became of the primary importance. Everybody would teach each other what they knew. Impromptu classes would be held throughout the day at various places on the island when someone had something to teach someone else.

Peter was an expert botanist. He knew all about medicinal herbs, having attended several seminars held in the forest while hitchhiking through the Mendocino coast of California. They had become a way of life for him, and he knew them all. He would talk of myrrh and mustard, balm of Gilead and bloodroot, lavender and lily of the valley. The list went on and on.

"God has provided a remedy for every disease that might afflict us," he read from Jethro Kloss's classic *Back to Eden,* and of course most of the herbs could be found on their lush island. He would make tonics for them and teach them how to recognize symptoms and which herbs were best.

"Leaves are for healing," he would say.

Helen was an expert seamstress. She could sew whole wardrobes with a professional's touch and an artist's craft. She taught anyone who wanted to learn.

Johnny knew much about abalone diving, having spent much of his childhood in the reefs near his home gathering food for his family. Sam was a top-class mechanic, June a gourmet chef...

Rena was by now an expert in baby and child care. Michelle was three years old and raising her was Rena's primary concern. She knew all about natural childbirth and would teach any young woman (or young man) who wanted to know. Michelle became quite the focus of attention around the community. Everyone loved and looked after her.

And...Rena was pregnant again.

And Heaven? Heaven was teaching his people to "breathe under water"...

"Open your heart," he would say. "Get as full an exchange of air in your lungs as you can, but remember the idea always is to get the oxygen into your blood. Pant before you go down so you will have as little under pressure in your lungs as possible. This is why dolphins don't get the bends. They store oxygen in their blood."

Bends was always a danger to any deep diver. He knew of many pearl and sponge (and abalone) divers who went for years without any symptoms, then suddenly developed the crippling sickness. The difficulty would arise upon surfacing, he knew, because of the lessening of pressure. Nitrogen stored in the lungs under pressure would dissolve into the blood, forming bubbles. The idea was to have as little in the lungs as possible and the rest in the blood. He spent a great deal of time working with Johnny to ensure his safety when abalone diving.

They would never be as adept as he, of course, for he had inherited certain dolphin genetic characteristics—from his father. In the muscles there is a pigment called myoglobin, which is like hemoglobin in blood, and joins readily with O2, storing it until needed. Dolphins have several times more myoglobin than land animals.

Still, he was a good teacher, and soon six minutes became not uncommon among the most dedicated.

And later, Heaven would teach them...sonar!

Heaven floated in the waves. He had seen the light again! He went under, going down two hundred feet. He looked through the dusky water. A dolphin appeared! It nudged him and Heaven got on its back. They took off, Heaven his arms around its neck. On and on through the sea they flew.

Just when Heaven thought he couldn't hold his breath any longer, the dolphin broke for the surface, breaching at the surface so they could both breathe. The whitecaps rose and fell and the wind blew foam spray. Heaven quickly gulped in air, and they went down again. The dolphin seemed to be looking for something. Every nine minutes or so the dolphin would breach at the surface, so they could breathe, then submerge.

Finally the dolphin dove for the bottom. It was dark at this depth but Heaven was using his sonar. There in the sand he "saw" a large open shell. He examined it closely. His clicks described a smooth, solid, round, surface within the shell. He reached in and grabbed it. It was a giant pearl.

All at once he saw a distant light! The dolphin took off for it, Heaven clutching his pearl. Suddenly they met, both stopping in the water. The dolphin's mouth came opened and it smiled. Heaven's head went back, as he looked again at his father, this time steadily, peacefully.

Michael reached out and patted the dolphin. It couldn't stop smiling. He showed a "book" to Heaven, an open book all of light. Written on the page were the words, "The dolphins rule." He leaned over and kissed his son on the cheek, then disappeared into the distance.

Heaven rested his head on the dolphin's neck. He closed his eyes and then they ascended.

On the beach, Heaven walked alone—

The dolphins are beacons in the water, he said to himself, beacons from the sea, constantly beaming a strong signal of love towards shore. This is how the energy of their great minds is used, since they have no hands with which to build. The outlet for the energy of their minds is love so strong it becomes a signal, a beacon of love actually able to cross long distances.

Slowly, secretly, he smiled, people are being—dolphinized!

Dr. Edward Smith clutched his martini, his third for the night. There would be more. Ever since he had read of Dr. Michael Hopes "death" some twenty years ago, he had retired and locked himself up in his mansion, and except for Sharon, who had become his mistress, would hardly see anyone. The unclassified CIA report was sketchy but troubling. He still blamed himself, as did Sharon herself, and they sought comfort in each other's arms. As he was independently wealthy, he had no desire or need to work, and Sharon enjoyed his money. He was seventy five now, but of such fortitude as to still be healthy, even with all the booze.

"You know," he said for the millionth time, slurring his words, "it was me who wanted the goddamned government contract. I had these visions of fame and glory. I could just see the head-lines: 'World Famous Surgeon Unlocks Dolphin Language,'" he gestured. "Michael wanted everything super secret and I wanted to win the Nobel Prize!"

Sharon walked in front of him, holding her glass. It was her third for the night, too, and a few tears came to her eyes. "We musn't blame ourselves any longer," she said sadly. "It's been so long now, though somehow it does seem like only yesterday." Her face brightened through her tears. "How's your research coming, dear."

Lately Dr. Smith had been spending much time in his own private basement laboratory. Ever since the incident with Michael he had vowed he never wanted to see a dolphin again, and had begun doing other things.

His latest project was a multiple heart organism which he thought could be used by medical students preparing for heart surgery. He had successfully sewn several living, beating hearts together, connecting their aortas and bypass valves, keeping the creation alive in a solution of blood, salt and water. This experiment was rather unusual, even for Dr. Smith, who had reveled in doing surgically what had never been done before.

He would sit and watch it for hours, the nine hearts beating at once: Lub dub, lub dub, lub dub dub dub. It fascinated him. Down deep he knew it was just a lark, something to keep his mind off dolphins, but he actually went so far as to approach the Harvard School of Medicine with it. His reputation was such they had watched with polite interest until about half way through the demonstration when they politely told him he had gone off the deep end and was drinking much too much. "How about a nice rest in the Caribbean?" they had suggested.

He had come home and brought out the organism and started watching it. Suddenly it went out of control and began dancing:

Lub dub, lub dub, lub blub blub blub blub. It flung itself around Dr. Smith's neck. He tore the thing off him and threw it on the floor. Then he stomped on it.

"I killed it!" he said.

Sharon was looking at the evening newspaper when suddenly her eyes saw a headline: "Mystery 'Dolphin Ship' Attacks Fishing Boat." She quickly read the story and then showed it to Dr. Smith. He too read the story:

"A sailing schooner named *The Dolphin* rammed and sunk a purse seine fishing boat in the Bermuda Triangle, sometime last week, said fishermen in Jamaica yesterday.

"'I'm not exactly sure what day it was,' the first mate said, who declined to give his name. 'My mind is a little foggy on that right now. All I remember is seeing this sailing schooner appear mysteriously out of the mist as we were pulling in a net of tuna. Then it rammed us! I saw the skipper swept over the side…and then a man riding on a dolphin picked him out of the sea!'

"When asked if there dolphins trapped in the net, he said, 'No comment.'"

Sharon and Dr. Smith both looked into each other's eyes.

"Is it Michael's son!?" they said at once.

They had learned Michael had a son, but had not any idea what ever happened to him. Dr. Smith was intrigued by the name of the ship and the incredible performance of it as described by the first mate in the news story. Such a ship must have cost a lot of money, he thought. He knew real wealth when he saw it, having a little of his own. "I think maybe he's a billionaire," he said. His mind began turning. "I wonder…" he said almost to himself, "if he continued the work of his father…

"Sharon…" he said suddenly, "how would like to go to the Caribbean?"

"We shall sail around the world!" Heaven announced. "Just for fun. We shall take sample counts of the dolphin population and determine if they are stable or not.

"Along the way we might do a little treasure hunting. All the gold in the ocean is ours. When we get to Bombay…" he laughed, "we'll make all the peasants rich. I shall give St. Teresa a million gold dubloons—and a dozen golden crosses. And ask her to bless my ship and friends."

He held an ancient golden goblet in his hand. He tipped the wine to his lips. "And when we return, we shall begin to build our underwater Shangrila, a port of call for our dolphin friends. And they shall be the architects."

"Before we leave, though," he said, looking at Rena and her swollen belly, "I will have a son."

Rena lay on a blanket on the sand. Torches lit up the night. The water lapped the beach and dolphins breached in the surf. Heaven gently massaged her head. Their friends quietly gathered around. Michelle stood by.

"I want to share this with my friends," Rena had said. "It's the way dolphins do it, isn't it?"

Helen knelt at her abdomen, ready to be her midwife.

Soon Rena started giving birth. The baby emerged quickly. Helen took the infant and laid it Rena's arms.

"I felt no pain," she said quietly, looking up at Heaven.

The child had brown hair and sparkling green eyes. Michelle held his little hand in hers and looked around at the others.

"He's baby Robby the Robot!" she said.

In a few days they were ready to sail! They had a great ceremony on their beach, then loaded the final supplies on *The Dolphin* and lifted anchor.

They smoothly sailed through the Gulf, passing the delta in the mouth of the Mississippi. They looked up the river through their telescope and could see a paddle-wheel steam ship.

"Huckleberry Finn lives up there," Heaven laughed.

"Barefootin' it through the bayous," said Rena, a scarf around her head, little smiling Robby in her arms.

The Dolphin sailed by…

Down the coast of Mexico they glided now. Sea gulls played in the masts, dolphins played in the waves.

Heaven stood in the mast watch, his binoculars to his eyes. They were in the middle of a dolphin ballet. There were dozens around the ship.

He called down through the loudspeaker. "Pipe a little Tchaikovsky over the intercom, Johnny. The dolphins have choreographed a ballet for us."

Soon music from *Swam Lake* was filtering through the breeze. The dolphins immediately picked up the lilting tempo. Everybody climbed on the ropes to watch.

"Their timing is perfect," Rena called through the wind up to Heaven. "It's almost as if they wrote it." She glided her way easily up the ropes to the perch, Robby in the papoose carrier.

"Here," he said, handing her binoculars, "opera glasses. We've got balcony seats."

They looked out on the fluid, glassy waves, where the dolphins danced perfect pirouettes on their stage of blue froth.

Soon down the coast of Brazil *The Dolphin* breezed.

Then finally—Terra del Fuego! Heaven called them all together. "It won't be long, now, until we reach Cape Horn. The weather there, I've read is almost always bad. Anyone have any second thoughts. We could always sail back through the Panama Canal."

He looked at all of them. They were silent for a few seconds. Then Johnny spoke up. "You kiddin', mon? *The Dolphin* could sail through a tidal wave!" The others echoed.

They all looked up at the night sky where the Southern Cross sparkled majestically.

"I believe you're right, Johnny," Heaven said. "It'll be a breeze."

In two days we will be at the Cape, Heaven thought. How many clipper ships have traversed those treacherous waters en route to Peru, hoping and praying for a miracle to bring them through.

But for now the water was smooth, the song in the sails playing a hymn to the southern stars.

Cape Horn is a rock, a speck in the sea. Between it and Antarctica the waters of the two great oceans, Atlantic and Pacific, converge and collide. Shipping presidents writing their sea captains in the sailing days of old would say, "The weather there is almost always very bad."

Heaven looked up at the whirling grey clouds. It was now beginning to snow. He pulled his fur parka around his face.

They were nearing the infamous cape. The change in the weather had been extreme. The water rippled with white tops.

Then the storm hit! pelting the ship with bullets of hail. Heaven ran for the masts. "Furl the sails!" he yelled. Peter scrambled up a mast-head as waves burst over the rails. It had become almost as dark as night.

Rena ran up to Heaven. "I'm afraid!" she spoke.

Heaven looked at her. "Go below with the children," he said as quietly as he could above the roar of the wind. "Strap them into their bunks and don't leave them 'till I tell you."

She studied his eyes. For a second she thought she saw something in them she had never seen before: fear. But it had passed so quickly she couldn't be sure if it was him or the reflection of her own eyes.

She held his arms. "All right." She ran for the hatch door.

Heaven grabbed the ropes and, with the others, began furling the main sail. Peter was on the mizzenmast, bringing in the canvas. Soon the masts looked like bare trees, sticking up towards the dark sky.

He ran back to the wheel, taking it from Johnny's hands. A gust of wind pelted the glass. "The compass says we're clearing the point," Johnny yelled. He looked ahead of him. "Why is it so bloody dark, mon?"

Heaven glanced at his face. He saw signs of strain, as if the tension, at any second, could bring him to his knees.

"We're right at the point," Heaven said, as he checked his compass. "We're rounding the cape!"

"But it's so damned dark," Johnny said, his legs shaking. He seemed about to fall to the deck.

Suddenly Heaven saw a light over the bow. He watched it closely. "Is it another ship?" Heaven wondered aloud. "Will we collide in this wind?"

"What?" said Johnny.

Then Heaven heard a voice in his mind: "Follow me. I'll guide you through."

Heaven held the wheel easily now. A calm seemed to come over the ship. He looked ahead to the light and glued his eyes on it, looking neither left nor right. Out on the water, the waves pounded the ship, but *The Dolphin* was somehow immune.

In a few hours the rays of the red morning sun began filtering in through the dispersing clouds. Everyone gathered around the wheel, looking over the endless water.

They had reached the Pacific Ocean!

The Dolphin sailed up the southwestern tip of Terra del Fuego, cruising in and out of the bays.

"The Indians live in here," Heaven said, looking over the side to the fog-layered, rocky shores. The rain poured down into the icy waters.

"What's let of the Yaghan tribe." The sea water around them was almost fresh from the abundant rain that incessantly fell.

Heaven looked intently toward the shore.

"There!" They all looked toward the hillsides, where the gnarled trees grew in proud defiance of the winds, and saw the shacks on the very edge of the water. Some little canoe-boats rocked in the waves.

Heaven turned to his friends. "Listen to me! These are the dolphin people of Terra del Fuego. They used to swim naked in these icy waters! and roll their babies in the snow to make then strong! and sleep naked in the freezing and howling blizzards. Now they are slowly dying out, long ago abandoning their old ways, forced to by the early explorers who couldn't stand their superiority.

"I must help them…if I can…"

He took off his jacket and boots and then the rest of his clothes. Pictures flashed in his mind, ones he had seen of their proud ancestors. The smiles on their faces were god-like, and dolphin-like, their eyes dancing, their hair thick and long.

"I'll meet you at the shore!" he yelled. Heaven dove over the railing and into the rain-swept, sub-Antarctic water. He had never felt anything so cold.

An Indian family came out of their shack as Heaven swam toward the beach. He looked up at them as he swam through the freezing water. They were smiling! as they watched him swimming towards them. Like the smiles in the pictures, he thought.

The Indians were standing outside their dilapidated, all but fallen-down, little board home. Their hair was scraggily, and they looked old before their time, caricatures of their once happy, proud, strong ancestors.

He lunged for the rocks and pulled himself up onto the shore, then stumbled and fell to his knees on the rocky beach. An Indian woman ran out of the shack with a thick blanket of fur. Heaven was nearly passing out from the cold. He felt the warmth of the fur wrap around him. A man lifted him up to his feet and they led him into their hut.

In the bright warmth of the fire, Heaven started thawing out. "Thank you," he shivered, clutching the warm fur tightly around him.

They could not speak English. He could not speak Yaghan. They sat around the fire smiling: they did not need to speak. The others came in from *The Dolphin* with gifts of fresh fruit … and dry clothes for Heaven. The new friends "talked" in sign language, showing their surprise and delight. The little children laughed excitedly at the fresh oranges.

A young man motioned to them he was going outside. They followed, Heaven still clutching his fur. The black-haired Indian and a couple of children got into their small boat and rowed a little way out. There, using long sticks, they gathered their primary food from the waters: urchins.

Later in the night they all shared a meal around the fire: urchins and oranges.

In the morning, Heaven and his friends left, waving.

"We love you, friends," Heaven yelled from the skiff.

The Indians smiled, their eyes dancing.

The Dolphin sailed smoothly up the coast of Peru. White-sided dolphins rolled through the waves, body surfing alongside the ship. The sky was blue and clear, with delicate lace clouds floating by.

Heaven lay on the deck, looking up at the sails, watching them move in the wind.

Rena walked up to where he lay, holding Robby in her arms. She kneeled down beside him.

"Hello, Robby," Heaven said, putting his hand on the boy's head. "See the clipper off the starboard bow?"

Robby looked around as if he were concerned about something.

"He seems so serious all the time," Rena said, "as if the weight of the world was already on his shoulders."

"Maybe Robby's going to be an ambassador someday," Heaven said. "An ambassador from the sea."

"Well, he can certainly wait a few years before he gets serious," Rena said firmly. She put him to her breast and shook her hair. "He's just a baby!"

"Ahoy!" they suddenly heard.

Heaven jumped up and walked along the side, watching as the schooner sailed past.

"Ahoy!" he yelled into his bullhorn. "Where bound?"

"The Straits of Magellan. We're sailing 'round the Horn."

"It's winter down there," Heaven shouted. "Be careful."

"Were you there?"

"Barely made it through. Needed a little help!"

"What?!"

"Dolphins led us through!"

"Sure, matey. Where bound."

"Alaska!"

"You got a ways to go."

"Should be there by Christmas."

"Good luck."

"Peace!"

Finally, after sailing up the coast of Mexico (with the dolphins dancing to mariachi music!) and Southern California, they reached the Golden Gate. The fabled bridge shone like copper in the early evening sun, as little puffs of lacy clouds played amongst its golden towers. Busy autocars zoomed back and forth, their headlights like a gigantic neon sign pulsating across the delicate thread of the strand astride the glistening waters.

Capt. Jones stood by Heaven's side, watching intently. "Is this where the hippies live?" he asked.

Heaven nodded. "Once, long ago," he answered. "They were a mythical race, like elves, I think, who wore feathers and beads and danced around like wild Indians to pulsating music. They loved everybody and stuck flowers into gun barrels and smoked hashish like the gurus of India and listened entranced to sitar ragas.

"Yes, those were the golden days of the Golden Gate. Now, dark times have come, I hear. The homeless beg in the streets and live in cardboard boxes, and bad hard drugs have replaced the peaceful ganja.

"There is little love here these days, free or any other kind," he said. "Only gang wars and mayhem. Yes, dark days have come to the Golden Gate."

"Can't anything be done?" Capt. Jones asked. "I feel sorry for all those kids here. I got kids of my own, y'know…grown, married…and grandkids. Hate to see little kids grow up in a gangland."

Heaven sighed. "I don't know," he said. "It'd sure take somebody pretty strong to do much good here."

"Strong like a bear," Capt Jones said. "I got it! Maybe…a werebear," he said, "that comes down from the mountains and runs through the streets at night, kickin' some ass. That's what they need," he laughed. "An ol' werebear!"

Heaven was startled by this outburst from the normally taciturn and silent old captain.

"Well," Heaven finally said, "we're sailing to Kodiak Island in Alaska. Maybe we can scare up a werebear. Maybe the Indians could cast a spell on a giant Kodiak and turn him into a hippie," he laughed.

"That's it!" Capt. Jones said. "Turn a big ol' Kodiak 'bar' into a hippie. Bring him down here and set 'im loose. Let 'im kick some ass! That's what they need, alright," he said, puffing on his pipe and peering over the rail into the San Francisco fog.

"A werebear!"

Soon they were sailing up the beautiful rock-bound coast of Oregon and then finally up the Alaska Inland Passageway. Tiny forested islands floated by, lace clouds covering the pine trees like angel dust. Then past Ketchikan, first port in Alaska, and Juneau the capital, and the great glistening diamond Glacier Bay, where the ice bergs floated like islands of frozen clouds, and finally they reached the beautiful ornate Russian church of Sitka, and Kodiak Island, home of the biggest bears in the world—the Alaska browns, the largest carnivores (partly) on land.

Now, killer whales, the largest carnivores in the sea, were following them, big black and white beautiful monsters, their flukes sticking proudly straight out of the water like flags of some warrior nation. These were the true monarchs of the sea, fearing neither man nor beast, dark giant cousins of the playful dolphins. Indeed, they were overgrown dolphins, as if a pet cat had magically been transformed into an African lion.

A pod of killer whales swam majestically by, but Heaven noticed one whale was set apart from the others. This lone killer stayed with *The Dolphin* when all the others swam off, acting aggressively, repeatedly charging the ship and turning away at the last minute.

Heaven wasn't sure he could communicate with the killer whales like he could the dolphins, but he quickly got his "megaphone" and "hearing aide."

"Hello, Sir Killer Whale," he said, hoping he had a dialect the whale could understand. "Why do you charge at us?"

First there was silence and Heaven feared the whale would charge them again. Finally he heard, "You speak our tongue!"

Heaven was elated.

"Why do you charge us, Sir Killer Whale?" Heaven repeated.

He heard: "My pod has cast me out, and I am...lonely...and I hate humans."

He was happy he could communicate with the whale, but felt sad for his predicament.

"May I ride on you, Sir Killer?" he asked.

The whale seemed to laugh. "You, human, would freeze," it sneered.

"I have a special suit for swimming in Arctic waters," he answered.

"Then come on!"

Heaven quickly got dressed and dove over into the ice-flecked water as the others watched open mouthed from the deck.

Heaven swam to the killer and got up in front of its flag-like fluke. He felt ecstatic on the whale, the icebergs floating around them, the magic blue waters sparkling and glistening under the turquoise sky and gleaming sun.

"Why did your pod cast you out, Sir Whale?"

"I killed a human man. My pod has a taboo against killing humans, as they are trying to communicate with them. Most other pods allow it if the humans try to hurt them, but ours is becoming more civilized...and dolphin-like," he sneered.

"Why did you kill the human?"

"We were swimming by a log chute and men were shooting logs into the water. As we went by, a man shot a giant log down and hit me. It tore my skin and hurt my flipper. I heard him laugh at me. I vowed to get that man.

"Every day for a month I watch him. Finally, one day he came down into the water in a little boat. The fool! I swam under the boat and capsized it. He screamed. I took him under for 15 minutes. When he finally floated to the top his body was limp.

"My pod cast me out for breaking the taboo. Ever since I hate humans. But you are different. You understand."

"You may follow us if you like, Sir Killer, "but you must promise not to eat dolphins any more."

The killer whale seemed to smile. "I will protect my little cousins," he said. "But what about…humans?"

"Leave them to me!" Heaven replied.

They trailed the ship for a while, Heaven on the back of the whale, and soon something unheard of happened: a pod of dolphins swam alongside, cavorting with the converted killer!

Heaven stood solemnly on the foredeck as *The Dolphin* rolled along (a pod of dolphins with their new killer whale friend swimming nearby), a Bible in his hand. They were crossing the smooth Pacific now. He looked at his people gathered before him and Johnny and his girl Frankie standing in the center.

"Friends," he said, "we have gathered together today to be witnesses to this very special occasion: the marriage of Johnny and Frankie!"

Everybody cheered wildly.

Heaven looked at Johnny, his dreadlocks neatly coiffured, and at Frankie, his pretty exotic-looking tan-skin girl friend.

"You are the first to be married by me," he said. "I feel almost overwhelmed by the solemnity of the occasion.

"Theirs is a love as true and pure as the dolphin's," he said louder. Everybody was quiet. Only the waves could be heard.

"Johnny is my first mate and Frankie his first lady."

Everyone applauded.

"And now they are man and wife."

He looked at the two for a second.

"Will you two please kiss each other," he said.

"Congratulations! Frankie and Johnny!" they yelled.

"Where's the cake?" someone else said.

Everyone laughed and gathered around them.

Heaven stood above in the mast watch, as they sailed the Pacific in sight now of Japan, observing the dolphins and the killer whale. The dolphins were herding fish for their giant cousin! If only humans could learn to cooperate like this, Heaven thought.

He climbed down the ropes and went below to the glass-bottom observation room. He fed new data into "Charly Tuna", their computer, on dolphin populations in the open seas, then sat and looked down into the ocean. *The Dolphin* seemed alive to him whenever he sat in this room, somehow becoming one with the whirling water. All different species of fish would swim by, some pausing to look through the glass before darting on. Dolphins rocketed by from one side of the ship to the other. Often they would stoop and peer up at him.

Sir Killer looked in. What a change had come over the truculent whale! Heaven thought. How much better to observe him here, rather through the translucent walls of a show tank! Here he could watch and observe them all in their natural environment. There were undersea microphones on the bottom of the ship, and he could listen to their joyous chatter. And all the while *The Dolphin* rolled easily along, almost seeming to breathe.

Johnny suddenly ran into the observation room. "There's something coming over the radio, Heaven, sir. Quick!"

Heaven looked closely at Johnny, standing and following him into the radio room.

Johnny turned up the volume knob.

"…on an isolated beach off northern Japan. The local fishermen are killing the dolphins to protect their fishing, stampeding them into a small cove, beating them with clubs.

"Greenpeace…"

"Turn it off!" Heaven yelled. Johnny immediately clicked the knob.

Heaven's eyes met Johnny's. His stare was glassy.

"Find out where the beach is," Heaven said quietly, "and when you have your location…set your course."

"Aye, aye, sir!"

Heaven turned and walked out the door.

"This is war!"

Heaven looked through his binoculars, the red setting sun glaring. He saw a scene of ghastly slaughter—a bay of blood.

"Oh God!" he groaned. He lurched for the railing and started throwing up. Rena ran and found a towel and then to his side, wiping his face. "Oh baby, oh baby!"

Somebody gave him a cup of water. He felt he was in a stagnant dream.

"Rena," he said, "take the women and children below. The men and I are going ashore. If the Japanese try to get to the ship…you know how to steer *The Dolphin*."

142

"Heaven…"she cried.

"Do as I say, sweetheart."

She heard utter finality in his voice. She grasped his hands. "All right," she said. She turned and ran.

"Peter!" he yelled, "get the skiffs ready!" Peter ran for the boats.

Heaven looked at his men. "If anyone wants to stay behind," he said, "they may with no questions asked."

Nobody moved. "We're with you!" Capt Jones said.

"Yeah!" the captain's men yelled. "We're with ya!"

"Get the rifles!" Heaven yelled, running off.

"To the boats men!" Capt Jones called out as they dashed across the deck.

Soon the skiffs were approaching the beach, Sir Killer following in as closely as he dared. Some Japanese were in a boat herding dolphins in. The whale immediately submerged and came up under the boat, tossing the men in the water like chaff in the wind. They screamed as they went under. More blood.

Heaven looked through the scope of his rifle. The dead and dying bodies of dolphins littered the shore, where the men were still beating them with clubs. Some of the dolphins had their mouths open and were crying, but not biting. Dolphins never bite men, Heaven remembered. Some dolphins had beached themselves. A painting of an avenging angel wielding a glistening sword came to mind.

"Fire!" His finger smoothly pulled the trigger. Shots rang out. Several men immediately screamed and fell onto the red-stained sand. More blood.

The other men started running around wildly on the beach. Several more shots rang out. Several more fishermen fell.

Heaven jumped over the bow and ran through the red surf onto the beach. He pushed a man into the sand with his rifle and lifted the gunstock over his head. Like Davy Crockett, he thought. The man cried out in the sand and Heaven rammed his gun butt into the man's mouth.

"Don't kill dolphins!"

In minutes, the fighting was over. The red setting sun shone on dead bodies of men that lay with the dead bodies of dolphins. Blood seemed everywhere.

Heaven counted his men. He had not lost one. "Kill any dying dolphins with a bullet," he ordered. "If you find any which could survive, try to get them back into the water. And if you can't—shoot them quickly."

Peter and Johnny ran and found a small dolphin in the surf who looked in good condition and attempted to push him out to sea, but he tried to swim back to his dying companions, crying mournfully.

"No, no, please," Peter said, "swim away, please swim away!"

Another came to help.

Heaven ran along the beach. He found an old wooden sign among some trash. He grabbed the sign and ran back to the bodies where he took off his shirt and dipped it in blood until it was saturated, then wrote on the sign:

"DON'T KILL DOLPHINS!"

Heaven stuck the sign in the sand. He ran to help the others in the deepening red-tinged gloom.

Soon they where back on board *The Dolphin,* stars above shooting across the darkening sky.

"A boat's approaching, mon!" Johnny yelled, looking through infrared night vision binoculars. "Flag looks like—risin' sun!"

Heaven took the binocs. "It's a coast guard cutter! Full speed astern, Peter!" he yelled into the microphone. "We're leaving them in our wake!"

The Dolphin took off through the water like a hydroplane, soon entering a fogbank.

"I think we lost 'em, but if we didn't...we'll ram the bloody bastards!" Heaven said gruffly.

"Right!" Capt. Jones said. "I just couldn't believe how the dolphins weren't biting..."

"You might say, Capt. Jones, with regards to men, dolphins turn the other cheek," Heaven said.

"I'd knock their bloody heads off, mon!" said Johnny.

Dr. Edward Smith and Sharon Bentley craned their necks toward the T.V. set in their Caribbean hotel room. Their mouths were open as they watched the news program showing the beach in Japan where the bodies of the dead fishermen were found among the dead dolphins.

"One final note to this incredible, tragic scene," the commentator said, "a warning left behind by whomever did this, a sign written in...blood."

The T.V. screen framed the old wooden sign.

"DON'T KILL DOLPLHINS!"

"This is..."

Sharon looked at Dr. Smith.

"He'll return...I think," Dr. Smith said.

The Dolphin sailed now slowly down the coast of India.

In Bombay, they found the charity of the Catholic Saint Mother Teresa. They walked into an office where a nun sat behind a desk, the rays of the hot afternoon sun shining in through slanted window slats.

The old wrinkled woman looked up at them.

"May I help you" she smiled, speaking in precise English.

Heaven and Peter carried a large bag. They emptied sparkling gold artifacts in front of her. The lady's mouth came open. "For you," said Heaven.

"But sir!" she cried. "There must be a million dollars here!"

"Then it should go a long way," he said quietly.

"Let me call the Mother," she said, picking up the telephone.

"No!" Heaven said forcefully. "I don't feel worthy right now."

"But who are you? What is your name?"

"Let's just say I'm someone who's trying to ease his conscience." He kneeled to her and lowered his head. "In the holy name of gentle Jesus," Heaven said softly.

He stood and turned and walked toward the door. "Please, sister," he said, looking back. "See it's spent wisely."

They walked out into the bustling streets and finally made their way to a park, where Indian musicians were performing. Flowing raga sounds filled the flower-perfumed air, the music a smooth swirl.

A young black haired man was sitting cross-legged, playing a sitar. His fingers whirred over the plaintive strings. Next to him sat an older man playing tablas.

"What magic sounds!" said Rena.

Heaven watched them, almost hypnotized by the exotic sights and sounds. The musicians wore bright robes, and decorated vases of jungle flowers were among them. They sat on exoticly colored rugs and pillows.

After the concert of "afternoon ragas", the friends made their way to the mouth of the Ganges River, where many people were swimming and bathing. Heaven saw the Gangetic River dolphins, swimming playfully around the feet of the worshipers, their outrageously long grinning snouts like Hopi clown masks. He ran out into the water, petting the smiling creatures. All at once Heaven felt he was on a "magic carpet" of cool flames, scarlet and gold. He felt he could fly across the Ganges!

He brought himself back, and Rena was holding his hand, standing beside him waist deep in the river.

"Aren't these cute dolphins," she said, petting one as it swam around her. "They look like court jesters."

Heaven whistled and laughed.

Finally they turned and walked out of the river, back into the fierce midday sun, the Ganges water quickly evaporating.

They next came upon a young fakir, performing tricks. He was smiling as he sang in English for some tourists:

"Gonna disappear,
Right before your eyes!
Gonna make the smoke fall
Gonna make the water rise!
Gonna pull a song
Right from my silk hat!
And if you watch me closely now
You might see where I'm at!"

He was playing an old American classical guitar, somehow making it sound like a sitar:

"Silk string magic I can make my,

Magic I can make my, magic I can make my
Fingers fly, oh!
Silk string magic I can take you
Magic I can take you, magic I can take you
To the sky, oh!
Gonna cut the cards, no sleight of hand,
You'll see this ain't no jive
And deal to you aces four
And to me jokers five!
Gonna talk in circles, sing in tongues,
And make the muse appear,
And play the lost and missing chord.
The sirens long to hear!

Gonna disappear, right before your eyes…!"

Ping! He played a harmonic on his guitar and disappeared behind a rising pillar of smoke. Then he was right before them, bowing. The tourists all clapped and threw him money.

Rena walked up to the fakir. "What a cute song," she said, Michelle holding her hand, laughing. "Where did you learn it?"

"From an American!" the young fakir said, smiling.

Soon they were sailing to the Holy Land.

In Jerusalem they walked about the dusty streets. A peasant woman ran up to Heaven. She peered into his face, then knelt at his feet and grabbed his ankles.

"Are you the Lamb? The Lamb?" she gasped in broken English.

"Mother," Heaven said, startled, lifting up the woman to her feet. "You are delirious. Can we take you a doctor?"

"Oh my son," she said, "my spirit tells me you have seen the Lord God. You have seen the One Who is to come!"

"I have seen an angel," Heaven replied, "the holy ghost of my father. But I am not your Lamb. I am only a man."

Tears were in her eyes. "I am sorry. I have embarrassed you." She bowed to his friends. "God bless you, children, and keep you safe." She disappeared into the crowd. His friends looked at Heaven.

"I think," Rena said, "we should leave Jerusalem."

"Yeah" said Peter, "let's find the Sea of Galilee."

Soon they were looking over the wave tops of the desert "sea." They walked on the rocks by the alkaline waters. Then they saw something out on the lake: a cloud came floating down from the sky seemingly in the form of a man! "walking" slowly toward them on the waves! the wind crying out suddenly.

They all stood silently, watching the cloud march across the Sea of Galilee.

"Is it walking toward us?" Rena whispered, her shaking voice blending eerily with the wind.

"What is it?" gasped Peter.

"Who is it, mon?" asked Johnny.

"I don't know," Heaven breathed.

The cloud was bathed in sunlight shining down in rays from above. The wind started blowing harder now, rustling the leaves in the trees around them.

"I've never seen anything so strange," Frankie said, holding tightly to Johnny's arm.

The others were silent. Then the cloud rose up to the top of the sky.

"It must be the wind," Peter said.

"Or maybe the second coming!" said Heaven.

They all laughed a little nervously, as the shining cloud ascended above them. The friends gazed up at it. The cloud seemed alive as it flew.

"Oh God!" said Peter.

"Anyone need to repent?" asked Heaven.

The friends finally found their way to the Jordan River, slowly tumbling through the green trees and plants. They all jumped in the river, immersing themselves, washing the dust off.

Heaven came up out of the water, his head back, his eyes closed, the others standing around. Water streamed off him.

He looked at them. "I feel new."

"I feel clean," Rena said.

"I feel light," echoed Peter.

The light from above shone down on them mutely as they all stood in the River Jordan.

"Jesus came up out of these waters once," said Heaven.

"Yes," said Frankie. "And John baptized here, two thousand years ago."

"Right here?" said little Michelle, on the edge of the river.

"Yes, right here," Johnny said.

Rena held Robby and carefully immersed him in the slowly swirling waters as Michelle swam out to them.

"Can you imagine those days," said Frankie, "all the people coming here to be baptized, and John the Baptist wearing animal skins and preaching to them."

"And Jesus talking to them about Heaven," Heaven said. "But they really didn't listen, you know. And they still aren't, I don't think, as least not with their hearts." His eyes sparkled.

"But I am," he said. "And so are ye."

They soon left Israel, sailing through the Suez Canal and the Red Sea, and finally were where they had started long ago: the crystal blue-green waters of Bermuda!

Heaven and Rena sat across from Pastor Otis and his wife. They had all decided to see their families while home in Bermuda after so long away.

"How are you Heaven?" the old black pastor asked.

"Fine, sir," he said.

"It's good to have you two here again, though I know you'll be leaving us soon. And Rena," he said, smiling at her, "you're still the prettiest girl in the islands."

Rena blushed, her hand on Michelle who sat on the rug by Robby.

"Your children are just beautiful," the pastor's wife said, smiling. "You are truly blessed."

Rena smiled.

"Your work with the dolphins has been successful, Heaven?" asked the pastor.

"Yes sir," said Heaven. "Very successful."

"Your father Michael loved them so," the pastor's wife said, a tear coming to her eye, which she wiped away.

"I know, ma'am."

"Heaven," the pastor said, "how about you and I take a walk outside, and let the women talk for a bit."

Heaven looked at the pastor. "All right, sir," he said, standing.

Pastor Otis stood slowly up. "We'll be back in a few minutes."

"All right, dear," his wife said.

The two walked outside in the warm evening breeze, where the stars shone clearly in the clean air and the waves glinted white from their distant lights as they rolled onto the beach, the surf restlessly frothing and foaming.

"Heaven," the pastor said, "I feel a…darkness about you which I never felt before, something sad and sorrowful in your spirit, in your soul. Is there anything you would like to…well…confess?"

A flash of blood was before Heaven's eyes, as he looked startled into the aged face of the perceptive old black pastor, who had been like a father to him, who had cared for him when his real father was…taken. Then he saw the dead men lying on the beach. He heard the dolphins crying.

"I got even with some people," he said simply.

Pastor Otis walked with Heaven in silence for a moment, then nodded his head and put his hand on Heaven's shoulder. "You're a soldier, like David. Retribution. God is with you."

Heaven and Rena were dancing together slowly on the deck of *The Dolphin,* as Sinatra sang over the speakers, the stars twinkling above them. He gracefully twirled her on her toes with his hand and then caught her as she fell into his arms. He stood her back up on her feet and lifted her up onto the rail, holding her at arm's length, gazing into her face.

"You look so pretty in the starlight," he said.

She blushed as he set her back down on the smoothly rolling deck, the ship rocking ever so gently on the silken water. Violins gushed a melody as he parted his legs and slid her between them and then brought her back up. She placed her hand and arm on his shoulder and felt the breeze blow her hair against her neck.

He lifted her up and the wind blew her dress into his face. He caught her in his arms and walked with her across the deck and swirled, holding her. She draped her arm behind his neck, watching the sky behind his face turn in circles. He set her back down in mid-swirl.

Then the song ended: "It turned out so right/For strangers in the night."

Above, the stars twinkled, and their eyes did too.

Alone in the on ship observation room (Rena and the children off to visit her parents for a week) Heaven listened to his "hearing aide" as a young dolphin was whistling a story to him, gazing up at him through the glass bottom: an ancient legend of thousands of years ago it seemed, a song passed through space and time from dolphin to dolphin:

"The creatures flew across the water. They looked down upon the water. When they landed they walked through the water.

"They lived in the land in the middle of the sea."

Heaven carefully studied his underwater topographical map of Bermuda, showing the hundreds of square miles of reef around the island, all of which had once been dry land.

"Then the land sank into the sea. All our brothers died."

Heaven looked closely at the map. He now knew what the dolphin was telling him.

"Of course!" he said into the "megahone." "Bermuda is the last remnant of the lost continent of Atlantis!"

He quickly donned his scuba gear and exited the escape hatch, where the dolphin met him. Heaven got on his back and down and down they flew through the dark water. Above, a storm rocked the seatop. Heaven immediately began echolocating.

They soon approached the coral floor. The dolphin swam to a small hidden cave in the coral and entered it. There was

153

barely enough room for the two of them as they swam through the passage. On and on through the tunnel they wound, finally emerging into a large undersea, underground cavern.

The dolphin stopped and Heaven "looked" before them. He switched on his headlamp, now, and got off the dolphin and swam to a sparkling wall of coral.

"Here," the dolphin said.

Heaven took a pickaxe off his utility belt and then began chipping away at the coral. The dolphin came and went to breathe at the surface as he worked.

He was almost out of air when his axe hit something very hard. He quickly scraped the coral away, and shone his light on the surface: It was ruby!

Day after day he and the dolphin went down, telling no one. This was between him and the dolphin. Day after day he chipped away at the coral wall inside the secret hidden cavern. Day after day more precious stone was revealed: ruby, emerald, pearl, gold, sapphire, opal. The shape of a small house began slowly to emerge, all in glittering stone, with diamond windows!

"Their homes sparkled like rainbows under the sun," the dolphin had sung. Atlantis, Heaven now knew, had been a city made entirely of precious and semi-precious stone!

Finally, one day, just as he was getting low on oxygen, his pickaxe broke through into an opening. He chipped away until he made a hole large enough to swim through, then entered carefully and shone his light around him: he was in a world of gems. All around him his light sparkled on the walls of solid gemstone, bouncing so brilliantly off the facets he was almost blinded. He swam from one room to another, his light flashing all about. From a wall of ruby to one of emerald he swam. He pushed open a pearl door and entered a multi-jeweled room. He swam through a gold framed open window, the diamond glass moving back and forth with the current. He wove around and through the labyrinth of rooms, so mesmerized by the rainbow world he had entered he didn't realize he was out of air until he had just enough time to take one final gasp. Then, just as he also realized he was lost amid all the sparkling sparkles, the dolphin showed up and led him out.

Over the next days he covered the stonewall back up, using under water mortar.

"The Spirit in the sky shook the sea and brought down their land," the dolphin had sung.

The "Spirit in the sky" had cursed the Atlanteans, Heaven was told, for becoming too greedy and had sunk their home. The place had "bad karma." As beautiful as it was, Heaven knew he could never return here again.

Heaven stood at the bow of *The Dolphin,* looking out over the green water. They were sailing finally into the Gulf of Mexico, back to their island home after so long away.

He had taken sample counts of the dolphin population and fed them into Charly Tuna, the computer. Charly had told him the dolphins were safe—so far. But if the present rate of killing them by the tuna industry continued, the situation could change drastically within ten years.

He knew, for instance, the dolphins most often caught in the nets were pregnant and lactating mothers. If these were unproportionately killed, this could lead to a dangerous mating imbalance, threatening the entire dolphin stock.

All he could really do for them, he knew now, was pray.

Heaven looked up at the sky and then to the shore: "It's good to be home!" he said. "And please, God, save the dolphins."

When they had resettled on their island home, now named Utopia II, Heaven started drawing—with the advise and consent of the dolphins and Sir Killer—the architectural plans for their underwater Xanadu.

"Use coral to build your home," they suggested.

Yes! Heaven thought. We'll use beautiful natural coral to blend in perfectly with the ocean floor and have windows with coral coverings which can be removed or set in place as we will. Our home will be in the coral under the sea...a giant "coral igloo!"

The dolphins can meet us at the door and we'll build an entrance for them to come into their inside swimming pool. (Unfortunately, Sir Killer is so big he'll have to stay "outside.") They will only have to push a button with their flipper or snout to enter.

Underground, undersea pipes would lead from the home to pumps on the island which would circulate the air. When their undersea "palace" was complete, they would be able to live permanently in the sea—true sea mammals.

We will share the dolphin's life, thought Heaven, living in their "state of grace." The sea will be our kingdom, and dolphin bliss will reign free. They have so many things to teach us, he thought as he swam down to the site, about love and felicity. And they want to teach us! All they know!

He held the plastic-covered architectural plans. Rena, Peter, all the others, were busy working, swimming about with the dolphins. Sir Killer effortlessly pulled a giant beam through the water; Johnny soared smiling by on a sea-sled...

Xanadu would be forty feet below the surface, in the coral. At this depth there would be no risk of decompression difficulties— no chance of anyone getting the bends. And besides, Heaven had designed the entire home as a decompression chamber, approximating a continual slow ascent.

He watched little Michelle, riding an undersea-sled with young Peter. She was already an expert diver. She waved, as did he. Someday, he thought to himself, as the bubbles rose from her breathing regulator...The world will hear from her!

Rena swam up to him, excitedly waving and gesturing to where she was working. He swam over with her. He nodded his head, and they touched face masks and then she went back to her work. It's getting there, Heaven thought. (He had just returned from a trip on *The Dolphin* to get supplies.) Robby smiled like a papoose...

Someday this will be home, our kingdom. True love will reign in peace, and we'll gaze at the stars through the waves and swim forever free with the dolphins. They will lead us in truth as the spirit and keep us together in love, for they know wise things:

They know the art of joy!

Dr. Smith and Sharon were fishing from a little dinghy in a bay. It was early morning. All at once without warning the sea became rough. "My gosh...we're going to capsize!" Sharon cried. Suddenly a brilliant white light soared by under their boat!

"What!" Dr. Smith yelled.

Then the water opened underneath them like a maelstrom and their boat was drawn down, swirling around and around, faster and faster. Sharon screamed, expecting to see Capt. Nemo and the Nautilus at any moment.

Just as the water was about to swamp them, a large air bubble covered their boat and they were under the sea floating down, down, down…

Now Sharon was thinking, "Curioser and curioser!"–Alice down the rabbit hole—too scared to even speak. Then the light approached the bubble, hovering in front of them, smiling!

Dr. Smith looked into the face before him.

"My God!" he gurgled. "Dr. Michael Hope!"

Sharon's mouth dropped open and she felt paralyzed as she gaped at him. Then she fainted.

The giant air bubble blew through the water. Fish and sea-weeds soared by. A grinning dolphin raced beside them.

"Edward!" Dr. Smith heard. "I have a job for you."

Then he too blanked out.

Heaven was dreaming when he heard his father's voice.

"Son," the voice said, "I'm sending someone to you. He can help you and you can help him."

Heaven awoke from the dream, got up and gazed out the stained glass window overlooking the beach. He saw a small boat slowly approaching their beach.

"Rena," he said. "Wake up. "We've got visitors!" He quickly dressed.

"Who is it?" Rena yawned sleepily.

Heaven was already out the tree house door and climbing down the steps.

"Hello, friends!" he called, as he ran out into the water to meet them. He led their boat to shore.

Dr. Smith and Sharon looked about dazedly. "The wind must have blown us here!" Dr. Smith kept saying.

"What are you two doing way out here in such a little boat? Are you all right?" Heaven asked as he dragged their boat up onto the beach.

"I'm not really sure," Dr. Smith began. "We were fishing in a small bay when the water quite all at once became very rough. I guess the wind blew us here…wherever we are."

"You're in the Gulf of Mexico," Heaven said.

"The Gulf of Mexico!?" both Sharon and Dr. Smith cried out at once.

"We were fishing in the Bahamas!" Dr. Smith gasped. "I didn't know there were islands in the Gulf of Mexico," he said, looking at Heaven.

"Only this tiny speck on the outskirts. It's not on every chart. We call it Utopia II which means 'nowhere.'"

"Well, it feels like somewhere to me," Sharon said. "'The Twilight Zone'."

"However you got here, at least you're still dry! And you must be tired and hungry. Come and eat with us."

Heaven helped the dazed pair out of their boat and led them up the beach to the tree house as others gathered around.

"Visitors," Heaven smiled as he helped the two up the tree steps.

Rena held open the round door as they staggered in and immediately collapsed on the star/dolphin rug. They sat silently, blank expressions on their faces, staring off out the stain-glass window. Dr. Smith shook his head and Sharon looked at him.

Dr. Smith now began slowly speaking, as though in a deep trance:

"We were working with dolphins in Key Largo," Dr. Smith intoned quietly. "I was doing mind maps and Sharon was my assistant. We were trying to communicate with the dolphins in their own language…and maybe go a step further, a step beyond, do something undreamt of, something unbelievable…

"Then I met him—a brilliant young scientist who loved the dolphins more than I liked most people, (excepting Sharon, of course)," he said putting his arm around her drooping shoulder.

"I admired this man more than anyone else I ever met…"

Dr. Smith's voice trailed off.

Heaven sat in silence, and then finally said, "And what was this man's name?"

"Michael Hope," Dr. Smith said. "His name was Dr. Michael Hope."

Heaven almost burst into tears, but caught himself. "He was my father. And you must be…Dr. Smith! Father said to exp…"

Rena quickly splashed cold water on Dr. Smith's face after he fainted, trying to revive him, while Sharon sat dazedly, leaning against the wall.

Finally Dr. Smith came to, staring wildly up at Heaven.

"You're…Michael's son?!"

"Yes, Dr. Smith. I'm Heaven Hope." He reached out his hand.

Dr. Smith slowly sat up and took Heaven's hand, looking closely at him. "Yes," he said, shaking his head. "I do see the family resemblance.

"Oh my lord," he said, now looking at Sharon, "I need a drink." He let go Heaven's hand like he was letting go of a life preserver in a stormy sea and clasped Sharon's. "We found him, somehow." Sharon silently nodded. Rena ran and got some wine in gold goblets and brought them to Dr. Smith and Sharon. Both gulped their's down like Kool-Aide.

"Did you continue your father's work?" Dr. Smith immediately asked.

Heaven studied him for a minute and then said, "I broke through. I completed the project."

Heaven quickly showed Dr. Smith the "megaphone" and "hearing aide" and computer readouts of the dolphin's language.

"My God!" Dr. Smith almost yelled. "This is it!" He grabbed his chest. "Oh," he breathed.

Heaven steadied him.

"I'm all right," he said, checking his pulse. He looked back up at Heaven. "You actually did it."

Heaven beamed.

"Sit down…Heaven," Dr. Smith said. "I have something to tell you."

Heaven drew up a chair and sat down in front of them.

"How much did you know about your father?"

"Well he…left when I was very young…

"I remember him getting shot on the beach at Bermuda as he flung me out into the sea…"

"What?!" Dr. Smith and Sharon both said at once.

Heaven quickly related the incident of the helicopter as he remembered it. "My father was holding me in his arms in the surf when suddenly he whirled around like a discus thrower and flung me out into the sea, yelling at me to 'Dive deep!' As I cut the water, I heard a violent ripple sound as bullets ripped the shore. When I finally surfaced, too scared to go up before I had to breathe, I saw my father's body floating in the water in his own blood…and a helicopter disappearing out over the ocean.

"As I was treading water, dolphins swam in and pushed him out to where I was floating and took him under. I seem to remember a greenish light around him. I dove under and swam to him. He had a peaceful smile on his lips. Then suddenly, his eyes came open like twin light beams, shining directly on me! The next thing I remember I was floating on the surface on the back of a dolphin and a girl swam out and carried me to shore.

"Then my mind goes blank, Dr. Smith."

Dr. Smith and Sharon were silent, nursing what was left of their wine and gazing vacantly again.

"I found some of his papers, hidden away in an old chest. He wrote of experiments with dolphins, but some of the writing had faded and I couldn't read it all. He mentioned you, Dr. Smith. Some things I couldn't quite make out, like smudged-out references to…transplants."

Dr. Smith came to.

"I remember feeling this constant overwhelming love from him," Heaven was saying. "And I know he loved dolphins very very much…"

"Heaven," Dr. Smith said slowly, "…your father was a dolphin…!"

"Project Love was your father's dream, Heaven," Dr. Smith was saying as Heaven leaned back in his chair against the wall, his eyes closed. "He believed dolphins are ethically superior to human beings and wished to transfer these qualities of love to somebody, to see if he, or she, could then teach others how to live at peace with one another. His dream was to transplant the mind—and soul, if you will—of a dolphin into a human.

"I had been working with the dolphins myself, thinking maybe of trying a brain transplant with a human, strictly for scientific research purposes…or I should say porpoises," he chuckled. "I had already succeeded in dolphin to dolphin transplants, and hoped maybe this might be a way for us to succeed in making dolphins speak English…or people speak Delphin.

"Then I met your father. You can imagine how stunned I was when I learned he had the same general idea. He was more interested in the possibility of morally improving the human race than I. But I came to see the superiority of his approach, and taking Sharon with me, we joined forces with your father in his laboratory.

"One day our main animal died—Cloe was her name—quite unexpectedly. We buried her at sea from our research vehicle. Just after her funeral, a freak accident occurred. A most unusually strong gust of wind blew our dolphin net down and one of the led weights hit your father in the head. It was a very serious injury, from which he would have died." Dr. Smith paused. "It was almost as though the gods had ordained, had willed that your father would be his own subject!

"Anyway, the last word he said, before he lapsed into what would have been a permanent coma, was 'Song!', the name of our other primary dolphin." Dr. Smith paused again.

"I transplanted parts of Song the dolphin's brain into your father and saved his life. Your father had the mind and…and soul…of a dolphin! And he recovered completely, I might add."

Heaven's eyes remained closed as he listened.

Dr. Smith paused.

"One day a National Security major showed up to see your father to procure data concerning the dolphin's language for military purposes. Michael refused to give him the data and when the major threatened him with a subpoena, Michael suddenly attacked the man—much like a dolphin attacking a shark!

"I fainted, and when I came to, the major was lying bleeding and unconscious on the floor. Michael was gone. He was later picked up in the middle of the Bermuda Triangle by a fishing boat! They took him on to Bermuda—after first radioing in they had picked up some one floating on a dolphin! With amnesia, they said. After receiving the report, Sharon and I quickly flew to Bermuda. After checking all the places the fishermen usually frequented, I finally found Michael—sitting in a ritzy bar with his new-found fishermen friends. We tried to get him to come back with us, but he refused…We never saw Michael again.

"I'm sure it was U.S. intelligence who ki…attempted to kill your father, to keep him from giving his top secret information to the Chinese or Russians or someone, I guess."

Dr. Smith took a drink of wine and looked back at his unexpected host.

"Now you know about your father, Heaven," he said. "And now I know a few things myself."

Heaven nodded his head. "Dr. Smith, you and Sharon must stay here and live with us on the island. Will you?"

Dr. Smith looked over at Sharon who quickly nodded her head.

"Yes!" they both said at once.

Heaven and Rena walked through the forest. The roses of the trees perfumed the air. Rena held his hand. He was very quiet and she walked silently beside him.

"My father," he said simply.

She leaned her head against his shoulder.

"Everyone loved him," she finally said.

"I still remember the girl," he said, "holding me in the water and the people on the beach."

He looked at Rena. His eyes were wet.

"They needed him."

That night, in a dream, Heaven was swimming with a pod of bottlenose dolphins at fifty miles per hour. His eyes were opened and he could hear their sweet ultrasonic chirps as they flew through the glistening world. He was soaring through an underwater multi colored tunnel, the love chirps yellow and green and blue. He could "see" sounds and "hear" colors. They were all talking to him ultrasonically.

They surfaced and a dolphin stood on his tail on the top of the water, looking at him. He was balanced perfectly on the tip of his tail. He moved his flukes and "walked" easily through the water. Then he dove.

Heaven leaped for his dorsal fin and they joyously swam together, chirping to each other. Heaven awoke–smiling.

Heaven and Rena were sitting on the beach, the sitting sun shining red, on this Saturday night. He looked out over the water. Then on the horizon he saw the first shape of a vessel come into view. He watched it more closely, as it approached the island, seeming to appear out of some uncharted region of the mists.

He stood up and called the others. They all came and stood around him. Peter handed him binoculars.

"Looks like an island rigger," Heaven said, looking through the high tech "spy-glass."

Finally they heard the sounds of music and laughing lilting from the boat. Heaven saw brown male and female faces smiling over the railing.

"I think," Heaven said, still peering intently, "…we're going to have a party."

"Hey there mon!" they heard. "Can we come to yer island?"

"Only if you want to!" Heaven yelled back.

They heard laughter. "Sure mon. We want to." A black man held a bouda bag a foot away from his mouth and squeezed wine in a spray. "Wine!" he yelled when he had drunk, wiping his face and laughing with the others. "Much wine!"

"You like calypso music, mon?" someone else yelled.

"Love it!" Heaven answered.

The islanders started climbing over the ship's railing with musical instruments, then waded ashore to the beach.

"Hey friends," one of the brownskins said. "Let's sing songs and dance in the moonlight, dance 'till the break o' day. Then we go. O.K.?"

"Okay!" Heaven smiled, remembering with a chuckle the Faulkner he had read in college, when the Negro "reiver" had said a white should spend one Saturday night as a black-man to really understand what it meant to be…"African American"…

They started setting up their instruments on the beach: conga drums, stand-up bass, guitars…One man pulled a harmonica from his pocket and started blowing a sweet blues. Soon the others joined in. Bouncing reggae tumbled down the beach.

"Roots, rock, reggae!

This-a reggae music," a man huskily sang.

The women started moving easily to the crazy cantering beat— like a drunken metronome.

Then the musicians broke into a calypso mood.

"Day-O!

Day-ay-ay-O"

Heaven got his mandolin and joined the musicians, the delicate instrument blending exotically with the island rhythms. He stood with them seeming almost in rapture as he fluttered over melodies. They smilingly looked at him, nodding their heads in approval.

Rena had her hands clasped and eyes closed and she swayed gently to the soft rhythms. Johnny and Frankie danced slowly together. Sharon and Dr. Smith sat at the edge of the beach and watched quietly. Peter bounced Michelle on his knee. Capt. Jones jitterbugged with a pretty young black woman.

Robby tottered in and out among the crowd. Some of the black women would pick him up, bouncing him gently to the music, laughing. Robby would laugh and kiss them on the cheek.

"Such a cute li'l boy," they would say.

The music went on and on through the night. Heaven put down his mandolin and walked to where Rena was standing, the silver gold moonlight shimmering around her.

"May I have this dance?" he said.

"Yes."

He took her hand and they danced together to the flowing sounds. Heaven moved his feet easily on the sand. He closed his eyes and dropped Rena's hand and picked up the tempo. Rena followed, watching him. He tilted his head back and shook his thick, long hair which hung around his neck almost like a lion's mane. He opened his eyes, smiling at Rena. "I was nearly transported."

Rena sighed and took his hand again. "Not without me," she said lightly. "I don't want to lose you. Ever."

"I promise," he said, "I won't go anywhere you don't."

In the morning, the bright yellow rising sun a splendid contrast to the silver/gold star/moon light of the night before, the visitors left.

"We didn't know this teeny island was even here, mon," the leader black said to Heaven. "It seemed to appear out of... nowhere! mon," he laughed.

"Well," Heaven laughed. "We call it Utopia II, and Utopia means, literally…nowhere. Kinda like Middle Earth," he smirked.

Everyone laughed in the morning sunshine.

"Maybe we see you friends agin someday," the black said. "If we can ever find this teeny island agin," he laughed. "It really is in the middle of …nowhere!"

"Please come back," Michelle said.

"Yes," Robby echoed. "Pleeeeese!"

"Of course we will, li'l darlin's," one of the women said. "Jest to see Michelle an' Robby."

The brown-skinned woman's eyes sparkled as she knelt down to them: "Yer es sweet es de dolphin!"

The years went by peacefully on their tiny island as the sea home was being built. Heaven and Rena raised their children and Michelle and Robby grew up healthy, strong and bright, learning everything they needed to know from those on the island.

Heaven performed more marriages and more children were born.

Capt. Jones and his men proved to be "able-bodied undersea carpenters." Peter and Johnny remained Heaven's closest mates.

Dr. Smith grew his hair long and took to wearing 24k solid gold-chain necklaces, becoming a "75 year old hippy." His great knowledge of subjects from medicine to astrophysics and almost everything in between was invaluable to Heaven in building their undersea home. (In fact, Heaven later thought, I couldn't have done it without him. What good fortune, he mused, that this mad genius materialized as if by magic out of the Bermuda Triangle!)

Sharon was the good doctor's constant companion. Neither of them ever told Heaven of her former relationship with Michael his father: they felt somehow he knew anyway, though he never once mentioned it.

Heaven loved Rena more with each passing year, and her beauty seemed to continually bloom. Like an elegant elf, he thought. They were rarely apart, and when the stars were shining, they could be seen dancing together quietly on the beach, as though listening to some distant music…

Heaven would often play sweet ballads on his mandolin, and the melodies would float up to the sky. The birds would whistle and chirp in the trees, adding innumerable harmonies, and the whole jungle became a magical orchestra.

They all lived in peace like the dolphins, with whom someday they would share their home of the wild blue/green ocean.

When Heaven was thirty years, their undersea palace was finally ready! They all donned their scuba gear and, carrying the last of their supplies on sea sleds, swam out to the coral. Their new home was completely camouflaged in the sparkling coral: someone swimming directly over it could easily miss it.

Heaven swung open the coral outer door, then pushed the button for the metal inner door, and they swam into the "water withdrawal room." He pushed another button and the door slid closed, water immediately draining out. They took off their scuba gear and put on dry clothes. Heaven pushed a third button and they entered a third door—the living room: sunken, with a soft thick carpet elaborately embroidered with seascapes, brightly colored pillows, intricate Indian rugs (Eastern and Western), with driftwood and shells decorating the walls and tables.

Priceless artifacts from many treasures, and pearls and precious stones finished the undersea decorum.

Windows looked into the sea where the fish swam among the coral. Sir Killer and a dolphin friend smiled in.

"Home!" Heaven said.

Everyone cheered. "It's worth all the work," Rena said.

Sharon and Dr. Smith stood together. They could still hardly believe it.

"Heaven," Dr. Smith said, "you are a genius. If I hadn't witnessed this with my very own eyes…"

"Let's have some wine for our homecoming!" Heaven said.

Then they heard splashing in the inside sea pool, in a large room just adjacent to them. They immediately looked through the transparent wall and saw two bottlenose dolphins.

"Our first official visitors!" Heaven laughed.

He pushed a button and they entered the "pool room." The dolphins had their heads out of the water and were floating vertically, their mouths open, their eyes shining. They whistled happily.

Heaven petted one. The dolphin jumped up part way on the side, turning his white belly over for Heaven to rub.

"My friends," Heaven said. "How good to have you."

All the others started laughing and playing with the dolphins.

"Our home is yours!" Heaven said.

"And yours ours!"

CHAPTER FIVE
THE SOLUTION

Dr. Smith and Heaven were in the elaborate laboratory the doctor had built for his projects and experiments.

"My latest invention!" Dr. Smith proudly pointed to a simple looking pair of headphones. "A 'dream machine.' Put these on and you're in dreamland, my boy—in technocolor!"

Heaven slowly put them on. Dr. Smith walked to a console and started whirling dials. Instantly Heaven was again in Alaska! the glistening, snowcapped peaks a rude contrast to the tropical waters just outside the window.

Indians were dancing around him (as he closed his eyes), where he lay coldly on snow. They were chanting wild words. He lifted himself up and out to sea saw the black and white flag of the killer whale nation. Auroa borealis danced above.

On the outside of the circle of leaping Indians, he saw a giant Kodiak bear rear up twelve feet into the air and open its mouth to let out a blast of a growl, like a cannon…

Then he was in a darkened one room cabin. Snow was drifting down around the window. He was lying in a bed.

He turned and looked to his side…Rena was sleeping beside him, looking as pretty as the last time he had seen her, sunning herself on their beach. There was only one difference: She was an Indian. He looked at his own skin: It was dark black.

A knock came to the door. Heaven got up as "Rena" said, "Someone's at the door, Ajax."

Ajax?! He stumbled across the room and creaked open the rough wooden door. An old Indian, his face covered with a fur parka looked intently at him, the ghostly sun shining almost like an aurora around his hood.

"Ajax! Just got a telegram for ya from San Francisco…It's serious, I'm afraid. Thought I better bring it right out."

"Come in, Billy." The dogs tied to the sled behind him were yipping and howling.

"Can't. Got more to deliver." He turned and walked to the sled, and then looked back at Ajax. "I'm mighty sorry," he said, his breath forming an ether-like frame around the icy portrait of his gnarled wrinkled face. Then he was off with a "Mush!" the dogs leaping down the trail.

"What is it, Ajax?"

Heaven opened the telegram and read in silence:

"Your sister had been killed in Oakland. Stop." Ajax stopped. "She was killed in a driveby gang shooting while visiting your parents there. Stop."

"Sis has been killed, Drena," he heard himself say. (Drena?)

Drena sat up. "Oh God!"

"Drive by shooting in Oakland."

Drena started crying.

Ajax silently put his clothes on. He got his wooden snowshoes down from the log wall and strapped them on his Caribou boots.

"I'm going into the village." He walked out the door into the gleaming white world.

As he walked slowly down the spruce-lined trail, he suddenly saw a huge form emerge from the trees. It was a giant Kodiak brown bear! Ajax was startled by the appearance of the bear, which should have been deep in hibernation now. It was not unheard of for a bear to wake up and wander around for a time in winter, but very rare. The bear loomed up to his full 12ft height, and Ajax recognized him as the same one he had seen at the Indian dance.

The bear walked up and licked Ajax's hand. "My name's Bear," he thought it said.

Ajax and Bear walked into the village together. Then he entered the Sourdough tavern. Bear lumbered in behind him.

"Holysmoke!" the bartender yelled, reaching for his rifle.

"It's all right, Pete," said Ajax. "This is a tame bear."

"A tame Kodiak!"

"Yeah," said Ajax, grinning like a killer whale, "just don't do nothin' to arouse him."

Pete put the rifle down. "O.K. If you say so, Ajax." Bear went and curled up by the roaring fire.

"Billy told me about your sister, Ajax. Real sorry. All the boys here are."

Ajax looked around. He hadn't even noticed his friends sitting around a table by the fire playing poker. Must have been dazed by the sun bouncing off the snowdrifts, he decided...or by this. He held up the telegram. He had crumpled it into a yellow wad in his fist as he walked. He threw it into the crackling fire, whistling it just over Bear's enormous head. Bear growled.

"Yeah," Frank Smith said. "We're all real sorry, Ajax. If there's anything the boys and me can do t' help, you just say the word." He spat into the fire.

Ajax looked at them: two whites and two Indians. He thought back to when he came up here to get away from gang life in the City. At first, Frank Smith had hounded him for being black, the only black here, the lanky white making jokes about how well he stood out against all the ice and snow.

They had worked together on the same fishing trawler, and finally Capt. Jones had decided to hold a boxing match between the two. "Get it out of their systems before they kill each other," he had growled.

The fight had gone ten rounds of bare knuckled gore, before Ajax was standing alone in the ring. Ever since, Frank Smith had been his best pal. "Anyone who calls ole Ajax a nigger," he would say in deadly earnest, "has gotta deal with me!"

Ajax sat at the table. "I'm going down," he said.

"Then we're going with ya," said Capt. Jones over a full house. "We'll sail down on the *Bounty*" (the *Bounty*?).

"And I'm taking Bear there along for the fight," Ajax said, pointing to the huge Kodiak stretched out like a giant bear rug before the fire.

"All right!" they all cheered, raising their glasses. "To Bear!"

"Hope Bear don't get seasick," Sam the Indian said.

Soon they were sailing on the *Bounty* down the coast of North America. Bear helped with the fishing, leaning over the railing to scoop in giant salmon. Sir Killer and a pod of dolphins trailed along side the trawler.

"We're gonna kick some ass!" Capt. Jones said, rubbing his hands together gleefully. He looked at Bear, sitting up on his haunches, his long reddish hair draping elegantly down his elongated snout. "When we set the ole werebear here loose, those hoods won't know hit 'em."

Nick and Sam got their bow-and-arrows out and started sharpening the obsidian and bone points.

"Yeah," Nick said. "We'll get 'em!" He looked at Bear and then looked back at Ajax. "You remember the dance on the beach, Ajax? This is the bear who walked out of the sea."

"Walked out of the sea?" Ajax said.

"Yeah," Sam said. "We were doing the incantation to the killer whales off shore when this here bear walked out of the water on its hind legs!"

"Sure!" Frank said, "and my last name is Frankenstein!"

No one laughed….Except bear.

Soon they were sailing beneath the gothic Oakland Bay Bridge under a full moon. Bear howled and roared out a mournful wail. They pulled up to a dock in the harbor and lumbered off the boat and into a labyrinth of foggy streets.

"Just follow me," Ajax said. "I could walk home from here blindfolded. I used to come down here to the harbor every day to watch the boats sail in and out, dreaming of the day I'd get out of town. I soon moved over across the bay, but even there…"

Now they were surrounded! A group of black youths, all brandishing knives, had appeared out of the dark!

"So you come back! Ajax," the lead one said.

"You should have stayed up at the North Pole," another laughed.

"Yeah," sneered the first. "I got your sister and now we got you."

They were closing in, when Bear reared up on his hind legs, looming 12ft. over the lead hoods head.

Bear let out a blast of a growl…

"What the hell!? Where did he come from?" the startled punk screamed looking up at the gaping mouth and dagger-like teeth.

Then a feathered tomahawk whizzed through the air turning in cartwheels and stuck in the chest of the sneering youth. An arrow zipped into the shoulder of another.

"Let's get out of here!" the wounded kid screamed, as Bear rose up over him like a Sherman tank. They madly dashed away down the street.

All of a sudden, fire erupted on the distant Oakland hills, looking like ordinances going off. A wall of red and orange flames shimmered against the black night, the flames racing across the horizon, eerily lighting the fog shrouded street.

"What's that!" one of the youths yelled as they disappeared into an alleyway.

"The end of the world!" Bear roared.

Ajax looked down at the bloody lifeless youth on the sidewalk, the feathered tomahawk sticking from his chest, his eyes staring up from under the blood-red mist shrouded street lamp.

"That score's settled," Ajax said.

They carefully made their way to Ajax's home, a 2-story pastel wooden house on a run down littered street. An elderly black matron peeked through the chain-fastened door.

"Ajax!" she cried out. "You've come." She opened the door.

"Mama," he said, holding her. "I brought my friends with me, and I brought..."

A big black Labrador rushed in from the porch.

"...my dog Bear."

"Well, come in. All of you!"

Pastor Otis walked out of a back room! "Ajax! You're here!"

"Hi, father," Heaven heard himself say. "We just got the guy who killed Sis. He's lying in the street, dead."

Pastor Otis stood behind the pulpit in the church. The black choir finished singing a gospel hymn.

"Brothers and sisters," the pastor cried out, "we must stop the senseless killing that is plaguing our streets. Those awful fires in the Oakland hills are God's final warning."

Ajax and his friends were sitting in the front pew, Bear curled up at their feet. The front church door burst open and a group of black youths stomped in. They marched quickly up to Ajax. The youth with the arrow wound, his arm in a sling, pointed with his other hand at Ajax.

"You killed our leader, Ajax," he yelled. "You and your bear!"

Ajax looked down at the big black Labrador. "You mean Bear, my dog?" Everybody in the church laughed.

"He had a great big grizzly bear from the North Pole with him!" the youth cried.

Another youth screamed: "Ajax turned into a werebear!"

Ajax stood up. "The only bear you saw was the grizzly bear in your own mind."

"Friends, friends!" Pastor Otis cried out, "can't we all...get along? Can't we all...love one another?"

Ajax reached out his hand to the other youth. After a moment which seemed an eternity, the black youth reached out and took Ajax's hand. Then they put their arms around each other, and the people all applauded.

Instantly Heaven was back in the laboratory and Dr. Smith was taking the headphones off him.

"Well, what do you think?" Dr. Smith said.

"What do I think? I think, Dr. Smith, you should either win the Nobel Peace Prize...or be arrested as a pyromaniac!"

Dr. Smith chuckled. "It's virtually reality!"

Dr. Smith immersed himself further in experimentation in his laboratory. He next started working with the dolphins' sonar, trying to break through into their three-dimensional sound world. Again he put a pair of headphones on Heaven, then blindfolded him. "What do you see, Heaven," he said into a microphone, holding up an orange.

"A...ball?"

Dr. Smith meticulously scribbled down notes.

"What do you...hear?"

"It's like a subconscious morse-code, Doctor," Heaven replied. "There's a definite pattern to it, depending on the shape and size and texture of the object."

"One day it just happened? you say.".

"Right. In the water. I was looking at Rena and I closed my eyes and...there she was! Clear as day."

"Well your father Michael obviously passed on to you some interesting dolphin traits. Your myoglobin is way up, which accounts for your ability to hold your breath much longer than any other human being in the world.

"And you can 'see' in three-dimensional sonar holograms— quite a trick! It took longer for these abilities to develop in you than in dolphins, who acquire them right at birth, along with the ability to swim instantly at very great speeds—an absolute necessity if they're going to keep up with the herd. You say you could swim by the age of one and a half years?"

"I seem to remember swimming as my earliest memory. My next earliest is lying in my crib, wondering where my mother was."

"Heather died in childbirth, you said."

"Yes, that's what my father told me."

Dr. Smith scribbled more notes. "Well, Heaven, from just a scientific viewpoint you can hardly imagine how fortunate it is that I came in contact with you, after performing the dolphin brain transplant on your father. To be able to, shall I say, 'study' the off spring of this man is a scientist's dream come true, to chart and calibrate, if you will, minute changes in your biochemistry and physiology, to…" Dr. Smith was walking rapidly around the room, almost as if talking to himself, as Heaven quietly took the headphones off.

"Dr. Smith," Heaven said with a wry smile. "I think I hear Rena calling."

"Sure, sure, my boy," the doctor said, lost in thought. "You run along, and we'll talk more later."

Heaven stood and without bothering to take the blindfold goggles off, turned and walked out the door.

Dr. Smith looked up. "Funny," he said. "I didn't hear anything."

Heaven and Rena together swam around the outside of their home, as he checked the structure once again with his sonar. Everything "looked" perfect. He was convinced their "palace" was totally safe. The dolphin's directions in building the home had, he knew, made the crucial difference. It seemed their underwater Xanadu would last forever.

As he swam intently around the site, he noticed something at the edge of the coral: a sparkling green light. He swam towards it, but the pulsating glitter seemed to stay constantly the same distance from him.

I don't seem to be getting any closer to it, he thought to himself.

Then, instantly it was at his fingertips: a perfect green emerald. Heaven looked into it. He shook his head. What was he seeing? They seemed to be little tiny angels, white with gold wings and smiles on their faces, flying through a sea of green.

He watched them flitter before him, then showed Rena.

Suddenly Heaven heard his father's voice! He looked up. A brilliant white light was shining above the water.

All at once they were encircled in a spotlight of gold! They heard a vague whistling sound...then whisked up out of the water and watched the sea fall below them.

Michael soared up to them! rippling through the air as though through water: feathery-white flipper/wings shining like sun on his shoulders.

"Welcome! Heaven! Rena! Welcome!"

Michelle and Robby were playing on the beach, when they heard a whoosh of air and looked up to see.

"Look!" said Robby, pointing. "It's Mommy and Daddy!"

"Michelle!" Dr. Smith said, in their living room, "what do you mean your mother and father have gone to be with God...?"

Michelle sat smiling on the couch, fingering a large pearl.

"Aren't they lucky, Dr. Smith?"

"When can we go, Dr. Smith?" Robby asked.

"Later, Robby," said Michelle. "They just went whoosh up into the air, Dr. Smith."

"Perposterous!" Dr. Smith guffawed.

"It's true," Robby said. "We saw them. If they don't come back, you'll have to take over, Michelle," he said to his sister.

"Oh sure," Michelle said to her little brother. "I'm very bright. But I might need some help, Robby."

"Sure!" Robby said. "I'll be your assistant. Right now, let's go swimming with Peter and Johnny."

"Good idea, Robby," Michelle said. "You'll make a great assistant. Come on!"

They ran out as Dr. Smith collapsed to the rug. Sharon, who had been listening on the side of the room, ran over to him.

"I'm all right," he said, checking his pulse. "I hope."

Michelle swam easily in her scuba gear under the water. Her golden hair trailed out behind her as she weaved effortlessly through the seaweeds. Robby swam beside her, holding her hand. They propelled through the water with the ease of young dolphins.

Johnny and Frankie swam above them and their two young children followed them closely. Peter swam alongside, pointing out different types of shells. They all undulated through the water like a small dolphin pod, and Michelle and Robby led them.

When they got back to their home, they all gathered in the living room. Dr. Smith was still there with Sharon.

"Still no sign of them?" he asked.

Michelle laughed and shook her head. "Well let's play 'Dolphin and Shark.' Dr. Smith can be the shark!"

Everyone laughed.

"I can't believe they just disappeared into the sky!" an exasperated Dr. Smith exclaimed.

"It was the Star Dolphins!" Robby said.

"The...who?"

"The Star Dolphins," Robby repeated. "They come from the water planet Shine. I see them in my dreams all the time."

"Me too!" said Michelle.

"Yeah," said Robby. "They have hands instead of flippers and they fly space ships..."

"Oh come now..."

"I believe Robby and Michelle," said Peter.

"So do I," entered Sharon, who until now had sat quietly. "I've had strange dreams myself."

"So have I," said Frankie, "dreams I didn't want to tell anyone because I was afraid you'd all think I'd gone..."

"Crazy, Frankie?" Johnny said.

She punched him. "See? I told Johnny my dreams of dolphins from outer space landing here and he said I was..."

"Imagining things. But last night I had the same dream!"

"You did? Why didn't you tell me, Johnny?" asked Frankie.

Johnny laughed. "I thought I was going..."

"Crazy, mon?" said Peter, laughing. "I thought I was the one who was going..."

"Crazy!" said Dr. Smith. "Well, we'll just wait and see if they show up, won't we," he said, a sparkle in his eye.

Over the next two years, Michelle grew into a beautiful young lady. Her skin had the dewy softness of almost constant contact with the water and her extra layer of female fat seemed to give her an added buoyancy so she cold float and swim for hours all the while looking content.

"Let's have a dolphin race!" she said one day. They were in the water over their home. "Down to the igloo and then back to the surface. And then back down and up again."

"Do you think they'd mind?" Peter asked. "I mean being used like sea-race-horses?"

"Oh no, silly," laughed Michelle. "They race all the time."

Robby started whistling. A dolphin surfaced next to him, smiling. He reached out and petted him.

"Let's 'plim'!" he said.

"'Plim'?" said Peter.

"Sure," said Michelle. "To play and swim. 'Plim!'"

Soon several more dolphins were on the surface. They all got on the dolphin's backs, holding them around their necks.

"Ready?" Michelle said. "Set?"

"Plim!"yelled Robby.

The dolphins submerged and swam down through the water, the riders bent over them and holding them tightly like jockeys on racehorses. Through the water they raced, streaking toward the coral. They were neck and neck for the first minutes as they swam down, the dolphins rhythmically kicking their tail flukes. Then they were at the bottom and they turned and swam up for the surface. They all gasped for air as the dolphins breached and blew off water, then resubmerged.

It was down again to the coral! First Michelle's dolphin would lead, then Robby's, then Peter's or Frankie's or Johnny's. Finally they turned for the light up above.

"It's up the stretch!" thought Robby.

The dolphins surfaced with their riders all gasping for air and laughing.

Michelle looked quickly around: "It's a tie!"

The ghost-like three-dimensional images danced suspended in space: fish swam seductively by, seaweeds placidly waved, water swirled by in rushes. Fish would suddenly disappear as they were gobbled by the invisible dolphin. Coral vibrated spectacularly. Clicks and clacks and whistles and pings sparkled the air.

"This," Dr. Smith said, standing in the darkened laboratory, "is how the dolphin perceives his world. In three-dimensional holographic sound!"

The doctor, having finally accepted the disappearance of Heaven and Rena as he had accepted other "impossibilities" in his long and "impossible" life, had reimmersed himself in sonar research, the scanty information furnished by Heaven proving to be the key he needed. He had invented and perfected over the past two years a computer device for receiving sonar communications from a dolphin, taking Heaven's inventions of the "megaphone" and "hearing aide" one final step, to communicate with dolphins as they communicate with each other in the depths of the sea when herding fish or fighting sharks—by passing back and forth three-dimensional sonar holograms!

Better than language for everything but the most esoteric of conversations, he told himself. And they have plenty of those, too.

He called his invention the "projector," and today was the premier showing of the "movie" he had made, decoding the sonar pictures of his dolphin stars. Everyone applauded.

"The dolphins are the most sophisticated creatures on the face of the globe," the doctor continued.

"They have no need for technology."

"Now you know you should love each other."

The dolphins stuck their snouts out of the water and nodded their heads and whistled.

"Yes, I think you have it!" Robby said, preaching to the dolphins like St. Francis preaching to the birds. Robby floated like a buoy alone in the waves, all the others having swam home for the day. As he was continuing his "sermon" (on the water)—

A large white yacht rounded the island from the back side!

He had not seen a boat come here since the island rigger years ago. The yacht stopped off the beach and some people dove overboard. Robby quickly "hid" amongst the swells.

In the gathering twilight, Robby saw a young girl on the beach, playing in the surf, as others lit a fire in the drift-wood. The girl walked away from the others and made her way down the beach to a small lagoon. Robby followed her, hiding between the waves. He swam towards her, then turned and swam swiftly out to sea, watching from between the gentle swells.

The girl ran out into the water, splashing herself. Robby dove under the water and soared up to her. He surfaced in front of her, smiling and treading water, his head just above the waves.

"Oh!" she cried out. "Who are you?"

"Robby."

He turned over on his back and swam in front of her, smiling. She started laughing.

"Where did you come from," she asked.

"Here. Where do you come from."

"Miami."

Robby turned and started swimming out to sea.

"Wait," she said. "Don't go!"

He swam back to her and offered her his hand.

"Come on," he said.

She took his hand and they dove down into the water.

"Oh," she said, "you're a good swimmer. But...where do you come from?"

"Here!"

"In the water?" she laughed.

"Yes." He swam easily around her. "And this is my island, too."

"This little island is yours?"

"Yes. It's home. I've always lived here."

"And those little tree houses...?"

"They're ours. Me and Michelle and Peter and..."

"Oh, we didn't think anybody actually lived here."

"It's A OK! You can play on our island if you want to."

"Marylou!" a voice called out from the beach. They looked back to shore. A man was waving at them. "Marylou, what are you doing? And who is there with you?"

"Oh! it's my father," she said to Robby.

"It's OK father," she called out. "This is Robby. He lives on this island!"

"Lives on this tiny island?" the man said in a rough voice.

"Yes, he says it's his, but we can play on it."

The man was silent for a minute. "Well, Marylou," he finally said, "why don't you bring you're young friend to meet the...family?"

Marylou looked at him. "Want to come, Robby?" she asked.

Robby said, "All right, Marylou." She took his hand and they paddled to shore and walked down the beach to the others.

"This is Robby," Marylou said to the people sitting around the drift fire. "And this is his island!"

"His island!" one of the men said.

"Where do you live?" a woman asked. "All we saw were little tree houses. We didn't know this island was even here."

"We did see a ship," Marylou's father said. "Do you live on the ship?"

"No," Robby said.

"Then where do you live?"

"Under the sea," Robby said.

"Under the sea?!" The cigar smoking man coughed smoke.

"And I'm Aqua-man!" another said, as they all laughed.

"Wait a minute!" said Marylou. "There's a story going around school of a super rich family living in the Gulf in an undersea home they built with sunken treasure money...."

"You told me those stories, Marylou," her father cut in. "Of course, I just thought they were only stories told to amuse children..." He looked intently at Robby.

"Then it's true? Robby," Marylou cried.

Robby suddenly turned and started running for the sea!

"Catch him!" yelled Marylou's father. Marylou screamed as they grabbed hold of him.

Marylou started hitting them with her fists. "What are you doing! Let Robby go!"

"Take him to *The Princess*, lock him in a room. If these...who knows? I don't believe in undersea homes, but if he does come from a rich family they just might pay a handsome ransom to get their little boy back," her father said, as Marylou sobbed.

"Don't worry, Robby," cried Marylou. "I won't let them hurt you!"

Michelle and Peter walked down the darkened beach toward the people around the fire.

"Excuse me," Michelle said, "but have you seen a little boy named Robby. We can't seem to find him."

"This is our island," Peter said briskly.

"As a matter of fact," one of them said, "we know exactly where he is."

"Oh great!" said Michelle.

"Where?" asked Peter suspiciously.

The man motioned out towards the lighted yacht. "On board the *Princess*," he said, as Marylou sneaked away into the water.

"Can you bring him to us?" Michelle asked. "It's past dinner time."

"Sure," said the cigar smoking man. "…for one million dollars…in gold."

"A million dollars!" cried Michelle.

"What are ya, the Mafia?" Peter yelled.

The man pointed a pistol at him. "You might say," he laughed, "we're treasure hunters." The women snickered.

"Peter!" Michelle whispered, clutching his arm. "Keep cool."

"How do we know you haven't already hurt him," Peter said.

"Robby!" the man said into a walky-talky. "Say hello to your friends here."

"Michelle!" a little voice cried out.

"Robby are you all right?"

"I'm all right."

"They haven't hurt you?" Peter said. "Have they tied you?"

"No. A man just keeps pointing a gun at me."

"Well be a good boy," Michelle said, "and we'll get you off there."

"I know," Robby said.

"He really is brave," the man waving the pistol at them said. "He didn't even cry."

"How do you expect us to get a million dollars?" Michelle said.

"Sunken treasure, maybe?" a woman laughed.

Michelle looked at Peter. Peter glared at them. "We'll be back!" he said. They turned away as Marylou reached the *Princess*. She climbed up it then crept down the hall and knocked where light was peeking.

"Father!"

"What! Marylou."

"May I talk with you. Please! It's important, father."

The door opened. Marylou pointed a derringer directly at her father's head.

"You taught me how to use this," Marylou said.

"Let Robby go!"

Robby dashed out the door, grabbing her by the hand and running with her to the side of the boat. "Come on, Mary Lou, you're going with me."

Marylou hesitated a moment, looking back at her father.

"Come on!" he said again and they dove together into the night water. They swam to the beach where he had left his scuba gear that afternoon, which now seemed an eternity.

"We'll share this," Robby said, as he hastily put the air tanks on. "Buddy breathe. First you take a breath, than I take a breath, OK?"

Marylou nodded her head, "OK," slightly shaking in the cool night breeze. Robby strapped his weight belt on. "Hold tight!" he said. They swam under beneath the waves.

They swam hand in hand down toward the coral home, Robby echo-locating to find their way in the dark, the two passing the mouth-piece back and forth. Suddenly they met Michelle and

Peter hauling a large plastic bag on an undersea sled. They exchanged surprised, happy looks and swam to the sea home.

"This is Marylou!" Robby said, introducing her in the water withdrawal room. "She lives with us now."

In the morning Robby looked through the periscope.

"The yacht's gone!"

Robby and Marylou held hands and dove under the water. They swam around each other, then ascended to the waves. They submerged again, schools of fish swimming near them without fear, and wove in and out among them.

A small baby dolphin swam up to them, about two feet long and fifteen pounds. Marylou reached out her arms to it and it swam into her tender grasp. She held him to her heart, showing him to Robby who nodded his head, smiling.

Then they heard the loving cries of the mother dolphin, swimming rapidly toward them. She circled Marylou who released the baby to his mother and the two swam over the coral. The baby turned and swam back to Marylou, who patted him on his head. The mother swam beneath her feet, and Marylou, holding the baby again, straddled the mother dolphin and they rose up to the surface. Robby quickly followed, finding Marylou on the dolphin's back, the infant smiling in her arms.

"What a picture you three make!" Robby laughed.

"She trusts me with her baby," Marylou said. "Oh I love him so," she said, holding him to her cheek.

Michelle swam over to them. "The baby's beautiful," she said, petting his little smiling face. "What a smiler you are!"

Peter swam in. "What did you catch, Marylou?" he said. "An angel?"

She looked over at Robby and then back at the little dolphin. "Two angels," she smiled, tearfully.

Michelle was in the pool room when the dolphin rushed in. She was squeaking pitifully.

"What's wrong?" Michelle said to it through the "megaphone."

She plugged the "hearing aide" into her ear. "They have my baby! They have my baby!" the mother dolphin kept crying.

"Who has your baby?" Michelle said.

"The boat people," she cried. "Oh I want my baby. Please get my baby."

Michelle ran to the periscope room and looked out onto the water. She saw a ship sailing away. On the side was the word "Marineland."

"Peter! Come quick!" Michelle yelled into the intercom.

Peter ran into the room. "A mother dolphin just swam in crying a Marineland boat has kidnapped her baby! We have to catch the boat and get her baby back."

"Let's get to *The Dolphin*," he said.

They were soon sailing rapidly toward the ship. Michelle had a bandanna scarf around her head as she stood at the wheel as did Rastafarian Johnny "Too Bad," his dreadlocks flowing from under his in the wind. Frankie watched from the deck.

"Full throttle, Peter!" Michelle said into the intercom.

The mother swam in the water alongside, as the ship cruised across the water. Finally they overtook the Marineland vessel and were by its side.

Michelle grabbed the bullhorn and ran to the railing as Peter rushed to her side.

"Hello, *Marineland*!" she said.

"Hello, *Dolphin*," a voice answered.

"Would you please release the little baby dolphin you caught? The mother dolphin down there is very anxious to have it back." The mother dolphin was jumping up the side of the boat.

There was a silence, and the man said, "How do you know it's hers."

"She told us," Michelle said.

"She told you?"

"Yes. Now please release the baby dolphin back to its mother. Look at her in the water. She's frantic."

"We want to a lot of trouble to get this little dolphin. We can't just let it go."

"Then I'm afraid," Peter yelled into the megaphone, "we can't let you go."

Peter ran and pushed the engine to full throttle, as Johnny blocked *Marineland* from leaving the bay.

"Hey! come on now," the voice cried.

"Please let the baby dolphin go," Michelle said.

"Please!" echoed Frankie.

"All right!" the man finally said. "All right."

In moment they saw the little baby dolphin drop over the side of the boat and splash into the water. There were instant squeaks of joy from the little dolphin and its mother as they recognized each other, and then swam off through the sea.

"Thank you!" Michelle said, as *The Dolphin* pulled away.

"Any time," the man said. "I suppose the mother dolphin told you the baby's name too."

Michelle and Frankie looked at each other and laughed. "It's Smilee Smile," said Frankie as Michelle held the horn.

"Right, mon," yelled Johnny.

"By the way," Michelle's voice said as the vessel left the bay, "this is 'Be Kind to Dolphins Week'…all year."

Marineland blew its whistle.

"Michelle," Dr. Smith said one day, "do you feel dolphins are more intelligent than people?"

"From what I know of people, I'm sure they are, Dr. Smith," Michelle answered.

Dr. Smith was now 90 years old. He was beginning to feel a little like Methuselah, and although still in remarkable mental and physical health, he knew his death was imminent. He desired to do one last great service for mankind.

"Well, I for one believe they are ethically superior, too. Michelle, I have an idea! Long before I joined up with your grandfather Michael, I was deeply involved in top secret research for Uncle Sam, uh, the United States government. I used to even have lunch with the President about once a month! If anyone still remembers me (!) with my contacts and credentials I bet I could get in to see President What's His Name. Why not set up an interview over short wave radio between the dolphins and Mr. President using the 'megaphone' and 'hearing aide.' Maybe the dolphins could teach him something to help mankind!"

"You mean 'solutions?'" said Michelle.

"Yes, exactly, solutions."

"Well it sure couldn't hurt, could it."

"I bet the President would grant me an audience and then… Michelle, just sail me and Sharon to Miami on *The Dolphin*…and I'll do the rest!"

Within the week Dr. Smith and Sharon were in Miami where they took a jet to Washington D.C. There on the basis of his reputation as a famous surgeon and dolphin expert and his former government research in biological warfare, Dr. Smith finally obtained a "brief" audience with the President, on a matter, he said, "of extreme importance, the very survival of mankind!"

"You have exactly 5 minutes!" the aide said as he showed the doctor in. "The Lithuanian ambassador has a luncheon appointment with the President next."

"Mr. President!" Dr. Smith said, extending his hand as he entered the Oval Office. "What an honor to meet you, Sir!"

"And I am delighted to meet you, Dr. Smith," said the President. "I've heard a lot about you. Everybody assumed you were either dead of being held hostage somewhere!"

"Mr. President," he said, "rumors of my death have been highly exaggerated, and as for being held hostage, well, let's just say I have been in contact with some extraordinary people these past many years, who, and this is top secret..."

The President nodded.

"...who have broken the communication barrier, using highly sophisticated computer devices of their own invention, to finally penetrate into the language of the extremely intelligent sea mammal we know as 'Tursiops Truncatus', the Atlantic Bottlenose Dolphin."

The President sat up in his chair. "This is interesting, Dr Smith." He looked at him. "I do recall your research with dolphins of some years ago."

"The ending was unfortunate, Sir," he said. "But the work eventually bore very real fruit. The son of the man I worked for and with did, indeed, finally break through this seemingly impenetrable language barrier. These people have been talking to dolphins for some twenty years now."

"My goodness, Dr. Smith!"

(Knock! Knock! "The Lithuanian ambassador, Sir!" "Tell him I've decided to use room service and to go ahead without me!")

"Would you care for lunch, Dr Smith.?"

"Thank you, Mr. President. Anyway sir, dolphins have proven to have an intelligence much advanced over ours…"

"Holy mackerel," the President breathed.

"And these people have agreed, on a top secret basis, to arrange an interview at your earliest convenience between you and several bottlenose dolphins via short wave radio, using these computer devices, Sir. For the benefit of mankind…"

The President was silent for a minute. Finally he said, "By Jove, I'll do it! Dr. Smith. But it well certainly be top top secret." He laughed. "If it ever leaked out the President of the United States was holding talks with…dolphins!…I'd be impeached, convicted, bodily removed from the Oval Office and then carried away by little men in white trench coats!"

Dr. Smith laughed. "All right, then, I'll arrange it at once, Mr. President!"

"Michelle!" the voice over the radio said. "This is the President of the United States…How are you today?"

"I'm fine, Sir," she said, "and it is a great honor to talk with you, Mr. President." She looked over at Robby, who excitedly leaned forward in his chair.

"Mr. President!" he said. "Can I say hi?"

"My little brother Robby wants to say Hi! to you Mr. President."

"Why of course," the President said.

"Hi! Mr. President."

"Hello! Robby.

"Michelle," he said more seriously, "Dr. Smith has told me a great deal about you. Of course I heard of your grandfather. He was a good man, one you should certainly be proud of."

"I am, sir," she said.

"Well, I am very interested in…talking…to your dolphin friends. We'll really be able to understand each other, you say?"

"Yes sir. We talk to them all the time."

"And they talk to us!" Robby said.

"Well, good for you! I have many things to ask. You know, Michelle, before we uh…get started…I should tell you about a book I've read, recently as strange coincidence would have it, *The Dolphin's Voice,* about world leaders who go to ask dolphins about how to save planet Earth from nuclear war. It was written by one of our inventors of the H bomb as a matter of fact. You really should read it someday, Michelle, you and Robby both…"

"We already have, sir."

"Oh yeah," said Robby. "That's one of my favorites."

"Well…" said the President. "Can we begin?"

"We have three dolphins in our pool right now, waiting to talk with you, Mr. President."

The President cleared his throat.

"My friends!" he said. "Can you…hear me?"

"Yes!"

"Yes!"

"Yes!"

"Wow! These are really dolphins?"

"Yes!" Dr. Smith said.

"Yes!" the President heard again.

"Wow! I can hardly believe this! Am I really talking to dolphins?"

"Yes!" Dr. Smith said. "I guarantee it, Sir."

"Yes!" the President heard again.

"Well how are you today?" he said.

"In fine health…Sir," he heard.

"Well good for you!" the President said. "May I ask you some questions?"

"Yes."

"We humans need a little help, as I'm sure you're aware. Maybe you can help us."

"We love you," he heard.

"And I must confess…I love you!" the President said excitedly.

"I've prepared a short list of questions for you. Maybe you have some solutions. Here's the first:

"What would you do about the nuclear arms race?"

"Give up," he heard.

"Give up?"

"Nobody can win," he heard.

"You're right, of course. But how?"

"Love one another," he heard.

"I think I've read that somewhere in the Bible," the President laughed.

"John 15-12," he heard.

The President gasped. "My God, they can read, too?"

"Yes," Dr. Smith intervened. "We set up a computer monitor for them and taught them to read…underwater!"

"Well, what would do about world hunger?"

"Herd fish for those who can't herd fish themselves."

"Well, yes. Exemplary!

"And how about criminals?"

"Set everyone free who's not a shark."

"Hmmm. I don't know what the attorney general would think, letting people out of jail instead of putting them in. But..."

"Michelle," the President finally said, after thanking the dolphins for their "valuable time," "how would you like a nice job in the United Nations?"

Michelle looked at Robby.

"Go for it, Sis!"

Dr. Smith read the newspaper in the Beltway coffee shop. Sharon sat across from him. "President Wants Jails Emptied!" the *Washington Post* headline screamed in bold red letters.

The people were milling around and talking to each other.

"I've never heard of such a thing!"

"Clark should be impeached, for Chrisake!"

"Why, can you imagine?"

"What would the streets be like?"

"Especially here in Washington D.C.!"

"What a compassionate President Clark is! I was in jail once..."

"It'll get him a lot of votes."

"But Clark'll lose a lot more!"

"I think it's a great idea. Give 'em a second chance."

"He's out of his mind! Just like all Democrats."

Dr. Smith shrunk down at his table. "My God, what have I done?" he breathed.

They finished their coffee and walked out onto the busy city street. The cross town traffic whirred and hummed and the sun shone down glossy through monuments and the tall buildings. They walked past a department store and there on the televisions in the display window was the President, smiling out at the people gathered around watching, giving the kind of long-winded, erudite speech for which he had become so famous, the speech Dr. Smith had helped him write and didn't want to watch.

"My friends," he was saying, "I have been thinking a lot lately about something I would like to call the American spirit, the spark. This great nation of ours, as we all know, was founded by the Pilgrims, who believed they were coming to a new promised land, a 'sweet promised land,' as Robert Laxalt of Nevada has so movingly written. This country was founded on this spirit and through all our history, this spark has not withered. It has flickered and sometimes smoldered, but never died.

"We have fallen into greed and violence, but this spark somehow endures. Alexis de Tocqueville, a French nobleman, was perhaps the first to notice it. He was first attracted to the words of Thomas Jefferson, who wrote in the Declaration of Independence, 'All men have the right to life, liberty and the pursuit of happiness.' De Tocqueville came to America in the early 1800's from the same nation which gave us the Statue of Liberty, and in a book called *Democracy in America* wrote very perceptively about what he saw here." The President peered over his reading glasses. "He noted our faults, which he said could divide us and indeed did so in the Civil War, but he also saw this spirit, this spark, and wrote, 'The future belongs to America.'

"Why did this aristocratic Frenchmen write this? What did de Tocqueville see?

"When Thomas Jefferson wrote the Declaration of Independence, he was drawing from an earlier work by the Englishman John Locke, who had written, 'All men have the right to life, liberty and property.' Jefferson specifically changed 'property' to 'the pursuit of happiness.' Why did he do this, you ask. Because happiness, not property, is important." President Clark smiled. "The Bible says, happy are the meek, happy are the righteous, happy are the merciful. How important it is then to be happy! Since Jefferson substituted happiness for property, then property, possessions, must not bring happiness." The people gasped.

"Think of dolphins!" he smiled. "They're happy all the time, and they own nothing!

"What does bring happiness then? Mercy, love, compassion. Which is why I've decided to issue an executive order ordering the attorney general of the United States to release all those poor souls in jail who really have no business being there." The people gasped again.

"I've also decided we should simply give up the arms' race with the Russians." More gasps.

"And I've introduced legislation banning all killing of dolphins by commercial fishing." He chuckled. "I know I won't be getting many votes from you commercial fishermen out there, but you guys are a very small constituency anyway," he said, peering intently from the TV sets, "and besides, I don't want the votes of known criminals like yourselves, anyway." He smiled and then looked back down at his papers.

"This great nation was founded..." he went on (and on).

The masked sun shone down in Dr. Smith's wan face as he watched the President deliver his speech. He was thinking back now to when Heaven and Rena had mysteriously disappeared, how Michelle and Robby had sworn they had been whisked up to the clouds, and how he given them a lie detector test and found them to be telling the truth, and though he had tried in his scientific mind somehow to cope with it and rationally explain it, he never had really come to grips with what had happened. Such things just don't occur in the "real world," not even on the outskirts of the Bermuda Triangle! any more then men walking around with dolphin brains (he chuckled) or people living in an undersea home in the coral! And what's more, he kept having this strange recurring dream of being in a giant air bubble soaring underwater, gazing into the smiling face of light of winged Dr. Michael Hope!

He vacantly looked at Sharon, "I do love you, you know," he said, gently removing her hand from his arm. "I have spoken with the dolphins..." he thought he heard the President say. Then he started running down the sidewalk through the people.

"Edward!" Sharon cried out.

"The dolphins are coming!! The dolphins are coming!!" he was yelling as he ran through the people. "Repent! Don't wait! The world is coming to an end!!"

"Who are you!" somebody yelled.

"Who's this old codger?"

"Hey! You bumped me, old man!"

"Wow! Dig this old guy."

"Please," he yelled. "We don't have much longer...!"

Sharon tried to catch up to him through the crowd. He finally stopped, panting on a street corner. "Listen to me." he yelled wildly. "Time is running out. God...oh..." He clutched at his chest and stumbled to the sidewalk. Some women screamed. Sharon ran up to where he was and knelt down to him. He reached his arms out for her. "...is coming!" Then he collapsed.

"Oh, Dr. Smith," Sharon said, holding him.

Michelle and Robby were ready to board the jet to fly to New York. She hugged Peter. "You have to look after the home now,"

she said. Then she hugged Johnny and Frankie and their two little kids. "I'm leaving everything in your care." Her business type dress fit her gracefully as she moved among them. "I'm just glad I practiced with these high heels, though I'm still a little wobbily," she laughed, a tear in her eye.

"Play with the dolphins for me," she added.

"And me," Robby said.

Frankie put her arms around her comfortingly. Her eyes were wet too. "You be careful," she said.

"And you look after your sister, Robby," Peter said, putting his hand on the boy's shoulder. Johnny gave him the "high five."

"I will," Robby said, taking her hand.

They climbed up the steps leading into the large jetplane, waving and looking back at their friends. The stewardess took their tickets and directed them to their seats. Neither had ever flown before, and their stomachs felt full of butterflies. They sat down, Robby by the window. Soon the engine began whirring and a beeper sounded. A stewardess came by and leaned over. "Fasten your seat belt, please," she said, pointing to the lighted sign.

"I already have," Robby said. "She's the slowpoke."

"Robby!" Michelle said. "I'm sorry," she said to the attractive lady stewardess. "We're a little nervous. This is our first flight."

"Oh," the stewardess smiled. "Well I hope you enjoy it." She quickly walked away. A few more people bustled through the aisle to get to their seats.

A voice came over the speakers: "Good afternoon, ladies and gentlemen. This is Captain Kirkland welcoming you aboard flight 363 nonstop to New York City. For those of you who have never flown with us before, the flight assistants will demonstrate a few of the safety features of our brand new Concord."

Robby leaned out to watch the stewardess in the aisle, demonstrating the use of life preservers and oxygen masks.

"I just hope it goes down over the ocean," Robby laughed.

"Robby!"

Soon the engine's whir began to increase, and the jet started slowly taxiing into position for takeoff. It stopped for a minute and then began rolling rapidly down the long runway. Michelle and Robby felt pushed back into their seats as the great bird finally lifted off the ground.

In a moment they were high in the air, and both Robby and Michelle looked out the window at the rapidly diminishing houses and streets below as they became abstract geometric patterns. Soon they were in the clouds where wisps and bundles of cumuli flew by their windows like turrets and spirals of a faery castle. Then there was a loud "bang!" as they broke the sound barrier.

"This is where Mom and Dad live!" said Robby.

Michelle stood at the U.N. podium before the people. She spoke quietly, clearly, into the microphone. "My friends," she said. "It is a great honor for me to address this great body of peace." The translators busily respoke her words. "And I bring you today a message of peace.

"Many years ago, my grandfather, Dr. Michael Hope, began doing research with a group of marine mammals called Tursiops Truncatus, the Atlantic Bottlenose dolphin, whom he believed had extraordinary intelligence and high moral values, indeed superior to those of mankind. He died before his work was completed, but his son, my father, Heaven Hope, completed his work and was able to communicate with these wonderful creatures!"

A hush swept the room. Delegates looked at one another, as Michelle told how the language barrier of the dolphin had been finally broken through. The Chinese ambassador took off his headphones, whispered to an aid, and then stood up and quickly walked out of the General Assembly hall.

"I have lived among the dolphins all my life and can testify they do have a superior intellect and in my opinion are more 'humane' then humans. I have been asked by the President of the United States to communicate this to you in the hope it might lead to more peace on earth and good will toward men and…"

She continued talking for ten more minutes. At the end of her speech, everyone stood and applauded. She gracefully bowed and then sat back down beside Robby in the U.S. delegation.

"You did it, Sis!" exclaimed Robby.

Michelle and Robby were in their New York hotel room when the telephone rang.

"Hello?" said Michelle.

"Michelle!" a voice cried. "Dr. Smith's dead."

"Sharon?" Michelle asked.

"Yes. I got your number from the President. I'm at the White House now. The President has invited me to stay until after Edward's funeral," she said through sobs.

"Hello, Michelle," she heard the President's voice say. "So sorry about Dr. Smith. He had become a trusted friend. Won't you and Robby come and stay at the White House, too?"

"Yes, of course, Mr. President," said Michelle.

"Good! I'll send a limousine around for you directly."

Michelle soon hung up and looked at Robby.

"We're going to the White House!" she said.

"Michelle!" the President said, when they were shown in. "How nice to meet you in person. And this must be Robby!"

"Yes, sir!" Robby said.

"I was so sorry to hear about Dr. Smith. I guess all the excitement. He was quite an elderly man."

"Sharon…?"

"She's upstairs. She's all right. I told her to stay until after his funeral."

"Will you be…?"

"No, Michelle, I'm afraid I really can't. The press, you know."

Michelle nodded her head.

"I was very impressed with your speech before the U.N.," he said. "It was quite a plea for sanity. And I must say, talking to those dolphins of yours was really an experience! I haven't felt the same since. It's almost as if," he said with a wry smile, "I've had just a little too much good French Bourdeau wine," he laughed. "The kind that's $300 a bottle!"

"They do affect you, Sir," she said.

"For the better, I think!" he said.

"Michelle," the President said intently, "I have the feeling some tremendous events are going to be happening in the world soon. I don't know what they will be, of course, but it's just this feeling I have, as if some cosmic events are about to unfold. You know," he said, "confidentially, and if you or Robby quote me on this I'll deny it, but NASA has positively determined the 'face on Mars' photographed by Voyager is an artificially constructed monument of very ancient origin" (both Michelle and Robby gasped) "and the pyramid-like structures are very similar to pyramids here on Earth! We've known this for some time now, though officially we deny it, of course. And Dr. Smith was saying how he believed dolphins were ancient emissaries from a planet in the Sirius star system!" Robby smiled.

The President sat down and invited the two to do likewise.

"He told me to read a book called *The Sirius Mystery*, which I found in the Library of Congress, and am finishing right now, as a matter of fact. It tells of a tribe in northwestern Africa called the Dogon, who have very ancient knowledge of an invisible star we call Sirius 2, a small dwarf star which orbits giant Sirius, the brightest star in our sky, every 60 years. Our modern astronomers did not discover this star until the 1950s but these 'simple' people have been worshiping it for centuries! This was well documented by anthropologists in the early years of this century, some thirty years before the star's discovery. Every 60 years, for the past millennium, they have a great ceremony, celebrating the orbit of Sirius 2 around Sirius, which is the exact orbit time of the star! They call it the 'Sigi.'

"They also tell of strange creatures, called Nommo, who came down from this star around the time the great Sphynx of Egypt was begun. These 'Nommo' were fish-like creatures who told the tribesmen they come from a watery planet..."

"Shine!" Robby called out.

"What!" said the startled President.

"They come from the water planet Shine," Robby said. "I see it in my dreams all the time. Nommo are just like dolphins except they have hands instead of flippers. They fly space ships and have been secretly orbiting Earth for...centuries! Mr. Spock on 'In Search of Space Dolphins' on TV last week..."

"I have the same dreams!" said Michelle

"Ever since I talked to those dolphins of yours, I've been having those dreams! I didn't dare tell anyone, of course, not even my wife, 'cause I was afraid she'd say I'd gone…"

"Crazy?" offered Robby.

"Quite mad," nodded the President. "Well, at any rate, strange things are occurring, there's no denying it. You two be careful," he said, standing.

Sharon was waiting at the top of the stairs when the pair were shown to their room. They embraced.

"You'll be coming back to the home with us, won't you, Sharon?" asked Michelle, wiping her tears.

"I don't think so," she said. "I've decided to move back into Edward's mansion. He left it to me in his will, poor dear. I think I'll just…retire. The cherry blossoms are beautiful this time of year. Besides," she said through her tears, "it's good to be back."

Michelle comforted Sharon at the funeral. "We'll all miss Dr. Smith," she said. "You'll have to carry on."

As they were getting ready to leave, Sharon handed Michelle a piece of paper. "If you ever need me." She opened her purse and pulled out a small radio and handed it to her. "It's a specially computerized, two-way, long-distance short wave radio. Dr. Smith designed them himself so we could always be in touch with each other. I'll always carry mine with me."

"Thank you Sharon," said Michelle through tears. "It's good to know we can always reach you."

Michelle stood before the U.N. podium.

"My friends," she said. "I have been asked again by the President of the United States to speak to you. As you all know, our beautiful world is in very desperate straits. The powers have enough nuclear missiles aimed at each other to annihilate the world a dozen times over. This, of course, is an intolerable situation. People must begin to change their hearts, to regard their fellow humans with care and joy (as do the dolphins!) and not suspicion. Otherwise...

"Please," she said, "repent of these evil ways. You're just being bullies when you aim your rockets at each other! Lay down your guns, dismantle your missiles! Just follow the example of the dolphins and love one another. The earth still has a chance, if we change now."

The people stood and applauded her. The Secretary General was by her side. He leaned and whispered in her air. "Maybe," he said, "maybe we're...beginning."

Michelle looked at him. There were tears in her eyes. And in his.

"Please," he said, in a thick accent. "Come visit us again."

Michelle and Robby were standing on a street corner, waiting for the light to change. It was night and they were just finishing some shopping. Suddenly, a black limousine pulled up beside them. Two men jumped out of the car and pushed them into the back seat! Michelle tried to scream, but a gloved hand came over her mouth and a rope was tied around her hands, and Robby's.

The limo roared through the red light, then sped down the street and, after a bumpy ride of underpasses and overpasses, finally turned into an isolated field. There the two were hurried into a small airplane and strapped tight into the backseats. The plane immediately took off.

The pilot said something into the microphone they couldn't understand.

"I think it's Chinese!" Robby whispered to Michelle. "Shut up!" the pilot yelled at them. He turned to Michelle. "The boss wants to talk to you." He handed the earphones and microphone to her.

"Hello," said Michelle.

A voice came over the head phone in thick Oriental accent.

"Betta tell us how you talk to dolphins," the other said to Robby.

"With our mouths," Robby said.

"Looky kid, one more smart remark from you and we shove you out door!" the man said.

The voice over the earphone laughed, a sinister Oriental laugh. "You be good children and you won't get hurt."

"You can't just kidnap us like this!" Michelle said.

"We're doin' it aren't we," the sinister voice over the earphone said.

"You're really not acting very nice, you know" said Michelle firmly. "The American officials will find you."

"Are you Chinese spies?" Robby asked.

"Shut up! Hey! Wha…!"

"#$%*&%+l!!!" the pilot yelled, pointing out the window.

"Daddy!!!" Michelle and Robby both yelled at once.

A cloud completely covered the airplane!

"I can't see! x@#$%^&*+l!" the Chinese pilot screamed.

Then the front doors came open and the two men were whisked out of the plane!

"!@#$%^&*-!" the men gurgled.

"They should have fastened their safety belts," Robby said before he blanked out.

Michelle and Robby woke up. They were still in the plane. It was flying itself! Then below them they saw a familiar beach.

"Michelle!" Robby yelled. "We're home! We're over our island." The plane easily landed on the smooth sand beach and coasted to a stop.

Peter and Johnny ran up to the airplane, followed by several others, including Frankie and Capt. Jones.

"What's going on!" yelled Peter. "We got a message over our shortwave saying you'd be landing here!"

"Kool plane! mon," said Johnny.

"Now I've seen everything," said old Capt. Jones, shaking his wizened head.

"How…what…are you two doing here?" Frankie gasped.

"Well," said Michelle, smiling, "it's…a long story!"

Several of the friends were in their coral home discussing the amazing events of the last days, when a whirring sound came over the speakers from their sensitive computerized under-water microphones.

"It's a sub!" Peter yelled.

Everyone stood up. Johnny ran for the console and pushed a button closing the outer coral coverings on all windows. They stood quietly and listened.

"It sounds like it's right over us!" Michelle cried.

They ran into the sonar-radio room. Johnny listened in the earphones. "I'm pickin' up a radio frequency real near by!" Then he took off the earphones and looked at them open mouthed. "I'm no language expert, but didn't you say, Michelle those creepy guys who kidnapped ya were Chinese?"

Michelle nodded.

"I think I'm hearing Chinese, mon!"

Michelle gasped. Robby grabbed the earphones. "It's Chinese, all right," he said. "It must be…them!"

"They found us," said Michelle, "…somehow…"

"But how?" asked Robby. "We never told anyone where the island was."

"Uh oh, mon! Maybe they coulda traced our short wave radio communications?" Johnny said. "President…uh…Clark called us a lot while you were there."

"What !?" Michelle said.

"Didn't you know?" said Peter. "We assumed you knew!"

"No! He never mentioned he was calling here."

"Uh oh!" said Peter. "He said he was very interested in our life here and asked lots of questions, strictly confidential, he said, like where the island was, and so on, and as he was the President we figured we had to tell him. You don't think the President would've have told the Chinese, do you, Michelle?"

"Oh no, of course not, Peter. Johnny's probably right. The Chinese must have monitored it."

"Yeah," said Robby. "With their spy apparatus."

"Wait a minute!" said Johnny. "Didn't ole Capt. Jones and his men go trout fishin' today up by the waterfall?"

"That's right!" said Peter. "They're on the island now!"

He raised their multi-mirrored periscope. "I can see the sub!" he said, looking through the eyepiece. "They're surfaced off the beach. Wait a minute," he said. "…They're lowering life rafts." He turned and looked at them. "They're going ashore."

"Oh no," said Michelle. "We have to warn the men!"

"And what about *The Dolphin,*" said Frankie.

"We must go ashore," said Michelle.

They carefully swam toward the beach. Several dolphins approached the shore with them. They all stayed submerged, sticking their heads above water just far enough to see.

Johnny peered through his dripping face mask. "I see men in dark suits," he said, "walking on the beach." The Chinese sub was partly submerged.

"There's Capt Jones!" Michelle cried, looking through binoculars. "He and his men are coming down the hill. They don't even see the sub!"

"We better try and sneak to the forest and meet 'em before they get down to the beach," said Peter.

They crept among some large rocks onto the beach, took off their tanks and exchanged flippers for the running shoes in their belt packs, then quickly hid their gear and silently ran up the hill toward the waterfall.

Suddenly Robby slipped on a wet rock and started tumbling down the hill! Michelle cried out and ran down toward him. Peter dashed after her.

"Oh no!" Johnny said. "The Chinese tong's spotted us, mon!"

Capt. Jones, carrying a string of fish, looked toward the commotion, waved and started trotting down the hill with his men.

They reached them, standing over Robby, who was rubbing his knee.

"I'm all right," Robby said. "But I think I blew it."

"Wha's happenin'?" smiled Capt. Jones.

Johnny ran up. He pointed down the beach. "There's a Chinese sub off the beach, old mon!"

"We came to warn you and get back to the home," Peter said.

"I think they've seen us!" cried Frankie.

All at once a shot rang out. "Come down here!" a voice yelled out in broken English, "or we shoot you!"

They all looked at each other.

"Well," Michelle said, "shall we go see what they want?"

They started down the hill.

"@#$%^&*!!" a man said in Chinese, pointing at Michelle. "She's the one!" They were all aiming rifles at them.

"Get in rafts!" the first man said, nudging them with his gun barrel.

They threw Michelle and Robby into a small barred brig on board the sub.

"I want to make a phone call!" Robby yelled to the guards through the bars. "I've read my civics books. I know my constitutional rights."

The guards laughed at him in Chinese.

"Communist atheists," Robby swore beneath his breath.

A man in an officer's uniform walked up to the cage. "We want the computer devices for talking to the dolphins…Michelle," he said, smiling at them sinisterly.

"Were you that guy over the radio?" Robby asked.

"SHUT UP!" the man said. "Now," he said, looking at Michelle, "the computers?"

"How did you find us?" Robby asked.

"The President is such a…how you say…boob! We traced his calls to you, of course."

Michelle was silent.

Michelle and Robby looked around them in the tiny, cramped cell. "They're on our ship," Michelle finally said.

"That's better," the man grinned.

"I'll take you to them, but you have to let the others go."

The man shrugged his shoulders. "OK. It's deal! But if this is trick…we kill you two both!"

The men put the captives in the rafts and started rowing toward *The Dolphin*. Without warning the boats began tipping over in the water! capsizing the Chinese men and the captives.

"!@#$%^&*!" the men yelled as they splashed into the sea.

Several went under and were now looking into the smiling faces of several bottle-nose dolphins.

"They won't hurt you," Michelle yelled. She and the others swam toward shore while the dolphins frolicked with the men, blocking from following the escaped islanders.

"Hey!!" the Chinese yelled again.

Michelle and Robby and the others got to the island, put on their scuba gear and then swam down into the sea. They were near their home when they saw several frogmen approaching!

Dolphins immediately swam between the two groups, smiling at the Chinese frogmen. The divers gestured frantically as the dolphins soared around them. Finally one of them pointed towards the surface and the frogmen swam up.

Michelle and friends quickly swam into their home.

214

"I wish the dolphins had rammed them!" Peter said, as the water was being withdrawn.

"Same here, mon'!" agreed Johnny.

"Love your enemies," Michelle smiled at them.

It was a dark and stormy night. Several black-dressed men had gotten on board *The Dolphin* and were carefully searching it.

All at once! their leader saw something out of the corner of his eye. He looked up...

Something–or someone—was glowing before them, shimmering above their heads over the ship's railing!

"Iiiiiieeeee!!!!!" the men screamed. They clambered over the side and dove into the sea.

"The sub's leaving!" Johnny yelled, watching the sonar. "At top speed!"

They all cheered.

"Something must have really scared them," Michelle said.

"Yeah!" said Robby. He shook his head. "Or someone! I just hope they don't come back."

Michelle closed her eyes. She saw her grandfather Michael.

"They won't," she smiled.

While the two had been away in the cities of the north, Peter had finally finished a project he had been working on for years:

buoyant "dolphin suits", with a skin texture as near to the dolphin's real skin as possible to allow rapid movement through the water. They had fin-like "mittens" and a large tail flipper which moved with an up-and-down movement of the hips, like real dolphins, and a back fin for direction and stability, and, of course, a face mask with a smiling dolphin's mouth!

Several of them, Peter, Michelle, Robby, Marylou, Johnny, Frankie, their children, tried them out one day.

"This is fun!" Michelle said through the smile mouth to Peter, kicking her tail fin smoothly with her legs. "This must be close to how a dolphin feels."

"Dolphins have such sensitive skin," smiled Frankie.

They all swam together.

After a few minutes Robby looked up toward the sky.

"The Star Dolphins are coming!" he smiled.

Then they all swam off through the water like a dolphin pod, joyously caressing one another…

Robby chased after little Marylou and rested his flipper on her stomach. She kissed him and they gazed into each other's dolphin eyes. He kicked his tail fin and dove under the waves. She quickly followed and they swam together. She rolled over him, playing, and then he chased her as they wiggled through the bright coral.

He caught up to her and pressed against her side. She rolled on her back and smiled at him as he swam over her. They cartwheeled together through the water and she held him with her flippers.

Ahead they saw Michelle and Peter and Frankie and Johnny and…The two shot toward them and joined the group. The others all smiled. They submerged, then surfaced together, laughing.

"Do you want to swim out to the rocks?" Michelle smiled.

"Umh hmh," the others smiled.

They dashed off toward the rocks and circled them.

Three dolphins surfaced in the middle of the islanders, carefully rubbing up against them. They whistled joyously. Michelle wrapped her flippers around one of them and he towed her smiling around the rocks. Michelle kissed the side of his face, laughing, then took off her dolphin mask and shook her long golden hair, which glowed like a faery queen's in the shimmering ocean sun.

Johnny and Frankie swam off together, and started body surfing on the waves. They rolled and tumbled over each other happily in the surf.

Peter swam up to Michelle, his mask off, looking like a knight with his visor up. He threw her a kiss with his flipper.

Michelle laughed. "You're cute!"

Michelle and Peter were swimming together alone. It was twilight. The setting sun shone like liquid gold, and Michelle's reddish blond hair hung all around her blushing rose-pink cheeks, while Peter's dark eyes lovingly adored her from under his thick bushy brown eye brows.

"Peter…" Michelle said, lightly brushing her hand over his hair and beard.

"Will you marry me, Michelle?" Peter asked her.

Michelle laughed, a silvery liquid laugh, holding her head back. Then she looked at Peter, her eyes softly, goldly shining.

Two dolphins glided to them.

"We are gathered here today…" Peter said to the dolphins. The dolphins whistled, and Michelle laughed again.

He pulled an ancient gold ring off his finger and placed it, glittering, on her's. It shone like the setting sun.

They looked at each other and then touched foreheads.

"I now pronounce us...man and wife!" they both said, slowly, at once.

He kissed her on her lips and then took her hand and they soared through the water together. They held hands and submerged under the waves, then swirled in circles through the sea, as though on an undersea merry-go-round. Fish swam by them, through them, and all around them as they made circles through the waves. A witness dolphin smiled happily.

They surfaced again.

"I love us!" Michelle said.

CHAPTER SIX
THE STAR DOLPHIN

Robby was sitting alone on the beach, his arms around his knees, leaning back against his favorite coconut tree. He looked out over the horizon and saw the star. The setting sun was hanging over the side of the ocean, a gleaming golden ball.

He thought he "heard" the star. It seemed to whistle!

He stood up, watching it closely. The whistling grew louder. Then the "star" was in front of him! whirling white…all of milky light, revolving just over the waves.

A "porthole" opened in the "star" and Robby saw two forms jump into the water and swim toward him. They surfaced in the water, their smiling heads bobbing in front of him: dolphins. He looked at the "star" again.

"Robby," a voice said from within. "Come on!"

It was his father's voice! Robby ran out through the water towards the voice. He could look directly into the "star", and saw shimmering forms.

"Father?" he said.

"Yes."

"Where are we going?" he asked as he ran toward them.

He got to the "star" and looked up. He saw his father and his grandfather Michael. They lifted him up into the sparkling "star." There smiled Rena.

"To the dolphin planet?" he asked. "I've seen it sometimes in my dreams."

"Yes, Robby, we were preparing you," Rena said.

"The dolphin planet Shine?" he asked.

"Yes, Robby."

The whirling starship lifted up off the sea. Robby turned and looked out the swirling opaque walls. He could see the ocean as a milky dream below them. Then Earth disappeared like a blue and white marble tossed into the distance.

"It's all water?"

"Except one large island where people live," Michael said.

Robby looked out the walls of light again. He could see the stars streak by him in a wavy haze.

"And the dolphin's rule?"

"Yes, the dolphin's rule? They are the dominant species on Shine."

The two dolphins swam off. They soon approached a small pod of bottle-nosed dolphins. They frolicked together for a while and then swam down to the coral floor. There they stood on their tails, having a meeting. First a messenger dolphin would speak, looking carefully at the others, the others listening. Then the Earth dolphins would talk in turns.

Finally, the two messenger dolphins took off through the water and the others dispersed.

They soon approached another pod of dolphins and then had their meeting, and again swam off.

Robby flew through space. He felt as if her were off on a comet! as the starship soared.

"And how do the dolphins rule?" Robby asked as he looked at the fleecy stars soaring by.

"By serving the people on the planet," Heaven said.

There was a light nudge as they leaped through hyper-space.

And then they were surrounded by greenish light and seemed to be floating slowly down. Robby could see waving water below them as they settled down through the blue-green air and landed with a great SPLASH!

"Hello, friends!" the first one said as he walked on the cloudy water toward them.

""Hello! Jessy," Michael said. "This is Robby!"

"Yes, Robby. You have finally come." He lifted his arms out to him. "Come out!" he said.

"Out on the water?" Robby asked.

"Yes. Out on the water, towards me,"

Robby sat down in the door of the ship, and, smiling at Jessy, eased out onto the water.

Jessy took his hands. "You're doing fine, Robby," he said, water-wings fluttering in the morning breeze.

Robby held Jessy's hands very tightly. Then his ankles began to sink a little below the surface. He cried out.

"Be calm," Jessy said.

Robby relaxed at the soothingness of his voice, and then he was standing on the water, by Jessy's side, effortlessly, and breathlessly—balancing.

"It's easy!" Robby said.

Then Robby saw a great white dolphin leap out of the water 20 feet into the air and dive in a graceful, perfect arch, the most beautiful dolphin he had ever seen. It was slender and long and streamlined, and seemed almost suspended in space as it jumped. It's skin was white as wool.

"The Dolphin King wishes to meet you," Jessy said.

The dolphin swam up to them, his smooth white head and smiling mouth out of the water.

("His smouth!" thought Robby.)

"Hello!" said the dolphin in a high sweet voice, like a musical squeak.

"He squeaks English!" Robby said.

"Fluently," said one of the others gathered around.

"And thirty other galactic languages, too," said another.

"Our dolphins have vocal cords," said a third. ("Ours don't," thought Robby. "Their sounds come from an air-bag near their blow-hole.")

"Hi!" said Robby.

The dolphin gently rubbed up against the boy. "Would you like to go down to the city under the sea?

"The Dolphin King wishes to greet you!"

"The Dolphin King?" Robby looked at Jessy.

"Yes, Robby," Jessy said. "Go with White Dolphin."

Robby got on the dolphin, inhaled deeply and then they submerged. Down through the gorgeous, clean, fresh water they flew. The water seemed almost like spirit to him. Down and down they soared and finally Robby saw something, reflecting even the faint light from above—the jeweled city!

All before him as they swam down was the most fabulous sight Robby had ever seen—an entire city made of jewels: Emerald walls and ruby terraces, sapphire roofs, a pearl gate…

The dolphin swam to the pearly gate and then stopped and pushed a button with its flipper, and the gate opened, and they entered a canal. The gate closed and water rushed out through the walls, as Robby gasped for air as they swam rapidly down the jeweled passageway.

They wound all through the sparkling tunnels. Many other dolphins passed them, smiling and squeaking "Hello," but the white dolphin did not stop.

Finally they approached a magnificent pearl and sapphire door at the end of a canal. It shimmered before them in the muted green light.

The dolphin pushed a button and the door slid open, and there, in the "throne room" floated: The Dolphin King!

Robby looked dazedly ahead of him; in the emerald green chamber the dolphin delicately moved in the water. He looked at Robby and smiled.

"Robby!" he said. "Come in."

The white dolphin floated in before the Dolphin King and Robby saw a very beautiful mark on its melon, its forehead: a shining white star. Then Robby's eyes suddenly noticed the Dolphin King's flippers:

Where the end of its flippers should have been, five long lacy fingers moved!

Robby stared at the Star Dolphin entranced, his mouth open. The star on its melon seemed to shine with an eternal, internal light. He had never seen anything as beautiful as this Star Dolphin—the Dolphin King!

Was he dreaming? Would he awake soon on his island, his head leaning against the tree, the morning sun in his face? Would he see Michelle and tell her of this newest dream and then have his breakfast of fish and fresh fruit?

Or am I really here? he thought, in this jeweled under-sea chamber with this dolphin with hands?

"Robby," the Dolphin King said, reaching out his hand, "I am very glad to meet you." A palm leaf was over the dolphin's head, waving slightly.

"You have traveled a long way." Robby held the offered hand, its skin the satin smoothness of a dolphin. He could feel the strength of it as it closed gently around his. "You have many things to ask, I know. Shine is a very old and a very young planet. We circle a tiny star we call Pulse, which you call Sirius II, which orbits giant Sirius, your brightest star.

"We have known of Earth a million revolutions. We love your people and," he said, smiling, "we love your dolphins, our emissaries to your world from long ago. We are the Nommo who visited the Dogon and assisted with the building of the great pyramids, just as we assisted those on your neighbor planet Mars when it still had water in its air. They live under the ice-caps now in cities much like this one which we helped them build."

"And the Face on Mars?" Robby asked.

"A great monument to…God, always looking above to the stars…

"Robby, I know on Earth no dolphins have hands. We are the…"

"Star Dolphins!" said Robby.

"Yes. We fly our 'stars'…"

"You fly…!"

"The 'stars' among the stars…

"White Dolphin," said the Dolphin King," Would you please show Robby around our city?"

"Yes! Star Dolphin."

They flew through the canals of the city. As they passed by a gold-plated window, a young man stuck his head out.

"Who is our visitor?" he asked.

"Hello, Jesu. This is Robby. He's from Earth, you know."

Then a young woman came to the window, so pretty Robby almost blushed, looking at her face.

"This is Thrace," the young man said.

"They're newlyweds," the dolphin whispered.

She waved her fingers.

"Won't you two come in and visit?"

"Sure!" said Robby.

A door opened and they swam into the hall canal.

"I'm very happy to meet you, Robby," said Jesu. He lifted Robby up to the living room, while White Dolphin floated in the hall. "We know a lot about planet Earth. We studied it in college."

"I majored in your classical music," said Thrace. "Mozart was my favorite—very light and happy, like dolphin music."

"Yes," said Robby. "He's my favorite, too—Mozart—and the Christmas carols."

"Yes," said Jesu. "You have many wonderful joys on Earth. They should be preserved."

"Earth people are crazy, though," Robby said with a sigh. "Almost all of them."

"They just need help," Jesu said.

"Then you'll come?" Robby said.

They all laughed.

"Thank you for stopping, Robby," said Thrace as Jesu set Robby back on White Dolphin.

"You'll have to come back," smiled Jesu, "Maybe you could help me with my chess."

"I usually win whenever I play Michelle. And our computer Charly Tuna hardly wins any more when he plays either of us!"

"Then you would be a master teacher," Jesu laughed.

The two sailed off down the canal.

"Goodbye, White Dolphin. Goodbye, Robby," called Thrace.

Robby looked back and waved. White Dolphin wove through the glittering tunnels.

Two dolphins swam around in a window above them. They opened their mouths and gaped at Robby. Then they disappeared and suddenly there was bubbling and they were floating behind them.

"Hello, Robby," one said. "Do you like our city?"

"You know my name!"

"Of course. We've been expecting you," the other said.

"You'll be staying with us, won't you?"

Robby looked at White Dolphin.

"Soon," White Dolphin said, smiling mysteriously.

They swam off, Robby waving goodbye.

They made their way through the canals. Other people riding on the backs of dolphins approached them.

"Hello! White Dolphin," they would say, as they passed slowly by.

"Hello, friend. This is Robby. From Earth!"

"Yes. Hello, Robby of Earth."

They toured all through the jeweled city. Lights sparkled everywhere.

Finally they got to the gate again. "It's time we went up," said White Dolphin. "Take a deep breath." The majestic gate opened and they swam out.

Up through the water they flew now, all manner of strange fishes swimming around them. Some swam up to Robby's face, the little mouths opening and closing, letting out air bubbles. They would then scatter before him. The coral shined like gold and sparkled with jewels: Rubies and sapphires and rainbows flashed at them as they flew by. Multi-colored fish whisked around them now, their colors flashing off and on, like neon signs. They dashed about, a sparkling magic show. Red, white and blue dolphins swam near them as giant turtles with sparkling shells propelled by, playfully chasing one another. Fans and bouquets of gold coral mingled with little pink tufts of satin sponges. Star-shaped rocks covered with colored mollusks were embedded in the sea walls. Little feathers of orange and green floated, suspended in the beds. Giant clams gaped red and white marbled flesh in the folds of their mouths; pink and purple friendly sea anemone waved their tentacles. Feather stars floated around them. Colonies of painted sponges nestled. Giant fans of red veins extended upward. The magic show of sparkling, flashing fish went all around. Soft coral, like bunches of colored snowflakes, waved at them. A rainbow of jeweled soft coral hung onto the rocks. Delight sparkled everywhere.

"This is the Dol-fun Sea!" thought Robby.

They surfaced near a small island with all manner of trees on it, some spiraling to the sky. Clouds lay on the tops of the trees. Robby looked out onto the white sand beach and the forest behind.

"This is where your brand new friends live," White Dolphin said.

Then Robby saw some frisky little lambs run out onto the beach from the forest. They had long, white wool hair which was so thick it almost hid them, so they looked like shining stars galloping.

Robby pointed to the beach. "Look, White Dolphin!"

"A drion!" said White Dolphin.

"Oh! He looks like a lion, only his mane is so shiny it looks like the sun. He's going to eat those little lambs!"

"Eat them? Oh no," said White Dolphin. "They're playing. Pretty soon the lambs will turn and chase the drion."

The drion stopped and lay down on the sand and the frisky lambs came and lay around him.

"They're the best of friends," said the dolphin.

"But…"

"Drions are fruitarians," White Dolphin said. "They only eat fresh fruit—preferably from the tangerine tree."

Immediately the drion leaped up and started prancing toward the forest. Then the little lambs jumped up and ran after him. They disappeared. Robby started laughing.

Then Robby saw a small boy with golden hair walk out onto the beach, towing a rope. At the end of the rope emerged from the trees…

"A giant bear! A giant panda bear!"

"He is large, isn't he," White Dolphin laughed, pointing his flipper at the giant black and white smiling bear.

The bear towered over the boy.

"It's his pet. They always walk together."

"Cool!" Robby said. "I want a pet bear, too."

The little boy stopped and waved. Then he tugged at the rope and they turned and walked back into the forest.

"You should swim to the island, now, Robby," White Dolphin said. "Your new friends live there."

"Yes, White Dolphin," Robby said, jumping into the water. He turned and waved and then swam to the beach. Rocks jutted up from the sand, orange and red and green moss hanging down on them like elves hair. Some tiny seal pups waddled up out from the water towards Robby. He patted them. "How sleek and soft you are." Then the mother seal ran along the waves. "Arf, arf," she barked.

"Are these your little pups?" She slid otter-like along the wet sand, through the ocean mist-spray. Then the pups chased after their mother and they disappeared into the sparkled waves. Bright green seagulls flew overhead, whistling like songbirds. "These gulls sing!" The spray seemed to dance off the rocks. He passed a sea cave with churning water.

Robby started singing a poem/song as he walked.

"Spray white! off the rugged rocks

And upward, in a dash to kiss the clouds

Your seadreams fly to me.

Smiling like a waterwisp

Your green eyes float to me.

And you are there to love and play with gently.

Do you know the path to home?

Along the beach and up the hill

Through heather gray with clouds

Above the great loud waves that wave

Their fleecy fingers as they sound along the shore
Then through an open door
That smiles like a sea cave!
It's just a mile through the spray!
Walk with me. I know the way."

Then he saw the face! through the ocean mistiness. It seemed almost suspended, smiling delicately through sea-green eyes.

"Hi," she shined. She ran up and kissed Robby.

Then she turned and scampered off into the woods. It happened so quickly Robby was barely aware of more than just a fluttering blur of opaque colors and the delicious softness of her kiss, but he knew it was a "girl."

He quickly dashed into the forest, looking for her. The sun-star was just beginning to set and reds and oranges and golds were filtering in between the leaves.

All of a sudden he heard the bushes behind him rustle. He looked around to see.

"It's a deer! A doe. Only…its ears!"

The deer's ears were large and flapping, almost like miniature elephant's ears. She was looking at him, waving her ears. She turned her head to lick her side, her tail flitting back and forth, and then looked back at Robby, her narrow delicate face framed by the giant ears which stuck out like catcher's mitts. She began browsing, eating the leaves.

"You're beautiful" Robby said, walking slowly towards her. She quickly looked up at him.

"I've never seen such ears before," he held his hand out to her.

She friskily romped around him. She started eating again. Then she pranced to one side, looking straight ahead, trotting around him again.

"You're circling me," Robby whispered.

Finally he stood very still, watching her. She flapped her ears, and then walked slowly towards him. He slowly reached his hand out and touched her nose. She licked his hand and then turned and, fawn-like, scampered off, and started browsing once again, ever so often looking up at him with her doe eyes, her ears out.

"I love you little deer…with the big ears," Robby said.

Then he saw something in the bushes. He lifted his eyes and there before him in the ray of light was the narrow elegant face of a young buck, with two little circular horns, like antennae.

"Oh! It's your friend," Robby said to the doe, who now ran up beside him.

The buck walked slowly through the trees, and stopped and looked at Robby. He turned his head and licked his side, his fail flicking. Now he looked back at Robby, and then—he knelt down on his front knees and lay down in the sun-ray before him!

"Oh deer!" Robby said, "how beautiful you look, lying in the light."

The young buck lay very still peering at Robby, the golden light of the setting sunstar bathing the handsome face and bouncing off his circular antlers. The sun/star light danced around his face in white shinings, almost cloud-like.

"You must be the deer-prince," said Robby.

The deer-prince lowered his head and light reflected off his antlers like a halo. He turned his head and again licked his side. The doe walked up to him and kneeled on her front legs and then lay beside him. She rested her head on his back. The buck turned and licked the doe's ears.

"Goodbye, sweet dears," Robby said, walking away.

He strolled through the woods again, and then in the far distance he saw the lambs chasing the drion through the forest!

Robby laughed, and then sat down, putting his arms around a tiny green sapling.

"Where did she come from?" he sighed. "Where did she go?"

He leaned his head lightly against the little tree.

"I love you," he heard. Robby quickly looked up.

"I love you," he heard once more.

He looked down at the tree. "I love you," he heard again in a small, whispering voice.

"You talk!" Robby cried.

"We love you," he heard around him, very very softly, softer than a breeze. He leaned his ear over to the tiny talking trees. "We all love you," they seemed to whisper, swaying like daisies in the soft breeze. He hugged one, then stood up, gazing down at the miniature trees.

He looked around. Jessy was standing before him.

"Your father has returned to Earth," Jessy said. "I will take you to our home." He offered Robby his hand.

They walked together through the forest in silence and finally they came to a clearing, and there, beyond a sparkling pond, Robby saw the mountains. He gasped. "They're so high."

"We live at the base of the Emerald Mountains," Jessy said as they walked beside the pond. "We're almost there now."

The mountains were rugged, but covered with soft green, their peaks disappearing into pearl-like clouds. Then, Robby saw on the far side of a lush meadow—a circle of tepees!

"You live in tepees?" Robby said.

"Yes," said Jessy. "They are made of giant leaves which grow further up in the canyons of the Emerald Mountains."

Robby saw some children running around the tepees. He recognized some of the others who had met him on the water.

"And now, Robby," Jessy said, "run off and play with the children."

Robby ran quickly towards the teepees. Some of the elders were sitting around a log fire, talking.

"Hello, young Robby!" one said to him. "The children have been waiting for you to come and play."

"What are you playing?" he said as he got to them.

"Dolphin King!" one of the children said as she scampered and fluttered around the campfire. "We're playing Dolphin King. I'm the Dolphin King. Can I bring you some food, Robby?"

"I am hungry," Robby said.

"Here!" She handed him a plate of fruit and fish and honey.

"Just like I eat at home," Robby said. "Thank you...Dolphin King!"

"You can sit here and eat it by the campfire." Then she scampered away.

"It's her!" Robby said.

A small boy ran up to Robby. "Did you meet the Dolphin King?" he asked.

"Yes!" said Robby. "He's very wise."

"Yes!" said the boy. "He's very good. We love the Dolphin King."

Later in the night as the sparkling stars came out, they all sat around the campfire, looking up at the pictures in the sky.

"There—Flying Little Lamb!" a child cried out, pointing.

Robby looked overhead. He could see the constellation: a lamb with shimmering wings lying down.

"Yes," one of the elders said, gossamer star-lit dove-wings glistening gold in the firelight.

"And there's the sword!" said another.

Robby looked. His breath was almost taken away: A giant long sword with jewel handle sparkled across the sky.

"Oooh," the others echoed.

"There's the dolphin!" a little girl squealed.

Robby looked on the horizon of the mountains where the girl was pointing. There was the dolphin! jumping over the mountain with a starry smile!

"I see him!" said Robby.

"And there's the King's Throne," said another, pointing straight up.

"And there's...Zardok!" They all booed.

Robby looked where the children pointed: A long tentacle of stars stretched across the southern horizon.

"Tell us the story of Zardok the evil space squid!" a child called out.

"Long ago," one of the elders began as the children all looked towards the south, "Zardok the evil space squid ruled the galaxy. His tentacles were light centuries long and he ensnared any dolphin-ships coming his way."

"Boo! Zardok!"

"Finally the Dolphin King decided something must be done. So he sent out a boy, much like young Robby here" (Robby gasped) "in a small dolphin-ship with a peace offering to Zardok.

"As the dolphin-ship approached Zardok, but still out of range of his tentacles, the young boy (let's call him Robby)"—the children laughed—"Robby said over his communication beam, 'I love you Zardock.'

"Well, Zardok had never heard anyone say, 'I love you, Zardok' to him before, and he went into a rage.

"'What do I, Zardok the Space Squid, care about love,'" he sneered.

"'I love you, Zardok,' Robby said again."

"This made the space squid even angrier. 'Love!' Zardok bellowed. 'I know not love.'"

"'I love you, Zardok,' Robby said again."

The children giggled and Robby blushed.

"Well, Robby kept saying 'I love you' over and over until finally it drove Zardok into a frenzy and he choked himself with his own tentacles!"

The children all said, "Hurray!" and "Yay Robby!"

"That strand over there on the southern horizon is all that is left of Zardok, the evil space squid. And this children, is the power of love. The sharks cannot stand before you—

"You can drive them away with love!"

(General applause!!)

In the morning Robby awoke early. He looked around him in the leaf tepee. The light was beginning to shine through. He saw the children lying in their hammocks.

He quietly got out of his and walked outside.

The two morning suns were glowing from between the mountain peaks, bathing him in warm rays of golden shine. He made his way to the forest and then down to the beach. Robby looked out onto the delicate lace waves, sparkling under the suns.

Then he saw, and heard, some distance away, a smiling foaming froth. A pod of dolphins were swimming towards him in a cloud-bank, conversing.

They stopped as they neared the beach.

"Hello!" one called

"Hello! Sir Dolphin," Robby answered.

"You're Robby of Earth, correct?" another asked.

"Yes."

"Earth! A fine planet. Lots of water!"

"And you have many dolphins, do you not?"

"Yes! Many, many dolphins!"

"Come on out!" one of the dolphins said.

Robby ran out into the water.

"No, no," the dolphin laughed. "Not in the water. On the water."

"I don't know if I can…"

"I'll help you."

Robby suddenly recognized the voice coming from the cloud, and then…There she was! her face and dazzling dancing laughing smiling green eyes before him!

"Here," she said. She offered him her hand.

He looked quietly on her face, then took her hand and easily walked out on the glistening sea—and they walked out of the cloud together, through the waves—beneath the suns….

Robby and the girl walked hand in hand over the wave tops.

"My name is Misty," the girl said.

"My name is…"

"Robby," said Misty.

"Then you were the girl at the camp who gave me food."

"I've been waiting for you."

"How old are you, Misty?" asked Robby.

Misty paused, then said, "Today is my 12th birthday."

"I'm 12 too!" Robby said. "12 ½."

"Last week I was a hundred."

"A hundred?"

"Tomorrow I might be three."

"Robby, there truths about time which people on your home planet Earth do not yet understand," Misty explained. "Time is a plaything of the universe, a jester it toys with until it grows weary of time—Then it gobbles time up in a black hole! and there is no more 'time' until finally 'time' escapes, again to rum amok, terrorizing poor human beings like those on your home planet Earth.

"We of Shine know that time is only a mask, an illusion, a court jester of the universe. It is to be toyed with, laughed at, made a joke of, but never, never, never taken seriously, and then as your cute French Earthlings say, viola! sent on its way.

"All the people back at the tepees—we all know how to 'bend' time, Robby. The little boy sitting next to you at the campfire last night might be an older today. The older telling you the stories last night might be a younger this morning!"

Robby was silent as he gazed upon Misty, who had his hand in hers. They continued walking on the silver-lined sea.

"But how about when you…die, Misty?" he finally asked.

Misty laughed. "We don't ever really die, Robby," she said. "You might say we…evaporate. We eventually revert back to our original state—water—and then…we merge upwards with the clouds."

Misty was silent now as they walked through the glistening and gleaming world of water, mist, light and spray.

Robby whispered, "What then, Misty?"

Misty smiled at him, a rainbow smile.

"We rain!"

Michelle and some friends sailed in *The Dolphin* around the tip of Florida. Robby had said he wished to stay home, alone, to "meditate" on the beach. Peter was standing beside her at the wheel and Michelle was teaching Marylou how to steer.

When night came, Michelle lay down in her cabin bed to sleep. "Goodnight, Peter," she sighed.

"Michelle," Heaven said to her in a dream. "Robby is on the dolphin planet Shine. Many UFOs have been their 'stars'. They are now ready to land—here.

"You must contact Sharon and have her tell President Clark and him Pope Jon-Paul. Pick them up in Miami in *The Dolphin*. Except one radio reporter, who is to be told nothing, no one else is allowed. No TV cameras—(yet).

"Now you must do exactly as I've said. The Star Dolphins will be landing in three days!"

Michelle woke up. She started smiling. "Peter! Wake up!"

"Sharon!" she said over her radio.

"Michelle?"

"The dolphins are coming!!!"

The Pope lay down the phone.

"Dolphins?"

"Ah mon dieu. Ah-but of course—Dolphins."

The President and the Pope stood smiling at the airport. They both waved and then boarded the jet.

"No one knows the meaning of this top secret trip of the President and Pope Jon-Paul," the commentator said into the camera. "The only comment has been no comment, and no one seems to have any idea what this trip is all about. We're not even sure where they are going.

"We do know the Pope flew all the way over from the Vatican in Rome on 24hrs notice, and now the two of them are boarding Air Force One.

"Just what…"

"Ah come on! Mr. President," the journalist said, "can't you give me some idea what this is all about? What's going on here? I know its something good! You, the pope, only one journalist, me allowed. Can't you…"

"No, John! Absolutely not. Besides, to be honest with you, I don't really know what is going to happen myself. We'll just have to wait and see together, won't we?" he said, smiling at the radio announcer.

"Uh stewardess," the President said, "a bit more wine, please."

The three Star Dolphins swam out to the *Star* and then into the submerged door. They floated in their water capsules, their long fingers pushing buttons and pulling toggle switches, looking out through milky walls of light.

"Is our passenger secure," the Dolphin King said.

In a few nano-moments the *Star* lifted up from the water.

Many people and dolphins were on the surface of the "Dolfun Sea" as the ship took off.

"Good-bye," said Jessy, waving his hand.

"Good-bye," called Misty.

The Star Dolphins blew off through space, floating easily in their water capsules, lacy fingers around the controls, looking out on their starry world. The *Star* seemed to cavort as it sailed through the sparkling void.

"This is it!" the Dolphin King smiled.

They jumped through hyper space and the blue oceans of Earth leaped up at them like a flung sapphire.

Heaven stood on a cloud over the ocean, as the faint star on the horizon came ever closer.

Then—a million dolphins leaped up into the air at once!

"Ladies and gentlemen," the radio commentator said into his microphone, "I am with the President and the Pope aboard a sailing schooner called *The Dolphin*. As soon as we landed, we were rushed to the Miami dock in Secret Service cars, and then escorted on board this ship by a young lady named Michelle Hope, who, as I remember, gave some very interesting talks before the United Nations this year.

"I still have absolutely no idea what this trip is all about. We have laid anchor, and now seemed to be waiting for something. Just what...

"Wait a minute! The President is pointing his finger up at the sky. The sun is just now beginning to disappear beneath the horizon, and the earliest stars can be seen. The President is definitely pointing at something, ladies and gentlemen. (What's he pointing at?) And now the Pope is pointing too! They're both pointing up towards the distant horizon…Yes, I see it now. (Is it a plane?)

"It looks like a moving…star!

"It seems to be sailing towards us!

"Yes, now I can hear it! It's…whistling. The star is definitely whistling, ladies and gentlemen.

"It's getting closer! And closer! Now…

"Oh my God, it's hovering directly over us. It's…it's…

"…a UFO! An Unidentified Floating Object!

"My God, I am nearly speechless. We are being bathed in the light above.

"And the whistling. It sounds a little like…

"The extraterrestrial space ship has landed!

"The extraterrestrial space ship has landed!

"It is floating before us here in the water. It appears to be a revolving ball of light, like the sun, but I can easily look directly into it.

"Wait a minute! Now a…door is opening! I can barely see some figures in the door, silhouettes against the pulsating white light.

"Now wait a minute…the door is opening further. I can begin to see the…creatures, (whatever they are!) more clearly now. They seem to be…

"Smiling!

"Now they're diving into the water!

"They're…

"They're…

"They're…

"DOLPHINS!"

The President and the Pope got into their wet suits and life preservers. The commentator babbled wildly in the background. Then the two climbed over the ladder of the ship's railing and down into the ocean.

Michelle quickly followed.

They eased into the warm Florida water and made their way slowly towards the Star Dolphins, vertically floating before them. A slight mist seemed to cover the dolphins, and behind them the whirling, milky *Star* floated on the waves.

The Dolphin King reached out his hand to the President, and then the Pope. And then Michelle. "You are Michelle Hope—Robby's sister, Heaven's daughter, Michael's granddaughter?"

"Yes," said Michelle.

"Mr. President," said the Dolphin King, "and Pontiff. We come as messengers of peace. Earth is a troubled, troubled world, but a very beautiful one. We have circled planet Earth in the past, observing you. We were hoping you could, on your own, resolve your many difficulties. However, it does seem you do need help."

The three Star Dolphins floated easily, erectly in the water, keeping afloat by rhythmically moving their tail flukes.

"Please!" the Dolphin King said, reaching his hand out to them, "we love you, we want you to be happy."

A rainbow mist of light covered them.

"Don't you love yourselves?" the second Star Dolphin said.

"Can't you help yourselves?" the third Star Dolphin said.

"But...but..." the President and Pope both blurted out.

"We know you have much good in you," the Dolphin King said. "You must believe in it and bring it to fruition."

"Let your light shine," said the second Star Dolphin. "We can see it. Can't you?"

The President and the Pope listened. Michelle smiled.

"The Spirit who made the waters wants you to live. Don't you wish to live?"

"Love?"

"Are you like your sad lemmings, who madly dash over the rocky cliffs to drown in the turbulent waters below?"

"Love one another, as brothers."

"And sisters." The Dolphin King smiled at Michelle.

"Help those who need help."

"Together you can stand. Divided you will be conquered."

"By yourselves!"

The President and Pope nodded their heads. They felt almost hypnotized as they gazed and listened.

"We love you," the Dolphin King said.

"Yes!!" said the other two.

"We don't want to lose you. We are concerned about the future of Earth. It is a very beautiful planet.

"I wish now to present you this gift which I made especially for you to share." He handed a gold satin-like bag to Michelle.

"Goodbye, friends," the Dolphin King said, waving his fingers.

Then the Star Dolphins turned and easily swam through the waters, back towards their shining *Star.*

"Good-bye, Mr. Dolphin King!" the President waved, a slight dazed smile on his lips.

"God bless you," the Pope intoned solemnly.

"So long, Star Dolphins!" Michelle said, smiling, waving. "Tell Robby hello for me!"

The Dolphin King turned to Michelle. "I will!"

Michelle looked now at the shimmering swirling ball of glowing plasmic pulsating beaming light. Then she seemed to see "someone" standing in the door! A human? She looked at the face, lit by the *Star* light. Yes, it was a young man's face! It seemed to glow radiantly, its brilliance almost impossible to look upon, but she continued gazing. His cheeks were like golden roses, his eyes the eyes of a friend, his brows thick and…glittering, his hair flaxen.

Michelle couldn't stop gazing on him. He almost looked familiar, but…

Then the young man stepped out of the door and stood on the water, easily balancing on the gentle wave tops. The backdrop of the shining starship seemed to illuminate fluttering wing-like flippers.

"Hello, Robby!" said the Dolphin King.

"Robby!" cried Michelle

"Oh mon Dieu!" cried the Pope.

"Jesus!" breathed the President.

"Friends!" said Robby, reaching his hands out. He smiled at them. A rainbow flew from his mouth as he spoke the word. They gazed at him in silence. He was a shimmer of love on the water. He took a step toward them.

"Friends!"

His voice seemed to carry forever over the water.

On *The Dolphin*, the commentator had fainted, but the voice found the microphone and flowed into homes all across the land.

In his mountain cabin in the Sierra Nevada, a young man listened attentively to his radio, thoughts of *The War of the Worlds* prank broadcast on a Halloween night years ago in his startled mind. But this was Christmas Eve, not Halloween, and he and his wife had been listening to a program of carols.

"It's some kind of Christmas show," he laughed.

"Friends!" Robby's voice came over the speaker. "The Star Dolphins have come to help us save our home." (Static seemed to interfere with the sound. "Did he say Star Dolphins?")

"We must not allow Planet Earth to be destroyed by our own foolish ways. Earth is too important. It is a critical link in the galactic ecosystem" ("What did he say? The 'galactic ecosystem?'") "a port of life in the stormy cosmic ocean. If planet Earth is not saved it will upset this entire fragile ecosphere.

"Friends," the voice said again, "the Star Dolphins..."

Now the voice faded out behind increasing interference...

Robby reached out his hands further towards the President and the Pope and his sister Michelle. He was a ghostly shape against the luminous globe behind him.

Then he turned and walked slowly back to the *Star*...and disappeared within.

Heaven watched as the *Star* lifted up from the water. Then it hovered near him.

Robby suddenly materialized in front of him! on the billowy cloud.

They watched together as the *Star* flew silently into the constellation Aquarius.

On the water, the three, the President, the Pope and Michelle, looked up, watching the *Star* disappear into the stars.

Then Michelle pulled a sparkling gold plaque out of the satin bag.

They all gazed upon it. On the plaque was written in jeweled rainbows:

"Verus amicus est tamquam alter iden!

A true friend is like another me!"

CHAPTER SEVEN
EPILOG: QUEST

In his rough wood cabin in the Sierra Nevada mountain range, Nick and his wife Nancy were (once again!) startled by the sudden replacement of "The Evangelical Hour" by the Star Dolphins…

Robby sat in the undersea television studio Dr. Smith had began building before he died. They were a "pirate" station, KFUN (laughingly called KDOL by some), capable of surreptitiously beaming at will into households all across America. The Star Dolphins had quickly installed super-sophisticated advanced systems, so they could, whenever they pleased, interrupt any program they chose and give their own. They had been "on the air" ever since New Year's Day.

Robby smiled into the camera. They had just beamed into the "Evangelical Hour," and Robby's smiling image had been superimposed over and then superseded the face of the paradise-selling preacher.

"My friends," the preacher had been saying, smiling broadly, holding several booklets in his hands, like items on an auction block, "what will you give for your soul...?"

"Hello, friends!" Robby's image said, fading in over the spiritual salesman.

"It's Howdy-Doody time!"

"Hi Kids!" said Peter in his Buffalo Bob costume. On his knee sat a computerized replica of the smiling, freckle faced, tousle headed Howdy-Doody puppet boy, hero of 50s daytime children's television. Peter slightly moved his lips and pushed a button in the puppet's back and the computer's sensors responded by relaying the "signals" to the puppet's mouth and its high, dolphin-like voice was activated.

"Hi! Kids! It's Howdy-Doody time, all right, Buffalo!" the puppet said, moving its head back and forth as it accurately mouthed the syllables.

Michelle was then smiling into the camera too, dressed up in blue overalls like Ellie May of the "Beverly Hillbillies."

"Gosh, Howdy," she said. "Ain't it a beautiful day."

"I couldn't say, Ellie May," Peter slightly mouthed as the puppet spoke the words. "We're underwater here!" (Canned laughter bubbled.)

Then a Star Dolphin put its hands to the window and peered smilingly in, its flukes moving rhythmically in the water.

"Look!" said Robby. It's the Star Dolphin!"

"Hello, Star Dolphin!" they all said at once.

"Hello, friends!" he waved.

The camera faded in and framed the smiling, beaming face of the Star Dolphin.

Nick didn't really mind that "The Evangelical Hour" had been interrupted; he only watched it to please Nancy his wife. But ever since the Christmas radio broadcast of "space dolphins" landing off the Florida Keys, he had begun to become apprehensive. He knew it was just a prank, something to increase ratings, like that *War of the Worlds* Halloween broadcast in the '30s, but here it was again.

They kept staring into the TV, somehow unwilling to change the channel. And were those flippers behind Robby or...

Robby was now speaking intently, and Nick recalled the distinctive voice as the one he had heard on the radio that Christmas Eve night, talking about the "galactic ecosystem." He had to admit the concept had caught his attention. He had even written it down. And there was something in the voice: It had a forcefulness to it, perhaps like Tyrone Power as a young boy, Nicky had thought. It seemed to penetrate his soul. He thought of his own son off at Annapolis.

"We have a special message for one of our special viewers out there," Robby was saying. Nick watched as the camera focused on Robby's eyes, which seemed to glow with white light. "For Nicky and his wife Nancy up in the Sierra Nevada Mountains."

Nicky's jaw fell open. "How the deuce did they know our names?" he asked his wife.

Nancy said, "Oh, you know how these television preachers are, Nicky. They know everything!" she smiled.

Then Michelle was on the TV. "Nicky," she was saying...as he looked at the attractive face on the screen. It seemed to glimmer with an unearthly beauty, the girl of his adolescent fantasies. Then the camera zoomed in on the ring of Michelle's fore-finger: It was a silver dolphin. Then it turned gold. Then turquoise. Then the little dolphin looked directly at Nicky and smiled!

Nick fell backwards in his chair and the next thing he knew Nancy was bending over him:

"Nicky, are you all right?"

Nick was looking down the shaft of the arrow in his power-bow at the great-antlered elk before him. He drew back the bow string, but then he stopped. "I can't do it," he said. The string went slack.

He was an avid bow-hunter—a poacher, actually—who regularly hunted deer out of season to keep fresh venison on the table. It was a good addition to the trout he caught without a fishing license in the remote mountain streams.

Nick was as libertarian writer, who resented any governmental intervention into his life. That was why he lived in a cabin up on Carson Pass south of Lake Tahoe all year around. Up here in the mountains he was his own man living like he pleased.

He and his wife had been hippies in the "psychedelic '60s" and "back to the earth '70s" and had never bought back into the "system" when the counter culture died in the '80s replaced by greed and Madonna. His son opted for Annapolis.

"Whatever happened to the counter culture?" he wrote once. "Why, man, they went behind the counter."

But now it seemed, a strange influence was taking a subtle hold of him. Only a day after the TV program, a large package had arrived via overnight express, postmarked Key Largo, Florida.

"Florida?" he thought. "I don't know anyone in Florida." He opened the package and there saw a small pair of "Gold-Feather" snowshoes!

"Snowshoes from Florida?" He laughed.

He remembered he needed a new pair of snowshoes. His old wooden ones were all but wore out after years of use hunting deer out of season in deep winter snow. This high-tech set was very different from the big ungainly ones hanging on his wall. They seemed to be a gold-tubular-alloy of some kind, paper thin, very small and feather light, shaped to a jet-like taper at the back.

He tried them on, thinking they would crinkle under his weight, but to his surprise they held. They were so light he felt he could run over the snow in them.

"Maybe fly!" he laughed.

He had them on now, the first time he had used them to hunt deer. He unstrung his bow and put it and the arrows back into his over-the-shoulder quiver. The elk watched.

Nick had with him too the incredibly light weight, pure white back pack he had gotten in his Christmas package, and neatly folded within was the odd piece of "plastic" he had also received. The label on it read "Molecular-Modular Micro Shelter." He got it out and spread it on the snow, looking at it shimmer in the muted winter sun.

Then it erected itself into an igloo! "What...!" Nick yelled, jumping back. It stood there seeming to glow in the lightly falling snow. Nick studied it.

He saw a flap and slowly opened the tent door and crawled inside. "Hmmm," he said. "Snug." He noticed how warm it was in here. He took off his parka and folded it on the tent floor, then reached over and fastened the velcro seal on the door-flap.

Instantly the walls became transparent! and he was looking through them at sparkling coral, with fish swimming through an aqua marine sea! A smiling dolphin with hands peered in!

It lasted only a second, so quick Nick wasn't sure if it wasn't merely an LSD flashback from his hippy days. He shook his head, staring at the pale green tent walls. Nick opened his pack again and took out the cellophane-type envelope that had also been in the brightly wrapped package with dolphins swimming on the glossy paper. The label read "see-weed." Inside was ground up kelp. He tasted it, a delicate salty flavor.

All at once he felt a wave of energy through his body, as if he could effortless run down the trail off over the mountain peaks.

Maybe fly! he thought.

Nick crawled out of the igloo tent. Standing directly in front of him was the elk with the great antlers, largest he had ever seen, that he had almost shot. Nick stopped still. Then the elk took off running, south, down the snow-covered trail.

Now the tent refolded itself into a neat little packet! Nick put it in his pack, put his pack on and started trotting down the Pacific Crest Trail, following after the bounding elk.

Nick had reached the stark volcanic landscape of Sonora Pass bounding like the elk in his tubular snow-wings. They seemed to propel him across the snow, almost like "jet-shoes." The "micro-shelter" had proven extraordinarily warm and wind-resistant, a little piece of tropics, it seemed, in the snowy High Sierra. And the granulated "see-weed" had met all of his food requirements.

As to what was happening or why, he gave it little thought. He only knew he was on a quest to the top of Mt. Whitney. He had done the PCT before in summer and knew the trail well and had seriously thought of trying it in winter some time. The time had arrived.

Suddenly, as he crossed a steep snow field, an avalanche unleashed! "Oh, God!" Nick yelled as the snow came rushing down on him. He had thought the slope looked dangerously convex, and it had snowed lightly just yesterday, but he had been so comfortable in the feather-weight snow-suit Christmas present he had also received in the "Care-Package", he had given it little thought, bounding along without a care in the world, until the world came cascading down.

He sought to make his way to the side of the avalanche path as he felt the snow give in under him. He started going under, but made one final effort and the snow-shoes seemed to carry him just over the tumbling dashing snow and he glided across the slope to the safety of the trees. There he turned and watched the awesome spectacle of the thundering, roaring "white monster" pour down the mountain.

"Whew! I'm lucky to be alive," he said, looking down at the sparkling gold snowshoes. "These things are incredible!"

Then he ran off between the trees, down the snowy path.

Nick was in the Sawtooth range now. The ragged/jagged peaklets seemed to cut the sky itself. Down in the peaceful valley below him was the ranching town of Bridgeport. Ahead lay the Yosemite North Country.

The huge elk with "horns like tree branches" (Nick wrote) stood at the top of the pass, pawing the dry snow with its antlers. Then it started browsing on the evergreen branches.

Nick found himself mimicking him! The crisp, snow draped pine needles tasted good, having many times more vitamin C, he remembered from his survival manuals, than oranges. Then the elk started eating the bark. Nick stripped some off and peeled the soft green inside layer and immediately ate it. "It has a pitchy taste," he said, to the elk he guessed, "but not bad," he had to admit.

The elk suddenly kicked up its hooves and bounded again off down the crystal trail. Nick took off after him, the "Gold-Feather rocket-shoes" propelling him over the snow.

The Yosemite North Country: a beautiful broad valley with an ice-bound brook coursing down the center.

Then Glen Aulen—a magnificent and strange waterfall which seemed to flow upward like a fountain from the great stone which divided its bubbling waters before they finally cascaded into the emerald-green waters of the Glen. Here there were remnants of a "High Sierra camp", the dilapidated canvas house tents quilted with snow.

Now across the beautiful wood bridge Nick ran, pacing himself, and up the trail to Tuolumne Falls, on up to the rocks that looked back out over the snow-blanketed North Country, and then off south to where the creek cut its path through solid granite, with smooth, glacier sculptured domes on either side like holy temples. Nick loved this place. The peace and serenity he had felt here in the summer was even magnified in the lonely white fantasy world that now surrounded him—like a kingdom in the snow-clouds.

But no time to rest: he had to get to the top of Whitney, 220 miles down the trail. "Why?" he wasn't sure, except, "It's there!"

Now Tuolumne Meadows—The great meadow, largest in the Sierra, named after the Tuolumne Indians, which once inhabited it in unimaginable bliss, stretched west to east like the endless, snow-dappled lawn of some monarch who lived in the castle crags above. The snow fall had been light this winter in the "drought-blessed" High Sierra. The elk was grazing—Nick did the same, kneeling and eating sweet grass like chlorophyll granola and washing it down with delicious snow water.

He lay on his back on the snow, his snow-parka and snow-pants effectively insulating him from the cold wet. Up above, slight lacy clouds were waving by through the ice-blue sky. Lambert Dome, an unearthly granite mound, rose up, the clouds playing around its crown.

All of a sudden, he saw a light blink at him from the top of the dome! Then the light rose straight up and flew away west, toward the fabled Valley of the Yosemite.

The light had startled Nick and tempted him to follow it down to the Valley. But his spirit had soared, pulling him in a different direction, on to the John Muir Trail, toward the higher and higher mountains of the southern Sierra.

He passed by the surreal diamond sparkling jagged peaks of the Sun Rise range off in the southwest distance, and then soared on to Lyell Canyon, the start of the High High Sierra.

The "Range of Light" lifted up to his left in an ascending crescendo of rock, leading up toward boulder-strewn Donahue Pass and over to the awesome spectacle of sentinel Banner Peak, standing majestic guard over the Ritter Range and the Lake of 1000 Isles.

Banner greeted him in all its austere majesty at Island Pass, its jagged profile magnificent in the gold, sparkling morning sun. On he flew now, to his single favorite spot—the spectacular sight of Banner rising over the snow-dappled islets did not disappoint him. Pure white clouds swirled around Banner like ghosts, the mountain's bulky hulk-like base ascending over the ice-bound frozen lake, a monarch on a rocky throne, its crown of precious diamonds reflecting facet-like the ever gushing sun as a spectrum of rainbow rays which careened off the "castle-strewn lakescape."

Nick had climbed up those imposing Banner snow-fields in his crampons just last spring, watching with awe how the slightly higher Mt. Ritter had played a game of "hide-and-seek" with him. No matter how close he had gotten to Ritter, it always seemed somehow faraway, eternally hidden in aloof grandeur.

But no time to climb Ritter again now—maybe next spring from Catherine Pass up from the magic isled lake. It was on to Whitney!

Now Garnet Lake—a granite bound islet strewed loch, nestled at the base of imperial Ritter; then down through the incredibly jagged Minarets, where mountaineer and writer Walter Starr Jr. had lost his life high on Michael Minaret, climbing in the early twentieth century, where Norman Clyde, who had more first ascents then anyone would ever have in these mountains, had found his body for a grateful Walter Starr Sr.

A handful of grass and Elk-man was dashing down the trail, the jagged peaklets like ornate guard towers, and there a-top the highest one, Clyde Minaret, right where Walter Star had climbed, the light flashed!

Runner's High!

The familiar feeling of exhilaration, mystic and peaceful and somehow "organic", filled him. He had just begun writing a short story called "Runner's High" in which the hero has to run the entire John Muir Trail (up and down-hill) to the top of Mt. Whitney in one week (the trail normally takes three) when the mystery package showed up, and now here he was doing it, in winter no less, in snow-shoes!

The light was following him now, peeking through wispy ice-cotton clouds swirling like unruly spirits around the stark spires of the exotic pillars of the lofty Minarets.

Nick passed Shadow Lake at a trot, and then "over the water-fall" plummeting down to the valley a thousand feet below, zipping along the curves and turns of steep rock carved switch-backs "like a race-car driver on a figure-8 track. Turn the 8 on its side, and you've got the infinity sign," he said aloud, "and if you go over the side, it will be infinity!" he reminded himself as he flew down the stone path, his breath a white cloud in front of him, his moustache lined with glistening ice crystals. The maneuver-ability of the snow-shoes amazed him.

He got to the valley and glided along and finally up and over to wild-flower rich (in spring) Agnew Meadow, and looked back at Ritter/Banner, the weaving clouds waving a friendly goodbye, a silent nod from the twin gods. Many people had died on Ritter, Nick knew. Nick himself had barely escaped death on its treacherous dark-mottled volcanic talus-strewn face, but now it seemed almost amiable. "Come back soon, Elk-man," the sentinels seemed to call. John Muir too had almost fallen.

Nick remembered back now to 1968, the magic summer he had graduated "with honors" from high school and had gone to the Tetons in Wyoming, and there had climbed the technical Exum route, class 5.6, up to the Mt. Olympus summit of the Grand Teton, standing on the 13,800 ft. "top of the world," as Alexander Dubchek had attempted to liberate eastern Europe from the grasp of the Soviet empire, as the hippies in San Francisco were being invaded by "meth freaks" and he was recovering from his first love—an ill fated affair with a petite, hobbit-like, blond haired (dyed) soon to be (locally) famous operatic singer who had the misfortune some years later of loosing her slip from her billowing dress as she played the lead in the *The Pirates of Penzance* which he had the dubious fortune of witnessing!

The climb had actually seemed easy at the time and he had even written a short story about his glorious experience and sent it to the *The New Yorker*, which, of course, promptly rejected it— (too erudite for their snobbish urbanity, he surmised) but there in the Tetons the rock was "good"—solid and stable—while here in the Sierra (except for the "dream-like" rock of Yosemite) it was anything but, crumbly and debris-strewn, especially in the volcanic Ritters, and technical climbing was something more dangerous—almost dubious? But glorious, even though one wrong move…

Now—down to Red's Meadow (named for the old-timer in the late 19th century who first "bought" this beautiful valley with riches acquired from planting crops and selling potatoes and tomatoes to the miners for $1 each, until he was lynched for rustling horses in the Sacramento Valley and bringing them up here to graze). The resort was tightly closed, the windows shuttered, but smoke was gaily wreathing from the snow-covered caretaker's cabin, where the hermit lived in splendid ice-bound isolation all winter-long.

After checking the premises for any female cross-country skiers who might be passing through (and finding none) he made his way to the out-door hot spring pool on the side of the hill behind the A-framed cabins. How glorious the hot, steaming spring water felt as he eased into it, the snow around him glistening in the white sun, the sky above pure blue.

He rested now, eating granulated "see-weed" and thinking, "I'm off to Mars next." Then he saw "the Elk," nipping bark off an aspen tree and he was "back here on Earth" again.

Robby sat in the "spectral room" in the undersea Xanadu, the windows gazing out on the watery universe, flowing music from the Planet Shine pouring out over the ultra-modern ultra-high-tech sound system the Star Dolphins had provided. He was in a deep trance, a virtual reality of sonar readings, as the various spectrums and prisms spun around the room, his sonar transposing this "light show" into a "sound show," the images filling in the "missing chords" of the music, so it seemed to become a living entity, almost beyond art itself. Or was it? Life itself is art, Robby thought, as the swirling images took his consciousness into strange realms of sound, space and timelessness. Space & timelessness, Robby thought, where image and reality mesh to create a third entity: truth!

The truth as Robby saw and heard it was this: Either Earth's ice caps were going to melt from the "green-house" effect and flood the world's shorelines, or the next ice-age was about to begin as a result of pollution blocking the sun. Either way, Planet Earth was about to enter the galactic graveyard.

Was there any way out? What if Planet Earth entered the galactic neighborhood, instead? Instead of being isolated and ostracized on the outskirts of the swirling spiral arms of the gigantic Milky Way Galaxy, what if the renegade planet became integrated into the vast Milky Way civilization?

The Milky Way Galaxy, he knew now, was one of the largest anywhere in the infinite cosmos. It was home of myriads of space cultures, all built, astonishingly, on a central theme—life mimicked life. In other words, once the blueprints had been formulated in the misty deeps of the cosmic soup, it repeated within very wide latitudes naturally throughout space. There were whales on most every sea-bearing planet out there. There were humans. There were birds and dinosaurs. There were flowers and Sequioas. There were dolphins. It just so happened the dolphins had obtained a degree of perfection which humans had not yet caught up to. Not that they couldn't, he knew. It would just be extraordinarily difficult, because humans, unlike dolphins, made war (at virtually every opportunity, it seemed!) against their own. Not only that, but they made war against their very world. The bottom-line, summed up in three words—Humans kill life. It seemed to be their primary preoccupation, Robby thought, except for those who create through the "art of life" (as opposed to the "art of war"), like Vincent Van Gogh, sad thief of light, or Ludwig von Beethoven, tragic deaf musician, or Hemingway, shotgun suicide case, or…More happily, Mozart, joyous master of sound and time, Raphael, glorious master of color and spectrums, or Shakespeare, marvelous master of words.

Here were the ones, not to mention (but he certainly should, he thought) Florence Nightingale, master of the healing arts, Saint Theresa, an artist of mercy—an endless list, really. For every Hitler there was a Swietzer, for every Capone an… "Elliot Ness, I guess," Robby thought. The kind teacher down the block at the local public school, the brave fireman, the "good cop", the loving preacher in the neighborhood church…For every evil, goodness, for every curse, a blessing, for every shadow, a light… at the end of a very long dark tunnel, Planet Earth's "tunnel of hate."

On! Through the orc mines, Robby thought. Frodo lives and so do Gandalf and Aaragorn.

Damn the mosquitoes. Full speed ahead!

As the poet Robert Browning wrote, "Some dolphin will be staunch!"

Marylou was beaming into the living room of Jane.

"Hi Jane, this is Marylou, Robby's friend," she said, as Jane's mouth fell open, "with a special message for you and Sally and Paul. The Star Dolphins will be landing again just off the beach in front of your home. You should gather your two children together and tomorrow night, at the rise of the eclipsed moon, swim out in your scuba gear to meet them."

"Really, now," Jane thought, "this is just getting to be too much." This prank, or whatever it was, had gone on long enough. She had been watching a black-and-white re-run of the "Beverly Hillbillies," when Ellie May had been replaced in color by the one who dressed in overalls but who talked like Marilyn Monroe. And now here was this girl who looked like Shirley Temple.

"Look, mom! Shirley Temple's visiting the 'Beverly Hillbillies,'" her little girl Sally said. "And she knows my name, too!"

Her son, two years older, said, "Think we better do like they say, ma. She's right, y'know. There's an eclipse of the moon tomorrow night."

Jane didn't know what to think. Her ex-husband, Sam, was a Coast guard captain, and even though they had parted in hostility they kept in contact, mostly "for the kids," he had said.

"Now don't you let the kids listen to this space dolphin nonsense, Jane," he had said over the phone. "There's some kind of pirate TV station in the Gulf somewhere, and we're going to track it down!"

"But Sam," she said, "the President's been on, too!"

She had remembered the night well, when President Clark had first appeared shaking hands with a "Star Dolphin" and smiling into the TV.

"Holographic projection," Sam had growled. "Either that or these…pirates got the ol' koot doped up on somethin'!"

It had been quite a scandal: The President had eventually resigned rather than face impeachment for "talking to dolphins," and had left Washington in the dead of night, and now often mysteriously appeared on TV during the evening news, like a ghost, Jane thought, materializing out of the air, talking about "emissaries from the Planet Shine," and "space ambassadors of the Milky Way."

And now they were talking to her, personally.

And now…this show was interrupted by another. A man was saying: "Attention all people of southern Florida coast! Hurricane Harvey is approaching land and should hit shore in 24 hours. We repeat…"

In all the excitement, Jane had forgotten about the "remote" chance of the close approach of the hurricane.

"Mom," Paul was saying. "Think we better do like she said."

Jane got out their scuba gear. Her two youngsters had been diving since early childhood, taught by their father as infants, Sam being determined his "kids" be like "fish in the water," he himself having washed out as a Navy Seal before reenlisting in the Coast Guard.

They walked down to the beach in the deepening twilight as their neighbors were streaming out. The waves were getting rough.

Out to sea they saw a Coast Guard Cutter!

They walked into the waves just as the partially eclipsed moon rose over the horizon, now peeking at them through the swirling cloud-wisps like a soft, red, glowing ruby.

Dolphins immediately surfaced around them in the eerie eclipsed-moon-lit water, whistling.

"Oh look," cried Sally, "space dolphins!"

Just then, stark flood-lights swept over the beach from the vessel, and a voice boomed out from loud speakers.

"It's Daddy!" the boy said. "Maybe we better go back!"

His little sister began to cry, petting the dolphins. "I want to see Robby," she cried out, "...and the Star Dolphins..."

"Alright, alright," her brother Paul said. Then, all three holding hands, they submerged into the waves.

Down below the turbulent waters, the three, Jane, Paul and Sally saw the green shimmering light. They looked as a gigantic glittering oval emerald soared up to them and dolphins swam out of the facets!

Then they saw the dolphins wave their hands and motion to them to follow. The three swam up to the emerald-sub, and then whisked inside. They were in some kind of plasmic "gelatin", swimming around as though suspended in mint jelly. They waved at each other, and smiled from behind their facemasks, as the sea-saucer soared off through the water, tinged green from light of the flying jewel.

Soon they saw eerie white shapes, like undersea ghosts, shimmering out on the sparkling coral beds, and people in scuba gear, children and adults, swimming about with dolphins.

They had arrived at Xanadu!

Silver Pass! 13,000 ft. up in the craggy snow-packed peaks, where the rock walls shone like mithril, silver untarnished and sparkling under their dappled coats of snow.

Then down the silvery staircase carved in the rock wall on the other side after gliding by a frozen pond. Here the negotiation of the steep ice and snow crusted switchbacks was tricky, but the snowshoes seemed to have a mind of their own, clinging to the slippery surface so surely Nick did not regret the ice-axe he had inadvertently left home—they hugged the icy trail as if installed with a gravity concentrator. In fact, Nick was beginning to believe gravity concentrators were exactly what they were, having examined them carefully several times in the warmth of his automated tent, as he wrote on the tiny "keyboard" also provided.

Nick felt totally free in them now, as if they had become an extension of his boots, of himself, as though he were a seal swimming in snow, an otter scurrying without a thought along the joyous path, as the pine trees laced with white powder flew past his peripheral vision.

Then Italy Pass! He made a diversion here from the John Muir Trail to stay in the higher timber-line country, turning east at the trail junction and flying up the rocks to the 13,000 ft. pass, past Italy Lake and over the top to where the heavenly peaks peeked at him from behind cloud shrouds, like beacons calling him on to an "other" world, where seagulls played in the mountain meadows and soared over crest tops—like their ocean brothers soared over wave tops.

Mt. Julius Caesar, rising in streaks of mottled mithril, reflected the daylight to his left while other unknown and unknowable peaks jutted the frozen moonscape to the right. Peaks, peaks and more peaks! And there far off to the southwest, pink, glowing, 13,900 ft. Mt Humphreys, its iceberg jagged top belying the incredibly massive base that rose up battle-ship-like out of the high dessert sea of Paiute Pass, where the early Poviatso crossed the Sierra to trade with the Modocs to the west...

And there—"like a beacon from Mars"—the light flashed.

Vic was listening quietly to his CD player late in the night when the Beatles were interrupted by a dolphin-choir singing in 14 part harmony! "What!" Vic was startled out of his headphones.

"Go to the Castle of Love

Wait for a sign from above

Climb up the stairs to a star

Watch for a sign from afar."

Vic took the headphones off and switched on the speakers. Yes. There were the Beatles singing, "We all live in a yellow submarine..." He put the headphones back on. There was the dolphin choir again! Vic shook his head, and tore the phones off and threw them across the room. "The Castle of Love?"

He ran upstairs, got his pack out and stuffed it with gear and slid down the banister. He hurriedly walked over and picked up the headphones and plugged them back in, hoping they still worked. A voice said, "Don't look back!...except in your rearview mirror." Vic took off and ran out the back door, the headphones still on his head.

"Now just take it easy, Vic," the headphones said.

"What! You're not even plugged in," Vic gasped as he opened the door to his '76 Volkswagen bus and threw his pack in and started the engine and roared out of the driveway and down the darkened street and through the stop sign and up to the green light and then switched on his headlights.

"We're with you all the way," he heard.

As the light signal turned red, Vic roared through the intersection.

Then he heard a siren! "Step on it!" the headphone voice said. Vic stepped on it and the old Volks bus suddenly hit 90mph, and as it was hurtling down the highway, he felt the ground rock under him.

"Earthquake!" He started to turn his head to look back, but then remembered what the voice had said: "Don't look back... except in your rearview mirror."

Vic looked in his mirror and saw a lighted billboard of the Marlboro Man riding across the plains collapse and fall on the rushing police car chasing him with lights flashing and siren wailing!

He rapidly shifted into high gear and soared off toward the Oregon coast.

He soon reached Bandon by the Sea, the beach with the weirdest rocks anywhere on the North American coast line, the wildest one of all, "Face Rock", looking up toward the sky, "probably exchanging glances with the 'Face on Mars'," Vic had thought. He pulled his bus to the side and jumped out and ran to the beach. There was the rock, surreal in the darkness, the water behind it rolling to the beach. The clouds parted and a moon ray fell directly onto the "Face", illuminating its eyes. Vic let out a whistle and then ran back to the Volks and careened madly down the winding, rock-haunted coast.

"Easy does it, Vic."

"Are you still there?" he said to the headphones still on his head.

"We're with you all the way."

"Yeah. You already said that."

By now the sun was coming up as he reached the ancient, beautiful series of concrete arches that was the Bridge Over the Rogue. He turned up the road on the south end of the bridge, took the phones off, got his running clothes on, jumped out and ran back onto the bridge. He looked over the placidly rolling water, thinking back to when he had bicycled down Highway 101 over this bridge, and there were the harbor seals playing happily beneath the ornate, antique span, the mighty Rogue, almost Mississippi-ish (to him it seemed so) rolling calmly into the sea at Gold Beach, where the early miners had long ago found flakes of gold. The white and black mottled playful seals smiled up at him as he waved down to them from the concrete bridge tower, doing backward rolls, their soft grey spotted bellies gleaming under the green liquid, their flippers playfully flapping the water. Then they would shoot down under the bridge to the river bottom, and soar like underwater birds.

"Hope this 'ol bridge don't collapse on ya," Vic yelled out and, and then ran across the bridge and north up the rock sculptured beach. The sand was firm and he seemed to glide as he ran through the stone statues that jutted up on the beach and out to sea like Michelangelo abstracts. He was heading for the cliffs about 5 miles up, to a place where he could sit sheltered from the wind and bask in the sun like a seal and watch the grey whales roll north.

As he ran, he recalled the time many years ago he backpacked twenty miles up the black-sand beach out of "Pirate's Cove" in northern California and he got to the old long-abandoned three story lighthouse (reminding of the tower by the sea in the opening of *Ulysses* which moody Stephen Dedalus had ascended) and camped up there two days watching the whales migrate to Alaska.

Ah, Alaska, there's another story, Vic thought as he puffed down the beach. He had lived in Ketchikan for a time having met a pretty Psimpsian Indian girl on the Inland Passageway ferry and the two had gotten married and divorced in the time span of one year, and he had left his great job in the junior high school library, babysitting a bunch of Indian, white, and half and half brats, and returned to the "States" why he wasn't sure except the "West" was "home."

The time he had hiked up to the lighthouse, he had been recovering from breaking off the marriage engagement to the girl he had been involved with just before he flew to Alaska to get away from…ah well..and then leave Alaska to get away from…

Funny, he thought, as he ran on the hard sand, I feel the same way today.

He finally reached the cliff and sat down in the rocks, the fine sun bathing him in gold warmth, the cliff walls protecting him from the north wind. Suddenly! Vic saw a light flash at him from atop the great rock-island about a half mile off shore. He knew there was no light out there, at least none he had ever seen before and he had run up this beach many times. And then it flashed at him again—"like a beacon from Mars," Vic thought.

He left the shelter of the rock jetty and ran back down the mystic black sand beach, in and out of the rock statues, the rivulets coursing down from the hills and emptying into the surf, the waves lapping the beach, the little white clown birds playing tag with the water, seagulls drifting in and out over the blue waves, past big piles of bulbous seaweed—"good to eat."

"And good for you, too," he thought

Now past the dead sea lion washed up on the beach. "Oh great," Vic had said out loud. He had noticed it as he ran up from the harbor but had blocked it from his mind, thinking only of the run. Now it could not be ignored.

But past the seal and toward the Gold Beach harbor, and up the road. Then second wind and runner's high kicked in as he raced back across the silver, sun-lit bridge to where the playful harbor seals did cartwheels in the river, watched their watery dance and then trotted back to the bus. He toweled off, changed his clothes and drove away.

Then the ground shook! Vic turned his head to look back as the image of the shattered bridge flashed through his mind but remembered the warning, "Don't look back, Vic, except…" and looked in his side-view mirror. The old bridge stood, standing serenely in the morning sun, its arches like marble, the concrete towers like turrets, overseeing the mighty rolling Rogue…

Now down the Redwood Highway, the great behemoths of the North California coast stretching their tendrils up to the morning moon. He reached the fabled Avenue of the Giants and turned off 101 and drove down the narrow sun-streaked road.

He got to the Darberville "Giant," the towering monarch, which seemed to easily penetrate the folds of the sky. There was only one thing wrong: The "Giant" was gone! And then Vic remembered hearing on the local news of the ancient "Giant" blowing over in a fierce coastal storm. The crash must have been apocalyptic, Vic thought, like Mt. St. Helens blowing up in the Washington Cascades.

If a tree falls in the forest and no one hears…

Yes, these were "strange days indeed," as John Lennon had sang right before he was gunned down by a deranged ——————. Strange days indeed! He gazed on the downed giant, lying like a grounded battleship!

The sky is going to fall next, just like Chicken Little prophesied, thought Vic, looking up.

He hurried back to his bus and roared down the Ave. of the Fallen Giants.

Nick had now arrived at Evolution Valley, where "The Hermit," a 13,000 ft. hermetic dome, waited serenely for him above the draping snow and ice curtained trees. He trotted past the fleece carpeted valley and up the hill to Evolution Plateau at the base of the "ol' Hermit." Indeed, this was the remotest spot in the Sierra, taking (in summer) between 3 to 4 days to reach, depending of whether or not you wanted to kill yourself getting here.

He decided to stay the night on the Plateau and got out his "Micro-Shelter," which automatically erected and assembled itself, and camped at the Hermit's base, overlooking frozen Evolution Lake.

In the summer this had seemed like the most perfect spot in the mountains, the very epitome of what a High Sierra lake should be: pure, sparkling emerald-green waters with a high-altitude, wind-swept—mosquito free (as compared to the valley below)—short-grass, purple wild-flower strewn meadow lapping up to its snow-melt depths.

Evolution Valley was the place, Walter Starr Jr. wrote, where the "artistic" soul would find what it most desired, where the considerations of the artistic and the aesthetic merged to provide the most sublime setting in the Sierra—remote, aloof, surreal—in a word: perfect!

He got into his shelter, feeling quite warm and snug, and brought out the tiny "keyboard."

"In the night storm, hammering my high-tech igloo with 'blaaasts'" (Nick typed) "of snow and wind, the shelter blew back and forth some with the gusts, but is surprisingly solid for something so light and flimsy, and as I lay on the tent floor, balmy without a sleeping bag in the middle of the night, the temperature outside a brisk -10 degrees counting wind chill (I checked when I want out to 'see a man about a horse, har har' with the 'digital thermo-meter' also provided—it was like going from the tropics to the arctic in a space of inches) I pondered once again 'Just Exactly' what the purpose of 'The Trip' was."

The next day he stepped out of the igloo to greet a bright, shiny, new, white world under a perfect blue sky, just a froth of lacy clouds around the Hermit's head like an ethereal crown. His "Vision Perfect" snow goggles, also in the mystery package, gave him absolutely "Perfect Vision" in the crystal bright-lit universe, and as his tent refolded itself he ate "see-weed", and it was off! up, up, up the hill to where high peaks, jagged, slightly sinister looking, stretched raggedly to the west, then over stark, rock mottled Muir Pass to the east, up to the Muir Hut, a stone one-story round castle at the top of the 12,900 ft. gateway to Le Conte Valley to the south. Indeed, Nick had long ago come to view these mystic "passes," whose rewards yielded themselves only after long and arduous, strenuous, upward always upward treks as mysterious passageways between two worlds, one world revealing itself on one side, the other on the other.

He pushed the door open and walked into the bleak stone-block room, and to his surprise found a note which read:

> "Dear Nicky!
> Hope you got here okay. There's some food for you in the sack.
> Have a great trip!
>
> >   Love,
> >   Michelle"

Next it was "the long and winding trail" down to Le Conte, past Lake Helen, and the high islands of little trees which provided perfect camping places in the summer overlooking the forest-green winding valley below, and then around south to the Ranger Station.

At the Le Conte Ranger Station, Nick met a Ranger! He was walking out from the snow-laden log cabin in a pair of great wooden snow-shoes.

"Well, hi there!" the Ranger said, surprised. "Don't meet too many folks back in here this time of the year, that's for sure. Where ya comin' from?"

"Carson Pass," Nick said.

"Carson Pass? Ya mean up by Tahoe? Hey, that's quite a trek in the winter! Uh, traveling kinda light, aren't ya?"

"Uh, got some new high-tech gear here I'm testing for a mountaineering magazine I write for. Just developed this year, as a matter of fact. State of the art. Gonna take over the outdoor world I bet. Works real good…sir."

"Whew, it better, I guess. Where ya headin'?"

"Top of Whitney."

"Whew! Mind if I check out this high-tech gear you talk about? Like the looks of those snow-shoes! Ya mind if…"

"Well, sir, I'm in a pretty big hurry…"

"Hmmm. Well, you got a wilderness permit I can see?"

"In the winter?"

"Oh yes, sir. Gotta have a wilderness permit any time of the year. Ya got yours?"

"Well, sir, I didn't think you needed one in the winter…" Nick said.

"Well, then I'm gonna haveta write ya out a ticket, and yer gonna have to go out over Bishop Pass here and down to the White Mountain Ranger Station and get a permit."

"Sorry," Nick said. "Ain't got time. Gotta fly!" He tore off down the snow-laden trail, shifting his "Gold-Feathers" into over-drive, and spewing up a spray of white powder in the Ranger's startled face.

"Hey, now, wait just a min…" the Ranger muffled out, as Nick disappeared down through the trees.

Now Nick was beneath the ethereal domes of Le Conte Valley, which towered above him to the west, hiding an even higher range which Nick had seen before coming over austere Bishop Pass to the east, the beautiful but slightly "sinister"—there's that word again, Nick thought—Dusey Basin above him, where jagged/ragged peaks looked disturbingly like the mountains of Mordor in Tolkien's *Lord of the Rings*.

Up the "Golden Staircase" it was now. The "trail" (it was more like a mountain climb, than a trial, Nick had thought. Whoever named this the John Muir Trail certainly had a sense of humor. Who ever heard of a vertical trail?) zigzagged in steep steps etched into the cliff side like a mountain sheep short-cut. He flew up it, the jet tapers in the back of the "Feather" snowshoes seeming to propel him forward.

He blasted past the frozen meadow, and then on: Palisade Basin! where the majestic Palisade Range, the one place in the Sierra where the western face of the mountains was as steep and precipitous as the eastern escarpment, greeted him in moody splendor. He gasped for breath—this "pitch" had been hard.

Nick stayed the night at Palisade Lake, "with peaks all round sparkling between the stars, the full moon pouring its gold out in profuse loveliness" (he wrote).

And "The Elk," the majestic Elk who had eluded him for some days now made his appearance again, the enormous antlers (which seemed even larger that before) framed before him under the "mountainous sky."

In morning light, "pink and blushing", Nick sailed up and over Mather Pass—thinking ahead to Pinchot Pass to the south—and he could look back on the Palisades, standing like a group of "child-gods" serenely gazing west over their private "ponds"—

upper and lower Palisade Lakes—nestled in the basin as though never before sullied by the visit of any one less superior than an angel.

"Come on!" Wendy whispered to her boyfriend Randy. "I've jumped the fence here before."

The fence at the San Diego Sea World was not as high in this corner and Wendy hoisted herself up and over it under the light of a parking-lot lamp.

Randy clambered after her. "I hope you know what you're doing, Wendy," Randy said, as he fell over on the other side.

It was 4 a.m., and the night lights lit inside the park mutely highlighted the shadows cast by the trees and shrubs.

It was quiet, and Randy heard the breathing.

"We're here!" Wendy said, standing by the dolphin "Petting Pool," where several dolphins swam sedately around the "over-size bathtub," as Wendy liked to call it.

"Great!" said Randy. "You're sure no one's around?"

"Just be quiet, and if the night watchman comes around, just disappear into the shadows."

They crept up to the edge of the pool. The dolphins kept swimming around in circles as though swimming in their sleep.

"Aren't they cute?" said Wendy, petting one, a small child dolphin, who slowed down for her. Then it jumped up on the side and rolled over, squeaking happily, for Wendy to rub its white, soft belly. "Hello, Leo," she said.

"Leo the dolphin?" laughed Randy.

"Yeah. He remembers me!"

"How long since you worked here?"

"It's been a month ago today since I got fired. Come on."

She took his hand and led him up the concrete steps and then wound to the right, and finally they jumped a gate and then…

"Holy smoke!" whispered Randy, as the killer whale appeared out of the night before them in the main arena show tank, the stars and muted moonlight bringing his black and white colorings into soft relief.

"Hi, Numu!" said Wendy, reaching out to pet the whale's gigantic snout as it lifted its head up out of the water.

"Remember Wendy?"

"You used to ride him?" said Randy, looking at her with new respect, even awe.

"Yeah, it was my job. I rode Numu in the shows…Yes, baby," she said, nuzzling the great jaw, "you miss me, don't you?"

"Why'd you get fired?"

"For putting up posters saying, 'Free Numu and the Dolphin Eight!'"

Randy laughed. "How'd they know it was you? Did you sign it 'Wendy the Whale-Lover'?"

Wendy laughed. "I used to kid my boss all the time about freeing 'Numu and the Dolphin Eight.' So when the posters showed up, he asked me about it. So I confessed," she shrugged.

"So you got fired for putting some posters up?"

"They didn't like my attitude, I guess. And then there was the time I made Numu spew water on some geeky tourists.

"But I guess what really got to 'em was when I made an obscene gesture to the audience from Numu's back—in my last show."

"What kind of gesture?"

Wendy showed him.

"Oh," said Randy.

"It was very discrete, really, not too blatant, but my boss happened to be watching me closely from the audience—you know, after the poster thing, and he caught it. So he fired me. I could see it coming.

"Yeah, I was wild back then alright." She took his hand and led him up the stairs into the bleachers. They sat down. "We got a show all to ourselves," she said, as Numu suddenly jumped up out of the night and did a giant belly flop, splashing them with water.

"Hey!" said Randy, shaking water off as Wendy laughed.

"Yeah, I taught him that trick, too," Wendy giggled.

"Wendy, what you doin' here?"

The two had fallen asleep in each other's arms, leaning back against the concrete wall in the last bleacher row. They awoke to pink morning sun shining in their faces.

"Hi, Marv," Wendy said as Randy came to. "Randy, meet Marv the night watchman." Randy gaped at the young Afro-American in a Sea World uniform.

Marv shook his head. "It's good to see ya Wendy luv, but if Boss catches ya here, climbing over the fence again…"

"What'll he do, call the cops?"

"What…?" Randy started.

"I don't know, luv, but…"

"Wendy, is that you?!" the man in a tan suit walking toward them from the other end of the bleachers called out.

"Hey, Boss!" Wendy answered.

"I'm off shift now. Gotta go!" Marv said as he smiled at Wendy, and then turned and walked quickly away.

"I oughta call the cops!" Boss said,

"Hey wait a minute now…"cried Randy.

"But I won't. Actually, I'm glad to see you Wendy. You want your job back?"

"Sure! But why…?"

"Numu just don't like the other girl. He's been pouting ever since you left, Wendy, and he just won't do some of the tricks you taught him for anyone else. So if you promise to be good…"

Wendy stood up and put her arms around the stocky man in brown suit and tie. "Thanks, Boss," she said.

"Your outfit's still in the locker. Why don't you and Numu get reacquainted?"

"Sure, Boss. Can I take Randy, too? I promised him a ride on Numu…"

"You did?" gasped Randy.

"Now, Wendy…"

"Randy's on the swim team at college," Wendy said. "Just moved here from Florida. You oughta see how he looks in a pair of tight trunks. And he's great in the water. Thought we might do a couple act…y'know, add a little 'spice' to the show…"

"Hey, that's not a bad idea. Tell ya what. We got about three hours before opening," he said, peering at his digital watch, "so go ahead. See what you can do. Spare trunks in the locker. Help yourself…Randy." He turned and walked away.

"Yeah!" smiled Wendy. "Boss is an alright guy…sometimes. Come on!"

"And now, ladies and gentlemen…Wendy and Randy!" Boss's voice boomed over the loudspeaker, as the audience applauded wildly. "With Numu, the Friendly Killer Whale!"

The show had been a great success, as the two had practiced and honed their act to a spectacle of precision synchronization where the young lovers stole kisses with one another as they performed acrobatics on the whale's back, the audience laughing with delight. Record numbers were coming to see the cavorting couple as word spread about the phenomenal new attraction.

"Aren't they great?" the voice said over the speakers to another packed crowd, as Randy lifted Wendy up and held her above his head at arms length as he rode astride the whale.

He set her back down, as she draped herself in his arms and he kissed her boldly on the lips, to ecstatic applause.

"And now for a special treat, Robby the Magnificent will perform a magic trick for you," the voice, slightly altered, it seemed, now said.

The two unlocked from their passionate kiss and looked at each other. "Robby the Magnificent…?" they both said.

"Yes, direct from the Florida Keys and recently returning from the Dolphin Planet of Shine" (the audience all laughed) "Robby the Magnificent will perform the greatest magic trick in the history of Sea World…or any other world!"

As the dazed pair gazed into each other's eyes…Numu floated up out of the water horizontally!

The audience gasped, as Wendy and Randy and Numu ascended to the clouds above…

Hidden within the puffy fog-clouds just above Sea World, Robby "The Magnificent" peered down from his dolphin ship, as the whale with Randy and Wendy on it rose up out of the park.

Suddenly, the pair were inside, as Robby and Michelle awoke each from their faint with a kiss.

"Ooops!" said Robby, "we just lost Numu," as the great whale fell back into the pool with the greatest belly-flop SPLASH Sea World, "or any other world" had ever seen, sompletely soaking the audience as it emptied the tank of half of its water.

"Robby!" Michelle said. "Keep your mind on your work!"

Robby whirled a dial and then Numu was floating up again and this time successfully "docked" with the dolphin ship, and they took off through the clouds, towing Numu securely underneath.

"Welcome aboard!" Robby and Michelle said.

Over the ocean, they unlocked the hyper-beam and Numu splashed down into the sea, looked up with a smile of "Thank you!", jumped jubilantly out of the water, and then started swimming north.

Back in the dolphin-ship, Randy and Wendy were coming to.

"Are you the ones on TV?" Wendy managed to finally ask.

"The dolphin-people? in the Gulf?" asked Randy.

"Yep," the two said. "It's Howdy-Doody Time !"

Vic had reached the turnoff to Pirate's Cove and turned west. The wildly twisting, narrow road wove through the coast range, up and down, around and about. Then, finally he was at the pass where he could look down on the black-sand, breathless beauty of the cove where low-flying clouds decorated the opaque scene with fleecy lace.

He tore down the road and reached the circling black-top streets of a housing development that had gone bust before any houses were built. The corkscrew winding road over the range had scared the prospective buyers away, he guessed, and he was quite happy, ecstatic actually, that the project went bust, leaving the wildly lovely cove in isolated splendidness.

Vic raced around the many deserted streets, honking his horn and playing his tape machine at the loudest possible volume, looking in his rear-view mirror for non-existent cops, as the clouds floated and played in and out over the bay. He finally got to the dirt lot where he had parked his car the first time he had hiked up this magical-mystical shore and stepped outside.

He breathed deep the sea-breeze, the freshness invigorating him, and then got out his gear, and put on his old Kelty back-pack, locked up the bus and started walking down the dirt path that soon gave out and led him down to the deep-black beach, where he struggled walking on the sand, the waves and sea-gull caws beckoning him toward the "Castle of Love"—the old deserted light-house twenty miles north up the wind-fresh shore. Yes, he had figured this out as he was winding his way over here through the mountains. The "Castle of Love" had to be the lonely lighthouse he had hiked to years ago to get over losing the only girl he had ever really loved.

"Ah, how sublime," Nick breathed, the crystal blue of the sky framing the frostiness of his breath, as he rested atop 12,500+ ft. Glen Pass and looked back north over the waves of mountain peaks spread out like frothy wind-caps in a stormy sea.

The hike up Past Rae Lakes had been long, but the rewards of this view now made it seem like "child's play" (Nick wrote) and he startled some cross-country skiers as he "flewwww paaast" (he wrote), waving and yelling "Helloooo…!"

After a thirty minute rest, lying on his back looking up at the few clouds floating by or sitting in lotus position and meditating on the "sublime" view to the north, where he could with great satisfaction ponder the spectacle of all those lofty peaks he had made it through, it was down the other side, again seeming to "fly" around the carved out switch backs where the adventurous cross-country skiers had previously gone leaving a vague trail in the snow.

Then it was past still more lakes, ("Lakes, lakes and more lakes," he wrote), including fabled Bullfrog Lake at Kersarge Pass, one of the most beautiful lakes in the Sierra, where thousands of trekkers huffed and puffed up from Independence, California, up famous Kersarge, the most direct way into the High High Sierra, to camp at its shores with the strange perspective across Vadette Meadow, where the perfectly cone-shaped Vadette Peak to the southwest looked like it was directly behind the lake when actually it was all the way across the valley, giving a depth to the view like looking into "one of those Easter-eggs with the inside scene," he wrote. In fact this placed had proven too popular and had been long off-limits to camping.

Nick decided to camp there for the night.

Nick saw the flashing light leading him on from the 13,000+ ft. distant top of Forester Pass, the highest pass on the John Muir Trail other than "Trail Crest" (Whitney Pass). The trail up the north side of Forester was a wandering affair, still following the tracks of the skiers he had passed like a cross country skater way back on the south side of Glen.

He blazed past the stunted trees and then up through the oblique walls on either side and finally reached the "pocket" in the vertical stone pass. Looking up at the "pass" as he had approached, it was virtually impossible to believe there was any way over, that the valley came to a sudden stop! here, and no "trespassers" were allowed into the mythical High High High! Sierra to the south, where he knew Big Horn Plateau, the single most magnificent place in the "Mountains of California" (the title of John Muir's second book) was waiting in "cool grandness" (Nick wrote), the gate to 14, 018 ft. Mt. Tyndall, 14, 375 ft. Mt. Williamson and 14,495 ft. Mt. Whitney!

From the top of Forester was revealed one of the finest views ("where the superlatives never end") in the entire "Range of Light," (Muir's phrase), back north, where the King's Canyon Nat'l. Park crescendo of "alpine landscaping " swept around in a grand curve, flowing around out of sight to the west, and the valley floor below provided the perfect setting for a "Santa's Village of sparkling Christmas trees."

Now down to Sequoia Nat'l. Park on the other side of the pass, down the absolutely vertical wall facing south, looking out over bleak, desolate Diamond Mesa…shining with "diamonds of snow-crystal splendor."

He soared past the mesa, across Tyndal Creek, and rocketed up and around to Bighhorn Plateau! the desolate, windswept home of the Sierra bighorn sheep. He had never seen the elusive bighorn in these mountains before. Maybe this time.

Pleeease…!

Wait! What? He noticed the flicking, long tail first across the field, and then the pointed ears. Mountain lion! Puma! Cougar! The long, nervously swaying tail was unmistakable.

Immediately it saw him and turned and loped off toward the trees. Then! in the opposite direction, up the barren slope, he saw the monarch of mountain sheep, its curving horns like ornately carved trumpets, pawing the snow with its hooves and tossing its "super-horns" back and forth at the vanishing cat.

Nick hailed the "Sheep-King", and then walked slowly across the plateau toward the pine-tree hidden meadow ahead where he knew he would finally be rewarded with the crescendo of all views (other than the view from the top of Whitney, he supposed)—the spectacle across the meadow to the cluster of highest mountains in the U.S., outside Alaska—the fabulous "Whitney Family"!

When Nick had crossed this magical place before in the summer, he had met here, right here, yes in the very middle of Bighorn Plateau, John Muir himself! Yes, it really was him, he thought. Anyway, the white haired, long white bearded lanky old gentleman looked like the John Muir in the old tin-type, antique photographs which decorated his books (all of which Nick had in his "libertarian library" at home).

They had stopped here to talk, Nick going north, toward Kersarge Pass, John Muir heading south over Whitney Pass and out at Whitney Portal up from Lone Pine.

The two had chatted for about ten minutes, no one else within the boundaries of existence, it seemed.

He was carrying a very small pack.

"You're traveling pretty light," Nick had said as he felt the weight of his own backpack, having just recently hiked up the single most difficult (non cross-country) stretch in the Sierra, the 100 (precisely) switchbacks on the east approach—the awesome vertical wall of Whitney Pass—gateway to the mythical Whitney back country!

The old man took off his pack and lifted it up with one arm!

"This is the result of doing the entire John Muir Trail five times," he said. "Over the years I've learned what to leave behind. Now I can do the whole trail in 17 days, no food drops. And I've eaten most of my food," he added smiling.

They talked about gear, tube-tents, freeze dried food and then Nick had told him a story:

"Yeah, I had this (Goretex) waterproof 'bivy-sack' which I bought the time I forgot my tent, when I went hiking one early spring (May 1) up at Spooner Lake across the highway from the east shore of Tahoe. Not having my tent, I made a shelter under a fallen tree, using spruce boughs for the roof, and camped there for several days in my lean-to shelter, building a fire to keep warm, listening to the coyotes wail in the middle of the night, and living off meadow grass, dandelions, mint leaf-pine needle tea and granola. I would go out toward the shore every morning and sit by the storm-cloud covered waters of Spooner Lake, where, I read, the Washo Indians used to spend their summers in total contentment before they were so rudely interrupted by the white gold-seekers, excepting John Muir himself, of course—although I also read, in one of his books as a matter of fact, *My First Summer in the Sierra* I think, that he did not have much use himself for the poor Indian, who he thought were encased with generations of dirt, though he greatly envied their effortless ability to find food off the land, y'know, grubs and the like, especially the time that first summer he ran out of flour to make his bread and nearly starved before more was brought up from the valley to the sheep camp he was working in—scaring off grizzlies, of which he himself was not afraid—before they became extinct in California. Happily, I might add," said Nick, who had no love at all for grizzlies except he was happy to clarify, the gigantic, long red haired, long snouted (rather like a dolphin, now that he thought about it!) Alaska brown, largest carnivore in the world, which were a distinct species or genus or something and less likely to attack than the smaller, irascible, and pugnacious Ursus Horribilis, "the last griz killed around here in 1935.

"Anyway," Nick continued breathlessly, "I camped out in the shelter for about a week, weathering some storms nicely and people would walk right past me sitting in my lean-to, going down the trail by the lake, and never even see me. The next year, I put up the new tent I bought, and within a half-hour of setting up camp, a highway patrolman came down from the highway and told me I was illegally camped and had to leave!

"Anyway," (Mr. Muir, he thought) "I stayed at Spooner until a heavy late-season hail storm blew in and partly disassembled my crude shelter—I've since learned to build better ones—and I hitch-hiked to Tahoe Vista and bought the water-proof bivy sack. Then I hiked up to Rubicon Lake in Desolation Valley Wilderness, crossing snow fields and semi-melted streams, and another storm blew in. I decided I really needed a tent. So I hiked back out to Tahoe to buy one. Ah, now I had both a tent and a bivy sack. Obviously more than I needed, for I put up my tent in a campground just across the highway from the shores of Tahoe (where I had grown up as a kid, by the way, over in King's Beach before it became a suburb of San Diego), and I was the only one camped there (if you know anything about Tahoe, you know this was early in the season) and I'd go to the pier across the highway and dive into the icy lake waters, rapidly come out and then go down to the local pub and drink imported beer 'til sundown and wander blissfully back to my tent.

"Now, this night, when I sauntered in, I saw smoking embers in the fire-pit! and I had not lit a fire. Then I heard someone rustling in my tent! 'Who's there!" I called out in a stern voice, instead of simply kicking the tent down, which in my beer-soaked frame of mind I really felt like doing. 'It's cold,' a somewhat whimpering voice said. 'Get out of my tent!' I angrily answered. He got out. 'I waited for someone to show up, but it was getting cold, and I don't have a tent of my own. Can I share yours?' 'Are you outta yer mind?' I somewhat slurred. He was a young kid. 'I just came up from San Francisco, looking for a summer job.' 'You came up here without a tent?' I yelled, momentarily forgetting I had forgotten my own. 'I'll buy one as soon as I get a job,' he promised. I sat down on the bench near the smoldering fire.

"'Tell you what,' I heard myself say, disbelieving, 'I got this great water proof ($80) brand new high-tech bivy sack I bought before I got this tent.' I handed it to the shivering refugee from the big city. 'Here,' I said. 'It should keep you pretty warm and dry. Just put your sleeping bag in it.

"'You do have a sleeping bag…?'" I asked. He nodded.

"'Thanks! uh…' he said, as though it were a $1,000,000.

"'Nick,' I said.

"'Thanks, Nick!'" he said, and then disappeared into the trees."

"Generous to a fault," Mr. Muir said, smiling. "Well, nice talking to you, Nick. Enjoy your trip. Been over five passes in five days, myself. Think I'll take it a little easy today." He waved and walked off.

"By the way," Nick called, "what do you do—when you're not hiking the John Muir Trail?"

"I teach school—in San Francisco."

"So long…Professor Muir," Nick said, as the old man vanished toward the Whitney cluster, "his favorite place," he had said.

That day, Nick had hiked all the way across Diamond Mesa and over Forester Pass, collapsing too tired to eat under the small, wind-sculptured trees in the cozy campsite on the north side, just as it was getting too dark to see.

Nick was at "Magic Meadow." Across the frosty expanse, as graceful as the great Elk standing serenely eating bark off an alder, stood the Whitney "Family," the mystic, divine God-peaks seeming to sway in the wind so "stylishly" did they appear beneath the marble sky. This was the grand crescendo! on the Muir Trail, where the great themes of mountain motifs finally resounded in perfect harmony, the "family" of highest peaks adding the finale-like ending to "a symphony of majestic magicness."

Getting down on his knees, Nick grazed with the Elk, nipping succulent alder bark, washing it down with snow.

From the cloud-wreathed heights of the Whitney peaks, he saw the light flicking back and forth among the tops, and he knew it was time to go.

Finally, Crab Tree Meadow, the advance position for the final takeoff to the top of Whitney—the vast, now snow-covered meadow from which millions of trekers from the west entrance of the Big Trees planed their final assault on the single most assaulted mountain in North America. Here Nick decided to rest for a day, "a lay-over being necessary to replenish my spirits," he wrote in his journal entitled "Confessions of a Runaway Snow-shoer". And it was a good day to lay snug in the tropic warmth of his igloo, for outside the snow fell down in dreamy wonder.

In the frosty morning of the next day, the sun peeking through wandering clouds, Nick saw again the great Elk, standing in the middle of the meadow, the sun slanting down on its massive antlers, which seemed even greater than before, as though attempting to touch the sky itself.

As Nick followed the Elk, he soon began to notice something strange, peculiar: a feeling as if antlers were beginning to sprout from his own head! He lumbered up the trail, after the magic Elk, and the weight of his "antlers" was becoming heavier and perceptively heavier. He had already put his hand up to see if there really were antlers sprouting up or not, and, of course (much to Nick's relief) could feel nothing, but in his mind there was no denying their existential existence, nor the fact the burden seemed to increase with each step.

He huffed and puffed past "Guitar Lake" under the base of the mountain (shaped quite like a frozen classical guitar!) and finally reached the final switchbacks up to "Trail Crest," (Whitney Pass, 13,500 ft.) and zigzagged up the trail. Now it was beginning to snow a light powdery beautiful floppy-flaked snow, the myriad-infinite hexagon designs floating down like lace artistry. He walked so as not to "startle an avalanche."

Nick was at "Trail Crest!" Below to the east were the 100 switchbacks leading down to frozen Consolation Lake and down and down, past Lone Pike Lake and Outpost Camp (with its gushing waterfall) and finally out at Whitney Portal. That was where Nick was planning to go after he ascended to the top of Whitney, to the little town of Lone Pine and a hot shower and a soft bed and a...

By the way, he wondered, how's Nancy taking this? Was she very worried about his unexpected absence (he certainly had not discussed this trip with his wife, not even knowing himself he would "take off" until the very instant he did so, under the influence of the strange Elk who even now climbed the trail up to the top). Nick turned up the trail (north by northwest) and followed his Elk-guide toward the still-distant summit as the antlers grew ever more burdensome for "Elk-man." Finally it felt like each step would be his last (one step forward, stop, rest, another step, stop), the air becoming thinner and thinner as he passed the 14,000 ft. mark right about where you could climb up talus slopes to Mt. Muir, really just a Whitney peaklet—then along the "cat-walk" past the pinnacles, where a wrong step on either side would send you off into windy eternity...

Now—the final, final approach.

Will I make it! Nick breathed. Rock by rock, step by step, the antlers becoming more and more and more cumbersome and then finally, the snow blowing down in designer shapes, he was at the great flat expanse summit of 14,495 ft. Whitney!!! He caught his breath, and all of a sudden! seemed to shed the giant antlers and felt as "light as a mountain blue-bird." He gazed north, and the endless expanse of snow-covered peaks before and below him looked like nothing else but an ocean of storm-swept white-caps.

Then the space-ship landed. On the flat summit of Whitney, Nick watched as the round-swirling ball of light descended before him. He had really been expecting it. Ever since the "antlers' mysteriously appeared, he had been receiving hints of what was to come.

And now, as he basked in the warm glow of this ultimate Runner's-High, after running the entire trail from Tahoe (almost) to the summit of Mt. Whitney (in snow shoes!), here came this whirling ship from the world of the...what?

The snow was falling all around him now and he felt like he was at the south pole up here. And then the door in the ship opened and out hopped...

Emperor penguins!!!???

Oh, it was too good to be true, Nick told himself. He hadn't known what he was expecting, but...penguins?

But wait. They were just the "butlers," it seemed. For now they escorted him into the ship, where the kid with the voice like a young Tyrone Power greeted him. "Hi, Nicky!"

"Hi, Nicky," said Nancy, who was there, smiling at him like it was the first time they ever met. (Which maybe it was.)

Finally, Nick was able to get his mind and breathing together enough (after a long embrace with his wife) to ask, "Hey, why did I just run the entire way from Tahoe (almost) to the top of the highest U.S. mountain outside Alaska? In winter."

And as the ship took off the mountain-top and then flew north, they were already over sky-blue Lake Tahoe before he had taken off his snow-suit.

Young Tyrone was telling him a story about the Washo Indians, who summered at the fabulous Lake of the Sky before the whites stole it out from under them. He was talking of the mythical "Ra" bird, which according to Washo legend lived at the bottom of Lake Tahoe. "The Ra bird is about to rise up from Tahoe's depths," he was saying, "and fly over Tahoe breathing fire, and 'Ice Lake' will become 'Fire Lake' and all the gamblers will cash in their chips, then...'head for the hills!'"

"Interesting," Nick the libertarian said. "But that still doesn't answer my question. Why did I run the entire High Sierra Mountain Range?"

"Because it's there."

"Not a good enough reason," said the ever-pragmatic Nick.

"To gather snow-samples, of course," Robby laughed, "on your computerized high-tech snowshoes. The Star Dolphins have chosen Mt. Whitney for their land-based center of operations, and need exhaustive snow-samples from throughout the range so they can completely analyze the water content. (There's someone hiking the Cascades now!) Did you know the Star Dolphins have over 1000 different words for 'water,' Nicky?"

"Like the Eskimos and snow?" asked Nick.

"Precisely," said Robby, petting one of the penguins.

Then the smiling face of the Dolphin King appeared on the screen over head!

"Welcome aboard Flight 1, Nick and Nancy, non stop to … Santa's Village!" he smiled.

"Now please meet Wendy and Randy…and Michelle and Michael and Heaven and Jessy and Misty and Robby and Rena and Heather and Pres. Clark and Pope Jon Paul…

"Oh yes…the ghost of Dr. Smith and Sharon and Marsha and Capt Jones and Frankie and Johnny and Peter and Paul and Marylou and Jane and Sally and Helen and Frank and Sam and Billy and Cloe and Song and Namu and Numu and…"

Nick looked out the opaque swirling walls of the ship and saw two dolphins and two killer whales swimming alongside through the clouds…!

"…and Vic and…"

Vic was watching intently from the upper story of the "Castle of Love." The twenty mile hike up the beach from "Pirate's Cove" had been quite exhilarating, if somewhat lonely. He had arrived at the castle late yesterday afternoon, and immediately climbed up the circular stairway to the top of lighthouse, where he could look out the empty window to the oceanscape. The stars had glittered over-head, and the Persian-like meteor-shower in the night had certainly been totally spectacular, some of the falling stars looking like comets as they trailed flashing down through the dark sky.

"Go to the Castle of Love—

Wait for a sign from above."

The hike up had not been without incident. He had passed a seagull with a broken wing struggling in the surf. It would try to take off over the water, but the waves would always dash it back. Vic had been quite depressed by this sight, but decided it was not his place to kill the bird with the piece of drift-wood he had picked up to put the poor thing out of its misery, and looking back several times, he had walked on, angrily flinging the stick into the sea.

He had to pass through a pasture with several mean-looking bulls protecting the cows, hoping if he must escape into the ocean the bulls couldn't swim.

His first night out he was almost run over by a flock of sheep, who, baaing madly, scampered away when he sat up in his sleeping bag.

But despite these hazards, he had made it to the castle. He stood in the top story, gazing out to sea through the binocs he had brought just for this purpose, watching for the great grey whales, which should be migrating north to Alaska.

"Climb up the stairs to a star—

Watch for a sign from afar."

Now he saw them! the greys rolling through the waves, their spouts rising up like graceful fountains. Then, through the binocs, Vic saw other shapes!

"Killer whales!" Vic shouted—their unmistakable black and white colorings, their proud flukes sticking straight up.

"A bit far south, aren't you?" He wondered if the killers would attack the grey whales!

But wait! Now there were other shapes out there, too...He focused the glasses more carefully...

"Dolphins! Dolphins are swimming with the killers!"

Vic surveyed the scene...the "sign from afar"—

"...the great whales are rolling north...and the killers and the dolphins swim along—sailing side by side!"

Appendix 1—Nick's stories and poems

A. The stories

Summer Climb

I sat on the porch, looking at the mountain, eating raisins and reading *Time*. Dubchek was in the news, bringing democracy to the conquered. He was a hero.

The mountain loomed like a gigantic edifice, the jagged summit reaching up into the very texture of the sky itself, where the light of the sun bounced and bounded like a celestial ballet. "I will climb it," I said. How could I not? The Grand was calling to me, and I knew I would.

The bus had dropped me off at the park camp, but there were no sites open, and so I had walked three miles down the road and put my army tent up in a little island of trees across the creek. All night I knew I was very alone in the forest. I wondered if grizzlies wandered down from Canada. I hoped not.

When the sun bravely reached through my tent walls, I suddenly remembered I had no food.

I got out of my canvas castle and sat cross-legged on a little hill, searching for God. I looked at a leaf covered with dew, but I could not find God.

I walked the three miles back to the park camp, dressed in a corduroy sports coat, levis, and cowboy boots.

On the bus I had got to talking to the young man next to me. He was going into the Navy soon. He was also dressed in sports jacket, cowboy boots and levis. We had talked about many things, like I how I was recovering from a love affair with a petit blonde-haired opera singer, whom I could have had one bright summer day in a meadow on Mt. Rose, but I had fallen asleep in her arms and she had wanted to seduce me. She was angry and went with my best friend instead. She was embarrassed, too.

"So I've decided to climb the Tetons," I said, "to forget her."

"Yeah, I've just broken up with my girl, too. Went with her for three years," he said. "So I'm going to Yellowstone before the Navy gets me."

The talk turned to music.

"Check out Joni Mitchell," he said. "*Song to a Seagull.* You'll love her."

That was how I heard about Joni Mitchell. When I got back home, I bought her album. He was right.

I stretched out in the seat.

"Are you comfortable?" he asked.

"I'm in ecstasy," I said.

"You have a low ecstasy tolerance," he said, smiling.

I eventually made it back to the camp. The store there had only souvenirs and raisins. I bought many little packs of raisins and sat on the porch, reading *Time,* writing poetry, and gazing at the Grand. I was very happy. The romance of the situation was perfect, getting myself ready to climb a great mountain because of a broken love affair. It was great for writing poetry.

The Matterhorn couldn't be better than this, I told myself between gulps of raisins.

That evening I got a campsite. The people next to me were interesting, a young man and wife. The man and I had several very long intellectual conversations. They reminded me of the talks of Settembrini and Naphta in Thomas Mann's *The Magic Mountain* which I had just read in honors senior English that spring. They went nowhere and everywhere at once. I can't even remember them now, but I do remember they were very intellectual. One, though, seems to have been about fishing, which I was not avid enough about to hold up my end of the conversation. I think he won that one. Another was about economics, which I also blew. Otherwise, I did pretty well in these campsite debates.

But then I should have. My friend, the one to whom my cute, disgruntled girl friend went to, was on the debate team.

Personally, I didn't like debate. Pick a side, any side, and baffle them with persuasion. Who needs commitment?

Who needs Dubchek?

Up on the rock, the holes opened like stops on a road map, leading me up the pitch. It was a practice run. I moved like a mountain sheep. I felt like the mountain was my playground.

I was suspended on the nearly vertical rock, the rope bowlined around my waist. I hunted carefully for holes as I moved straight up. I felt like I was playing a great musical instrument, and the sounds of nature around me was the music!

When I got down, a woman said, "You looked good up there, Nicky. Very smooth."

"Thanks," I said. I felt ready.

The next day, I hitchhiked 20 miles to another camp to take a shower and do my laundry and get some food. I got picked up by a man and two children in an open jeep. We whizzed along the highway, beneath the mountains.

"I'm climbing the Grand Teton," I said as we talked.

"Good for you!" the man said. He seemed like a Boy Scout leader. "Good for you," he repeated. "You seem like a good, bright boy. You'll do fine!"

"I'm a hippy," I announced, though I had neither long hair nor a beard. It was 1968 and the hippies were just appearing.

The man looked at me with a pleading smile. "You're not a hippy!" he said. "Not if you're hitchhiking twenty miles to take a shower!"

"I'm a hippy who likes to take showers," I replied.

"You're not a hippy!" he said again.

I was right and he was wrong.

Later in the day, I tried to hitchhike back, but I did not get picked up.

I walked a good long ways, before the sun started going down. I stayed on the road until it was absolutely dark, and then I was sure I would not get picked up. I walked into the woods, thinking about bivouacking and how I had an extra pair of levis I could put on. Then I noticed I was near a campground.

I walked into the lodge and sat down at the counter. A young waitress came up to me.

"Hi," I said. "Uh, I'm stuck here. I tried to hitchhike to Jenny Lake Camp but couldn't get picked up. Any chance someone here could give me a lift?"

"Sure," she said. "Don't worry. Me and my girlfriend are going that way soon. We'll take you."

It was too good to be true. "Oh, great," I said. "I thought I was going to have to bivouac."

She laughed sweetly.

Soon, I was riding in the backseat behind the two girls. It seemed like sailing on smooth water as we glided through the dark woods.

"I'm climbing the Grand," I said.

"Oh really!" the girl driver said.

The other girl turned to me. "Wow. That sounds great."

"It'll be fun, I think," I responded. I felt like we were driving through the heart of love itself, as I talked quietly, almost mystically.

"Yeah," the waitress said. "You'll like it. I'm going to climb it too someday," she said.

"Me too," her friend said.

They let me off in the rain at my camp.

"Be careful on the mountain, Nicky," the driver girl said.

"Thanks for the ride. It would have been a soggy night."

The waved and drove off. I walked to my tent. The rain pounded down on the canvas, but I was snug.

I sat on the porch the next day, looking confidently at the great Grand. I was right. The mountain was mine.

"You'll be more tired than you've ever been in your life," the old mountain-climbing instructor told us on the morning we began the climb. "But you'll keep going and you'll make it." He was very serious. "Trust your guide."

The sun absolutely streamed down when we started the long hike to the base camp. We took small steps up the zig-zag path and finally got to the "U" shaped valley at the base of the peak, carved out eons ago by a large glacier. The peak rose up like a great monument to the sky above us, and we watched the sun go down like a big orange globe, before we entered the quantsit hut to sleep.

The next morning, in the dark, we began the climb. And when the sun crept through and then splattered the crystalline azure sky with red orange light, the heavens opened and angels were flying through the rays. And the peak like Everest peeked down at us through the crevices we were inching up. Yeah! I thought. God's country.

All this for a girl, I thought, looking up the rock wall. I held the rope coil like a life support tether.

"On baley!"

I climbed up through the crevices, slowly, carefully, finding precious foot and hand holds. The climb went smoothly. Only one time, as I was sliding unroped across a surface, did I almost slip. I looked down the thousands of feet to the valley and made it across quickly.

There's death, I thought gaping like a jaw. No, there's beauty. The earth's a jewel.

On and on, pitch by pitch, we climbed. The granite seemed almost like a living mass as I made my way angularly up its face, finding the holes like so many treasures beneath my finger tips and climbing shoes. Spread eagled or bent over or leaning out or leaping, it was all dance like.

And then the summit! We climbed the last yards to the top. We congratulated each other as sat on the tip of the Grand, and looked at the appallingly awesome view of the mountain peaks and valley below us. I felt like a god on Mt. Olympus, surveying the mortal world below like Christ on Mt. Zion.

Storm clouds were rolling in and we had to leave quickly. We repelled down walls like kids on a jungle gym, bouncing off the hard rock surfaces as though they were marshmallows.

We got to long snowfield. "We're sliding down this," our guide said. "I want to get back soon." He sounded almost bored. "If you don't know how to glissade, just sit down and pretend you're on a toboggan. If you need to steer, use your feet to guide you."

I had never glissaded in my life. I sat down and took off. I saw a rock sticking up through the snow, straight ahead of me. I hoped he was right about the steering, or this rock and I were going to meet. I used my feet and glided around the rock like a mountain stream. (I have since perfected the art of glissading!)

Then we walked the long trek back to camp. The old mountaineer had been right. I was more tired than I had ever been. But like he said, I made it.

I was very disappointed later when I learned Dubchek was arrested.

Mars

"Hail to thee! Olympos Mons," said the speck, as it marched across the red-rock strewn desert.

"Hail to thee!" cried the speck again, struggling against cold wind blowing red dust everywhere.

Martin sat in the opulent splendor of the Highest Mountain Priest's castle, looking out on the familiar scene of Olympos Mons sparkling like a desert mirage in the red-tinged distance. The top of the mountain disappeared into the sky, pink clouds hiding its mysteries in perpetual secret.

Martin knew though that at the top of the Mountain dwelled the souls of the departed Mountain People, the people of Mars who lived on the plain at the base of the Mountain—the largest, he knew well, in the entire solar system!

Olympos! It rose out of sight, up into paradise, finally merging with the sky itself, where Mars and the infinite red-tinged sky became one, where the souls of the Mountain People aboded in perfect eternity.

Nobody, of course, other than the souls of the deceased, had ever been to the top of Olympos—and lived. Even flying over it was punishable by "particlization."

Martin walked out and checked the rifle-ray on the balcony outside his lavish abode. It was the Canyon People, who populated the vast Canyon Marinarias, which stretched two thousand miles through the desert. The Canyon People lived in cave abodes above the cascading waters of the River Marinarias, riding the strange fish-like creatures—like the Mountain People Rode their glider-horses. They were the only ones who ever dared attempt to climb sacred, forbidden Olympos Mons!

Martin looked through the range-finder of the rifle-ray toward the Mountain, sparkling like a giant jewel in the peaceful morning Martian sun.

Yes, just where he had expected. Their attempts were becoming more frequent now, he noticed. He focused in on the wildly scrambling Canyonman, his long red hair blowing out from his head, a red robe hanging from his muscular body.

Martin had to admit he admired their spirit—these wild Canyonpeople, male and female, young and old, who risked everything to climb the walls of the sky up to heaven itself!

Yes, he thought to himself as he pushed the button on the ray-rifle, you have to admire their…There he goes, clambering madly up the rock fissures, vainly trying to hide…there! Now he's dust! Yes, you have to admire their courage!

He looked intently through the viewer—where once their had been a living creature there was now a puff of white. "Very efficient," he said.

He sighed and turned and walked back into the opulent splendor. "Will they ever learn?"

The siren rang out again! "Another one?"

He walked slowly back to the ray-rifle and looked in the viewer. "Yes, there he is!" Martin looked closer. "Wait…It's a Canyonwoman this time." He focused on her face.

A ruby-like cloud passed from in front of the sun and he could see her face clearly now.

He suddenly gasped. "My lord," he said. "She's beautiful!" He looked at her carefully.

The fierce ardor in her eyes only seemed to magnify the breathtaking beauty of the young woman frantically scrambling up those unbelievably high cliffs, agilely bounding from crevice to crevice, like she must have done a thousand times in her canyon home, thought Martin, a tear coming to his eye now. "What a marvelous creature!" he said. He had never seen such a look on a woman before, certainly not on the "civilized" Mountainwomen who lived here at the base of Olympos. He thought of the irony. The "Mountain People" never attempted to climb the Mountain. That would be sacrilege. Only these curious Canyon People.

He pushed the button…and she was gone…

Martin sat down. Something had happened to him—this time. It was the wildly beautiful look on the young woman's face. She had looked directly at him. And she had smiled!

Martin sat looking out the opaque windows toward the Mountain. He shook his head and then held his head in his hands.

"No, no," he cried. "Not this!"

He had felt the feeling grow for some days now, ever since he had particlized the incredibly beautiful Canyonwoman madly dashing up the sides of Olympos.

He knew too well what the feeling was. Other Mountain Priests had experienced it, but had dutifully confessed (to him!) and been dutifully obliterated. He knew too well—He, Martin desired, more than life itself—to climb the mountain!

Martin gazed now at the picture of the young woman the ray rifle had taken just before it had particlized her—her wild red hair flowing around her face like an unruly but proud spirit, her lips set in her mouth like the finest rubies from the Canyon Marinarias ruby mines…her mouth was smiling at him just like the smiles on those river creatures these people rode.

Martin knew now he had to find the girl's family. The Mountain People, with their sophisticated ray weapons and gadgets

had long ago subjugated the Canyonfolk and used them as labor-
ers in the ruby mines. He would go under pretext of question-
ing the family—this was sometimes done—using the picture as a
means to identify the beautiful trespasser.

When the family was finally located, Martin made ready to
depart. First he looked at the pictures provided by the archi-
vists—he was stunned! Here was the woman's mirror-image
among the surviving members (the Canyonman he had also particlized that day had been the woman's brother) of the Canyon
family. The young woman, he read in the report, had an identi-
cal twin sister!

Martin mounted his glider-horse and it gracefully spiraled up
into the sky, under the clouds of Olympos Mons. He soared away
from the those sparkling walls of sky toward the canyon. Soon
he was over its ornate curves and twists etched in the red Martian
surface by the River Marinarias far below looking like a scarlet
ribbon at the bottom of the "Grand Canyon." The Canyon, he
knew, was an unbelievable 2000 miles long, stretching beyond
the Martian imagination across their small planet, just like Olympos soared up beyond the imagination 20 miles into the sky!

His glider-horse soared down through the canyon walls, finally
landing at the outpost of the Mountain People, a crude castle
carved into the red stone with laser gates and guards to greet
him.

A laser guard saluted him stiffly. Martin tersely snapped back
a perfunctory salute and entered the headquarters. "Act as natural and complacent as you can," he told himself, as the com-
mander of the base immediately jumped to attention.

"Your Holiest," the man said, kneeling.

"Be at ease," Martin said.

The man sat down. "We received your message, sire. It is somewhat irregular, is it not, to question a Canyon family in their own home? Are you sure you would not like them brought here, as usual?"

"I wish to personally make an inspection of the abode of this one," he said, bringing out her picture. "I strongly suspect, because of the circumstance of catching two of the same family on the Mountain the same day, that they are ring leaders, and I desire to look for clues that may implicate others of daring to climb Olympos Mons."

"I see, sire. I will arrange a guard detail at once."

"Don't bother, general." The general looked carefully at him. "I have my ray pistol. I wish not to arouse their suspicions, as I am actually going to try to convince them" (he chuckled) "that I wish to make an attempt, under cover of night—to climb the Mountain!"

"Very clever, sire. Well, here," he said, unrolling a map, "is where she lives."

Martin's glider horse glided down to a rock ledge overhanging the roaring red-glazed river. He tethered the glider and knocked on the door. It creaked open and he was gazing into the beautiful scarlet-hair framed face of the girl he had seen on the Mountain!

"Who are you?" she said in the curious dialect common to the Canyoneers.

"May I enter? I'm a...friend."

"You're a Mountaineer," she breathed.

"I've come about your sister…"

"She's not here," she whispered.

"I know. I have news…"

The door opened further. "Alright," she said. "Come in."

He entered the darkened cave-abode. Soft bubble lights danced on the red clay walls, highlighting the stark interior. Martin quickly took out the picture.

"Is this your sister?" Or is it you? Have you returned from the land of the dead?

The girl started crying. She nodded her head.

"I'm very sorry," said Martin, "but…"

"She is dead."

"Yes. She was attempting to climb…"

"The Mountain!" she cried.

"Yes."

"Did she get far?"

"She almost made it," Martin lied.

"Who are you?"

Martin paused. He took out his ray pistol. The girl flinched. He handed it toward her. "You know how to use this?" She shook her head, "No," stepping back. "Just point at me and push the button. I am Martin the Highest High Priest of the Mountain. I killed your sister. And now you may kill me. Here."

The wild girl looked at him silently and took the ray pistol. The beautiful face turned to an animal grin, but then softened.

"Why?…" she groped. The ray pistol fell to the stone floor.

"I fell in love with her the instant I saw her. It was love at first sight! And now I want to climb the Mountain." Suddenly Martin took the young woman in his arms, holding her tightly. "I never want to lose you again. Never!" She did not resist. "We will climb the mountain together. You and I!"

"We can't both ride on my glider-horse. I couldn't take off."

"We always ride on the river dolphins."

"Alright. As soon as it gets dark, we'll go. Are they hard to ride?"

"No. They're very friendly."

They waited until the red Martian sun sank over the tops of the cliffs and under the light of the two moons, climbed slowly down the stairs carved into the walls to the river. The girl whistled. A long-snouted dolphin swam to the side, its smile like a chain of pearls.

She got on first and then offered Martin her hand and he swung up behind her and the Martian dolphin swam down the river.

They sailed past the guard house. Martin saw the chief guard. He thinks it's the plan, Martin laughed to himself.

Soon they were out in the middle of the Great Martian Desert. They stopped along the shore and got off the dolphin and started climbing the steps toward the star-crusted top of the canyon. The young Canyonwoman almost seemed to bound up the walls. Martin followed easily. The Mountain Priests constantly stayed in top physical condition—it was part of the religion. I'm just glad we're not on Earth, he thought. He had done exhaustive studies of their blue-green neighbor and knew gravity there would not have allowed the kind of gymnastics they took for granted here. It was what made the Canyon People try to climb Olympos—the feeling one had of being able to leap tall mountains with a single bound!

just like in the Supermartian holographic funnies so popular with the Monks of the Monkey Martian Face.

Even the Mountain Priests never went into the sanctum sanctorium of the Monks. The Monkey Monks had strange powers which the Highest Priests treated with respect. He knew, though, they had a labyrinth of underground canals, but as they never attempted to climb the Mountain like the Canyoneers and were pacifists by religion, the Mountain People left them to their scroll libraries inside their quaint pyramids.

But he would go to the Monkey Martian Face when (& if!) he got back from the summit of Olympos, to tell the Monks what he had found. They had no taboo against climbing the Mountain. Only out of deference, he was sure, to the Mountain People's ray guns did they keep a healthy distance! And they were sedentary!

They reached the top of the Canyon, where in the dark distance they knew loomed the Mountain!

They walked across the rocks hand in hand…

They finally reached the cliffs as Phobos—the meteorite-battered artificial moon whose ancient settlers eons and eons ago perished—was setting behind the wall of sky.

"Now we must put these on," Martin said, handing her a light cloak. These were the secret robes of the Chief High Priests—only a select few had these—they neutralized the ray-gun alarm and were used during exercise periods when the Chief High Priests desired to exercise on the cliffs—only the bottommost cliffs!—at the base of the mountain without tripping the alarm system.

He put his on, then helped her with hers and then the two, Martin and Maria, for she had finally told him her name as they ran across the twin-moon light splattered desert, began bounding up the ledges of the cliffs of Olympos Mons.

The climb seemed more like a dream (actually a nightmare) to Martin than real. They transcended zone after zone as they made their way first this way then that way among the boulders, through the canyons, along the streams, past waterfalls, through the trees (200 different species Martin had counted, some never before known to exist) as different species of animals ran by and howled from the distance (he had counted an equal number of animal species, some never known of before), as the sun rose and fell. But what really got to him were the dark-faced creatures living in the caves as they finally neared the summit!

The Monks had outsmarted them after all! Martin thought of the irony of the ancient Monks actually living on their sacred mountain. They had outsmarted the Mountain Priests after all!

But it seemed they were all leaving! They were hurriedly scrambling down long dark tunnels toward the base of Olympos, talking in a Martian dialect Martin couldn't understand. Must be a secret language, he thought.

All at once he felt the ground shake! Marsquake! Martin held to Maria.

"If we are going to climb the Mountain," she said, "we must hurry!" She took his hand and they hurriedly climbed (Martin was too dazed to question) up and up toward the stars which seemed to be almost touchable.

Up they climbed. Luckily for them, Martians had eons ago developed a kind of gill system which allowed them to extract even the slightest traces of oxygen from their thin atmosphere, but still it was becoming harder and harder to breathe up here.

Martin looked toward the still distant summit and saw the sky above turning red. He also noticed it was getting hotter and hotter as they ascended…and red snow was melting…

When finally they obtained the summit Martin and Maria saw: the gigantic lake of fire.

They climbed as quickly as they could back down to the caves of the Monks. Martin was almost crazed with fear and anger. They had been deceived, duped, all these eons. Paradise indeed!

The pair finally reached the caves and plunged down the tunnels which wound around the inside of the sacred mountain, torch lights lighting the way. Other hermits were still madly plunging down the stairs, trying to reach the base of the Mountain before…

After what seemed an eternity of darkness lit only by torch lights in the walls, they reached the lower tier, where there were caverns and a large underground canal, where all the mountain Monks were boarding smiling river dolphins!

Maria and Martin got on one and raced down the canal. Finally they saw a bright light. "Where are we?" asked Martin. They got off their river dolphin and climbed stairs and then Martin, the Highest of the High Priests of the Mountain met the Highest of the Martian Monks.

"So now you know," the Monk said to Martin in a dialect he could understand. "So now you, Martin the Highest of the High Priests of the Mountain, know the truth of the Mountain!"

"How do you know my name?"

"Every Monk knows your name—Martin," he smiled.

"What is going to happen?"

"Mars will soon be destroyed by your sacred mountain. We the Monks of the Great Face of Mystery have known for eons this would someday occur, for we are the descendants of the ancient settlers of Phobos—who learned the dark truth of The Mountain as they observed and studied it from above. Most of them committed ritual suicide in despair—but not before beaming down the scrolls of knowledge, which are still in our scroll libraries. Our ancestors became absolute pacifists and began building the Great Face after receiving this terrible knowledge.

"You of the Mountain Priests, who call us the Monks of the Monkey Martian Face—your cute little joke. We know you've had many a laugh over it. This is the ancient Face of Mystery! older than time itself, always looking up, searching for…"

"God!" said Martin. "We thought God was on the top of the Mountain."

"God is on the top of a mountain," said the Monk, "but not your mountain. God dwells on the top of a mountain in the deserts of another world…Planet Earth!"

"So the face is looking…"

"To Earth! But we could never tell you of the Mountain People, for you are the descendants of those who did not take the vow of pacifism, who refused to accept the truth. Your ancient ones perpetrated the myth which you, Martin, have spent your life defending—and the lives of others—the Canyoneers, who still try to climb Mons. You would have particlized us—for sacrilege. And now your own people will particlized! by your sacred mountain.

"But the Canyon People will be saved, those who make it here past your ray-rifles, for the river dolphins will warn them.

"Only here, underground, is there any hope for survival, for when Olympus Mons erupts, as it will surely do soon now, it will start a chain reaction and all the other volcanoes of Mars, the largest, as you know, in the solar system, will also erupt. And the atmosphere of Mars will be– particlized!"

The speck marched rigidly across the red-strewn sand, struggling against the cold-dry wind toward the smoke-spewing behemoth rising out from the distant horizon like a spectre from the grave-yard of the gods. The black smoke disappeared up into what was left of the sky, the top of the smoldering mountain looming some twenty miles up into the atmosphere.

"Hail to thee! destroyer of Mars," said the speck, said Martin the Martian, (former) Highest High Priest of the Mountain. He adjusted his circulation pack and then shook his fist at the monstrous apperage, as red rivers flowed down the wall of sky which stretched end to end across the horizon like a wall of plasma.

"Hail to thee, Olympos Mons," the speck said again.

"Destroyer of Mars!"

Martin then turned and strode rapidly away from the sacred mountain across the stark desert toward the distant outline of the Great Face, appearing against the horizon as an eternal mystery—looking directly up at the distant hills of Planet Earth.

Walden Pond, California

"Walden Pond, California," the sign overlooking the Pacific Coast beach said, "home of Henry David Thoreau's distant cousin Hippie Harv."

I turned into the beach cottage driveway, got out of my '67 white Rambler Classic, and walked up to the door.

Knock! Knock!

"Don't need any today!" I heard Hippie Harv's voice say from within the log cottage.

"It's me," I said.

"Oh, you. Well come in you!"

I walked in. Hippie Harv was lying on a white polar-bear rug in front of a crackling fire place.

"How are you?" he said as I entered. "And by the way, who are you?"

He was gazing into the flickering flames, his head in the lap of a pretty girl with long straight blond hair.

She was holding a cigarette in front of Hippie Harv's mouth so he could puff on it. She looked at me and smiled a Cheshire cat smile.

"I'm Alice," Alice said.

"Where's the caterpillar and hookah?" I laughed.

"They're at the Mad-Hatter's today," said Harv. "Some kind of tea party of somethin'."

"I thought that was in Boston," Alice giggled.

"Hippie Harv," I said seriously, "man, I been reading a strange book recently and I can't understand a word of it. Maybe y' could like enlighten me, y'dig, man?"

"Sure. What book?"

"*Finnigan's Wake.*"

"Ooooh, that is a puzzle, ain't it," said Harv. "You say you can't understand a word of it?"

"Right, Hippie Harv. Not a word."

"Let's see, *Finnigan's...*"

"*Wake.*"

"uh…*Wake.* I remember. Didn't Jack Kerouac write *Finnigan's* uh…"

"*Wake.*"

"uh *Wake.*"

"No. James Joyce."

"Oh yeah. The same guy who wrote the *Odyssey?*"

"No, Harv," Alice said. "That was Homer, silly. James Joyce wrote *Ulysses.*"

"I know, I know," Harv said, chuckling. "I was just joshing 'what's his name.' Let's see…got my 'Classics Illustrated' version of *Finnigan's…*"

"*Wake.*"

"…right here. Hmmmm. The reason you can't understand a word of it is because—there aren't any words in it, y'dig?"

I walked over to the round window and looked out over the crisp blue waves wandering into the white pebble beach.

"Ever see any whales out on the pond?" I asked

"Sure," he said. "When they's migratin' north."

"How about dolphins?"

"See 'em all the time when I'm surfin'. Ride right in with ya. Keep the sharks away!"

"Have you ever wanted to be a dolphin, Hippie Harv?"

"Sure. Swim lots better 'n me, for sure."

"Listen." I started making high pitched squeaking and whistling noises. "Know what I just said, Hippie?"

"Not in English," Harv admitted.

"I was talking delphin," I said.

"What did you say, dolphin boy?" asked Alice.

"Wouldn't you like to know, Alice," I smiled.

"Well, Hippie Harv, I guess I'll be on my way. Thanks for the enlightenment."

"Any time. By the way, who are you?"

"Your long lost cousin," I said, walking out the door.

"Y' mean...?"

I shut the door...and looked out over Walden Pond, Ca.

Hardy Boys in Outer Space
Space Detectives!
(an animated adventure)

Joe and Frank Hardy are walking home after school. As they pass the vacant lot next to their house, Joe Hardy suddenly yells,

"Look, Frank, a flying saucer!"

In the lot, partially hidden by trees, a small flying saucer pulsates. The two Hardy Boys run to the saucer. The door to the saucer opens and the Hardy Boys carefully crawl in.

"Wow!" Frank says. "Where do you think it's from?"

Then they see an electric guitar against the wall. "Look," Joe says, "an electric guitar!"

"Wow," says Frank. "Maybe there from around here."

Joe picks up the guitar and starts playing it. Then they hear applause and the space craft takes off!

As they fly through space and stars rush by the small window, the view screen suddenly shows a shimmering face.

"Welcome, Hardy Boys!" says a deep booming voice.

"Who are you?" Frank asks.

"We are the Gleeshons, from a far away planet…At least we used to be from a far away planet. You see, this is why we've come for you. You are the best detectives in the galaxy, Hardy Boys, and we need a mystery solved."

"Wow!" Joe exclaims.

"Space detectives!" Frank chimes in.

"What's the mystery, Mr.Gleeshon?" eagerly asks Joe Hardy.

"We have lost our planet!"

"Your planet!?" both Hardy Boys say at once.

"Yes. We were on an intergalactic space mission and when we returned, our planet was missing."

"How could you lose your planet?" Frank Hardy exclaims.

"This is the mystery you must solve, Hardy Boys. And as time is of the essence, to make sure you do your best space sleuthing we have, by means of reverse relativity, accelerated your aging process. So you will soon be the Hardy Men if you don't solve this mystery."

"The Hardy Men!" the Hardy Boys exclaim.

"Yes," says the deep voiced Gleeshon. "And to help you may use Delphi, our computer."

Delphi flashes on in front of the Hardy Boys.

"Hi, Hardy Boys!" Delphi says in a high pitched voice.

"Wow," says Joe. "A smiling computer."

And so, as they zing through the galaxy toward where the Gleeshon's planet used to be, Joe asks Delphi, "Where could an entire planet hide?"

"Insufficient information," Delphi responds.

"What about a black hole," Frank asks. "Could a black hole have swallowed the Gleeshon's planet?"

Delphi's lights quickly flash on and off. "A black hole is a collapsed supernova," Delphi says, somewhat mechanically, "with gravity so strong not even light can escape. But the Gleeshons had long ago foreseen this possibility and surrounded their home planet with a strong antigravity force field which would propel it away from any black hole trying to eat it. Besides, the Gleeshons have only been gone a few hours."

"A few hours!" Joe exclaims. "How do the Gleeshons go so fast, Delphi?"

"By wishing," Delphi responds.

"Wishing?" Frank exclaims.

"Sure," Delphi says, "they simply wish upon a star."

"Well why don't they just wish for their planet back," Joe says somewhat sarcastically.

"We've already tried," the Gleeshon's deep reverberating voice sadly tells the Hardy Boys. "That's why we have come for you. It didn't work, and now we don't know what to do."

The Hardy Boys keep asking Delplhi questions. Joe, the oldest, runs his hand over his cheek as he is thinking and feels the stubble of a beard.

"Wow!" he says. "Now were the Hardy Men!"

All at once, the flying saucer enters a multi-colored prism of light.

"Where are we now, Delphi?" Frank cries out.

"Insufficient information," Delphi responds.

Frank and Joe look at each other and see they now have white hair and white beards.

"Wow! Now we are the Hardy Old Men!"

"Didn't something like this happen in *2001 A Space Odyssey*," Joe asks.

"Where are we now, Mr. Gleeshon?" Frank asks as they look outside the window at the pulsating glitter.

"I do not know," the deep voice says. "But we should be where Planet Love used to be."

"Planet Love?" exclaims Joe.

"You come from Planet Love?" asks Joe.

"Yes, and now we are lovesick!"

"Oh, no," moan the Hardy Old Men.

"It's almost like someone's playing a joke on us." Joe says dejectedly.

"That's it!" Frank exclaims, grabbing his brother's arm.

"What's it?" Joe Hardy asks through his long white beard.

"Someone's played a trick on the Gleeshons and made their planet disappear."

Delphi's lights flash on and off. "That is correct, Hardy Old Men. That is correct."

"A trick!?" the deep-voiced Gleeshon booms out.

"Who would play such a trick on us?"

Then a face appears in the view screen!

A face in a multi-colored jester's cap!

"Ha, ha, ha!" the face laughs. "Here's your Planet Love back, Gleeshons!" the jester merrily cries out, as pulsating Planet Love appears in the view screen.

"Ha, ha, ha, ha, ha, ha, ha, ha, ha!" he laughs. "Goodbye for now, Gleeshons! Ha, ha, ha, ha, ha…!" and then disappears.

Soon the Hardy Boys are above the vacant lot.

"For solving our mystery, Hardy Boys," the deep voice says as the flying saucer lands, "we have made you both honorary Glee-shons!"

"Thanks," Joe Hardy says, looking at his brother.

"I'm just glad we're the Hardy Boys again!" Frank Hardy says, as they crawl out the saucer door.

Rings

When Roger MacIntyre examined the photographic plates of the Magellanic Cloud taken the night of Jau 56, the seventh day of the Saturnian "summer," from the floating space station Titan III between the third and forth rings, he immediately noticed the unusually bright light, where their had never been one before. He was not, in the usual sense, a scientist, but, instead, an artist, a "space photographer," he modestly called himself, who specialized in dramatic, artistic "photos" of galactic and intergalactic space phenomena, photographs so beautifully awesome, taken with the most elaborate, and sophisticated cameras ever dreamed of in the minds of men, equipment perfected over the past 500 years (to which Roger MacIntyre had added his own personal touches) that space images seemed more like living, breathing organisms than astrophysical phenomena. Mr. MacIntyre's plates commanded unearthly sums, and hung on the walls of the homes of the wealthiest lords of the solar system. From the moons of Neptune to the undersea gardens of Venus, Mr. MacIntyre's plates were as famous as Van Gogh's paintings and commanded almost (though not quite) equal sums. His "Five Moons of Jupiter" adorned the main dining room of the lord's castle on Mars, a "photo" that seemed almost, due to his perfected use of "depth persuasion" techniques, as large as its subject matter. When one stared in wonder at this marvel of advanced space art, one was not "observing" the sublime, beautiful scene: one was suspended in it, floating blissfully above Jupiter's giant "Red Eye," between Io and Europa. Viewing his "Milky Way Over the Asteroids," well, one, to use his own cliché in describing his works to those few unfamiliar with his work, one simply "had to be there." And this, of course, was the goal and purpose of all Roger MacIntyre's works; to actually "Put you there," as he would say. No wonder his work commanded billions of earth dollars, second only to the best Van Gogh's or the most majestic Da Vinci's.

Needless to say, his long awaited series from the rings of Saturn was commanding huge sums and great acclaim. The lords and ladies of the entire system were waiting in line for the most "unbelievably beautiful" plates of all, plates which suspended the viewer in various states of "space bliss" more powerfully than even the best myrhh from Mars, for one was simply "there," and the state of mind was so pure the viewer felt he was tapped into the very universal essence.

Lord Cavilish had remarked when first viewing MacIntrye's "Rings," which now adorned the study of his undersea castle on Venus, "My God, the stars are alive. I've never known it before: yes the stars are alive!"

"And the rings?" Mr. MacIntyre asked.

"The rings," Lady Cavalish said, "are the jewelry of God!"

Roger MacIntyre nodded in agreement, as the three stood in the showing room.

Lord Cavilish was astounded. "I'm floating above Saturn like a child before a Christmas ornament." He groped for words. "The rings circle before me like...cosmic highways. I feel as though I could walk on the rings themselves…I feel as though… I am."

Lady Cavilish was even more poetic. "I feel," she said, "…I feel I'm in the presence of the most fabulous treasure in the universe, that God has shown me His most precious jewel…and is wearing it over His heart."

The new plate, the last of the "Saturn" series, was to be his ultimate masterpiece, actually taken from between the rings themselves and focusing on the vast Magellanic Cloud. Its title was, "The Rings and the Cloud."

On the night of Jau 56, as he contemplated the strange new light that had appeared on the plate, he immediately recognized it for what it obviously was: a supernova! A giant star had exploded in the Magellanic Cloud, and the result was an entity more powerful than an entire galaxy! Which star had exploded was for the scientists to determine. His only concern was the artistic value of this unexpected occurrence.

He instantly realized the significance of this event for what was already his greatest work: a supernova near enough to the Terran solar system to be readily observable to the naked eye, for he had immediately gone to the nearest observation station to check it and it shone before him like a Christmas light. He had then donned his space suit and gone outside and floated beneath its beauty, so as to completely absorb its essence into his artistic soul. This would be the one they had waited for—the best of the best.

When he came back in, he enhanced the image of the glowing supernova, deciding to focus on it from between the rings. The new title would be "Super Nova Through Saturn's Rings." The nova now shown like a cosmic search light seeking out life itself. He worked over the new print for months.

"I've never felt anything like this," he said to himself as he worked on the plate. "It's as though the very essence of the universe has been focused in this one ball of light…as though I were being drawn to the source of all eternity."

He was well aware of the power of his own works. He knew the kind of hypnotic attraction they exerted over those viewing them. His total mastery of "depth persuasion," a technique he had himself invented some 20 earth years earlier, rendered his work as living entities. But his very knowledge of the hidden technique of this art, a technique he had kept secret and that no one else had been able as yet to discover, gave him a certain aloofness when viewing his work, like a magician who knows what the magic trick is as compared to the viewer who is totally absorbed in the effect. In comparison to himself, his patrons were like children before Houdini. He understood it and therefore had power over his art. His viewers were mystified and therefore his art had power over them. He could remain aloof to the extent necessary to maintain professionalism, while his patrons became absorbed to the degree where they had believed Mr. MacIntyre, like so many great artists before him, was somehow more then mere man, and his works, like Da Vinci's paintings, more than "mere art"…but touched with "something" from beyond.

But this one even had him.

On the night he finished it, he placed it in his showing room and stood before it, gazing on the bright new light from between the multi-colored, prismatic, circling, flashing, shining rings. The new star was even brighter in the sky than the distant sun. He had always avoided taking close "photos" of the sun—for obvious reasons—he did not, after all, wish to risk blindness. His previous plate "Sun through the Rings" had exuded a warmth that seemed to draw viewers like moths before a flame. With this culminating masterpiece he desired to fling his viewers, as it were, into the very depths of the galaxy from between the circling rings.

And now he viewed it, and it terrified him. He was plunged into the void and drawn into his own vision like never before. It shook him to his soul. He quivered and gasped as he confronted the supernova, the most powerful entity in the known universe, from between Saturn's sweet rings. His mouth was drawn back around his teeth and he could feel his head being forced back on his shoulders, as though he were riding a roller coaster through the stars. He became a child, he became an old man, and just in time he stepped back and returned.

Roger MacIntyre was becoming concerned. If this new work had this kind of power over him, who understood the technique, what would it do to those who viewed it? Would it drive them mad? What would happen?

He decided to hold it back from the public for some months while he delved the depths of this new work. Every entry (which he called viewings of his works) left him shaken and drained. A supernova was truly an extraordinary phenomenon, he concluded.

He became determined to test his new print on one person, his friend, Lord Cavilish of Venus, who had desired to purchase the plate when complete, so as to see what he might expect.

Lord Cavilish immediately flew to Saturn when informed of the plate's completion.

He talked to his friend, prior to the exclusive showing. "Lord Cavilish," be bowed, "I must tell you in advance that this plate is more powerful than any I've done before. You must prepare yourself for the experience. It exerts a strong effect even over myself, and I am somewhat immune to my own art," he confessed.

Lord Cavilish was a hearty though sensitive man, a former officer in the King's Solar Squadron, a man not accustomed to fear. "I'm ready for anything," he jested light heartily. "Ours is not to wonder why, ours is but to do and die," he laughingly said. "Lead me on, Roger. I will follow you to the ends of eternity itself."

As they stood before "Super Nova Through Saturn's Rings," Roger MacIntyre carefully watched his friend.

"Oh!" Lord Cavilish exclaimed. "How beautiful! How sublime! This is your most wonderful work yet, Roger. The light! I've never experienced…"

Suddenly he was cut off in mid-sentence. His head was pushed back and he screamed. "My God…it's…God!" he yelled and then he collapsed.

Lord Cavilish recovered slowly in the hospital on Titan, and was never again the same. He talked over and over of the star with the rings.

As the months went by, a curious phenomenon occurred. The supernova did not fade, as all supernova eventually do. It remained as bright as ever! And, what is more, scientists on different space stations, moons and planets throughout the solar system, in observing the phenomenon, had not been able to determine which star was responsible, which star had blown up. All their most sensitive equipment could not determine the progenitor star. Indeed, their readings showed that all previously known stars in the sector were present and accounted for. Of course they could not be 100% certain, but, nonetheless this was causing great consternation through the system. What, exactly, were they observing?

This occurrence greatly excited Roger MacIntyre. He made further "entries" into his work, and finally he decided to risk it all, and not hold back, to loose the awareness of technique that kept him from the full experience. He accomplished this through self hypnotics, and then he too confronted "Super Nova Through Saturn's Rings" in all of its totality, and then he too saw the rings around the star!

If his experiences in entry had been awesome it was now overwhelming. But not frightening as before. The rings of the nova reached out like the strong arms of a loving wise father, and he was aware of a bliss so pure as to be beyond imagination. He was suspended between the rings of Saturn and the rings of the nova. He could actually look down to those rings below him and up to those rings above and felt he was dancing in eternity. And then he entered the rings of the star and merged with the infinite. He heard a million voices singing a million songs all in perfect harmony and the nova bloomed like a Van Gogh sunflower, and he remembered the words of his friend. "My God…it's God!"

When he returned, which he was able to do with an extreme effort of will, he knew he had changed forever, but that he had changed for the bettor. He took long afternoon walks now in the atrarium, with its myriad whistling flowers—something he rarely did before. He watched the sunrise in the mornings, magnifying the brilliance of the luminous disk appearing like a sunflower sprouting up through the rings.

He decided to show his work to a select audience, to properly prepare them in advance, so as not to repeat what had occurred to his friend Cavilish, who still remained under psychiatric observation in the Titan hospital.

He assembled his audience. "Friends," he said, "you must not hold back in any way. Simply 'go with the flow,' as they used to say in an earlier time. Be childlike in wonder and awe and I promise you an experience which you will cherish and keep all the days of your life. Just relax and do not resist the power of the nova."

They stood before "Super Nova Through Saturn's Rings" quietly, and as Roger MacIntyred watched, they vanished…

Mr. MacIntyre sat down. He knew what had happened. Even though he had hypnotized himself to eliminate his professional aloofness, enough residue had remained to allow him to resist just sufficiently to remain corpeal. His friends, he knew, were gone forever—floating blissfully in the rings around the star.

There was no way he could explain the disappearance of forty people who had entered his laboratory. There was only thing to do.

He worked quickly and designed a solvent which would make the plate disappear completely in a matter of minutes—just time enough for him to follow his friends and never return.

He applied the solvent, and then entered "Super Nova Through Saturn's Rings." He felt added strength drawing him on, the strength of his friends, and he was gone.

At precisely the instant the plate dissolved, scientists around the system noted the vanishing of the supernova. They breathed a collective sigh of relief.

The universe, as they knew it, was back to normal.

B. The poems

If You Remember

If you remember
There were trees there
Marble skys.
If you recall
It was green there
Very nice.
I saw a girl with green hair
And a dolphin smile
And she lived were the river meets the sun
Horizon.
And love flowed
And they rowed their boats just for fun.

It you think back
Their faces came out at night
Kaleidoscopic stars
Smiling, above us in the height!

Mozart's Tree

The music grows like a plant,
This Mozart woodwind quintet
Up to the sky like a thing growing high
Like a tree with vines all around,
A tree made of sound!
I soared up the tree for what to see—
I saw eternity.
I saw an ocean blue as the tree still grew,
Or was it a cloudless sky?
Or did sky and sea meet
Horizon at my feet
At some sweet bye and bye.
I looked down, down, down...
And the earth was round
And covered with moss so green.
I looked around, 'round, 'round
To see the sounds
And birds were in all the leaves!

And when I finally flew down the tree
I looked up at the ceiling sky.
The players had paused to greet our applause—
And Mozart was gone with a sigh.

Innocence

Whatever happened to innocence
And where, oh where did it go?
Tears stream down,

As I search the fawn's den.

Into the Forest I Would Go

Into the forest would I go
And build my home by the water breezes
The purple mountains like horses would neigh at the stars
And I think no more of wars
And the clouds would be like God shining
And the birds as angel flocks
Swirling, swirling, swirling…
Forever!
Oh, into the forest I would go,
And dwell with children and angels!

No Choice!

When the masters of war
Try to take your life
You hit them as hard as you dare.
You have no choice—can only strike back
And no choice—but to care!

Free!

Free!
I smile at the girl with the dolphin smile
Slam!
The shark is dead.
Revolving through the ocean green water
We swirl through all the waves.

The island before us foams
We bless the fish and run through the waves
To our home.

I kneel in the sun on the ground, my friends gathered
around
The light makes—shimmering angels.
We are
Very
Important

I kill the sacrificial lamb
Where we watch the blood seep into the sand
My wife holds my hand
My little children hold hers

We
Are
Free!

Easy Stream

I lie beside the easy stream
It bubbles from a spring
Between the black rocks.
In stair steps, moving stairs
Water downward flows
Among the emerald mosses.
Pearls dance!
Sunlight white
Then phantasia of color—

I drink it in.
Huddling in the sand in the breeze,
I dip my hand into the forest stream.
I turn my head, looking up the flash of water lights
Beneath the pining sun, at the gurgle cascade.
There light sparkles
Where the pools eddy and swirl
Rippling through the watery cosmos
Like rainbows of love.
I drink the water
Stand up
And walk away
Into the trees.

Petals

The petals of the flower like a wheel turn.
In the morning hour
With a wild yearn
While the last stars still faintly burn
I am taken by the power
And softly
Learn

Vision

I see a dream!
And peace is in its folds.
I see a dream!
And fast to me it holds.

And like a star-struck king
A child is on a throne.

Girl

The girl is love.
Wheel chair moves her
Crying soothes her.
"You are the best," she says.

Pyramid Lake

There would be alone.
Buttes fan out
Reds glow
Land lies
Low
Painted is the word used
It does seem so
Paints flow.

I walk between them in the dry air
Sagebrush crackles beneath my boots
The desert gives you time to stare—
And shares your lonely search for roots.
And shares your lonely search for roots.

Over rise—now the sky's reversed.
Blue below
What!?

Project Love

This scene was long ago rehearsed
Indians saw it first
Indians saw
Pyramid Lake
First

Pegasus

There, where the halo of the highway light
Blends into the forest,
I see the horses, straining over the fence—
Waiting, on all fours, for me to come to them.
Around me now, the sky is dark, darker even
For the light in front of me which
Blocks out the stars.

Out the other way, the mountains fade into the deep night,
But here it is friendly, for they are waiting.
I remember my tent as I walk toward them,
Three miles down mountain highway,
Then down dirt road, across the brookling spring…
On up the hill through the trees which will
Sparkle under the stars like lighted tannenbaums.
Then through the forest. But I will find it easy.
And for now these horses seem as sweet
As they clover they are eating,
Their eyes lighted as the lamp.
For it is cool…and they have come to laugh.
They neigh like cats purring, rub their noses on my arms,
Examine my hands for oats, and shake their manes,
Tossing their locks about like shy children.

I know they have come from the sweet stars
And as soon as I leave will sprout wings
And fly away with Pegasus!

June
(a love song)

If the waves could tell the story
Of my love for you,
If the sun could show its glory,
Would it then come true
If the stars above could light the page
On which these words are writ
Then perhaps my dear you'd see
The love by which they're lit.

Oh my dear I long to hear
Of your love for me.
Could it really happen
Can it really be?
Or is it just a dream I have
When I see your face
Just the way your golden hair
Lies on your golden lace.

June oh June I long to hold
Your heart next to mine
June oh June I long to taste
Your love sweet as wine
And June I'd love to walk with you
Into the rosy dawn

And hold you there forever
Just like in this love song!

June, I love you
Come dance away with me
Walk with me beside the waves
Of love's enchanted sea.
Out to love's oasis
Between the rippling sands
Where sugar pines brush the stars
And make a lover's stand
And we'll gaze upon the Pleiades
Standing hand in hand!

The Last Star

The last star
Is far away
Einsteinian space curves
Limits accelerate
To the ends of time
And, as you are aware
$E=mc2$

Daylight Sparkles

Daylight sparkles
The glee of heaven!
Murmuring, blazing, soaring
Amazing Grace
The sun shines down

Scott Campbell

On the leaves of grass
I read Walt Whitman
In the shade of a tree
And wonder if the angels
Think of me

PART II:
THE SMILING
INVADERS

CHAPTER ONE
THE WINDOW

The mirage approached in the early morning desert sun—a man riding a glider horse—light around him a muted aura. Behind the figure a second glider followed, snow-sheeted Mt. Whitney rising up out of the sage-covered valley like a "wall of sky," as they said on Mars when talking in muted tones of Olympos Mons. A long white desert robe-jacket hung loosely from his shoulders, reflecting the light bouncing up from the rocks. Dust bounced behind him in little puffs as he slowly approached.

Down in the valley before him slept the movie town of Lone Pine. Across the valley behind the town where the sun rose red and dusty were the rainbow-ribbed White Mountains. The Owens River tumbled between the two walls like the river in the Valley of the Hunzas high in the Himalaya. The only difference was that it was near sea level here, and just over the Whites in the "Valley of Death," the bottom dropped out at Badwater—225 feet below the sea.

Michael rode slowly toward the town through the prehistoric looking Alabama Hills, the dark-rock "movie-set" used in a hundred westerns.

They were filming now.

"Haven't I seen you before?" the director had asked Michelle, as he interviewed her for a part as an "extra."

Michelle had only smiled.

Light! Camera! Action!

Michelle rode her horse easily through the Alabamas at a stiff trot. She now had the leading role! The director had become so enamored by her innocent charm and wild good looks, he had decided to make her the "star." The movie was about a young lady who was trying to get through the Army blockade around the base of Whitney to reach her boyfriend who had been abducted by the "Grinning Invaders," (the name of the movie) and was being held captive on the far distant, sparkling summit of Mt. Whitney!

"I'm not the best horse-back rider," she had told the director, "but I'm a good swimmer. Do you have any water scenes?"

"Now don't you worry honey," the director had said, patting her cheek. "You'll do just fine. Just sit there and look pretty for the camera."

As Michelle trotted across the sage stage, she suddenly kicked her horse into a full gallup, flying through the rock obelisks of the Alabama Hills.

"Hey," the director called out. "We're shooting!"

"Keep shooting!—honey," Michelle yelled over her head. "Keep shooting!"

From behind a rock, Michael suddenly appeared. "Hurry," he said. Michelle quickly got off her roan and jumped on the neighing glider. The two took off and soared directly above the camera man, who instinctively raised his camera to film the "action," as the director looked into the sky, where Michael and his granddaughter Michelle rose up against the spired silhouette of Whitney like doves against the setting sun.

"The best special effect they ever had!" said Michelle, waving down at the folks below.

As they soared up to the summit of Whitney, Michelle remembered back to when they had left their under-sea home in the Gulf in the Star Dolphin's sea-saucer.

The sub-fleet had shown up over Xanadu, and they had all barely escaped into the saucer, taking off through the submarines like a giant turtle through a school of barracudas.

They had fled their home, and most of the pod now lived in the compound on Mt. Whitney with the Star Dolphins, as though in a besieged castle.

The glider horses coasted in between Whitney's ray-like peaklets and they were again at the fortress, the giant igloo-like geodesic dome the Star Dolphins had quickly erected last winter—a fait d'accompli, a smiling coup d'etat.

Michelle and Michael looked down to the valley where the startled movie makers were still filming "The Grinning Invaders."

Michelle laughed. "Bet it's a smash!"

They entered the giant igloo, which covered the entire broad expanse of the Whitney summit, through the tunnel-like entrance—the command center, sparkling in a myriad of flashing lights, flicking on & off, on & off.

The huge holographic globe of Earth was suspended in mid-air in the center of the room, where Star Dolphins swam around canals past their myriad computer monitors. The globe was replete with whirling weather systems—snow falling down from clouds here, tornadoes there, hurricanes, squalls, earth-quake tremors—some mild, some strong—volcanoes, geysers, dust storms, migrating geese, ocean currents with microscopic dolphins…all rolling around the gargantuan holographic sun—complete with sun spots and solar flares…

Mars was here, too, red with white polar caps and endless can-yons and giant volcanoes.

Michael stopped in front of Mars, looking intently into the "micro-viewer" at the red-tinted plain at the base of Olympos Mons…

Across the red strewn desert, Heaven loped toward the unend-ing wall of Olympos Mons, climbing gear in his "space pack." He would climb the mountain—not because its there—but because the Martians would not accept him into their society unless he did. And unless he was accepted by the strange, remote "people" who inhabited the half dead/half alive world, they would never help his people on Earth in their struggle against the new "Earth Power" regime which had coalesced from among the old nations of Earth to resist, violently, the coming of the Star Dolphins, join-ing forces with the international drug cartels and crime syndicates to wage war against the "grinning invaders," as they called them.

And, just as in WW II, it had been vital to get the United States into the war against the evil Axis powers, so now was the help of the Martians equally necessary.

Such strange creatures, Heaven thought, as he loped across the plain. Why must they insist on adhering to their ancient customs so devoutly, especially now! I can't even use the flipper wings the Star Dolphins made for me! They insist on me climb-ing "Mons" the "old-fashioned way," the way they've climbed it to test themselves for "Martian-hood" for eons. Only tether ropes and grip-shoes.

He knew they were watching him closely from their citadel at the Great Face even now as he raced across the desert toward the distant cliffs, rising up like "walls of sky" before him. Luckily, Martian gravity made the quest possible, but still...

He had hoped Rena would be his climbing partner, but Martian tradition had insisted he climb Olympos alone. He had never been away from Rena before and felt very alone out here in "the middle of absolute nowhere," the Mountain, the incredible "wall of sky" meeting him like a visage from the Land of the Giants, while Rena waited back at the Great Face, in the underground pyramids, searching the ancient Martian scrolls for clues to the "Mystery of the Mountain."

Heaven spoke into his radio.

"Find anything, yet, Rena," he asked.

He had no time himself to search the scrolls as time was, as they said on home planet Earth, "of the essence," so Rena would have to be his guide.

"Yes," she said. "From what I've heard so far of the scrolls White Dolphin has translated" (White Dolphin had flown to Mars and the Great Face, specifically for this difficult task, using his vast knowledge of galactic languages to transcribe the scrolls verbatim) "you must head first for the crevice 17.5 degrees north by northwest of the giant boulder."

"That's right," chimed in White Dolphin, from his water capsule. "That's where the route, the only route to the top begins. If you miss it the climb is impossible."

"I won't miss it," Heaven answered. Earth depends on it, he thought.

Michael walked now to Earth and focused the micro-viewer on the Southwest deserts of the United States.

Outside the hogan, Robby sat cross legged before a sand-painting of silver dolphins swimming among golden stars, completing the "painting" by sprinkling colored rocks from between his fingers. The painting seemed to come to life as he worked intently over it. A young maiden came out and sat beside him, holding a little "papoose" in her arms.

"You're a very fine sand-painter," she said solemnly. "For a 'white man,'" she giggled.

"Uncle taught me well," he said, "—the best medicine man in the county."

The door flap to the hogan came open again and Johnny walked out, his long locks of hair hanging down from under his brightly colored headband.

"Will it work, mon—Dr. Hope," he laughed.

"It better," Robby smiled. "My medicine-man reputation depends on it."

Off across the desert floor, the pickup truck came into view, dust trailing behind.

It pulled up in front of the hogan, and the Navajo couple got out, the woman dressed in a long traditional dress, a tiny infant crying in her arms.

"Ye-ta-i!" the Navajo man in a cowboy hat called out.

"Ye-ta-i!" Robby responded.

Robby stood up and took the infant from its mother and placed it on the sand-painting—as if riding on the sand-dolphin through the glittering stars.

The crying baby began to laugh...

Michael now looked in "The Window" just south of Mt. Whitney...

(Ex) President "Joshua-tree" Clark stood at the top of New Army Pass, watching below him as the convoy of green jeeps and marching soldiers made their way slowly up the steep switchbacks toward the top of the 13,000 ft pass at the base of 14,000 Mt. Langley. He focused the laser-binoculars carefully, and scanned the line of vehicles.

"No doubt about it," General Peter Bryan said, standing at the (Ex) President's side. "This is no mere 'exercise,' like they said. They've launched an all out invasion. They're trying to surround Whitney from the south!"

Ever since the Star Dolphins had taken over the Whitney summit, the new "Earth-Power" regime had been attempting to "take back the mountain."

Helicopter flights over the summit had simply disappeared, and jets couldn't get low enough to do anything except strafe the Star Dolphin's compound, which was impervious to their firepower. Peter just hoped they never tried nuclear weapons. The anti-matter force-field around the compound would protect it from the blast, but the repercussions, locally, would be devastating.

A fully armed Marine platoon had marched up the Whitney Trail toward the summit, but had not gotten past the magnetic-fence which the Star Dolphins regularly opened for any "private citizen" wishing to climb to the top.

This was their newest tact, and General Peter Bryan and (Ex) President Clark knew it must be met decisively.

Then the snow began. It fell in big dry flakes, a myriad of hexagons fleeing to the earth, tumbling all around the advancing legion in a blizzard of soft rocks, as if some cosmic sling was propelling magical stones of beautiful design to ensnare the caissons. In minutes, they came to a standstill—they could not advance further up the steep switchbacks.

"We can't see anything!" the lead jeep radioed. "It's a total white out."

They stood still in the thickening white tornado.

"We gotta get outta here or we'll freeze!" radioed the platoon sergeant.

They froze in solid white statues and never again did anyone attempt to come up New Army Pass.

Down in the western lowlands, the rains began in earnest. It rained for 10 days straight and the towns along the Mad River and Eel River were flooded. Cars were washing down the streets and houses became bathtubs.

Two little children were being swept crying down the water! their mother crying out from the top story of her house.

Two river dolphins appeared! swimming under the boys, who clasped their little arms around them. "Mommy! We're all right. Funny looking dolphins have saved us!"

348

A legion of river dolphins swam through the streets, into the houses, under the bridges, saving all the people and bringing them where a giant starship floated, eerily still in the middle of the raging Mad River.

The people went into the starship in twos and families, like the animals had marched into Noah's Ark.

At last the winter of floods and eternal snow came to an end—in July. On the Fourth, Nick was in Mammoth, looking up at the snow covered peaks which surrounded the resort town. They were still skiing upon the mountain!

Nick sat in an outside café, eating breakfast and reading Carl Jung's *Syncrinicity* which Robby had given him, a book the fabled psychiatrist, who took a decidedly different path from his contemporary Freud, had written about meaningful strange coincidences. Nick now knew there was really no such thing as random coincidences—they all had a connection caused by forces and powers even Nick, who had been extensively trained by the Star Dolphins for his commando-type mission in the High Sierra, had really little understanding of. Nick just knew they existed and had purpose—like when he had been camping up on the High Trail and reading how Jung had been helping a patient interpret a dream about a scarab, when a rose aphid, the closest European relative to the fabled golden Egyptian bug, had flown in the window. Jung had caught the aphid, handed it to his patient, and said, "Here, Madam, is your scarab!" As Nick had been re-reading once again this section, a shiny rainbow colored rose aphid had flown into his tent!

Now Nick believed. And how!

He laid the book down, reclining in his chair, drinking coffee with much cream and gazing again on the snow covered peaks. "Incredible!" he said again out loud. "On the fourth of July!" He had heard it had snowed here 10ft in one day!

He knew Mammoth's funky parade would begin soon, which he didn't want particularly to see—the whistles and sirens and cheap floats and fire engines and police cars and etc.—so he paid the check, got his pack and wandered over to the highway leading up to the Mammoth Lakes back country. He had just gotten to the side of the road, ready to hitchhike, when a pick-up truck pulled over.

"Hop in!" the driver said. "The parade's about to start and then you'll never get a ride!"

Strange coincidence…

Many strange things had happened already this summer of ice and snow—languid backpackers unable to get to their favorite glens and meadows because of winter-like conditions in the high country, languished in the lower elevations.

And articles were appearing in the local newspapers about how the Mammoth volcano was the most likely one to come alive of any in U.S., as mysterious gases were appearing around the base of the mountain. Several times Nick had caught the ominous odor of sulfurous gas. It brought back the "Mars" short story (strange coincidence?) he had written while in the compound on Mt.Whitney, which, luckily was decidedly non-volcanic.

But here at Mammoth, some 100 miles north as the crow flies and 200 miles down the John Muir Trail, it was a decidedly different situation. And the area was quite seismically active, as well.

In fact an earthquake had happened here about ten years earlier in the Thousand Island Lakes area, rolling huge boulders down the side of Banner Peak. All together, an "active area."

But, just in time to relieve the gloom, a Highland Games Festival had come to the Mammoth Town Park—the clans and bagpipes and the folk singers and—most amazing of all—the caber tossers, who threw huge logs across the lawn. What a festival! It had reminded Nick of a medieval country fair, and just in time to refresh the spirit of folks tired of a winter which seemed to never really end.

Nick wrote a "poetic journal" about his ramblings in the mountains this summer.

He called it: "The Sierra Speaks".

The Sierra Speaks

1. Icarus Soars

>I walk up the desert way
>toward the mountain—a wall
>of sage and brush—leaping
>to fluffy clouds and blue sheen
>of desert sky
>over monarchial heights.
>Behind me now, the desert
>floor drops away as if
>someone above pulled the
>drain plug of the sage sea
>and all the sage and
>grass and rocks swirled
>away, down, down, down
>swirling down, deliriously,

and now all I have left
is the mountains before me
and the draining desert below!
Whew! What sights from the
heights—what rushes of
oasis salvation reach out
as if crying, "Put the
plug back in, I don't wish
to disappear, dissolve,
down the mad rush of your
flight to the pinnacles—up
there—up there—in the
kingdom of the sky. Forget
not the Earth in your
dash for the oxygen-less
loftiness of sunlit crag and star
crusted nights!
Forget not the Earth. You
once walked here too!"
Forget! Ah who could?
I'm just testing my wings.
Icarus taught me well!
"He fell!" you cry. Yes
he did. But (knock on wood)
not I!

2. Deluge

The snow-clad majesticness of
90 degree desert! What? I gasp.
Down in the valley, where
The lacy days of summer

Unfold one after a lazy 'nother
Where the grass already wilts
Under the blaze of the sky,
One looks up to see the
White mountains of the Sierra
To the magical west, where
Water walls gush and torrents
Roll, where thick coats
Of snow still cling to
Their seats of power
Or to the Sierra of the White
Mountains to the east—
The desert peaks too still
In ice-mantle—Happy
Fourth of July, y'all!
The fireworks happened
Last winter—the floods
Made inland seas of the
Western lowlands
And the history making
Deluge did not stop
Until Noah's Ark came to
Rest atop Mt. Whitney!

3. All the Beautiful Stars

All the beautiful stars are out tonight
Framed by dark bows of pine
Like ghosts they swirl out of sight
Just like in Van Gogh's mind—

All the beautiful stars are out tonight

They're lovely—and they love us so
All we have to do is treat them right
And it's heavenly here below—

Yes, all the beautiful stars are out tonight
You can count them one and all
Connect the dots above the mountain peaks
Before the mountains fall.

4. Portrait of a Desert Sea
Now before and below me
Across the gray sage
And green/red sentinels
Of pine, strewed across
The Sierra hills,
The valley, the long valley
Opens where worlds collide,
The watercolor scene of the
White Mountains across the
Desert floor, rising
Like earth-whales
Out of a sea of sage
And buoy-like poplar trees.
The watercolor dark-white
Cumuli clouds float
Like—well, like—like clouds!
And watercolor lacy
Sheets of desert rain
Cool the whale's back
Then! a lightning harpoon
Shatters like a tinker toy

Tossed at Moby Dick!

5. You shaped valley

> God—did You shape this valley?
> This U shaped glacial masterwork
> Of snow-sheeted rocky spirals
> That glissade "glacierfully"
> Down to the tiny green
> Postage-stamp of a meadow—
> From which fingers of
> Summer—yes summer!—snow
> Reach achingly up to
> The white draped
> Traverses beneath the
> Battle tested crags of
> Unearthly splendors.
> Norman Clyde walked
> With You, as he climbed
> More Sierra peaks for
> First ascents than anyone
> In those achingly pure
> Days of the early century—
> Before wilderness permits
> Or hunting seasons, of
> Need for hiking quotas.
> You were closer then
> Weren't You?
> But You're here now, too
> Hovering over Clyde Peak
> And the valley You shaped.

6. The Sierra Society

    Uncle John wants you!

John Muir's ghost

Still walks these hills

His words are ringing yet

He wants you too

To join his cause

The Sierra Society—you bet!

The Sierra Society

Where all who dare

Will walk untrummled, he said

A few good men

And women too!

Who walk where angels tread!

Up to those lofty, lofty heights

Where clouds have their domain

Where eagles of gold

Still soar so bold

And silver sprinkles rain!

The Sierra Society wants You!

7. So there!

    I could be down in the town below

I could be weary and blue

Thinking about all those important things

And particularly about "you know who."

But instead I'm up here in the mountains

Where purple violets line my path
And little yellow marigolds talk to the sky
And bluebirds sing in a waterfall bird-bath!

Yes I could be down in the valley
Where people talk all day at a roar
Or sit forever before their MacIntoshes
Eating apples to the core*

So instead I'm up here in the Sierra
Where even the dirt is clean
And the only time you're ever sad
Is if you rip your jeans!

Yes I could be down in the town
My tears falling like a sad clown
But instead I'm up here.
So there!

*Don't get me wrong—
I married a computer too
On which I wrote the GAN
But making love to my IBM
Is not my idea of FUN!

8. Frosting Lake
Finally, after a grand prologue
of desert rising to mountain
loftiness, I am in the
Alps—the Palisades—
alpine perfection rising

out of a lake still
covered in blue/white ice
melting where the
waterfall gushes
from snowy walls of
white frosting—
Icing dripping down to
meld with the
slowly thawing water.
And above, The Crag
arches in graceful
perfection, while
here on a rock as I
sit writing, a tiny
chipmunk scampers.
Blue of sky meets
white of cairn,
faint, faint laces of
cirrus icing
floating above
Frosting Lake.

9. Milk and Honey
Liquid ice flows in
Ecstatic rushes
Down the stream
From Icing Lake.
I drink the
Bubbles of champagne
I taste the
Milk and Honey

Snowfall 200%
A cold spring
Suddenly it's
Summer! 90 degrees
And all the snow
Is melting fast.
Fast, fast, the
Milk and Honey
Liquid ice
Rushes gladly,
Gladly free of
The bondage of
Eternal winter,
Living water
Leaping for joy
In such display
Of water power
As never before
Seen since the
Summer of
Creation!

10. Puffball Clouds
Puffball clouds
down in the
valley—a scene
from Zane Grey—
rising to heights
like a mountain
covered with

Himalayan snow
(Zane Grey in Tibet).
The mountain
moves, takes shape,
grandly floating,
now like some
sailing schooner
from the stars,
sails catching wind.
Now sailing, now
flying, the
cloud hovers
over the valley,
across the
Owen's Sea.

Puffball clouds
which Mother
Nature uses to
put Her
make-up on:
Her pastels and
golds and
oranges and pinks and
grays and reds
and blues and silvers and…

11. Glen "Livitt" Pass
Ah! The view from Glen Pass
is like good Scotch:
sublime, delicious,

intoxicating,
mellow, the snowy
peaks like ice
cubes, "on the
rocks," as they say,
and even though I
drink my Glen
Fiddich straight,
for this ceremony
of living life
to the fullest,
drink the draught
to those who toil
up those infinite
switch backs carved
into solid rock out
of the steep side
of a stony
Glen—a toast!
Look out over
the view to the
north, where you
wearily made your
way through those
icebergs.
A toast! to you and
Me and Glen!

11. Norman Climbed!
    Norman Clyde
    climbed and climbed

and climbed.
His pretty, dear wife
died when she was
young. She went to
Heaven—and so
did he—into the
Sierra to climb
every peak he could
see, in the early
days of the century.
And right on through
to yesteryear, climbing
more peaks than all
the rest. Day after
wondrous day he
hardly ever took
a rest from carrying
his 2 ton pack with
books of Greek and
anvil for his sturdy
twenty lace!
hobnail boots and
guns and fishing
gear and everything
of which he might think
except, of course,
the kitchen sink!
Norman "Superman"
Clyde flew over
mountains with
a single bound!

and then he flew
'round and 'round
as if angel wings
grew from the
sturdy back
which carried his
jet pack!
Norman climbed as
if his life
had "slipped the
surly bonds of
space" in the words
of some other poem—
the poem of the
unknown pilot who
"reached out and
touched the face of
God."
Norman Clyde just
As surely flew—
and climbed and
climbed and climbed!

12. The Highland Trail
   Up
   The Highland Trail
   The High trail
   —as it is known around here.
   You take the
   Vail trail
   And I'll take the

Highland Trail
And I'll get to Scotland
'fore ye will.
Aye, me bonnie lass
Will you come with
Me—where wild
Mountain Thymes
Bloom along the
Spring decorated path
Leading on to the
Home of the
Twin gods of
Ritter and
Banner,
Looming like lofty
Friends
Greeting a long
Tarrying wayfarer from
The vale of tears—
Where Bob Dylan's
Sad-eyed lady of
The low-lands entices
With her nuptial
Charms and her
Celtic drum.
But you welcome
Me back with
Open arms—and
The snow melts
Slow this year, like
The first year of the

New Ice-age, just
Over the hill from wooly
Mammoth! And to
The west, the
Keawahs bask in the
Sun, weaving their
White frocks and
Waving smiling
Fingers toward the
Higher still mountains
Of the crest to
The east and
Then to the east
Roll like one
Strand of waves
Onto another
Larger current,
As if waiting to
Cascade down
And deluge the
Town below!
The creeks are high
This summer,
The white caps ready
To pounce like snow
Panthers on the
Daydreaming hamlet…

But the piper band
Marches in the town square,
The caber tossers in their

Red plaid kilts
Toss the trees across the
Lawn—The clans parade and
The red-haired girl sings
Scottish songs of love in
The First Annual Eastern
Sierra Highland Gathering—The
World's Highest Highland games!

13. Shadow Lake
I scrambled up the steep
green slope, green from
the weight of too much
(200% "two much") snow,
sagebrush like heather
this summer, this strange, strange
summer of snow covered
peaks and frozen lakes!
But across the glacial valley,
Shadow Lake is thawed,
sitting in the perpetual SUN
rays, which collide off
its rocky cistern, holding
the water like an ornate
bathtub! The most ornate
beautiful cold-tub ever
designed, as if prepared
for a God or
Goddess to ease themselves
into and then gaze
dreamily up to the white

marble-crusted Minarets
standing like gothic
spires—art work for a
king—and the Picasso-
like sculptures of the
two peaks of Ritter and
Banner—out of his
Cubist period no doubt—
Priceless masterpieces…
And the luxuriating
God or Goddess reclining
in Shadow Lake must
feel very—clean.

14. Rainbows Falls
　　Rainbow Falls flows over
　　Its rocky, striated
　　Cup of streaked rock
　　Flinging water droplets
　　Everywhere this year of
　　Eternal spring—heaviest
　　Snow pack in 100 years!
　　And the rainbows at
　　Rainbow Falls are out in
　　Profusion! Rainbows,
　　Rainbows—everywhere.
　　A rainbow here—a rainbow
　　There. Rainbows all
　　Around you. See the
　　World's greatest display
　　Of rainbows! Step

Right this way! Come
One! Come all! To
Rainbows Falls!

15. The Enchanted Valley
So I got tired
fightin' the sno' in the
high country and came
on down to the
enchanted Valley itself—
Yosemite Valley, where
the waterfalls crash as
never before in the
middle of Augustian summer!
Yosemite Falls, as John Muir
once said, is a revelation
of water dancing and
dashing down the perfect
cliffs. I could find
no words to describe this
awesome sight, except to
say, "There's God!"
So I decided to run
the trail to the
top, 3 miles straight up!
Early, early morning, cool
and clean, I skip
breakfast and run up
the switchbacks (most of
them, anyway, the others
I fly up) and get to

where the upper falls
are pouring like white
wine. "It was a very
good year," I say to
myself, as the bottle
is poured over the
cliffs into the lower
two falls, where the earth,
dry from two many
lean years, greedily drinks
in the intoxicating
bubbles, and I too feel
the effects of the effervescent
spray, thinking, "This
is the best year for white
water you'll see," then
spring on up the trail,
running, flying on to the
top, where the gushing,
still flooding! Yosemite
creek gracefully cascades
over the falls, the dancing
falls of Yosemite!
Now, down in "Mellow Meadow,"
I sit writing poetry, and
looking to the white ribbon of
the drunken falls of
Yosemite, while to my right,
Half Dome rises like the
Half Moon, its scoured wall
looking for all the world

as if some mighty
Awanee Indian of ancient
times gazed up into
the sky, had decided
two moons was one too many
for our night (made it too
light—hard to sleep) and brought
the moon's twin brother down
to earth and hid it in the
most isolated beautiful place
he knew—His own home
of Yosemite!
Climbing on the moon
is what the hearty souls do
here when they dangle suspended
in space from Half Dome's
sheer moon-like expanse...
Climbing on the moon!

I recall now my own
climb, in Wyoming, when
we pitoned our way up
the straight, strong rock
of the lofty Grand,
up the regal Teton,
a mountain climb
of the highest kind,
where sunrays sparkled off
rock so true, it seemed

to lift one in wings of
light. I wonder at
the wall scurriers—is it
really mountaineering?
But who am I to judge
another's dream?

Then—I ran up the Vernal-
Nevada falls trail—up the
Mist—where those two
Grand waterfalls display
Their might and beauty
In graceful, awesome perfection,
Pacing myself to get to the
Top of the mystic Nevada Falls,
Water flowing in such
Majesticness as to make
One gasp—which I
Do –and finally I am
At the top of the falls
Looking over into the
Intoxicated
Enchanted Valley.

And at the other end—
El Capitan! Whom not even
Glaciers could move from

His post—The Captain! Standing
As if he could hold back
Time itself! Indomitable!
And on the wall, microscopic
Climbers bravely make their
Way up this greatest
Of Cliffs—which the Awanee
Thought would keep out
The white man! As I look
Around, I see they were wrong.
But the captain has not
Left the sinking ship.
Will he steer
Yosemite clear?
Will the sailors
Mutiny? Time has crept
Its way into the Enchanted
Valley—and only time will tell…

16. Spirit Hike to Mono Lake
I made my way up to Tuolome
And left the Enchanted Vale
But the singing falls of Yosemite
In my mind will surely avail
Themselves to me, to endlessly reveal
The sure, eternal mystery
Of the Spirit's medicine to heal
The tired soul in minutes of repose—
In Wordsworths' own immortal song—
Sweet Nature's symphony to compose!

I flew on past the sculptured marble,
Grand statues of abstract spires
Along the shores of Lake Taneya
Named for the Indian squire
Who long ago his people led
In dealing with the white man
Who long ago his people fed
When reeling from the strange new foe
Who came like Custer's legions
Who dealt a mortal blow!

I stood beside the purple highway
My backpack like a sentinel
When a pickup truck stopped beside me
And an Indian maiden so sentimental
Said, "Would you like to hike with us,
My people are now retracing
Their ancient route. Get in the bus!"
I happily accepted her invitation bold
And swung up into her pickup truck
To hike the honored route of old!

I joined the honest Indian band
Where we hiked along the holy trail.
I even got the task to drag
Three willow sticks which seemed too frail
To make the trek on up the hill
To build a holy sweat lodge
Where in the light of moonlight still
They gathered there to sweetly chant
Their timeless songs to the Spirit's kin—

Timeless power to enchant!

The meadow there was green and pure
And wind-swept clean by nature's broom
Which blew away all things unclean
And only left in nature's womb
The flowers and the trees to grow.
So nothing evil this way comes
They set sentinels all in a row
To guard the honored camping ground
And then they went into their lodge,
And passed the pipe of joy around!

And from this pipe glad songs arose
Like William Blake once sang himself
"Piper pipe songs of purest gold,"
Gold from their God—the only wealth
The holy spirit will ever coin.
And in the morrow they sang a tune
To greet the golden rays which join
The bringer of this world's dawn
And those by whom the rite was done
To leap and play like Nature's fawn!

And with the song of morning sung
While diamond rays did cross the mounts
They gathered up their humble packs
And led their horses, noble mounts,
Packed down with all their needful things
While youngsters, elders, all the tribe
Walk up the trail, clothed with the wings

Of Spirit's grace to trek once more
Across the high and lofty pass
Their ancients walked in days of yore!

Peaks on either side rose up
Like battlements of Nature's fort
And on the tips of lofty cliffs
The bighorn sheep did now cavort
And spy down at us from sentinel high.
We look up to watch them there afar
And glad I was they now survived
Just like this peaceful Indian band
Another relic from times past
Whom God had lent a helping hand!

Far up the trail we could now see
Mono Pass, which crossed the reddish rocks
Where soon we stopped beside a lake
Carved in the stone like a Scottish locke
And waterfalls did stream down madly
To feed the home of silver fish.
We laid down our packs, and I quite gladly
Conversed with a young Indian maiden
Who with her daughter, a youngster fair
With eyes of doe, did talk with souls unladen!

"At Crater Lake I make my home,"
She told me as we took our ease,
"At Oregon's priceless jeweled spring
Where Mt. Mazuma crashed and ceased
To be a mountain high and formed

From death the living waters
Which now the graceful forest so adorn
To make all who come to view and wonder
At the ageless skill of Spirit's art
To mingle blessed water with the thunder!"

We once again adorned our backpacks
And mine weighed forty pounds or more
To walk again down God's steep back path
 Carved in stone of blood which bore
The hues which named it Bloody Canyon—
Or was it named for the grim battle
When here history did abandon
Their ancient ones to foes of steel,
The white man's army in hot pursuance,
Against which no supplicant could appeal!

Down again we wound through high peaks
And there before us were such sights—
Off in the desert far below us
Mono Lake, an ocean from the heights
A piece of sky which did forsake
Its former home to float on the earth
And then another smaller lake—
Lake on lake, and above the sky
Like the spectral waters of the cosmos
And the reason we walked I now knew why!

They had trekked up from Yosemite Valley
Along a path where across the view
Half Dome like the setting Half Moon

Had lit their way, their path anew.
Young and old, all ages proudly
Had walked this path of truth and hope
Had witnessed sights proclaiming loudly
They had reasons to follow the bighorn sheep.
I too had reasons to follow this long path
Even when it dove so deep—
Even when it climbed so steep!

When they had finally hiked all the way down Mono Pass, a steep and long walk, the Indian woman and her daughter had given Nick a ride in her pickup to the shore of Mono Lake.

Nick was exhilarated! From mountain paradise to desert wonders. No question why the Indians had chosen such a path for their timeless migration—

On Mono Lake, the beautiful blue briny lake with the island in the middle where the pelicans nested, they stayed the night at a small cabin where a white friend of Diana, the Lakota Sioux girl who lived at Crater Lake with her daughter with the beautiful eyes like the eyes of some child e.t., was caretaking the cabin for his friend who as off on trail construction in Yosemite.

He had a long white beard down to his chest—an elder hippie.

After sharing some homebrew beer, which tasted like sherry, they talked about recent cosmic happenings.

"What do ya think of this space dolphin stuff?" asked Dave, jiggling his long white beard, which made him look like a desert elf. "Pretty amazing if it's true."

This was better than when Nick had been talking with someone in a bar at Mammoth over a couple of beers.

"What do you think of the Star Dolphins?" Nick had asked innocently during the course of the slightly intoxicated conversation.

"A bunch of nonsense if you ask me. Those jokers on the TV ain't got nothin' better to do than play some silly prank to get ratings up. Even the government, whom I don't usually trust, says it's all the work of computer pirates who have somehow infiltrated the airwaves."

"Personally, I believe it," Nick had said in response to both.

"Yeah. Me too," Dave said, taking a swig of homebrew.

"Ever hear about the Roswell incident?" Nick continued, looking at Dave, whose eyes were glittering.

Nick didn't wait for an answer, but enthusiastically went on saying, "As a matter of fact, I just read a book all about it…how a flying saucer had crashed in the New Mexico desert near some town named Roswell, and this 'ole cowboy riding the range came upon this strange debris. Couldn't herd his sheep through it. It happened in 1947, the year flying saucers first appeared. The government covered it up…"

"I was born in 1947," Dave smiled.

"No kiddin'! What a coincidence," said Nick excitedly.

Dave and Diana seemed to be two of the contacts Nick had been told to make. He hadn't been given any names, just instructed to seek out those who seemed sympathetic to the Star Dolphins.

"Yeah," Nick went on, looking on Dave, who sat somehow seemingly strangely serene, "they found this 'stuff' out there unlike anything from this Earth, especially in 1947. They found large pieces of metal which were virtually weightless, light as a feather. They found pieces as thin as aluminum foil which they couldn't even dent with a sledge hammer. They couldn't cut it or burn it or anything. They found stuff they could curl up in a little ball, and set it down and it would roll completely flat, no marks on it at all. They found these pieces as light as balsam wood which was impervious to everything and had strange writing on it. And then they found…"

"Yeah," Dave drawled. "Well, as a matter of fact, I have an ancient friend who lives around here who told me he was in the Army at Roswell when the whole thing happened. He saw the crash, he even saw the bodies of the creatures who were in the saucer—little guys with six fingers and big eyes. One of them was even still alive!"

Nick almost fell off his chair. He was very tired, anyhow. "Wow! A friend of yours. No kidding. What a coincidence!"

Funny, but Nick had never thought to ask the Star Dolphins about the infamous incident, but had just happened upon a newly published paperback about it in the bookstore in Mammoth Lakes.

"'Course the government covered it all up—agents threatened to actually kill people if they talked, said they'd take them out into the desert and nobody would ever see them again, deadly serious, or dock their pay, or put 'em in jail. But my friend says the wraps are about to come off. The government just can't keep it a secret much longer. It's no secret anymore, anyway," Dave said, leaning back in his chair, looking out the darkened window.

Dave stretched his arms and then slowly stood up.

"Yep. It makes ya wonder." He looked at Nick. "Ever wonder about the meaning of life, Nick?"

"Sure," Nick replied.

Dave then showed Nick a cartoon—it had an old man with a long white beard clothed in white robes standing on top of a mountain. A man was climbing up to him.

"Life," the hermit in the cartoon was saying with a bewildered expression on his face, "is just one darn thing after another."

Nick laughed. "Ah," he said. "I've been searching for the meaning of life all my life. This is the answer I've been looking for."

Diana's nine year old daughter, named Pearl because, Nick supposed, of the amazing luminosity of her e.t. like eyes, which seemed to gaze at you from some heavenly place deep within her soul, asked, just like a child, "Why is life just one darn thing after another?"

"Leave it to a little kid like Pearl to ask 'Why?'" chuckled Dave, who had been around life long enough to know there was no "easy answer" to such a question.

"Well," said Diana, who walked in from the kitchen. "I don't know the meaning of life, but I do know one thing. This home-brew beer tastes just like sherry!"

Acting Pres. Zachary, also known as Pres. Zak, had had a bad day. He knew the Star Dolphins were for real, but couldn't let the public know he knew. This morning's press conference had been a nightmare.

"Pres. Zak, are there or are there not dolphins from outer space on this planet," the old lady reporter, the one who always posed the toughest questions had asked.

"No, ma'am. There are not. This is all the work of a group of computer nerds, effete snobs you might say, who are trying to disrupt the country to push forward their own agenda."

Pres. Zak also had his own agenda. He was in close contact with the Columbian cocaine mafia to work out plans to co-ordinate all the drug syndicates in the new world to create a police state type federation in the Western Hemisphere to combat the "grinning invaders."

Pres. Zak had become acting president by pushing through an "emergency measure to constrict the constitution" to allow him as chairman of the Ways & Means committee in the House to assume "extraordinary powers to deal with the threat of internal subversion." The V.P. had suffered a nervous breakdown when (Ex.) Pres. Clark had first appeared on TV shaking hands with a Star Dolphin, and the Speaker of the House, next in line to become President, had declared "The Dolphin King would make a great President in my view," and had been promptly arrested for "sedition and treason and consorting with known dolphins."

Now the entire government was in chaos, and Pres. Zak, as Ways and Means chairman, had ended up holding the reins of power. The FBI and CIA and Pentagon had gone along with him. He was the only leader left who seemed to have retained "a sense of gravity," in the words of one commentator, a man with "dollars and sense," another had proclaimed.

In short, he had become dictator. It suited him. He was "the right 'wing man' for the job," the General of the Air Force had proclaimed, a "no nonsense kind of guy," etc. etc.

He liked being dictator. First of all, he absolved congress. They had divided not along party lines, but whether they viewed themselves as "dolphins" or "sharks" and had even renamed the political parties "The Dolphins" and "The Sharks," though no one was sure which was which. The two main parties of Democrats and Republicans had simply ceased to exist, as the senators and congressman had regrouped.

The Dolphin party had, of course, immediately been outlawed as subversive by Pres. Zak, and all its members hauled off to jail as "political detainees." That left The Sharks. Pres. Zak simply told them to go home and "police your own neighborhood!"

That left Pres. Zak and the Supreme Court. The Supreme Court was in a quandary, for without a congress to pass laws for them to review, they had no jurisdiction. This went all the way back to "Marbury v. Madison."

"I suggest a recess," Pres. Zak had told the Chief Justice. "The executive wing of the government can fly just fine on its own!" (Pres. Zak had been an Air Force man.)

And there it was. The Executive Branch of the government, which now held the purse strings too with the abolition of Ways and Means and had the police and military under its reign, had accomplished a coup d'etat and were ready to meet the challenge of the "grinning invaders."

Nick and Diana and her daughter had arrived at Crater Lake. Nick had decided this was a good place to go at the present time. He had come to realize, as the two had talked, that Wizard Island in Crater Lake would be a perfect base for the Star Dolphins in the Northwest.

The setting was an ideal one—it appealed to the romantic poet in him—the image of Star Dolphins swimming around Wizard Island with a little domed "dolphin-port" delighted him. He should have written such a sci fi short story long ago!

Along the way, they had stopped at Mt. Shasta. He had some friends who lived in a hippie commune at the base of the beautiful, mystic mountain, long believed by the faithful to be the center of all contacts with anything not of Planet Earth.

His friends there did not disappoint him.

"Nick, the space dolphins have a base in the center of the mountain. They've had it there for years. We've seen their space ships come and go in the night, flashing lights—they even look like flying dolphins!"

"Yeah. They're amazing, Nick. They've got this base in a secret cavern in the mountain, where they're sending out secret messages in space sonar to people all around Mt. Shasta."

"Yeah, I got a message myself just last night. They told me you were coming here. With a beautiful babe, too! They said they have come to save Planet Earth and set up a new government based on peace and love..."

"Yeah, they're coming to bring on the New Age of Aquarius—now!"

This, thought Nick, smiling at his friends as they sat around a campfire under the sparkling stars which made a cosmic picture frame for looming Mt. Shasta above them, is more like it.

"True believers!"

Actually, it was all true. The Star Dolphins did have a "secret base" inside Mt. Shasta. And they had had it there for years, ever since the days when the Shasta Indians had been the only inhabitants of the area! With their monumental level of technology, the Star Dolphins had long ago tamed the volcanic activities of the mountain, so as to insure its stability.

And they really had been sending out secret messages in "space sonar," which was probably why there were so many "spaced out" people around the mountain.

As a matter of fact, Dr. Smith was there now! He was floating in a "rehabilitation capsule" in the Star Dolphin's laboratory
within the mountain. He was slowly being brought back to life,
for the Star Dolphins had long ago secretly typed his DNA patterns and were "rehabilitating" him. He floated semi-conscious
in a warm liquid, aware of some slight feelings. He was about to
open his mouth and utter his first sounds. "Goo goo, gah gah,"
the little baby boy finally said.

Michael was there, having flown from Mt. Whitney to Mt.
Shasta just for the occasion, vaguely remembering when the
elder Dr. Smith had hovered over him in the laboratory in Key
Largo. Now things had gone full circle. Funny, Michael thought,
looking down on the tiny baby, I thought Dr. Smith was always an
old man. He chuckled to himself.

How much does he know now, I wonder, he thought.

"Dr. Smith" was waving tiny arms at him, and then he smiled a
tiny smile. He seems so innocent, so very naïve, Michael thought.
Can this really be the sophisticated man who seemed to know
everything? Who saved my life? The baby's eyes sparkled up at
him. And what would Sharon think? Sharon was on Shine, he
knew.

Of course, Dr. Smith would not be a baby for very long. His
growth hormones would be accelerated in the rehabilitation capsule, which would automatically grow as he did, and he would
within a matter of weeks instead of years become the same Dr.
Smith Michael had first seen when coming out of the brain transplant.

Full circle, Michael thought. Dr. Smith "goo goo gah gahed"
again.

Full circle.

CHAPTER TWO
HAZEL

"This is war," Pres. Zak had said aloud when he first heard the fate of the Army battalion making its way up New Army Pass toward the fortress of the Star Dolphins atop Mt. Whitney.

He surveyed those sitting around the table—the Chiefs of Staff of the Pentagon, the top ranking officials of what still remained of the FBI and CIA—those who had not committed high treason by declaring they thought the Dolphin King should be "drafted" to be President—even emperor—and had been taken away by men in white coats—and the leaders of various crime and drug cartels who sat smiling to be sitting at the same table with officials of the U.S. government.

They were in the special bunker deep, deep underground in Colorado, the room reserved for the President and other high ranking leaders in the advent of nuclear war.

Here they hoped the Star Dolphins would not be able to use their sophisticated spying gear to eavesdrop on this Top Top Secret Emergency meeting.

Actually, they were right. Even the Star Dolphin's super sophisticated gadgetry could not penetrate this room built to withstand a direct atomic blast and lined with lead ten feet thick. Even Superman couldn't see through lead, Pres. Zak had told himself.

"I suggest nuclear weapons," said the Army Chief, "obliterate the mountain!"

"I don't think it would work, general," Pres. Zak said. "Our intelligence suggests they have energy fields capable of resisting even nuclear weapons, and the fallout would blow all across the country. No, we're going to have to be careful.

"I suggest waiting them out. Our information is that these dolphin-like space creatures are incapable of direct aggressive action toward humans. Y'know, like dolphins never bite people…not even if you try to kill them. Pretty stupid, I'd say. Any creature dumb enough as to let a human kill it when it could bite your arm off if it wanted, and not even defend itself is bound to make a mistake sometime."

"But they'll fight sharks," interjected the erstwhile leader of the Shark party.

"That's true," said Pres. Zak. "So we're going to have to be careful."

"How about, Mr. Pres.," said the Bolivian representative through his personal interpreter, "we infiltrate our newest destabilizing drug into them, you know, uh, maybe send somebody in disguised as an innocent hiker with a vial of 'happy gas.' If he could get inside their, er, compound, he could release it. The stuff makes you cuckoo. Even a tiny amount released into the air, and everybody starts singing "'Auld Lang Syne.'" Laughter. "On the Fourth of July, ha, ha," the greasy looking man laughed. "My government has been working on it for years—in conjunction with your CIA here. I even happen to have a small tube of it with me…"

The man brought out a tiny test-tube and held it up.

"I don't see anything," said Pres Zak.

"Of course you don't, Sir," chimed in the CIA chief. "It's super-concentrated, but invisible, odorless, impossible too detect. We've been trying to perfect it for years, something to covertly destabilize governments, but never could. Getting in touch with the South American drug cartels, though, made the difference. Those people got some genius chemists working for them—who provided the final missing ingredient. It's perfect. No one, not even out best chemists, can detect it, partly because it only becomes active when it's released from the vial and mixes with oxygen. In the vial it's a perfectly inert gas, like helium, but once released, well anyone trying to analyze it will begin to giggle and say inane things—for the rest of his life—ha, ha!"

"Put it away!" Pres. Zak said quickly. The Bolivian representative shrugged, and put the tiny vial, the size of a paper-clip, back in his pocket. "Ha! ha!" the man laughed through his interpreter. "There's no funny gas in there. I was just showing you how little it takes. Fooled you, though, Mr. President."

"The real stuff is safe in our lab, Mr. President," the CIA man said, chuckling slightly.

Pres. Zak looked around at his confederates. Being a male chauvinist, they were all men.

"Men," he said, "this is no time for jokes." Then he smiled broadly. "Then again, maybe it is time for a joke on these silly space dolphins. I think we have a plan. Pick the best man—no, no, let's make it a woman. They'd never suspect some pretty little thing innocently out for a hike in the mountains, would they. Find the best gal you can for the job, someone in the CIA, and train her until she'd even fool you. Then we'll let her loose on those space dolphins!"

Hazel Macelroy was not your normal pretty girl. She had been placed by the CIA as an informer against "eco-groups" in a college in the Northwest. She had nothing against trees—she just thought it was "glamorous" to be working for the CIA. She even chained herself to a tree once in a demonstration against logging in old-growth forests during the protest at Sugarloaf Mt. in southern Oregon, all the while keeping mental tabs on who showed up at the rallies, who seemed to be the leaders. She was very good at informing, and the CIA eventually took her back to Washington D.C. to train her as a full-time agent.

She was strikingly good looking. She had blonde hair and calendar girl features, and looked like she was president of her sorority at college. And, she had been president of her sorority at college—her election showed why the CIA had been right to recruit her. They had picked the right girl!

Hazel was by nature a very conservative business major type who would have done very well as secretary of the college business club. And, she had been secretary of the college business club—another triumph which proved the CIA had recruited the right girl. And there was a third triumph. She had successfully changed majors from business to organic chemistry in her senior year. She had minored in chemistry previously, thinking of starting her own pharmaceutical company when she retired from the CIA.

Hazel Macelroy was very smart though a little confused. Her parents had been East Coast hippie types, her father had had a clandestine laboratory in the basement of their home in New York City where he concocted various "potions," as he called them. This was the primary reason she had been recruited.

Her parents had been finally busted when she was just 16. In a deal with prosecutors, she had not been charged with anything in exchange for information on other neighborhood "potion" dealers.

She had proved so efficient at this job (partly because she felt betrayed by her junkie parents at a young age) that the CIA had provided her with a new name and bio, helped her kick the habit, and helped her to get accepted at a Northwest college where she majored in business and chemistry and spied on local eco-groups. Her good looks and hard bitten charm and tough determination had made her quite successful in college—as a student, as a social queen, and as a spy.

In short, Hazel Macelroy was simply too good to be true. But she was! and the CIA finally brought her back to the east coast for full-time training in domestic clandestine spying operations.

What's more, she was in good physical condition, as the agency insisted she stayed fit so she could go to eco-rallies in the mountains. She regularly worked out on her CIA bought exercise machines, while watching her favorite soaps. She was perfect for the job!

And now, Hazel had her next assignment. "A bigee, this time," she said to herself. "No more small-time eco-spying for Ms. Bitch" (she liked to call herself Ms. Bitch—made her seem more macho—particularly when she was at the CIA target practice range—as in "Good shot, Ms. Bitch. Got the _____!")

Even she did not know just quite how "big" her next assignment would turn out to be, but she knew it was "reeely big," this time.

She was to take AmTrak from Washington D.C. all the way across the country to Los Angeles and from there hitchhike up Highway 395 to Lone Pine, California, home of Mt. Whitney.

Once there she was to hike up the Whitney trail and try to get into the space dolphin compound posing as an injured hiker.

"Hitchhike?!" she had gasped when first told of the plan. "Why hitchhike?"

"These space dolphins," (the CIA chief had had to tell her there really were space dolphins, who had a base on Mt. Whitney in California) "are very advanced technologically. Who knows what spy capabilities they might have. We must be very careful. This is why you're to take the train instead of flying out there. We want you to appear as innocent, and poor, as possible. If you were to fly directly there—well these space dolphins are monitoring our air space and all air travel for all we know. They probably have hidden spy cameras above our atmosphere. Who knows what they can detect. We must be extremely clandestine. Taking the train is much less likely to attract their attention than flying. And hitchhiking out of L.A.—well you'll just look like some poor girl trying to get out of the big city, without even enough cash for bus faire. Get it?"

"But isn't hitchhiking out of L.A. dangerous?" she asked.

"Honey," the CIA man had told her, "with your training, I feel sorry for anyone who tries to molest you. We've already given you the antidote to the 'happy gas,' just in case of accident. All you got to do is pop open a vial, and anyone trying any hanky-panky with you will suddenly start singing 'Auld Lang Syne' at the top of his lungs. He'll pull over at the very next bar he sees and you just hop out. Get it?"

"Yeah, Chief. I see what you mean. It's foolproof. Can I punch him out, too?"

"Only after he's pulled over. Then sure, why not?"

The train trip for Hazel was eventful—even before the derailment.

She had a plethora of strange encounters with strange people…almost like in a Flannery O'Connor nightmare story.

Hazel hated Flannery O'Connor's stories. She had had to read them for a modern English lit elective she had taken in college. The strange, even bizarre landscapes, peopled by strange even ludicrous characters who seemed more suited to an insane asylum than real life, had actually terrified her. The story of the young man riding across the country in a train, encountering nightmarishly funny figures, had, in fact, terrified her the most. What's more, his name was Hazel!

And it seemed now to Hazel that she had entered such a carnivalesque world herself!

She had never really had a boy friend. She had had a lot of flirtatious encounters with men—her good looks made this inevitable—but the extent of her involvement with the CIA had precluded any real chance of romance. What's more, she had feelings for men which were somewhat cold—possibly, deep down, because she felt betrayed by her father. And sometimes she even wondered—just for an instant—if maybe she perhaps liked— "Oh, never!" she would gasp—after all, she had felt betrayed by her hippie mother, too.

No, Hazel was just cold, period. "Asexual, I guess," she would think to herself.

She viewed men with misgivings. They were not to be trusted. "You never know what they'll try next," she would think.

But she was always being approached by men. They were "ubiquitous," a word she liked to use and then smile at her superior intelligence. Actually, she really was smart. She had scored very high on the CIA intelligence test, which was one more reason she had been given the job of infiltrating the Star Dolphin's fortress. She was resourceful. She could certainly outthink most of the men who came on to her, but they were a "nuisance." She had to be totally involved in the mission, and even her "trainer" had told her to "keep your pretty little mind on your work."

She loved her work. Clandestine operations were a thrill for her, the challenge of outwitting a foe on his or her own turf.

But these guys who kept approaching her on the train! Everybody seemed a little strange these days. Everyone had an opinion, one way or the other, about the "dolphins from outer space."

"They are so real!"

"They are not!"

The conversation on the matter would get heated often as not. People all around her on this train were having the same "discussion." Even when a man sat down by her to make a pass, the conversation would get around to the man saying, "And how about those space dolphins, huh? And what do you think about it, my dear?" ("Your dear, my ___," Hazel would think.)

Unlike the rest of the passengers—unless there were agents here and there—Hazel knew the truth: the space dolphins were definitely for real. But she had signed a strict oath—like the government employees in the Roswell incident—to never tell anyone what she knew.

She wouldn't have anyway, even without the "silly 'ole oath." Hazel didn't trust anyone these days. Everyone seemed to be one glass of sherry over their limit!!

"You know," she said to one man who approached her, "I think you're drunk."

The man in a western shirt and cowboy hat had been saying in a thick southern drawl, "Funny thing about these here space dolphins, though ma'am, they seem to know a lot more about us than our government, who's 'sposed to be protectin' us from extraterristral species, knows about them. Like this Robby kid who's on TV all the time. I mean, he looked right at me one time and said, 'Billy'—my names' Bill, by the way, right glad to meet ya—he said, 'Billy, you're lookin' a little worried out ther. You've got a mortgage to pay and alimony to pay, and you're wonderin' wher the 'ole money is a comin' from, ain't ya?'

"Although, ma'am, he didn't say 'ain't.' Nope. He talked more like one of them ther movie actors, you know, uh like Tyrone Power, ma'am, the young good lookin' one with the deep voice. Yeah, Tyrone Power. Boy, they don't make movie actors like him nomore do they? Remember him, ma'am, in the *Captain from Castille* and those swashbucklin'sword duels. Yes sir, ma'am, they don't make movies like them kind no more.

"Anyway, as I was asayin', ma'am, wasn't I? Robby looked right at me and then he said, 'Santa Claus is goin' to be real good to you this year, 'ole Billy boy.' And you know what? I was out prospectin' for gold down in Texas and I found me a…"

"I think you're drunk," Hazel interrupted. She stood up. "Excuse me, but it have to rearrange my makeup."

She walked to the lady's room, where a woman was changing a diaper on her baby. Hazel looked into the mirror at the attractive face before her, and took out her lipstick.

"You'd think the whole world's gone crazy!" the young mother said out of thin air. "Even my eldest can't talk about anything else except…space dolphins. What I don't understand is, if it's for real, where are the space dolphin Saturday morning cartoon shows, or the space dolphin lunch boxes of the space dolphin whatevers. If they're real, they'd have all this stuff wouldn't they?"

"You're absolutely right," said Hazel, smacking her pretty lips on a piece of tissue. "So obviously, there's nothing to it, is there?" She smiled at the nervous mother and walked out, this time toward the view car.

The entire trip had been like this. "What next," she wondered. She sat down in the view car, looking overhead to the clouds going by the windows above her. They were in Arizona now. The wide expanse of nothingness rolled by, flat spaces of sun parched sage and cacti and Joshua trees...

They were nearing a trestle over a river bed. Suddenly there was a jolt! The train had derailed! They were about to plunge into the dry river bed when Hazel looked up to see a brilliant white light above the roof-top windows. Then the train was suspended in mid-air. Everyone was screaming and yelling, except Hazel. Her extensive training came into play, and she merely sat very still, observing the scene.

The pulsing light seemed to engulf the car now, and then the train landed over so gently on the other side of the gorge. Then the light disappeared.

Soon people were walking around bewildered outside the train. It was still on the tracks! Behind them could be seen where the track had been derailed.

"What happened?" people said in unison.

"Did you see it? The bright light?"

"My God, the train derailed!"

"We all could have been killed!"

Hazel was confused...again. She knew, of course, what had happened. Her quick mind had easily assessed the situation. The AmTrack had been derailed—an act of sabotage—an all too common happening these days it seemed—and the Star Dolphins had miraculously prevented a catastrophe. Just like Superman! the level of technology necessary to ensure such a smooth landing on the tracks on the other side momentarily dazed even her.

The Star Dolphins had saved her life. She felt she should be grateful, but she had a job to do.

"It was the space dolphins!" someone suddenly called out. "They saved us all."

"Ah, maybe they caused it," sneered another.

"Then you admit they exist," said a third.

"Ah, who knows. Maybe it was Pecos Bill," the man grumbled, walking off.

Hazel was now beginning to be concerned. She had taken the train, her superiors had told her, to elude the scrutiny of the space dolphins. But were they on to her mission anyway? She wondered.

But she'd continue as if the saving of the train had nothing to do with her—just a strange coincidence.

After about 15 minutes, the conductor called out, "All aboard!" and everyone got back on the train.

The train continued down the track, just as if nothing had happened. Now began the strangest past of all—most people acted as if absolutely nothing had occurred!

"Beautiful day, ain't it miss," the cowboy, who had followed her back to the view car said to her. "It was good to get out and stretch for a bit back there, weren't it."

Hazel looked at him aghast.

"Right beautiful country around here," he continued to drawl. "Right pretty—like you, ma'am," he said, doffing his Stetson.

Other people were watching the view go by, as if nothing out of the ordinary had occurred at all.

Hazel felt she had entered an upside down "Through the Looking Glass" world. She knew something very strange had just happened. Had everyone else simply put it out of their mind, unable to deal with such an event? She was so focused on her mission, she certainly would not forget. Not her!

Finally, she looked up at the cowboy. "____ off! fella!" she said.

"Why ma'am, I was jest…"

Hazel quickly stood up and struck him sharply in the solar plexus. The man instantly crumpled. When he finally straightened back up, he doffed his cowboy hat again, and said, "Nice day, ma'am," and smiled and turned and walked off.

Hazel sat back down and glared out the window.

From the L.A.train depot, Hazel easily hitched a ride to the town of Lone Pine…where the man had pulled over at the very next bar, singing "Auld Lang Syne" at the top of his lungs.

Hazel now knew the stuff worked—and the antidote.

"Like a charm, Ms. Bitch," she thought, then crumpling the man to the dirt.

Hazel felt a slight twinge of remorse. The man had been a perfect gentleman. But she was so curious about the "happy gas."

"So long, sucker," she sneered.

She got her backpack out and walked over to the road leading up to Mt. Whitney. At least she didn't have to worry about a wilderness permit these days!

She stood in the shade with her thumb out and in moments she had a ride.

"Yeah, I'm as curious as the next guy," the man was saying "about these supposed space dolphins."

As they were going past the Alabama Hills, Hazel suddenly said, "Stop! Turn here, and I'll make it worth your while, sailor."

The car turned onto the dirt road, spewing up dust. She had just then remembered her boss telling her that some big-shot Hollywood director was filming a movie at the base of Mt. Whitney, called "The Grinning Invaders." She was surprised, and pleased they were still here. In the distance she saw a bunch of people standing around movie cameras. "Stop here!"

"Thanks for the ride, sailor."

"Hey, sister, I thought…"

Hazel immediately let out some "happy gas" from a vial. "May ol' acquaintances be forgot…" the man started singing, and immediately turned around and headed back for Lone Pine. "Same bar as the other nerd, I hope," Hazel said with a laugh.

When asked if she was to disrupt the filming, her boss said, "Nah. If they make a movie of it, nobody will believe it anyway!" She hauled her pack over to the man sitting in the director's chair.

"I'm an actress," she said with her best plastic smile. "Need an extra extra?" She giggled at her joke.

"An extra extra, ha, ha," the director laughed. "Extra extra, read all about it—dolphins from space invade planet Earth." He looked at Hazel. "Sure kid, with a sense of humor like yours and your pretty face, we can use you."

"You've been filming here a long time now, haven't you?" inquired Hazel, curious as to what the man might know that could be useful to her in her mission.

"Yeah, we gotta finish this film if it kills us. Which it might. It'll be the smash hit of the year—if we can ever get it done. You see, my dear, these space dolphins like to play little practical jokes on us. I guess they think it's just a riot when they make our cameras go backwards suddenly, or our night lights blink off and on at a critical moment. Not only that, they even abducted our leading lady and flew her off into the sky toward Mt. Whitney."

"No kidding," Hazel said.

"No kidding—we got it on film!"

"Hey—can I be leading lady," Hazel suddenly asked.

"Sorry, kid, we got a replacement already. Say, you wouldn't happen to be a stunt person, would you? Our last stunt lady got hurt last week on a climbing scene."

"No kidding," said Hazel, who had been trained intensively in mountaineering for her eco-terrorist surveyance jobs in the mountains—as a way of convincing paranoid EarthFirst types—particularly after one of their leaders was seriously injured by a car bomb—that she was who she said she was. She had been given an intensive refresher climbing course specifically for this mission, in upstate New York.

"As a matter of fact, I am," said Hazel. She was thinking fast now. This might be the perfect way to get up the mountain without unduly drawing suspicion on herself. She was just the stunt girl. What a stroke of good luck, she thought.

Then she had another thought.

"Did the space dolphins cause the girl to fall?"

"I don't think so. As a matter o' fact they rescued her and took her up to their compound! She radioed down to us, said they were taking very good care of her, not to worry, and she would be all right in a few days. We haven't heard from her since, though."

Hazel gasped. "They took her inside?"

"Yep. Sure enough did. This guy flew down on a horse with wings, leading another one of the creatures, and put her on it, and off they flew. Just like when they abducted our leading lady.

Got the whole thing on film! What a movie this is going to be—If we can ever finish it."

"Can I have the job?" immediately asked Hazel.

"You got it, little lady," the director grinned.

Hazel now had a plan. It was risky—but she was committed. "To an insane asylum," she grimly thought.

For the movie they wanted the most spectacular climbing sequence they could have. Up the 5.8 technical route on the sheer east face of Whitney. Hazel had had enough climbing experience where she felt she could fake an accident and hang in her harness from the climbing rope, feigning unconsciousness. She would carefully place her piton so as to insure it would hold her, climb up a few feet above it, and then pretend to slip—and slide down the rock to where the piton (hopefully) would hold her suspended. She just hoped the Star Dolphins were observing today.

She made her way expertly up the sheer cliffs, unmindful of the spectacular view below her. "Well," she said, when she got to a smooth, isolated place on the rock. "Here goes." She let go her grip, and slipped down the rock. Debris rolled down after her and one good sized rock hit her on her climbing helmet, and her head bounced into the wall, and she really was unconscious!

She dangled there in her climbing harness, while people scurried below.

Suddenly! Vic repelled over the side, down from the top of Whitney!

Vic Adams had been watching the grey whales and the killers and the dolphins from his view atop the old light house. He finally put the binoculars away, and as the sun went down, he prepared his dinner and waited for the stars to come out. He wondered if there would be another shower like last night, when meteors had streamed down across the sky like a spill from the Milky Way!

As it got dark, and more and more stars appeared, he looked up out the window to see if any "fell."

Then he saw one move! It went straight up—then it went straight down—Then it went zigzag!

"What..."

This was hardly your typical meteor. Now he heard faint music—like whistling.

"Oh boy..."

Next, a bright light illuminated the old light house from above!

"Whoa..." breathed Vic.

Then he had blanked out.

When he awoke, he was lying on a table, with soft glowing lights around him. He slowly opened his eyes: forms of humans stood above him. He would have said something, but didn't know what to say. The whole thing was too amazing for words. First the zigzagging star, moving in the sky like no Earthly flying machine could move, then the light from above, transforming the old abandoned light house into a real light house again! And now here he was lying on a table in an oval room with smiling people around him.

Vic blinked his eyes—and then simply smiled back. No words were spoken...but he understood now what was happening. "I'm a UFO abductee," he thought, "and I'm surrounded by other abductees…and they're all smiling!

"Nothing to get concerned about, Vic 'ole boy," he told himself. "Just relax and enjoy the ride."

Vic repelled down and reached the unconscious girl. He attached a tiny anti-gravity generator to her, and easily towed her up the cliff and over the summit. He then lifted her up and carried her past the two neighing tethered gliders and into the glittering opal compound, where Star Dolphins swam around their canals, viewing their various computer monitors, so absorbed in their work they didn't even seem to notice them.

Vic carried Hazel into his own room and laid her on a couch. She started to come to. "Oh, oh, my head," she moaned. Vic took off her climbing helmet and examined her skull.

"Can you move?" he asked.

Hazel started moving her head up and down and back and forth and then flexing her arms and legs.

"Yes," she said. Her eyes came open with a start. She looked around at the softly glowing lights. "Where am I? Who are you?"

"You're on the summit of the mountain, ma'am," Vic smiled.

"You mean…I'm in the space dolphin fortress," Hazel blurted.

"Yes, ma'am. Now just take it easy. I think you're all right— just knocked a little silly."

Hazel grinned up at Vic. "I'm actually in…" she said.

"Yes, ma'am. Here you are!"

Hazel sat up. This had worked out better than she had even hoped for. Here she was! Perfect.

She looked around the oval shaped room. Then she noticed 3D paintings on the wall…dolphins swimming in what looked like liquid opal. She gazed at one, instantly mesmerized. She felt like a mermaid! drawn into the almost depthless image and a feeling of peace came over her like she had never felt. She was almost ready to abandon herself to these luscious feelings, when her well-hued instincts, enforced by much training, came back into play, and Hazel remembered her mission—why she was here—not to cavort with the enemy! no matter how enticing but to sabotage them! Evidently, the gas hidden in her special pockets had passed any detector! She pulled her thoughts together, thinking quickly. She musn't tip this guy off as to her real identity, but she musn't succumb to the intoxicating powers of the paintings, either. She closed her eyes.

"Wow," she said. "When do I get a look around?"

"After you've rested, ma'am."

Another part of her mission was to get as much information as to the comings and goings of the space dolphins—how they went about their work, etc.,etc.—before she released the "happy gas"—so she could gather as much intelligence as possible on how they worked—"And then zap them, Ms. Bitch," she said to herself, chuckling inside, satisfied with her determination to carry out her job. She was, after all, a trained scientist, a qualified observer. This was another reason she had been given the "mission of the century," as she had come to view her assignment.

"Assignment bezerko!"

"When do I get to have a look around the place," Hazel asked nonchalantly as she drank of strange but nice smelling "tea." "And what is this stuff. Tastes good."

"Seeweed tea, ma'am. It'll restore your strength."

"I already feel completely recovered." Which was true. She made a mental note about the tea.

"Then come on," said Vic, standing.

He smilingly offered her his hand, which Hazel begrudgingly accepted.

They walked out into the main control room, where the Star Dolphins were very seriously swimming around in their canals, viewing their myriad of computers. Hazel watched, open mouthed. So here were the space dolphins! In the middle of the room pulsed the holographic Earth.

Hazel pointed to it. "What's this?"

"The most amazing thing you ever saw in your life. It's the Earth!"

"A replica of the Earth," said Hazel.

"A real replica. And it has a view screen that's like a window on the world, so you can look down any place an' actually see what's happening there."

"Are you kidding? Can I have a peek?"

"No. I'd let you have a look for yourself, but I'm not qualified to program the microviewer, and as you can see, the Star Dolphins are too busy to stop and Michael's not here right now…"

"Michael?"

"Yeah. Dr. Michael Hope. He and Michelle, his granddaughter, are off in the Star Dolphin's secret base inside Mt. Shasta."

Oho, thought Hazel. A secret base inside Mt. Shasta. That must be why they have all those weirdos around there.

"Who are these people?" asked Hazel.

"Dr. Michael Hope is the one who had the dolphin brain transplant years ago. He's the one who first established telepathic contact with the Star Dolphins. Or, I should say, they established contact with him."

Hazel researched her memory. Dr. Michael Hope. She recalled something in the CIA records of all dolphin cases handled by the agency. This one was the top secret case of the scientist assassinated covertly on a beach at Bermuda.

"You mean he's alive," asked Hazel incredulously.

"Very much so," said Vic.

She'd make a note. "And Michelle is the young girl who was on TV?"

"Correct." She'd make another note.

"I'm afraid," said Vic, "this is all I can show you. The power room is off limits even to me."

"I see," said Hazel.

He escorted her back to his room. "Pretty impressive, huh."

"Yeah," said Hazel.

"By the way," said Vic. "I'm Vic. In all the excitement, you haven't told me who you are."

"You hadn't asked," Hazel replied. "I'm Jane."

"Jane…"

"Doe. By the way, is the other girl still here, the other one you rescued."

"Yep. What a coincidence! Both you girls winding up here. She's still recuperating. She'll be perfectly all right soon, though. These Star Dolphins are amazing healers, Miss Doe. Well… Jane..I sure am happy to meet you." He put his arm around her. "Now don't you worry about a thing."

Vic was rolling around laughing on the floor, as Hazel stood up from the couch. She clasped the next vial of "happy gas" and walked out into the control room, where the Star Dolphins seemed oblivious to her presence.

She felt a slight pang of regret. But not for very long. She uncorked the tube.

Suddenly, the Star Dolphins stopped swimming and looked over at her. Those eyes on her almost made her swoon, but she held steady.

Then—all the Star Dolphins now began doing flips and cartwheels! just like her CIA boss had predicted: The Star Dolphins were turning into show dolphins! just like at Marineland, except—they had hands instead of flippers. This fact made their flips and jumps and dives somewhat less than perfect, but nonetheless impressive. "Put these uppity dolphins back in their place," her boss had said.

"Now, if I only had a bucket of fish for you," she laughed. "But now I gotta get out of here."

She ran for the hatch door, but to her surprise, she was unable to unlock it! Hazel was really surprised she hadn't considered this possibility in the first place. She had been so intent on doing her job, she hadn't even thought if she's be able to get out once it was done.

And now here she was—trapped!

Michael had called back to the Whitney Castle from Shasta, looking at the viewer at the unbelievable scene inside. The Star Dolphins, who never cavorted about, were doing flips and cartwheels! He couldn't believe his eyes. What was happening?

White Dolphin, who had left Mars, looked on too from his water capsule, with Michelle standing nearby. "What's going on?" Michael said.

"I have absolutely no idea," said White Dolphin.

They looked on, with mouths open, at the cavorting Star Dolphins, who always kept a decorum about them. In fact this was one of the crucial differences between them and Earth Dolphins, who always seemed to be cavorting happily. The Star Dolphins were almost somber by comparison.

"What should we do," asked Michael.

"I think..." White Dolphin said, "it's time to awaken Dr. Smith."

"But he's only 10 years old by now," Michael said.

"True," said White Dolphin. "But he still knows more than any of us do about such aberrant behavior, since he was, or I should say is, a psychiatrist, too."

True, thought Michael. Among his many other skills, Dr. Smith had also been a licensed psychiatrist.

"OK," said Michael. "Let's do it."

10 year old Dr. Smith looked up at them from out of the capsule. "What's happening," he asked. "Why am I being disturbed?"

"We have an emergency, Dr. Smith," said Michael. "Do you recognize me."

"Yes. You're Dr. Michael Hope. What's the emergency?"

"You'll have to come and see for yourself."

Young Dr. Smith looked quietly on the strange scene.

"Yes. This is quite serious." He walked over to a whirring mega-computer and inputted some data. He looked at the results on the three dimensional holo-screen, and suddenly turned to them and said, "Sabotage!"

"Sabotage!" the three said at once.

"Yes. Sabotage. Someone, somehow has introduced a gas into Star Castle, which has caused the Star Dolphins to become like Earth's show dolphins. They're doing the kinds of tricks they would do for a trainer at Marineland."

They all looked at the screen.

"What do we do," asked Michael.

"Well, first," said Dr. Smith, again walking to the computer, "I have to figure out an antidote—if there is one."

Finally, Dr. Smith discovered the molecular structure of the "happy gas." Then it was just a matter of time before the genius with an IQ of 180 figured out the antidote. "Luckily, there is one. Now I administer it to all of us, except you White Dolphin, who'd be better off here, and, we go to Star Castle."

"Is it foolproof, Dr. Smith," Michael asked, looking at his granddaughter.

"Absolutely," said Dr. Smith.

They arrived quickly at Star Castle, and entered. The Star Dolphins were still doing their circus stunts in the canals, the computers making strange whining sounds from hours of neglect.

As Dr. Smith administered the antidote to the Star Dolphins, Michael and Michelle searched throughout the compound for other victims.

Michelle walked into Vic's room. She found Vic on the floor, giggling and singing "The Star Spangled Banner," very off key. With him, also laughing and carrying on as if she were at the final game of the World Series, was a pretty young lady. Hazel Macelroy! Her antidote had finally wore off, and she, too had succumbed to the "happy gas."

"My goodness," gasped Michelle. Dr. Smith entered the room, followed by Michael. The antidote was quickly administered, and soon the unlikely pair were sitting quietly on the floor, shaking their heads.

"What happened?" groggily said Vic.

Michael sat down by Vic. "Sabotage. Somebody…" Michael warily looked at Hazel, "drugged you. Dr. Smith…" he pointed at the young boy, "found the correct antidote and administered it to both of you. You're all right now."

"And the…Star Dolphins?" quickly asked Hazel.

"They're fine, too."

Hazel almost felt relieved.

Dr. Smith looked intently at Hazel. "Who's she," he asked

Vic said, "This is, uh, Jane. Jane Doe. I rescued her on the wall of the mountain. She had a climbing accident—like the other girl."

Dr. Smith peered at "Jane." "Your name's not really Jane, is it…Jane."

Hazel shook her head. The "happy gas" had succeeded in curtailing some of her intensive training, along with the effects of the magical paintings still smiling at her from the opal walls.

"No." She felt an overwhelming desire to confess completely as to her mission. "My name is Hazel Macelroy. I was specially trained by the CIA to infiltrate your compound and attempt to sabotage your operations."

She brought out the remaining vials of "happy gas." She handed them to Dr. Smith. "Here's the rest of the 'happy gas.'"

Young Dr. Smith took the vials and peered into them closely. "Amazing. Totally invisible. An absolutely inert gas, which I would guess, only reacts when it mixes with oxygen."

Hazel nodded. "Right. It's a super-secret, destabilizing gaseous compound, designed by the CIA, in conjunction with South American drug cartel chemists" (Hazel had gleaned this information from clandestine research of her own) "designed to sabotage an enemy—in this case you. I was to gain entry to your compound here and administer it. I did so," she said somewhat proudly.

Vic looked at her with open mouth. "You sure fooled me," he said. "You really were knocked out when I rescued you on the mountain."

"I hadn't exactly planned that part," she said a little sheepishly. "But it worked like a charm," (Ms. Bitch, she thought.)

"I realize now, though," she went on, "I was wrong. You people…and dolphins" (she quickly added) "are really quite nice. I would like to make it up to you." To her utter surprise, she was sincere. "How about me working for you as a double agent?"

"I was thinking exactly the same thing," Dr. Smith said. "Of course I'd have to give you a special lie detector test to check on the sincerity of your, er, repentance and conversion to, uh, dolphinism," the young boy said, searching carefully for the right words.

"What a nifty idea," said Michelle, smiling at Hazel, who found herself becoming fond of the young lady who was, in some ways, not all that different from herself, like a potential "girl-friend."

"I even have a plan," said Hazel, thinking quickly, finding herself suddenly feeling betrayed by the CIA, having the same negative thoughts about them she once reserved for her parents. She looked again at Michelle.

She looked at young Dr. Smith. "Do you think you could create, with your vast technology here, a variation of 'happy gas', which would not be affected by this antidote?"

Dr. Smith thought for a moment. "Yes, I'm sure it could be done," he finally said.

"And its own antidote?"

Dr. Smith thought again. "Wait a minute," he said. He walked out. After a few minutes, during which the new "friends" engaged in small-talk, Dr. Smith walked back in.

"I had to check with the computer to be totally positive, but yes, I could do it."

"Fantastic. Here's the plan: Michelle," she had quickly surmised this must be Michelle Hope, "goes back to Washington with me—pretending to be a victim of the 'happy gas.' I call my boss and tell him I've captured Michelle, that she has all sorts of information about the space dolphins—which I'm sure is true. Then I would say, 'I'll only let her talk to President Zak himself.' When they ask me why, I would say something like, 'I'm calling the shots now!' I'm sure they wouldn't refuse, not for Michelle herself. I'd insist on meeting the President in the Oval Office, where they could pick up Michelle. I'd insist on 'ole Pres. Zak being there. Then I'd tell him I even had Robby hidden away somewhere, zonked on 'happy gas,' and if they did exactly like I said, I'd hand him over too. All you have to do is make sure Robby doesn't appear on TV again." (Hazel was beginning to feel like a triple agent. She might not completely abandon her mission after all. She might get some small concession from the dolphin-people out of her failure to complete her assignment!) "Don't you see? It would be a coup d'etat. You'd actually have

someone in the White House, because I'd insist on Michelle staying there. When they ask why, I'd say, 'Because she saved me
on the mountain,'" she looked admiringly at Vic, "'and I feel
I owe her. I never forget a debt, and I don't want her in some
smelly 'ole jail cell.'" (It was true too. Being a business major,
she never did forget a debt. And she remembered back to the
Star Dolphins saving her on the train. She had to keep the led-
gers balanced.)

"But I'd give 'em another reason." Her mind was wheeling
and dealing now. "I'd say, 'Have her appear on TV with the
President from the Oval Office on a daily basis! It'd be a coup,'
I'd say. I'd tell them the 'happy gas' had had the unexpected
side effect of making Michelle turn against the dolphin people.
Instead of Michelle on TV from the pirate station somewhere,
there she'd be in the Oval Office, cooperating with Pres. Zak
himself. And this way, I'd know she was all right, too. Then, and
here's the best part of all, on national TV, Michelle could suddenly open a vial of the new and improved 'happy gas', to which
she and I would have already taken the antidote prepared by
Dr. Smith, but nobody else there would have. Then, in front of
everyone, 'ole Zak would go zonkers, and Michelle could quickly
revert to her real self, and tell the people the dolphin people
had taken over! And because Michelle would have several vials
of the new and improved 'happy gas' on her, if anybody tried any
hanky-panky, she could just zap the creeps.

"Well, what do you think? Of course," she said, looking at Dr.
Smith, "I'd need a couple of things. Techno-gadgets."

Everyone looked at Hazel in open-mouthed amazement.

"Well," Dr. Smith finally said, "I'd have to be sure of the sincerity of your commitment, which I should be able to ascertain from
the lie detector test. But if you pass the test…"

"I think it's too risky," Vic suddenly said.

"Be quiet, Vic," said Michelle. "I think it's a great plan! I would love to see the White House again, anyway."

Dr. Hope sat quietly. "I don't really like the idea, myself. But if Dr. Smith believes Hazel is sincere, and if Michelle really wants to try it, well it's up to her."

Michelle gave him a kiss. "Thanks, grandfather," she said.

Down in his hogan in Arizona, Robby received the message of Michelle's bold plan and an account of what had recently occurred at the Whitney Castle, along with instructions not to broadcast TV from the hogan until further notice. He had not been too concerned about his temporary inability to get through to the compound—this had happened before when the Star Dolphins had not wanted to be disturbed or to suddenly appear on Robby's "New Howdy Doody Show" on TV without warning. Robby had insisted on spontaneity for the show, believing (correctly) this added an important and even essential element of honesty to the program, but sometimes the Star Dolphins were not in a mood for playing with puppets. When the computers were neglected, the screening device had automatically kicked in—a precautionary device suggested by (the original) Dr. Smith, so as to prevent them going on TV if they didn't wish to. It would never do to have anything go out over the air waves but something they wanted to have go out. Robby would have gotten concerned had it continued for very long, but happily the situation had been remedied quickly.

He was a little worried about his sister, but had to admit the plan seemed like a good one. He shut down the micro television broadcasting equipment in the hogan and sat cross legged across from Johnny and Frankie. Frankie was nursing her and Johnny's new baby.

"Well, we're off the air for a while." He told them about Hazel.

"Whew!" said Johnny. "You wanna repeat that?"

"I'm worried about Michelle," said Frankie.

"I am too," admitted Robby. "But Dr. Smith…"

"Dr. Smith," gasped Johnny and Frankie.

"Yes. They brought him out of the capsule to deal with the situation at Star Castle. Dr. Smith seems to believe Ms. Hazel is sincere in her desire to help…"

"Whew!" repeated Johnny. "That is really something."

Frankie giggled. "How old is Dr. Smith now, anyway?"

"The same age as Howdy Doody," said Robby.

They all laughed.

"Are we still going to Roswell, Robby?" asked Johnny.

They had planned on doing a "remote" from the site of the 1947 UFO crash.

"Sure. We've got nothing better to do."

"I'll pack a picnic lunch," suggested Frankie. "We could just have a picnic there…"

"And look around some," said Johnny. "Who knows, maybe we'll find some left over debris."

He looked over at the special "treasure hunting" apparatus standing by the door, which they were to have used on the broadcast.

"Maybe…" said Robby.

Michelle and Hazel were on the Amtrak going east. They had decided it would be best if Hazel used the round-trip ticket the CIA had given her. Hazel had ample emergency funds with her to buy a ticket for Michelle. And, she had insisted. "Let the government pay for it."

The two talked as the train made its way. Hazel told Michelle her life's story, and Michelle told Hazel many of her experiences, about which Hazel made mental notes. She really had been sincere when Dr. Smith had given her the lie detector test. She just made mental notes out of force of habit.

The same type of strange encounters occurred as when Hazel had come west on the train. Michelle only smiled as she observed the effects the arrival of the Star Dolphins was having on ordinary people. "Well, everything seems to be going as planned," she whispered to Hazel, as they listened to the many debates among the travelers as to the existence or not of the "dolphins from outer space."

A young man sat down across from Michelle, looking at her closely. "Haven't I seen you on TV," he said. "Why you're..."

"People are always asking me that question," said Michelle quickly, feigning exasperation. "I must look like this dolphin girl."

"You do, miss. You could be her twin sister!"

"I know. It's terrible. I don't even like dolphins," she said. "Silly creatures, always smiling. Why don't they go back to where they came from? The government should have more stringent immigration laws in this country, that's what I think. Imagine, allowing any 'ole extraterrestrial creature in. And then lettin' 'em on TV!" She popped her bubble gum. "I may not be the smartest person in the world, but I'd never let 'em across our borders if I were President!"

"They come from outer space, ma'am," the young man said patiently.

"They do not," some else chimed in. "It's a communist ploy to take over the government."

"And it seems to be working like a charm," quickly added Hazel.

"Maybe the communists didn't lose the cold war after all!" someone else said.

The first young man said, "They really are from outer space, just like they say on TV. They've come to help us bring in the new age of Aquarius. I'm from Mt. Shasta, and I know. They even have a secret base inside the mountain!"

Hazel quickly looked at him.

"How can you be so sure," she asked.

"Everyone there has gotten mental messages from them," he said. Which was true, "telling us to prepare for the 'beginning of the world.'"

"You mean, the end of the world," another said.

"No, no, the beginning of the world. The new world."

"You mean the new world order?"

"No, no. That went out with Yugoslavia. I mean the real new world. They said they're on their way right now to take over the White House" (Michelle held in a gasp. Hazel intently peered at the earnest young man, wearing bell bottom pants.) "and when they did, planet Earth would be finally integrated into the galactic society, just like Robby said on television."

"Robby's an imposter."

"Yeah, a clone."

"No, he's real."

"Yeah, he's real, alright. A real brat!"

It went on and on, as Michelle watched in fascination.

They finally arrived in Washington. Hazel kicked in her plan. They went to a hotel. She called her boss, attaching the device she had gotten from Dr. Smith which did not allow the call to be traced. He was aghast, but passed the message on to the President. Finally Pres. Zak was on the line.

"How do I know it's really you, Mr. President," said Hazel, after he had quickly ("A little too quickly," Hazel had thought) totally agreed to her demands.

"Do you have a TV?

"Turn it on."

She did so. "Special Presidential Message" was written across the screen. Then there was Pres Zak, talking to her on the telephone. "Are you there," he said to her over the phone.

"We're here," she said.

"Put Michelle on." Clever, thought Hazel. The old boy's clever. But not quite clever enough.

Pres. Zak looked into the camera. "Ladies and gentlemen, I have on the phone with me Michelle, the young lady who's appeared on your TV, claiming to be allied with the so-called dolphin people. Are you there, Michelle."

"Yes, I'm here," said Michelle, looking at Hazel.

"Michelle, are you ready to come on TV and tell the people the whole dolphin caper is just an elaborate, admittedly quite sophisticated, sham to bequile the people and set them up for some kind of communist coup."

"Well, Mr. President," said Michelle, thinking quickly now herself, "I wouldn't say we were communists. I'd say we were more eco-nuts." She smiled at Hazel.

"I see," said the President. "So you admit the space dolphins are not real?" He knew they were, but hoped the "happy gas"

416

had rearranged the girl's thinking. The full effects of the sub-stance had not been totally examined in the rush to get it out for the mission.

"Yes, sir," said Michelle, reverting to her Ellie Mae voice. "We just made 'em up," she giggled.

"And you're willing to come on television right here in the Oval Office with me so the people will know it's really you and tell the American people and the people of the world the truth, the whole truth and nothing but the truth?"

"So help me God. Yes sir, I am," she said truthfully.

"Then we'll all look forward to seeing you later, Michelle," Pres. Zak smiled into the camera.

Robby and friends were at Roswell. They were sitting around a campfire in the middle of the desolate field where the extrater-restrial craft had crash-landed so long ago.

"This is eerie," whispered Frankie, looking up at the twinkling stars. There was no moon tonight, and the sky was completely plastered with the sparkling lights of the Milky Way.

Robby had to admit she was right. It was eerie. Actually a little too eerie. He could feel goose-bumps on his arm. He almost felt as if someone somewhere was doing something to him.

"Ever read the story 'Nightfall,' by Isaac Asimov," said Robby looking up too at the mask of stars across the sky. "The sky tonight, with all the stars out, reminds me of it. It's about a planet in the middle of a galaxy—maybe ours—where night hap-pens only once every thousand years because the planet has two suns in close enough proximity so it never gets dark enough to let stars come out—except once every thousand years when the two suns align in a certain way so as to allow 'Nightfall.'

"It's a totally amazing story," Robby continued, still looking up. "It's based on this quotation from Emerson—ever hear of Ralph Waldo Emerson, the transcendental philosopher of the 1800s who was a close friend of Thoreau, who wrote *Walden*—ever read *Walden*?—which said, 'If the stars only came out once every thousand years, how all the people would look up and marvel!'

"Anyway, when the stars finally do come out, they come out completely covering the sky, like tonight only ten times more so, because they're near the center of the galaxy, but instead of marveling, all the people go quite mad and burn down their towns to get light, because they can't take the darkness, and even though there are so many stars covering the sky, it's still dark. Amazing story," concluded Robby, "in a perverse kind of a way."

"I've read it," said Johnny.

"I haven't," said Frankie, "and I don't think I want to!"

"Look!" said Robby, pointing straight up.

A light was approaching them! Soon a small craft landed in the sagebrush, seeming to pulsate as though it were going in out of a different dimension. Robby tried to stand up, but couldn't move. A luminous being appeared.

"Look at what," he heard Johnny say, as if from a great distance.

"I don't see anything…"

Finally, he heard, "Robby quit playing a joke on us. Come out, come out wherever you are. Oly Oly oxin free. All home free. Come on Robby. You win. Stop hiding…"

"Who are you," Robby felt himself ask. He could see nothing but pulsing lights around him in human-like shapes.

"We are the most advanced beings in the galaxy," he felt one of the lights say. "We are to the Star Dolphins as they are to humans on Earth. We exist in a different dimension. We are able to slip in out of this dimension so as to travel virtually instantaneously.

"We have been carefully, secretly preparing you, Robby, for years, so you can travel in out of these dimensions too."

"Why me," asked Robby, who had been quite content sitting around the campfire with his friends. He had often wondered at the "strange" feelings which seemed to come over him "out of nowhere."

He heard light, far-away laughter, almost like giggling.

Are they laughing at me, he felt himself think.

"To teach you," he "heard."

"What..."

"What we have taught the Star Dolphins. And perhaps a little more. You know, of course, how it is possible to travel faster than the speed of light." Robby remembered back now to White Dolphin patiently explaining faster-than-light space travel to him.

"First of all," White Dolphin had said, "it's all a matter of perspective. If you have the correct perspective, then, and only then, can you derive the right theory. If you have a faulty perspective, or I should say, a faulty premise, you will have a flawed theory. In other words, if you ask the wrong question, you'll get a wrong answer—no matter how well it fits in with the question—understand?

"Now here's where Einstein went wrong, shall we say, though meaning quite well, when he derived his theory of relativity and the ultimate barrier of 'c', the speed of light. E=mc2. His premise was, suppose you could catch up with a beam of light in a space ship. What would it—the light beam—look like as you caught up with it. He finally concluded, based on this perspective, you could never catch up to it, because as the speed of the space craft 'E' increased relative to the light beam, which was a constant, so would its mass 'm'. Understand, Robby? Thus, the mass 'm' would become infinite as it 'caught up to' shall we say the light beam. This led to all kinds of strange anomalies, such as the light beam always staying the same distance in front of the space ship, no matter how fast the space ship traveled, and other perplexing things.

"However, though, to Mr. Einstein's credit, some parts of his theory of relativity were, relatively, correct." White Dolphin went on. "For instance, space really is a matrix of space-time, just like he said, and gravity really can bend a light beam. Just like he said. But the fact gravity as a 'field' can bend a light beam should give you a clue as to the flaw in Einstein's theory in relation to the speed of light, the flaw in his perspective." Robby didn't have a clue.

"It's all in the premise. Einstein set up his premise as trying to 'catch up' with a light beam." Again Robby heard the polite laughter. He had to admit, the image of some imaginary space craft trying to catch up with a getaway beam of light was somewhat funny. Who'd ever do such a thing in the first place, he thought. He could almost see them flinging an imaginary rope toward the beam, as if trying to lasso it!

"No, no," Robby now heard the light humanoids saying.

"It's all in how you approach the situation," he could hear White Dolphin say. "You have the light beam, right. But instead of attempting to catch up with it, going parallel with it, you approach it from a field, an anti-gravity field. You don't go parallel with the beam—you jump over the light beam. Do you understand, now, Robby. You jump over the light beam—just like a dolphin jumping over a suspended rope at Marineworld!"

"Then," he heard one of the light humanoids say, "you enter the 'ether'—hyper space. You're early scientists in the last part of the 19th century, prior to Einstein, were actually pretty much on the right track when they talked about the 'either,' the nebulous substance of the cosmos. Once you enter the 'ether,' you enter different dimensions, where instantaneous travel obviously is easy—We were with Dr. Hope after he was 'chosen.'

"And now, Robby, we are with you."

Michelle was standing next to the President in the Oval Office, looking into the television camera.

"Ladies and gentlemen…friends," the word came out of Pres. Zak's mouth like a sneer. "I would like to introduce some one to you all of you should be familiar with. This is Michelle Hope, the young lady who has appeared on your TV many times in the past, spreading propaganda about these so called 'Star Dolphins.'"

He looked at Michelle. "Now, tell the people the truth, young lady, just like you told me earlier on the telephone, 'bout how the space dolphins are only a cover story, a ploy for a sinister international plot to covertly undermine nation states in order to set up a world-wide socialistic government run by the United Nations, where you Ms. Hope, as I vividly recall, appeared before the Chinese communist infiltrated General Assembly, spreading more lies about talking to dolphins. Now look the people out there straight in the eye and tell them!"

Michelle cleared her throat and looked straight into the camera. "It's all true," Michelle nodded her head. "Every bit of it."

"You see, ladies and gentlemen, Ms. Michelle Hope admits what I've just said is all true. Every bit of it."

Well, this is it, thought Michelle. Desparate times call for desparate measures. And these are desparate times. I really hate to do this even to you, Pres. Zak. She brought out the tiny vial of the new and improved "happy gas" and unplugged it.

Pres. Zak started jumping around the room like a monkey!

"It's all true," he was saying, loudly. "It's all true. Don't you believe for a minute what the network newscasts try to dish out to you. It's all true. The Star Dolphins are here to help all of us." He gestured frantically at the camera. "You, me, everybody. They're here to save us all. 'We have met the enemy and he is us.' Didn't Pogo say something like that? He was right, ladies and gentlemen. Pogo was exactly right! We are the enemy, and the networks are the biggest enemy of all. Why? Because the networks are us. You, me, all of us. You watch the tube every day, right? You watch all those stupid ads" (he stretched his arm across the room.) "They've turned your minds into mush. You watch all those silly programs. The cop shows have turned our country into a police state, for God's sake. Don't you see it? You're being programmed for a take over by television—network television! And the Star Dolphins have infiltrated the networks to save you, me, all of us."

The new "happy gas" which Dr. Smith had come up with was, in truth, truth serum.

Suddenly, Hazel Macelroy entered the studio—armed with a semi-automatic rifle!

"All right, I'm taking over now," she said.

She was like Professor Moriarty to Sherlock Holmes. Even Dr. Smith himself could not completely outwit Hazel Macelroy.

Michelle awoke to find herself once again in her prison cell, alone. No, it wasn't just a bad dream. Each morning for the last two days when she woke up and looked around in the dim light, she had hoped it were.

Across the hall, in another cell, (Ex.) Pres. Zak was still going on about the insidious television networks.

"He's right about the Star Dolphins," Michelle said out loud, "but I wish he'd shut up…"

Suddenly, she heard a voice. "Michelle!"

"Robby?!?!"

"Yes. Don't worry. You'll be out soon."

"Where are you?"

"I can't really tell you. In a different dimension. There are ten, you know, but its too difficult to explain. I don't even understand it, but I'm here. Here I come!"

Then Robby was before her! looking a little dazed, but none the worse for wear.

"Robby!" Michelle fell into his arms.

"We've got get the guards in here, so we can get you out of here."

"But what about the cameras. They are on surveillance all the time!"

"We zapped 'em" said Robby.

"Why don't we just go out like you came in," asked Michelle, who was ready for anything at this stage.

"Because you haven't been properly prepared for multi-dimensional vector travel."

"By who?"

"Michelle, dear sister," Robby said, "as Hamlet said to his friend, 'There are more things in Heaven and earth, Horatio, than dreamt of in your philosophy.' There are beings as much more advanced than the Star Dolphins as the Star Dolphins are of humans. They have been in contact with me for years, though I never knew it. They exist in multi-dimensional space, able to slip in out of different dimensions. Why they contacted me was because I was the youngest and easiest to 'train'.

"Now, start making a lot of noise so we can get those guards in here. When they see me, they'll open the door, and then watch the fun begin."

Michelle started screaming, "Help!" at the top of her lungs.

Soon, the outer door clanged open, and a couple of husky guards ran to Michelle's cell. They saw Robby smiling at them like the Cheshire cat!

"Hey! What are you doing in there," the guard gestured at Robby. "She's in a private cell, isn't she, Mac," the prison guard said to his partner, who quickly looked at his roster just to double-check. Behind them could be heard (Ex.) Pres. Zak still going on. "You there," the guard said to him. "Shut up!"

"Yeah! Get 'im, whoever he is." The cell door quickly swung open, and the two guards rushed in.

"Watch this," said Robby.

Suddenly, the two guards screamed, and disappeared into vector flashes of color.

"They weren't prepared for vector space travel," said Robby.

"Where did they go?" asked Michelle, still looking where they once were.

"Nobody knows—not even the multi-dimensional beings know where people go to not properly prepared for vector space travel. They speculate, though, there are beings somewhere in the universe as much more advanced of them as they are of the Star Dolphins, who do know where—but," he added, "they're not telling. It's a mystery. Come on."

They ran out of the cell. "Now, we zap the cameras back into action." Robby started jumping around in front of the camera, waving his arms. Soon the outer door opened as other guards rushed in. It was like a multi-colored fireworks display as they all disappeared into vector space.

In the Oval Office, Hazel Macelroy leaned back in the Presidential chair. It was a very comfortable chair. After Pres. Zak had "freaked out" on nation-wide TV, the remaining brass had agreed Hazel Macelroy had a lot of "brass," rushing in like she had, and was as well qualified as anyone else to be President.

She had delivered Michelle Hope, hadn't she, who was safely tucked away in maximum security. And she would deliver Robby—if they did exactly like she said.

CHAPTER THREE
THE RUN -IN

Down in San Francisco...strange strange things were happening.

"San Fran—City by the Bay...

"Here it is," wrote Jean in his journal. "Here is where the Earth ends forever—at least until it begins again in the pearl sea!"

Jungle Jean (his stage name) played "folk music" in the cafes of "San Fran," as he liked to call this "exasperated, exasperating city." He made $100 a night (when he was playing), singing his soul into other people's empty lives—those tired, dressed-up folks who sat at the bar, waiting for the bartender to tell them they could go "home" now.

"Wherever 'home' might be," Jean wrote. "Home is in the stars, is what I think."

He looked around in his "backyard tepee"—a real authentic Native American teepee he had ordered for $250 and had the good fortune of having a friend's backyard to put it up in. Various colorful Indian artifacts decorated it.

Otherwise, he would have left "good 'ole San Fran" long, long ago—he would not live in an apartment in the earthquake-prone city. He would have taken AmTrak up to "'ole Reno," stopping in Truckee long enough to see the museum at Donner Lake State Park—and go out to where "the doomed dying Donner Party had camped under a great old pine giant when snow had been unlucky 13ft. up the trunk over from Donner Pass—where AmTrak goes through the most amazing tunnel through solid smooth granite rock above the tree-pined shore of amethyst Donner Lake, where I looked on from the rocks above once, under clouds in a aqua-marine sea-sky, Donner a picture-window into the depths, the rocks like castle crags, just south of Crystal Pass and luminous green Castle Peak, which I scrambled up to see the sky—the great, never-ending blue sky—except when it dies at the edge of outer space—and then births again into the never failing love.

"Love, now is it," wrote Jean, who was seriously mimicking Jack Kerouac, the legendary "beat" writer, mimicking, but trying to instill the one thing he felt "St. Kerouack" lacked—some poetic discipline.

"Just a little poetic discipline, pleassse, Jack. Be like the fisherman who hauls in the net and discards the muck but keeps all those flashing silver fishes! C'mon 'ole boy" wrote Jungle Jean about his icon, the misunderstood Catholic mystic, "not a beatnik at all," Kerouac once wrote of himself. "You can do it. Forget the sinister junkie Burroughs (whose name we must never mention.) You're it, Jack Kerouack, if only you'd come back...But, just like James Dean, you had to die young..."

Jean looked at the framed words he had hanging in his tepee, out of Kerouac's "Piers of the Homeless Night." It was the "Paragraph of paragraphs," which Jean had edited ("What, edit Jack Kerouack?!") "just a smidgen," Here it was—America in a capsule:

"'Where?' I say, looking out the window all over the horizon at those marshes of night...–all you is see is marshes and great black distances of night and far off, on hills, the little communities with Christmas lights in their windows blearing red, blearing green, blearing blue, suddenly sending pangs thru me and I think, 'Ah, America, so big, so sad, so black, you're like the leafs (sic) of a dry summer that go crinkly ere August found its end, you're hopeless,...there's nothing but the dry drear hopelessness, the knowledge of impending death,' (editor's note–Kerouack died at the ripe old age of 47) 'the suffering of present life, lights of Christmas wont save you or anybody, anymore you could put Christmas lights on a dead bush in August, at night, and make it look like something, what is this Christmas you profess in this void...(sic) in this nebulous cloud?'"

One of Jean's artist projects (he had several) was to "edit Kerouack." He liked to misspell his name with two 'k's.' It gave his name the same beginning and end, which was somehow like his writing, even his life.

Jungle Jean was amazed at the fact Kerouac had been born and died in the same year as his own father! 1922 and 1969. They even looked similar—both handsome with wavy dark hair.

Jean had found an old arcane copy of Carl Jung's "Syncrynicity" in an antique-looking second-hand book store here in San Francisco. Jean was a "fan" of the psychiatrist who had taken an almost mystic approach to group psychology in startling contrast to Sigmund Freud's clinical, repressed memory, sexual perspective. The book about random meaningful coincidences was Jung's longest and most involved work. Jung (whose name in

German means "young"—coincidence?) had had serious mis-givings about even attempting such a study, but was compelled to do so because of the vast amount of data he had gathered over his long career in helping his many patients to understand the workings of their own minds. Too many "coincidences" had occurred in not only the lives of his patients, but his own as well. The list was almost endless. He advanced a theory of "noncausal-ity," in direct opposition to the "causal" approach of the so-called rational sciences, in which "series" of incidences had to have a casual relationship. X implies Y. Science itself was based on this approach. Anything else was purely random chance.

However, Jung had documented too many cases of noncausal experiences, experiences which carried great significance for his patients—For instance, a wife suddenly believes her hus-band, who had traveled to America on business, has died, and in her distress immediately wires a cable to him. The answer comes back her husband had died at the precise time she sent the cable!

Too many such noncausal incidents had occurred for Jung to ignore…the result he felt of the "collective unconscious."

So—Jean's father and Kerouac had been born and died in the same year and even had a similar appearance. This was a bit much for Jean. There the similarities between the two virtu-ally stopped. Virtually, because one trait they had in common was drug abuse—in his father's case, alcohol, in Kerouac's every-thing under the sun, though primarily alcohol there, too.

Jungle Jean's father was a very conservative man. He had actu-ally voted for Richard Nixon! He had been an accountant—not an iconoclast. He had been a fighter pilot in World War II, flying Corsairs off of aircraft carriers in the star sprinkled night, when the sky looked like the sea and the sea like the sky, where pilots regularly succumbed to vertigo and dove into the sea, thinking it was the night sky—not a merchant marine, like Kerouac—yet even there...

St. Experary, the fabled pilot-author who wrote the children's classic *The Little Prince* also wrote the tiny, strange novel *Night Flight* about a night airmail carrier in the early days who died in a storm. The author himself eventually disappeared in a night-flight of his own...Jean had read the little book—with strange strange opening of an airplane "herding" the fields below like cows!—immediately thinking of his own doomed dad, who drank himself to death at the ripe old age of 47...

Two people could not have been more different than Jean's father and Jack, and yet...Strange coincidence–

"Imagine," Jean had thought. "Kerouack died in 1969. What timing! What a coincidence! The end of the sixties, which he, maybe more than any other person, helped gestate. He died with The Beatles! What a way to go!"

The man was compassionate, Jean would say to those cynical souls who asked why he'd waste time on such incoherent ramblings.

"And a great writer. He just needed an editor!"

"The timeless hippies seem to be reappearing," Jungle Jean wrote, "like peeking from behind street signs, like elves, tentative, illusive...but happening!"

It did seem to be true. The startling appearance of the Star Dolphins on everyone's TV was having a particularly interesting effect in the City by the Bay—official birthplace of the hippies, home of iconoclasts of all types.

The talk in the taverns, like where Jungle Jean played his "folk music," hearkened back to the days of the beats and folkies and hippies.

The atmosphere was seething with the poetic talk of seething times. It was unmistakable. It was a landslide. It was a gold rush!

It was: "Jefferson Airplane cds and Bob Dylan and Beatle songs and Quicksilver Messenger Service and Country Joe and the Fish from Bezerkely and Janis Joplin and Big Brother and the Holding Co. (instead of Bad Co.) and Jimi Hendrix and Creedence and Kesey and the Dead and Cassidy (Hopalong and Neil and Butch) and Ralph Ginsburg and Alan Watts and Gary Snyder and King Kerouack (but not the man whose name we must never mention—let him go off with the nova express) and Grace Slick (sober for a change) and Lightfoot (sober for a change!) and Steinbeck and Gertrude Stein and Earnest Earnest, Faulkner stumbling drunk out of the Mississippi bayous and Mississippi John Hurt finger pickin' and smilin'…" It was all this and more…

Soon, seeweed was making the rounds. Vic had brought the substance down to the Bay, and opened the "Tea Tavern," specializing in all manner of "healthful herbal teas" with the "special mystery ingredient—Seeweed!"

The word began to circulate about the "seeweed," and every night the place was jammed-packed with people drinking seeweed herbal teas, talking in hushed voices and listening to Jungle Jean and other "folkies" ply their wares.

Soon Jean became the "house folkie," for Vic had taken an immediate liking to his "folk-baroque" guitar style and singular songs, particularly after he had sung one called "Rainbow Miles":

> Rainbow Miles lined with smiles
> Go on around the bend
> Rainbow Miles lined with smiles
> They seem to never end!
> (verse)

Dorothy went over the rainbow
To see the Wizard of Oz
She found a tin man
And an 'ole scarecrow
And a lion to help her cause
The tin man needed oilin'
The scarecrow needed a heart
The lion was afraid of his own growl
But together they did start.
They marched on down the yellow brick road
Where the Witch of the West was waitin'
But they mellowed her down to a pool of gold
And ended all of her hatin'.
The Wizard of Oz was a little 'ole man
Behind a great big mask
But they saw right thru his phony façade
And took him there to task
Rainbow Miles…

(verse)
Alice went down the rabbit hole
White Rabbit led her on
The Queen of Hearts was waitin' for her
But Alice just sang her a song
And Tweedle de Dum and Tweedle de Dee
Danced on the Beach of Nowhere
The 'ole Cheshire Caterpillar
Smoked a hookah smilin' there.
The Mad Mad Hatter drank capuchino
At his Very Merry Unbirthday
But Alice said, "I cannot stay
For today is my ninth birthday."

Rainbow Miles…

(verse)

Davy Crockett wore a coonskin cap

When he grinned that 'ole bar down

Pecos Bill rode his wild whirl wind

Right through the middle of the town

Paul Bunyan and his Babe Blue Ox

Fought to save the spotted owl ground

John Wayne at the Alamo swung his Betsy all around.

Robert E. Lee he said to me

"I'm fightin' 'gainst' my own brother

Fightin' some one who has the same mother as me

An' there's just one chile in my family

An' the ghost from his rifle I can see."

And the fiddle and the fife

And the Yankee Doodle dandy

Went off to fight the 'ole Red Coats

And shot 'em full of candy…

Washington crossed the Delaware

Benjamin flew his kite

Thomas Jefferson declared,

"Our independence is in sight."

And Abraham Lincoln freed the slaves

That all men might be free men

The Kennedy's freed them once again

To try and save the Union.

And Bobby Dylan and Johnny Lennon

Led all of us in a new song

Lightfoot in the wilderness

Waved the Canadian Railroad on

Hank Williams in the barroom

Joni Mitchell by the sea
Woody Guthrie, Neil Young
Martin Luther and Bobby McGee.
And John Muir's trail leads to the sky
Paved in gold and precious gem stones
Interstate 80 don't stop at the sea
And spacemen fly home moonstones.

Rainbow Miles lined with smiles
Go on around the bend
Rainbow Miles lined with smiles
They seem to never end!

Soon, something else began to occur in the City by the Bay, where the sun stole in over the bridges and the span-dappling clouds. An idea began to circulate among the questers. The idea of "The Great Run-In."

The seeweed had had the effect of turning all these free-floating folks into—runners! Everyone was running. Everyone bought brand new, expensive running shoes. Those who couldn't afford them were given a new pair by local charities. People were running all over the city—young people, old people, rich people, poor people. And since the city was the one, the only San Francisco, somebody—nobody was quite sure who (but the rumors were (Ex) President Clark himself, like a leader in exile, was the mastermind!)—began to stage a "run-in." But not just any "run-in:" The "Great Run In—The Run-In for Peace and Love."

"We're going to run all the way across the United States," the speaker at the rally said, to a sea of cheers. It was the popular

Ex-President on the podium! "Just like Forrest Gump!" (A tidal wave of cheers.) "We're going to run right up to the Washington Monument!"

The rally was soon over, as everyone had a running workout schedule to keep. And everyone ran off.

Vic and Jungle Jean, along with (Ex) President Clark, had become the de facto leaders of the Great Run-In, partly because Vic's Tea Tavern was a center of activity, but like a giant school of dolphins or an extended Indian tribe, there was no one real leader. It was grass-roots democracy at its best. After all, everyone would set his or her own pace...

Vic had brought large amounts of concentrated seaweed down from Lone Pine over Tioga Pass through Yosemite in his old van. After the Star Dolphins picked Vic up from the lighthouse, they had secured his van, like a small whale, and brought it up to Whitney Portal, and placed it in the hikers' parking lot. The hikers there trying to get through the magnetic fence were treated to the rare sight of one of the "dolphin ships" hovering over them and lowering the old Volkswagen van down—complete with a shimmering force field around it so curious onlookers wouldn't get too close, or try to take a souvenir—like one of the doors...

The seaweed spread through San Francisco with the speed of sound, as Jungle Jean, who knew the streets, had set up a "delivery system." In the first place, everyone who got any wanted to share it with his neighbor. It was easy to set up a "pyramid-type" system of distribution, with selected "givers" passing the packets on. It was hailed by the underground press as an "anti-drug." Soon the San Francisco *Chronicle* began doing a series of stories on the new "anti-drug" circulating through the city, how old, interim street people, wandering around lost on the streets pushing grocery carts with all their worldly goods, were all of a sudden clad in new running shoes and suits, jogging up and down the cable-cared hills! (Vic had also brought a large amount of cash as donations to local charities, with the strict stipulation it be used for "running gear for the poor." Where had the cash come from? When Vic had asked a Star Dolphin this question, the dolphin had only smiled.)

Jungle Jean led the first group out over the Oakland Bay Bridge, up Interstate 80, toward the Sierra Nevada foothills. First they wound up from the Bay, the cloud painted scene of the sparkling waters behind them. There were so many people running, only a few cars were on the highway. And even the cops helped out by acting as guards, like a parade—a long, long parade which would eventually spread all the way from sea to shning sea—the New Summer of Love. All along the way, seeweed was taken on ahead, and motel and hotel owners opened their doors to the joggers, as did private homes. Those who could afford to pay, paid twice or three times the normal amount just out of generosity. Those who could not afford were welcomed anyway.

Soon they approached the Sierra, the golden tinged foothills beckoning on the runners up toward marble-domed Donner Pass. They chugged and puffed their way around the pine-tree lined curves, up, up, past Blue Canyon and Immigrant Pass and Rainbow Road, where the Yuba River rippled through smooth rock, tree dotted, through the granite Taj Mahals, past Castle Peak, the highest mountain on the pass, where Donner Lake opened up like a rippling blue window. Many went swimming here, thinking nothing at all of seeing dolphins in a mountain lake!

Vic had led the second group out over the cloud dappled bronze towered Golden Gate Bridge, using his old van as a "pace car" for the ultra ultra marathoners. They paced themselves through shimmering Marin county, passed the first redwoods, and on up Highway 101—the Redwood Highway. Soon they were at the hippie capital of Garberville, the marijuana growing capital of the U.S. Here, seeweed spread through the area at the speed of light! Old hippies, young hippies bought running shoes with the money they had from selling their weed. The stores were selling out! There was a run on running shoes! But Vic just happened to have a large supply with him—and just in time a Dolphin Ship landed in a lush meadow near the town, startling some grazing cows, with enough running shoes for all! (When Vic asked a Star Dolphin where they got all those running shoes, the dolphin had said, "From Planet Shine.") It was a perfect way to get the grass-roots people on the side of the Star Dolphins—like dropping down leaflets—but instead it was manna from Heaven.

Next happened the Big Camp-In. The grass-roots leaders got together and decided they would like to camp out all through the Redwoods. They asked Vic about it. Vic asked the Star Dolphins. The Star Dolphins said, "Sure!" They gave out to the leaders very lightweight pieces of "plastic" looking material, which turned out to be shelters. The leaders dispersed these to the people; the people dispersed through the trees.

"But what about water," the people cried. The leaders asked Vic, "What about water?" Vic told a star dolphin, "The people need water."

The Star Dolphins said, "Tell the people to look for cathedrals in the forest. There they will find water."

"Cathedrals?" asked Vic.

"Yes. There are places in the forest where the giant redwood trees grow in circles, where they form living 'cathedrals' to the sky. Here, the people will find 'water-falls.'"

Vic told this to the leaders, who went before the people, searching for the "cathedrals." When they found these enchanted, magical circles of giant trees, they also found "water falls"! water spraying down like a waterfall from the sky.

Everyone was happy.

Vic was told by a Star Dolphin of Nick being in Vic's home state of Oregon up at Crater Lake with an Indian girl named Diana and her young daughter. Vic was to drive his van up there, spreading seeweed as he went, and join them at the park.

"Great!" said Vic. He had become homesick for Oregon anyway, and it had been a couple of years since he had been at Crater Lake.

Vic made his way on up the Redwood Highway, back up the way he had come down on his quest to Pirate's Cove—turning east just south of the Oregon Border, going over the pass to Cave Junction (passing out free seeweed and more running shoes) and finally coming out in Ashland, home of the Shakespearian festival. *The Tempest* was playing! the great comedy, one of the only plays of the "immortal bard" where Shakespeare actually supplied the entire plot himself, about shipwrecked people on the magical, enchanted isle of Prospero, the wronged man of great arcane knowledge, who played tricks on his hapless captives, before revealing himself as one of their own.

Vic was able to get a ticket to the play which he enjoyed greatly. He decided not to worry about the seeweed and the running shoes here. Everyone runs in Ashland, anyway, he thought. He wandered around beautiful Lithia park, with the swans in the pool and the gorgeous antique Italian statue in the fountain. He then drank some of the fabled "lithia water," which contained "many healthful minerals." It certainly tasted like it did, the effervescent liquid like a natural soda. Then he noticed the water seemed to have the same effect as seeweed! Had the Star Dolphins somehow improved the potency of the spring? he wondered.

Soon Vic continued his journey up to Crater Lake.

Along I-80, the runners had reached the old railroad town of Truckee. At least it used to be an "old railroad town." Now, it was a quaint tourist trap, with board sidewalks, renewed train depot, refurbished shops, taverns—a very bustling place, as it sat at the crossroads between Lake Tahoe to the immediate south and the interstate. Normally, cars (and trains) zoomed through in a constant stream, but the roads were strangely quiet now. Seeweed had infiltrated this mountain community too, and almost everyone was off running, along the trails which permeated the hills here, or down the two highways going toward Tahoe.

At Tahoe, runners were circling the ice-blue lake—and of course dolphins were swimming in the waters! Nobody knew where they came from, but there they were. Actually, they had been dropped like paratroopers behind enemy lines from dolphin ships. Everybody was so astonished to see these smiling creatures swimming along their speedboats, some immediately turned around and flew back to the piers! Obviously, rumors of dolphins from outer space were REAL!

Meanwhile, back at I-80, the runners cruised into Reno, "The Biggest Little City in the World".

They had planned on cruising past Reno, not stopping longer than necessary to play a quick slot machine just for fun. But, the Star Dolphins, who enjoyed playing pranks, made the slots pay continual jackpots. It was a bonanza! the gamblers loaded their money into their satchels and raced down the highway. Some even hit multi-million Mega-Bucks jackpots, which the casinos smilingly paid out—or risk a riot. Now they had all the money they needed for their cross-country jaunt.

Then it was across the eternal eastern Nevada desert, past the endless rows of desert mountain ranges which rippled off into the vast distance like some sort of windswept sea, past Lovelock and Elko and Wendover…

Now, it was the Utah border, past the Great Salt Lake and through Salt Lake City, the Mormons looking on in open-mouthed amazement at this tidal wave of humanity invading their citadel. Some joined the throng, but here, the seeweed had a curiously muted effect. Most of the folks simply threw up their hands and ran back into their homes, instead.

But the deluge passed through Utah and made it finally to the Rockies of Colorado, up the steep passes and over to "The Mile High City" of Denver—where Robert Redford, and old man by now, met them with—what else?—a camera crew!

Vic had made it now to beautiful Crater Lake. He found the house where Diana and her daughter lived, where Diana worked for the National Park Service—which was in some disarray these days. National Parks seemed to be low on the priority list of (former) Pres. Zak, and no one had any real idea what was going to happen next.

Nick introduced Vic to Diana, and immediately beautiful sparks flew between the two. It seemed to be love at first sight. Nick was glad for both of them. Diana had been like a sister to him. They had had long conversations on the way up about everything under the sun. About how she had left her Indian husband because he tended to abuse her—which she was not going to take. About how Nick had grown up with a family in Nevada with a father in a wheel chair—not his own, but a family who virtually took him in when his own "family" was becoming dysfunctional. About common stereotypes perceived between the two antagonistic races of "Indian" and white. The conversations had gone on and on.

But Nick had not really felt any romantic inclinations toward Diana, even though she was very beautiful—partly because he was already married to Nancy, whom he very much loved. Nancy had been his partner through all the rough spots in his life and had shared his good times too. She was up on Shine! he knew, taken there by the Star Dolphins. He wondered what she was doing up there. He wondered when he would see her again. He hoped it would be soon. But he would be faithful to her forever if necessary. He hoped it wouldn't. For now he'd console himself with some of Dave's homebrew beer which they had brought with them. Even if it did taste like sherry!

Vic and Diana walked along the road by Crater Lake. The moon was out tonight rippling through the depthless waters of the purest, bluest (now that Tahoe had been polluted) lake in the world. Crater Lake! The perfect place for a moonlight stroll for two young lovers. The endless stars sparkled above the luminous depths like sparkling diamonds.

They exchanged small talk, and gradually Vic had begun to tell Diana the truth about him and Nick—how they were "secret agents" for the Star Dolphins—how the Star Dolphins were about to establish a base here at Crater Lake on Wizard Island!

Diana laughed and looked at Vic. "Well," she said, "my daughter believes in them."

Vic said, "I could see by her eyes!"

"Pearl does have beautiful eyes, doesn't she?"

"Like a beautiful space child," said Vic.

"Maybe they've already been in contact with Pearl," mused Diana.

"Sure they have. You two were chosen, just like me and Nick."

"Well," said Diana, "I'll believe it when I see it!"

"You may not have to wait too long," whispered Vic. He put his arm around her and they continued their stroll by the steep, rocky shore of the lake. The golden moon lit up Wizard Island like a cathedral on the water.

"It would be a charming place for a dolphin port," Diana had to admit. "I can just see dolphins swimming abound Wizard Island in the moonlight! Wow! What a scene it would make!"

"Right out of a Walt Disney animation," agreed Vic, nuzzling Diana's neck.

He could smell the sweet whiff of her perfume.

"I'll believe it when I see it," laughed Diana.

"You will."

The runners had reached the midwest. It at least it was flat here. They made better time. Not one person had dropped out of the run. The seeweed made all the difference. Up ahead of them, Jungle Jean, who had grown a long Forest Gump beard by now, was leading the way.

The flat expanses of Kansas spread out before them like endless seas of gold.

Down in New Mexico, Johnny and Frankie were searching for Robby.

They had all three been sitting around the campfire looking up at all the beautiful stars when they had entered a trance. When they came out of it, Robby was gone.

Looking around the sagebrush for him, they suddenly heard a faraway voice say, "Don't worry about me."

"Robby! Where are you hiding. Come out, Robby."

"I've entered a different dimension. You can't see me."

"C'mon, Robby. Stop playing a joke on us! We know you're hiding around here somewhere."

"This is what you are to do. Listen carefully. Go to the Hopi mesa pueblos. The Hopi are the original people of North America, having arrived here earlier than anyone else. They did a timeless migration before settling on their barren mesas. First they marched all the way east to the Atlantic, then they marched all the way west to the Pacific, then they marched all the way south to the Gulf of Mexico, then they marched all the way north to the glaciers. Then they marched here, to settle—thousands of years ago, having sailed across the Pacific from the Mongolian highlands in special watertight boats the Star Dolphins taught then how to construct, centuries before they were teaching the ancient Egyptians how to build the Pyramids, or the ancient Babylonians to write, before they visited the Dogon of Africa to tell them of the secret invisible star, Sirius 2. The Hopi were the first."

"Why did they have to march all over creation," asked Johnny.

"So they would see they had chosen the most barren place in the new world. Here, they would learn the secrets of the earth, how to bring forth abundance, maize, from a parched place, how to most effectively manage the environment. In this way, they would become masters of the earth. The First People.

"The 'kachinas' were playful spirits given to them by the Star Dolphins to teach and reward them."

Johnny knew well of the kachinas, the wildly imaginative masks and costumes the Hopi wore during their ceremonies to celebrate the infinite variety of the Great Spirit, the many faces of their god, from playful to somber, from loving to stern, from forgiving to wrathful.

"Go to the mesas. Tell the people living there in the stone pueblos you have been sent by the kachinas."

"Are you kidding!" gasped Frankie. "They'd shove us over a cliff!"

"Or laugh us out of town."

"I will be with you," they heard. "Along the way, play the tourist. Visit the sights, become aware of the mysteriousness of this ancestral land. After all, this place of glistening beauty is where the first Americans landed—not at Plymouth Rock."

The pair drove to the Four Corners area—Monument Valley, spirit home of the Navajo, where the strange, weird monuments rose up like Indian sculpture. What a perfect place for the Navajo, thought Johnny, looking in awe at the monumental statues of sandstone. It's almost as though they created these wonders themselves—The Grand Canyon, where colors danced and pulsated in waves across the striated walls, changing endlessly with the sun, temples of pink rock glittering like ornate Hindu temples—Mesa Verdi, where the Hopi Anasazi ancestors had their homes etched in elegant cliffs, dwellings hued out of the sides of solid stone, like some stone age metropolis.

The two wandered through these timeless wonders, in awe of the never ending, ever changing changing panoramic beauty around them.

They finally reached the Hopi Mesas, just south of the Grand Canyon. After the overwhelming vistas of the magic land they had just visited, this area of low shrub-grass and stark mesas seemed desolate, empty. But it did have a beauty all its own to it—the very desolation in comparison to the art-show like beauties of the rest of the region lent it its own austere grace. Here the "first people" had honed their skills of bringing forth maize from the parched land. Here the "first people" had purified their spirits in the area where only the strong—and the imaginative—survived. The endless, incredibly imaginative kachina spirits had taught them all real beauty lies in the realm of the spirits. As wondrously beautiful as the wonders were around them in every direction, they were to look up toward their snow-decked San Francisco peaks—where the kachinas lived.

So the pair landed at first mesa, and wandered wonderingly up toward the pueblos on the mesa tops. How surreal they seemed! as if overlooking their domain.

They were soon approached. "The mesas are closed to all outsiders," the Hopi said. The Hopi were notorious for defending their ancient homeland from peering "foreigners," as they looked upon all not of their tribe. "No 'belacona,'" he smiled, using the Navajo word for whites. "We're not belacona," said Johnny. Well, here goes, he thought. "The kachinas have sent us."

The Hopi looked at them open mouthed. Then he began to laugh. He laughed and laughed. "The kachinas sent you! That's the funniest thing I ever heard." The small man stopped laughing. "Actually, though, it's not very funny at all. You'd better..."

Uh, oh, thought Johnny. "No really. The Star Dolphins have sent us to you. The Star Dolphins created the kachinas to be your playful guides in this desert sea, so far from the oceans of the earth. We have come from the Star Dolphins."

The man peered at them. "We have heard rumors of these... Star Dolphins. We were not sure to believe them or not. But how can we know if you speak the truth."

"Gather your people in one place, here on the mesa, and they will appear to you."

The Hopi man stood silent.

"Alright. I will do as you say. If you lie, we'll throw you over the cliffs. Though really," he smiled, "we'll merely send you away. After all, 'Hopi' means 'peaceful.'"

The people were gathered soon on the top of the mesa, as if ready to watch one of the kachina celebrations. Everyone was talking or giggling, looking at Johnny and Frankie.

Johnny had no idea what was going to happen, but at least it seemed their lives were not in danger.

The Hopi who had met the mysterious "emissaries" addressed the crowd from the flat roof top. "My people, these two claim to come from the kachinas!"

Laughter echoed across the mesa.

"They say, they were sent by the Star Dolphins, of which we have heard mysterious rumors." Everyone was suddenly quiet, the wind whispering through the ghost-like pueblos. "They say they will prove it to us."

He turned to them.

Suddenly, the people all gasped. "Look!" they cried.

"The kachinas!"

They were all pointing up to the sky, where a fireworks display was under way—the kachinas were appearing in the night sky, their endless variety emblazoned against the stars. First one kachina, then another, more outrageously wild than the first, like an endless succession of clowns, one trying to outdo the last in outlandishness. It went on and on.

The kachinas had finally, after thousands of years, flown down from their Olympian home in the San Francisco Mountains.

The Hopi looked at Johnny and Frankie, tears in his eyes. "How do you do this, my friend," he asked.

Johnny was just as astonished as the Hopi. "I wish I could tell you," he said, as he gazed at the endless display. "The Star Dolphins…"

The man nodded his head solemnly. "They are truly…true," he said, looking up again at the pantheon.

At Crater Lake, Vic and Diana were jogging around the lake on the paved road which encircled it, under the moon-lit splattered night-sky, pacing one another as they ran. Nick was babysitting little Pearl.

"I still don't know whether to believe you," Diana said as they trotted beside one of the natural wonders of the world.

"You'll see," said Vic.

They encircled the lake, feeling invigorated at running in such an environment as this, munching seaweed for energy as they went.

As they were finishing their lap, feeling a peaceful "runner's high," suddenly…

"Oh my," breathed Diana.

A light was slowly coming down from the sky! a gigantic, multi-colored light, pulsating in every hue of the rainbow.

"I told you," said Vic, who himself was overcome at such a display. He had not expected the Star Dolphins to show up here in such a magnificent manner.

It was the largest Star-Ship he had seen yet—the Star Ship of Star Ships. It filled the sky above them. It made strange whistling and horn-like musical sounds as it slowly settled down onto the surface of Crater Lake, almost seeming to fill the crater with its size. It was like the ship at the end of the movie *Close Encounters of the Third Kind*, where the unbelievably grand space saucer had descended on Devil's Tower. However this was the real thing— and at Crater Lake. It was like God descending in a circular chariot, like Ezekiel's wheel of wheels. It was the most beautiful sight either of them could ever imagine—it was like every Christmas display rolled into one!

Now Nick and Pearl ran up to the side of the lake and stood silently beside them. Diana took hold of Pearl's little hand.

"It's true!" said Pearl.

They stood in silence, watching the spectacle…

The runners sped on across Kansas, and on across Iowa…

And on and on…

They sped on past the wheat fields.

Helicopters were hovering over them now.

Meanwhile, back in Washington, Pres. Hazel Macelroy watched the newscast on her TV in the Oval office of the runners making their way patiently, relentlessly eastward. (Ex) Pres. Zak stood grinning by her side. Hazel had finally administered the antidote to Dr. Smith's "truth serum" to the poor man, and he had returned to his true self—the competent liar. He had become her "Sec. of State."

The escape of Michelle Hope, to which (Ex) Pres. Zak would have been an unwilling (but truthful) witness had he not blacked out, had been the cause of no little concern among the "brass." As a matter of fact, they had truly considering "impeaching" Pres. Hazel Macelroy in the wake of this, but she had reminded them that only the Congress could impeach and convict a sitting president, and the Congress had long since been permanently disconvened. They had to admit she was right; besides they still couldn't think of anyone else who could do the job any better than Hazel. After all, she had delivered Michelle Hope. It really wasn't her fault she had escaped. And, she had actually been inside the Star Dolphin's compound. She knew more about the enemy, the "grinning invaders," than anyone else around there.

The disappearing of the guards, flashing off into vector space, was even more troubling.

"You say, Zac, they just disappeared.?"

"I blacked out when I heard Michelle Hope talking to someone in her cell. I seem to remember the guards coming in. When I came to again, everyone was gone. That's all I remember."

"What are we going to do about it," asked the General, the erstwhile Chairman of the Joint Chiefs of Staff.

"There's not much we can do about it, is there General," Hazel replied.

"What are we going to do about this," Sec. Zak gestured at the incredible sea of humanity running down the highway, like a hundred marathon races in one.

"How are they doing this mile after mile?" the General asked.

"It's this stuff they have called 'seeweed.' I had some when I was in the Star Dolphin's compound on Mt. Whitney. It was very potent. It made you feel like you could run up and down mountains."

Hazel looked on in silence.

"Send out the Marines! is what I think we should do," yelled out Sec. Zak.

"SSshhhh," whispered the CIA boss, standing nearby. "We must talk in whispers, very, very softly. We're even taking a risk talking here at all. We still don't know what spy capabilities the space dolphins have. We should be underground in Colorado..."

"No way," whispered Hazel. "I don't want to be down in some 'ole smelly bunker under the ground. I want to stay right here in the White House. My White Hose! I like it here. I like the view over the rotunda. We'll just have to talk in whispers, that's all. And turn the television up loud! And besides, even down there you couldn't be 100% sure they couldn't hear anyway, now could you?"

The CIA boss had to admit she was right. "Who knows what these space dolphins can do!"

"We've received intelligence that the lemmings plan to hold a large but peaceful rally here at the Washington Monument," continued Hazel. "I don't think sending out the Marines is the best course of action. They seem to be able to influence all those who they come upon to join their cause. They might even sway the Marines, and then where would we be?

"No—I think we should lay a trap for them. Keep the Marines in their barracks for the time being. Keep them away from any television or newspapers. Let these lemmings reach the Washington Monument. Let them have their peaceful rally—" Suddenly Hazel stood up. The television camera had focused in on one silvery-gray haired man, jogging in the middle of the runners. "There's Pres. Clark!" she gasped.

"And there's Pres. Clark!" the TV commentator was saying, "right in the middle of this rippling river of humanity. The President seems to be keeping a good pace for an old man." It was true. "He seems to be running smoothly. He's even smiling up at the camera. Now he's waving at the camera! Hello, down there, President Clark," the commentator said.

"Mugging it up as usual," Sec. Zak said.

Hazel was now beginning to become just a little concerned. It seems these "lemmings" had a plan after all. Was Pres. Clark going to attempt to put himself back in the White House?

"We'd better think of something. Fast!" Sec. Zak said.

She pushed the button on her intercom. "I already have a plan—General, have all the troops issued gas masks.

"Get the CIA lab chief on the line immediately," she whispered into the intercom.

"Just before the runners show up at the Washington Monument, we'll put some 'unhappy gas' into the water in the pool. We'll zap 'em!" Ms. Bitch, she thought.

"CIA lab? This is the President calling. Have you got the stuff ready yet. Well, hurry it up over there." She clicked off the intercom.

"But what about the antidote—maybe they've taken the antidote," whined Sec. Zak.

Hazel incredulously looked at Sec. Zak. Was the old man beginning to crack? "What do you take me for?" Hazel said. "I've already thought of that. In the first place I doubt they could make enough antidote for all those people. But just to be on the safe side, I've had the CIA lab and the drug cartels working around the clock to develop a new, top secret destabilizing compound. I just got the word last night they had come up with the mother of all covert destablizers."

"What does this one do?" asked Sec. Zak, thinking back to the nightmare of his own experience of telling the truth for a change. What a chilling experience. He shuddered to even think about it

"It's really quite incredible." Hazel had had enough of "happy gasses" and truth serums. "When 'unhappy gas' mixes with water it strays inert—until...and here's the genius part...it becomes activated...by sound waves. You know how sound travels four times as efficiently in water as in air." (Sec. Zak didn't know this.) "We administer this substance into the water at the base of monument a couple days in advance. We close the area to all visitors, saying we have repairs to do on the monument, so as not to take a chance of activating it too early. When the lemmings, er runners, show up, we let them in. Pres. Clark will give a speech, I'm sure of it, telling them how he is the rightful 'heir to the throne.' When the sound waves reach critical intensity, say right when Clark is waxing his most eloquent, like Martin Luther King and his 'I have a dream' speech, right when he's telling about how he's been to the mountain top of the Star Dolphin's fortress on Mt. Whitney, the aqueous substance will be activated—by sound waves..."

Hazel paused for dramatic effect.

"And?" said Sec. Zak. "What then?"

"What then? As the TV cameras are focusing in on close-up shots of Clark at the podium, right as he's becoming the most emotional, suddenly—everybody—it's really quite simple really—dies."

"You mean kinda like autumn leaves, all floating down to the ground?" smiled Sec. Zak.

"I couldn't have put it better, myself," said Hazel.

At Crater Lake...

The pulsating Star Ship had landed on the star dappled waters of the lake, floating like a floating, rainbow flashing castle. All the people around the lake were lining the abrupt shores of the crater—looking on in quiet wonderment. The Star Dolphins had surely outdone themselves this time. The lights twinkled like multi-colored stars, sparkling off the lake waters, under the moonlight.

Star Dolphins leaped out of saucer doors, swimming with their hands over to Wizard Island.

Nick looked at Vic and Diana and little Pearl. "Come on," he said. He led them down the steep switchbacks through the pine trees to the lake. They got to where a small speedboat was moored to a pier. They all four got in, and sailed over to Wizard Island. "They told me they were coming," Nick said. "But I decided to keep it a surprise for you. Were you surprised?"

"I'll say!" said little Pearl.

The little boat swiftly made it across the lake to the island. They moored it and scrambled to the shore. The Star Dolphins were happily cavorting about the island, which Nick and Vic found intriguing as the Star Dolphins had almost seemed somber in the past.

A Star Dolphin swam up to them, his cosmically smiling face looking up at them from the sapphire sparkling waters.

"Hello, friends!" it squeaked. "This is the most beautiful place under the stars," it said. "This is why we are so happy tonight."

"Except for Tahoe," Nick said, who even still was partial toward his own beautiful mountain lake, even as it had been turning green ("Yccccckkk!") with algae from pollution, the once peerless sky-blue lake in danger of becoming a "green monster."

"Except for Tahoe," the Star Dolphin agreed. "And one day, Tahoe will be returned to its original, pristine glory."

"How?" asked Nick.

"We already have a plan."

"Tell me," pleaded Nick.

"Well, it's rather complicated. It will be a massive undertaking. And it will require infinite patience. But basically it's like this. First of all, everybody moves down over the Carson Mountains to the Nevada deserts. There's enough room there for all. Then we irrigate the waste-land. The water in Tahoe has to be drained…"

"Drain Tahoe?" gasped Nick. He all of a sudden had an image of somebody pulling the plug in the tree-covered mountain basin holding the immense waters of the lake and all the water running out, like a bathtub!

"Slowly. Slowly. We will irrigate the desert all the way to Great Basin National Park on the eastern border. Parched desert will become rich land capable of growing every plant under the sun—and they have lots of sun in Nevada. Once all the water is emptied out of the Lake—which we have to do if we are to purify it from the immense amount of pollution and algae which has permeated all the way down to its infinite depths" (Nick remembered reading a newspaper article about how the pollution in

Lake Tahoe could never be cleaned out, like they had success-fully done at shallow Lake Eeirie in the Great Lakes, because the incredible depth of Tahoe—almost the deepest lake in the world—precluded such a remedy) "and after we've reinstated the old Virginia-Truckee railroad," (the old steam locomotive used to haul timber from the Tahoe Basin to the silver fields of Virginia City and kept in operation until the early 1950s) "we'll level all the buildings at the lake—the casinos and mansions and gas stations—and load the debris onto the train cars and haul it out into the Nevada desert and bury it—"

"You mean like burying radioactive waste?" said Nick. "Out in the middle of the Nevada wasteland?"

"Yes. Exactly," smiled the Star Dolphin. "Bury all the refuse deep in the middle of the desert."

"How are you going to get the water back into Tahoe?"

"Well," smiled the Star Dolphin, "this will be the easiest part of all. We simply seed the clouds directly over the empty Tahoe Basin. It will rain—or snow—non-stop until the Basin is filled with pure, pristine waster once again! Here we need a little help from Mother Nature. Only pure rain and snow water—and we are experts on water, Nicky—only pure rain and snow water can ever return Lake Tahoe to its former glory. We give Mother Nature a little help. She has to do the rest."

"How long do you think it would all take," finally asked Nick. "Forty days and forty nights?" he laughed.

The Star Dolphin, smiled, somewhat sadly. "Let's just say a long time. A lot of wrong has to be undone. But good things take time, don't they Nicky?"

Nick had to admit this was so.

Just then Nick felt a tap on his shoulder. He looked around to see Nancy! in a dripping wet suit, having swam through the frigid waters from the Star Ship. They embraced in a watery embrace.

"Nancy! I'm so glad to see you again."

"I'm getting you all wet," laughed Nancy.

"Hey, friends, this is Nancy, my wife. She's been up on the Star Dolphin's home planet of Shine. Nancy, this is Diana and her daughter Pearl. You already know Vic."

"Hi!"

"Hi!"

"Hi!"

"Guess what," said Nancy.

"What?" said Nick.

"We're getting married."

"Getting married?" asked Nick. "I thought we already were," he laughed.

"No silly. You know how people sometimes get married all over again, just for a special occasion?"

"Yeah," said Nick.

"Well we thought it would be nice…"

"Who's 'we?'" asked Nick.

"Me and the Star Dolphins," said Nancy. "We thought it would be nice if we got married all over again—right her on this cute little island. It'll be nice double wedding…"

"Double wedding?" said Nick, looking at Vic and Diana. "Oh, I see now," he said, as the couple blushed under the moonlight. "When?"

"After the wedding chapel is built."

"On the island."

"Yes. On the island."

"I thought the Star Dolphins were going to make a dolphin port on Wizard Island."

"No. They want to keep it pristine. A small chapel would be much nicer," smiled Nancy. "Don't you agree?"

Within a few days, the small chapel was erected on Wizard Island. A smiling preacher was brought in from Ashland, "I sure guess these Star Dolphins are for real, alright!" the preacher kept saying, looking astonished on the glittering Star Ship floating pristinely on the pristine waters of Crater Lake, and the blessed double ceremony occurred.

The two couples stood together in the quaint chapel before the ever-smiling preacher. Little Pearl was the flower-maiden.

The chapel was small, but very beautiful. The walls were of myrtle, the rare wood flown in from the Oregon coast just to build this chapel. The miniature pipe organ was quite compact, certainly no where as large as the largest pipe organs in cathedrals, but because of the highly advanced degree of engineering the Star Dolphins had put into their "wedding gift" to the two couples, the sound was the complete equal in sumptuousness of the biggest, most magnificent organs anywhere. And what was even more amazing, it never sounded too loud, even in the tiny cathedral. The sound seemed to delicately caress them. The organ lady brought in with the preacher said she had "never heard such a lovely sound."

The preacher performed the wedding, while the Star Dolphins swam happily around Cathedral Island.

The runners were getting closer to their goal of Washington D.C., the Capitol, and the Washington Monument, symbol of all just causes. Nothing could stop then now in their just cause of equality of the species!

They wound their way down the turnpikes, over the overpasses, through the tunnels, under the underpasses, past the belching factories, and the car dealerships, and the shopping plazas.

Nobody stood in their way, as seeweed had preceded them, and people lined the streets, waving white handkerchiefs, waving them on—or those who hadn't gotten the mystery potion, booing at the top of their lungs—

"Dolphins go home!" some signs read.

"We love you, dolphins!" others proclaimed.

(Ex) President Clark was somewhat surprised they had met no resistance as they made their way. It seemed too easy. He wondered if maybe it might not be some kind of trap…

Well, he could only hope everything was going all right. He certainly could not stop this tidal wave of humanity now—even if he wanted to!

The finally reached their goal! There before them loomed, pink like a cherry blossom in the early morning sun, the Washington Monument, inspiring spire!

The vanguard cruised up to the pool at its base. People soon filled in the area around the placid water. Behind them, the vast sea of humanity, those who could not get close enough to the Monument itself, had trekked off to other areas of the Capitol grounds, to the Lincoln Memorial, the Library of Congress—but not the White House itself. They had all been given strict orders, passed along from runner to runner—stay clear of the White House! This was to be an orderly demonstration.

The rest of the runners, as they arrived, circulated into the poorer parts of Washington D.C., through the glum slums that so shamed the capitol city of the "Free World." Through the desolate neighborhoods, past the "projects", the running ambassadors of love, hope and charity, dispersed. They were to seek out those who would let them stay in their homes with them to watch the mass demonstration at the Washington Monument on their TVs (even the poorest of families had televisions).

The drug dealers were so astonished at the mass of runners invading their "turf" they did nothing but stand on the corner and stare glassy-eyed, open-mouthed.

Now the long anticipated "happening" finally began to happen. First, the singers and musicians in the throng got up on the stage, where an advance crew put together by Jungle Jean had already set up ultra high-tech microphones and micro-speakers provided by the Star Dolphins and carried along by the lead pace car, and sang one song after the other from the glory days of the sixties—the sound clean and pure.

> "If I had a hammer
> I'd hammer in the morning
> I'd hammer in the evening
> All over this land!
> I'd hammer out danger
> I'd hammer out warning
> I'd hammer out the love between
> My brothers and my sisters
> All over this land!"

> "How many roads must a man walk down…"

> "All we are saying, is give peace a chance!"

> "Hey, Mr. Tambourine man…"

> "Where have all the flowers gone…"

Then, Jungle Jean got up on stage. He looked out over the never-ending sea of people. "Wow," he thought. "What an audience." He got out his guitar which had ridden along too in the lead car and began to sing some of his best protest songs:

Well, we're marchin' to the sea
Yeah, we're marchin' to our victory
Well, we're marchin'to the sea
And peace will be our victory!

"We're gonna bring our brothers in
We're gonna give 'em strength to begin.
We're gonna bring our sisters in
And show that together we all can win!

And we're marchin'to the sea…
And love will be our victory!

We're gonna make the armies go
We're gonna march'em out on tiptoe
We're gonna let the soldier go
And maybe light the fire so he will know!

That we're marchin' to the sea…
And hope will be our victory

We're gonna turn the politicians around
And make 'em speak without a sound
We're gonna turn the politicians around
And maybe ride the bad ones out of town!

And we're marchin' to the sea…
And truth will be our victory!

We're gonna save our mother earth
Save our mother earth!
We're gonna do all that we can
Sound the alarms!
To make sure that no man
Robs the last of her sweet charms!

And we're marchin' to the sea
Yeah we're marchin' you and me
Oh we're marchin' to the sea
And life will be our victory!

What a moment! Jungle Jean had actually gotten the crowd to sing the choruses along with him. They were all "Marchin' to the Sea"!

Next he sang his song "Liberty and Justice for All."

Liberty and justice for all
Is what the Pledge of Allegiance says
But liberty and justice for some not all
Is what the reality is!

Second class people in the land of the free
Can this be?
We must give a hand to those who have less
Than you and me.
There are so many who need the help
Of those who can see.
Second class people in the land of the free
No this cannot be!

Liberty and justice for all
How long will this take to come true?
Two hundred years have come and gone—
Will two hundred more pass thru?

Another golden moment!
Finally, he did his hymn, "Someday."

Someday
There'll be love for everyone
Someday
When the world shall be as one
Someday
Read the writing on the wall
Someday
When we hear the trumpet call
Someday
On the oceans we will stand
Someday
When we're walking hand in hand.
Someday, someday…
Someday
There'll be peace throughout the land
Someday
When the world will understand
Someday
When the child will lead the bear
Someday
There'll be flowers everywhere
Someday
On the mountains we will stand

Someday
When we're standing hand in hand!
Oh, someday, someday, someday.

The crowd was cheering.

"When do reach critical mass?" asked Sec. Zak.

"It takes a while," whispered Hazel. "Because the compound is in solution in the water, before it becomes sound activated, it has to become saturated with noise. This is what it takes to trigger the chemical change caused by the sound waves. It must reach the saturation threshold. Because the CIA did such a rush job on this stuff to get it out, nobody is exactly sure just when the sound saturation threshold is reached."

"What you mean, Ms. President," Sec. Zak whispered somewhat sarcastically, "they're not sure it will work at all!"

"Well if would have been better if they had a loud rock band playing," admitted Hazel. "Then it would work for sure," she chuckled grimly.

"Well, is it foolproof, or not?" demanded Zak.

The CIA man was standing in the background, watching the proceedings on the television. "Maybe I can answer that," he said.

"Well I wish someone would. Who ever heard of such a thing anyway—sound activated compounds!"

"Oh it's the newest thing," assured the CIA man. "But it does have certain flaws, a few wrinkles which haven't been completely worked out yet."

"Such as," demanded Sec. Zak.

"Well, we're not completely certain if the kind of sound is critical or not in reaching critical mass or not. Like Pres. Macelroy said, if they had a loud rock band playing, we could be much more certain of it working, because it would be the right kind of sound—loud and booming. With the kind of non-descript noise they have going on right now, it's not quite as certain if it will work—or not."

"All we can do is wait and see," said Hazel.

"Oh great," whined Sec. Zak. "You probably don't even have a backup plan do ya?"

"Oh I have a backup plan all right. In the first place, it might work...even without the rock band. Hopefully right when Clark has raised the crowd to a fever pitch. But if it should fail to reach critical saturation mass, then, and only then..." said Pres. Macelroy, "we put plan B into operation."

"Which is..."

"Top Secret," smiled Hazel.

"What do you mean, Top Secret, Ms. Presidenti," he sneered.

"I mean Top Top Secret," said Hazel. "I'm not taking any chances of leaks on this one, and besides you don't have need to know status anyway."

"Who else knows?" he asked.

"Top Secret, I'm afraid," she said. She suddenly pointed at the television.

On the TV (Ex) President Clark had at long last reached the podium. He was standing before the microphone. Finally he began to speak, as a hush came over the crowd.

"Oh, just great," whined Sec. Zak.

"Friends," he began, "we have finally made it! I must admit I'm just a little winded, but I feel great. How about you?"

A roar went out over the crowd.

"That's more like it," said Hazel.

"We have come a long long way together, all the way across the United States of America. Who would have thought it was even possible? Just a few short months ago, many, many of you were wandering homeless and hopeless up and down the streets of San Francisco, way across on the other side of this vast land of ours. You were desolate and despondent, you were hungry and cold, you were young and you were old!

"But now here you are at the Washington Monument!

"You were bank executives and ad writers and policemen and firemen and teachers and doctors, you were in all walks of life, and some of you were near death. But now here you are. And why?

"Because the Star Dolphins have come!"

A huge roar went up, engulfing the monument.

CHAPTER FOUR
THE HERMIT

Heaven felt like a speck, as he inched his way up the immense side of Olympos Mons. Such a sight as loomed above was so far beyond the reach of the normal senses as to make one swoon.

Mons was like three Everests piled one on top of another!

He had read much of the ancient customs of the Martians concerning the Mountain, of the quest each Martian had to make to be considered one of the "tribe."

Strangely, but not so strangely if you thought about it, after Olympos Mons had blown like ten Krakatoas and virtually destroyed their small world, a technologically advanced Eskimo-like culture and a primitive Apache-type culture had evolved on their "angry red planet."

Most of the survivors had migrated north or south to the poles, where the largest concentration of water was, in the ice-caps. When the already thin atmosphere of Mars had been blown away, the surface water, which had been quite plentiful, quickly evaporated. Only underground springs here and there had remained.

At the two poles, these had developed a Martian variation of Earth's Eskimo culture. They lived below the shifting ice. Luckily for the survivors, the Star Dolphins had arrived to help them establish their new home, tunneling down into the ice and building "Martian igloos" which were engineered to withstand the incredible forces of the shifting ice.

Here, the full force of Star Dolphin technology had been brought into play to build a shimmering, under-ice city of wispy ice-like spires which flexed with the changing flow—Echoes of the yet written poetry of distant Earth—those "caves of ice" in Xanadu–

Heaven had visited this technological wonder. Even the Star Dolphins had been taxed to the maximum in designing such an ice-city. How they did it was to design the structures with a circulating system which made the ice melt as it came in contact with the surfaces, creating water flows which cascaded around the structures, and then quickly refroze when it streamed past.

The ice under the poles was continually shifting, like a sea of ice. The use of sound vibrations through the walls of their ice-castles caused sympathetic vibrations in the ice, momentarily liquefying it. The sounds were ultrasonic, even for Martian hearing, which was quite good, like a gazelle—which these shy, strange, creatures, though two legged, in some ways resembled—and as the ice flowed by it created a soothing kind of ice-music, which the Martians enjoyed.

Heaven had still not gotten use to their antlers! Not horns, he thought—They were not like the devil creatures with pointy tails and two horns which Heaven had read of in Arthur C. Clark's science fiction classic *Childhood's End*.

Childhood (innocence) ends for mankind when the saucers land on Earth, bringing with them vast amounts of seemingly beneficial technology. The people of Earth divide into two factions—those who oppose the "Overlords," as the creatures call themselves, and those who applaud them.

At first, there was no visual contact with these overlords, only vocal contact, during which "audiences" the space visitors tell the Earth people they have come to give turbulent planet Earth stability.

But at what price?

Here was the question. Finally, the Overlords reveal themselves to mankind—the very devils of religious tradition—complete with pointed tail and two curved horns on their heads!

And the price—the people's souls—or their minds—their mental extrasensory powers, brought out by the ouija board, which the Overlords use to help power their spacecraft! through the infinite cosmos. The people become mere "pawns in their cosmic game!" In other words, Heaven thought to himself as he climbed, the humans lose their humanness in a high stakes trade for stability—

They were stable, all right—so are lobotomites...

Actually, Heaven had learned that Clarke was not so far-off as one might think. There actually was such a planet around a neighbor star, where such creatures really did exist! with a high level of advanced technology, who had learned how to tap into the mental powers of people in various types of trances—voodoo rites, satanic rituals. They tap these poor creatures' minds, or souls, and divert the energy to their own (under)world by means of telepathic channeling: séances, occult practices, etc, etc, were all fair game. Persons like Hitler, or Alister Crowley (the beast), or Stalin, or Levy (the San Francisco warlock), or the child sacrificers of ancient (and not so ancient) times, or the black magic inspired ancient Aztecs, or vampire-worshipping

Transylvannians, etc, etc, ad nauseam, had all been dupes for these advanced creatures, capable of using the negative energies as a power source, like leeches or parasites, for their own selfish ends...

However, these antlered creatures of Mars, though often violent, were not like this in any way, had indeed fought their own epic battles with this ancient foe.

As a matter of fact, one of the reasons for the traditional climb up "the Mountain of Mountains" was to instill in young Martians the mental and physical discipline necessary to resist the temptations which the Overlords insidiously brought to bear.

And like Jesus on the mountain, fasting forty days to withstand the temptings of the chief Overlord himself, they too could eat no food during "the climb"—were allowed only the "mineralized-mist" in their circulation tanks. Heaven also would fast the entire climb. And the other stipulation was, there would be no outside help. If he had an accident and fell and died up there, as had so many Martians over the long centuries—so be it.

As he slowly bounded from rock to rock, feeling almost molecular in size, he thought again of his "Martian friends." No, he had not yet gotten use to their antlers, nor the way they used them in fierce mating rituals—mortal combat affairs which ended often in the death of one of the combatants, while the doe-like female looked on.

These blood-rites had not taken hold among the technologically advanced Eskimo-martians of the ice-caps, for like the Eskimos of planet Earth, they had, under the benign influence of the Star Dolphins, resisting these violent traditions, opted for the peaceful Eskimo-type custom of wife-sharing!

In the first place, logistics in the ice-cities somewhat precluded such rituals, as space was at a premium, as everyone necessarily lived in close proximity to one another. So instead of duels to the death for a mate—they went the other direction.

Too hedonistic for me, thought Heaven with a small smile as he made his way carefully up toward the cave on a ledge where he would spend his first Martian night on the Mountain, where he would carefully check the "aide climbing" gear he carried in his "space-pack." Soon he would become like the wall climbers of Yosemite, who literally hung from the vertical sides of moon-like Half Dome, sleeping in hammocks hung from pitons over sheer cliffs.

And here, now that he had overcome the initial disadvantage of not "knowing" Olympos as the Martians knew it, living "in its infinite shadow" all their lives, is where he would have to fling his radio off the cliff. For here, from here—he was on his own!

The Apache-type Martians who roamed the desert, traveling from hidden spring to hidden spring, had rejected the technological offerings of both the Star Dolphins and the Overlords, reverting to ancient Martian aboriginal customs—even worshipping the Sphynx-like "Face."

Heaven recalled the first mating ritual he had witnessed out in the desert. It was a gruesome affair of the two gazelle-like human-oid creatures crashing into each other with their antlers—like knights of ancient Earth going at each other with lances from horseback. The Martians would charge each other like bucks, but these duels were often to the death of one of the combatants, the victim offered to the "Great Face."

What's more, they took their "mineralized-mist" masks off for the ritual. Their oversized lungs, like dolphins, allowed them to hold their breaths for long periods, and, as a matter of fact, victory seemed to come invariably to the one who could hold his breath the longest.

Ah well, thought Heaven, as least it keeps the tribe strong.

And they had to be strong to survive the "windy season" on the Martian plains, with its swirling windstorms…which these wraith-like creatures were also adept at riding! "Riding the storm" was another test the young, only male for some reason, Martians had to undergo to achieve full status—only after climbing Olympos Mons first– This too he would have to do!

And without my flipper-wings! thought Heaven. He knew why the Star Dolphins did not use flipper-wings: They preferred the waters below the firmament and the "waters" above the firma-ment—the oceans and hyper space.

"Well, Rena, this is where I sign off," he spoke into the radio. He did not wait for her reply. He took the radio and then flung it off the red cliffs below him. With the relative weakness of Martian gravity, it sailed a good long way off toward the plain below before crashing into the rocks, and making strange squawking sounds.

Robby and Michelle had escaped into the prison yard.

"Now what?" asked Michelle, looking forlornly at the great barbwired walls surrounding them. The towers were eerily lit by flashes of multi-colored eruptions, as vector space claimed the remainder of the hapless guards.

"The great escape!" said Robby. They quickly ran across the empty yard.

Suddenly a milieu of convicts rushed out the doors behind them!

"Hurry!" screamed Michelle.

A helicopter-like dolphin ship appeared over them, hovering above the prison yard. An "energy ladder" lowered down. Robby

472

pushed Michelle up the ladder and then quickly followed. The dolphin-copter took off just as the mob arrived.

"The Star Dolphins decided to have mercy on the convicts," explained Robby.

"What next!" gasped Michelle.

"Next..." said Robby.

"Wait!" said Michelle, holding up her hand. "I don't want to know!"

"...we climb Mt. Everest," said Robby.

Michelle punched him.

After the wedding, Vic and Diana decided to go on a honeymoon—but where? Nick and Nancy volunteered to baby sit little Pearl, so the two newlyweds could be alone, although Vic had grown to love Diana's cute little girl so much he hated to leave her behind.

"Where shall we go?" said Diana. "People come here for their honeymoons."

"True," said Vic. "This is a pretty hard act to follow." He looked out on the peerless waters, still marveling at the sight of the Star saucer sparkling on the lake. "But I love to fish, and I was thinking the Siskiyous, down in the Trinity Alps in northern California would be nice. It's not very far away, and they have plenty of campgrounds and the fishing's great. What's more, it's really rugged, secluded country, with lots of backcountry trails. We could do some backpacking, too!"

"Okay," said Diana. "Sounds nice."

They loaded their things into Vic's van, then said "goodbyes" to Pearl and Nick and Nancy and waved at the Star Dolphins, Diana saying, "I still don't believe it!"

Off they were on their honeymoon. What a fine time it would be for both.

They drove down the Crater Lake highway to Interstate 5 and turned south, past Ashland and Yreka and Weed, and turned west at Mt. Shasta on the road winding its way over toward the coast, through the Trinity wilderness area.

"Maybe we'll see a sasquatch!" said Vic as they drove past a rough-hewn wooden statue of the mythological, erect, hairy ape-like creatures in one of the little towns they passed through. The river rumbled past on the side of the highway.

"For some reason," said Diana, "I thought you were going to say that."

"Do you believe they exist?" asked Vic.

"Well, the Indian people have ancient legends of meeting the poor things in the woods, so they must have thought they did. Or maybe they were just stories told to keep their little kids in line—You know, like the boogey man, who would come and carry a child off to its cave if it misbehaved."

"Why did you call it a 'poor thing'? Maybe they're quite happy—if they exist."

"I think they're lonely, like hermits, you know. They hide back in these rugged mountains, because they know if people caught them, they'll haul them off to zoos, or 'study' them—or put them on talk shows on TV," she giggled.

"Yeah, you're right. Imagine being forced to go on the 'Tonight Show' if you were a sasquatch?" laughed Vic, "sitting there in one of those chairs under the hot lights, in their thick fur, their hairy legs crossed just so, and trading inane jokes with Jay Letterman, or whoever it is these days. And listening to all those stupid sasquatch jokes.

"Why did the sasquatch cross the road?"

"I don't know," said Diana.

"Whoa!" said Vic. "Did you see that?"

"See what!?" gasped Diana, looking.

"Nothing," said Vic, grinning.

Diana punched him in the arm.

"Hey," said Vic, "that's my fishin' arm!"

The sun had set rust red over the hills. It was getting dark, and the headlights peered down the gloomy, forest lined road.

Suddenly, a doe and two fawns scampered across the highway! Vic punched the brakes, and the family just made it across in front of them.

"You alright?" Vic said, looking at Diana.

"Yeah. I'm fine. That was close. Maybe we better stop for the night."

"Yeah," said Vic. "The next campground we come to."

They pulled into the campground and found a secluded spot to put up their tent. Vic built a campfire, and Diana started to prepare dinner. After they had eaten, they sat next to the warm fire, Vic's arm around her shoulders, peering up at the star filled night sky.

"Boy, am I a lucky man," said Vic, holding her tighter.

"You deserve it," said Diana.

"Yeah, you're right. I guess I do."

Diana kissed him.

In the lovely morning, they put their stuff into the van, and got their backpacks out. A trail climbed into the back-country wilderness from here.

Vic kissed her. "Married like ain't so bad, I guess," he said.

Diana punched him again.

"Hey! My fishin' arm. Boy, I can't wait to do some fishin' from one of these mountain streams they got around here."

"I can't wait to do some sightseeing," said Diana.

They loaded their gear on, and sauntered up the trail, through the rugged, dense tree thicketed hills. "Watch out for poison oak," said Diana. "It's all over the place around here. You know what it looks like, don't you?"

"Do I look like a boy scout, or not. 'Leaflets three, let it be!'"

"Just checkin'," said Diana. "When it comes to poison oak, an ounce of prevention is definitely worth a pound of cure."

"Yep," said Vic.

They kept hiking until they finally came to a nice little meadow with a creek tumbling down the middle.

"Well, how about here?"

"Looks swell," said Diana.

They set up camp, and Vic got his fly fishing gear out. He walked over to the tumbling creek and expertly cast the fly up the waters, the line making tight little arcs as he flicked it.

"Hey," said Diana, "you're pretty good at that!"

"I should be. Been doin' it since I was a little kid. My dad, who's dead now, bless him, was a pro. He taught me at the age of 5...Whoops! Looks like we got somethin' here." Vic expertly hauled the struggling fish out of the water.

"Hey," said Diana. "Good catch!"

He flung the fish over to her.

In a few minutes, he had caught another trout, and in the waning sun, they had fish dinner under the trees.

Then they sat by the fire as the stars appeared.

"Look," said Vic, pointing toward the stars above the tree lined ridge. "See that constellation?"

"Which one?"

"Well, that one, right there just over the trees, is the sasquatch. You can see…"

Diana pinched him.

In the morning, after a breakfast of fresh mountain trout, the pair hiked back out to the campground. It was almost night by the time they arrived at Vic's van, the full moon rising.

They decided to sleep in the van instead of putting up the tent. As he was rummaging around, Vic came upon the headphones he had heard the Star Dolphin's message in.

"Hey Diana," Vic said. "Look! Here are those headphones I had on when I first heard the Star Dolphins talking—er, singing—to me." He quickly retold the story of the night the Beatles had been interrupted by the dolphin choir.

"I thought I'd lost 'em, but here they are!"

He put them on. Silence.

"Nothing now."

He took them back off, and the two got their connecting sleeping bags out for the night. They crawled in together (and after an hour of frolicking like lovesick dolphins) blissfully went to sleep.

Suddenly, in the middle of the night, they were awakened by the shaking of the van! Earthquake? Diana screamed.

Vic looked out the window to see a hairy—hominid!—face peering in! Diana screamed louder, and the creature shook the van again.

"Ssssh!" said Vic. "You might scare it!"

"Me scare it? What is it?"

Then—Vic heard strange squawking sounds coming out of his headphones!

"Put me on! Put me on!" he heard.

Vic grabbed them and quickly put them on, as the shaking stopped.

"I am sasquatch!" Vic heard.

"What are they saying?" asked Diana.

"It's sasquatch!"

"Roll down your window. I will not harm you."

"He wants us to roll down the window."

"No!" screamed Diana.

"I think we better do like it says."

Vic slowly rolled down the window.

"What do you want?" asked Vic, feeling just a little stupid.

How could "it" understand?

"I am Auk. I understand your tongue, but cannot speak it except through the interpreter of my thoughts," the headphones said.

"Who is the interpreter?"

"The magic starfish," Vic heard.

"Y'mean the Star Dolphins?" asked Vic.

"Yes. They can read my mind...interpret my thoughts. They told me you were coming. They told me you—a man—would listen to my story...someone would finally understand me."

A nice honeymoon surprise, thought Vic.

"I am the most intelligent of my kind. The smartest sasquatch that ever lived.

"We hid away from you, uh—homosapiens. We can hear and smell like the animals, and with the instincts of mountain lions and the intelligence of your little children, we have successfully eluded your capture for all these years—but we exist!"

"I see," said Vic.

"I am an aberrant, the smartest of my race. All my life I have felt ancient longings to contact your race—the 'wise ones.' We have superior senses and strength—like animals—but you have superior minds—have invented frightening things. But we have learned over the ages to elude you.

"This was not always so. In the beginning, my ancient ones were often killed by yours. As a little sasquatch, I heard many stories, passed down from age to age, of how our early ones died at your hands. But we learned quick—and survived!"

Vic remembered the incredibly poignant novel by William Golding the great British novelist, *The Inheritors,* about a tribe of ancient Neanderthals who came in contact with the more "advanced" cromagnum homosapiens during the ice age. Vic had thought Golding could never write a better book than his first monumental novel, *The Lord of the Flies,* about a group of "homo-sapien" children shipwrecked on a deserted island, who revert to particularly "homosapien" kind of savagery, but *The Inheritors,* his next work, was even so much better it had seemed to Vic the British genius had reached an "epiphany of poignancy." The portrayal of the gentle giants brought emotions to Vic he hadn't known he had—feelings of mysterious, aboriginal pathos—as he observed the day to day simple world of the Neanderthal family rent asunder by the sudden, swift, frightening appearance of a tribe of ancient homosapiens…with bows and arrows and spears and nets and fire and alcohol—and bones in their noses.

All in all, a nightmare.

Vic looked out the window at Auk, who was kneeling down to look in the window. Diana huddled against Vic's side, trembling. Vic thought about it for a moment. Diana's "ancient ones," the Lokata Sioux, had also come in contact with a "superior race"— his own!!

"My kind drove me out, because I wished us to make contact with your kind—the enemy. Mine would have killed me with stones, but I escaped, and my superior intelligence has allowed me to elude my own kind as well as yours.

"I have become a hermit.

"One night, as I, Auk, was sitting on top of a hill, gazing up at the stars and meditating—one of the stars moved!

"I stood up, watching it! Then the strange star started to whistle! but I, Auk, was not afraid. Then, it came and hovered over me! I stretched my arms up to it.

"Suddenly I heard talking in my head! The talking said, 'We are the starfish. We know of you desire to talk with your smaller, distant cousins. We know your desire to learn the mysterious things they know—and more! We know you, Auk, are the most intelligent of your kind who has ever lived. We, the starfish, will teach you the language of your cousins so you can understand the things they say.'

"They told me you would be coming here and that Auk could talk to you through the interpreter. Auk is here!"

"But what do you want?" asked Vic.

"I want to learn to read! I have found your books sometimes in the woods…leaves with strange tiny markings. I want to know what the marks are saying.

"I want to see into the sky. The starfish said you have windows which look through the shield of the stars." Auk swept his hand across the sparkling sky. "I want to see beyond the stars!

"I want to know how these things," Auk shook Vic's van, as Diana softly cried out, "go so quick down the mysterious highway that leads into infinity. I want to know where they go. What's at the other end of the mysterious purple ribbons?" Auk stopped.

Vic was silent. He thought of Ishi, the last surviving "wild Indian" who had walked out of these hills in the early part of the twentieth century, to be clothed in white man's clothes and sleep in a white man's bed, eat white man's food, who learned many strange things before he finally died. Another hermit, the last of his wild kind, who had decided to contact the "superior" "civilized" white race.

"Auk wants to go back with us," Vic said to Diana.

Diana screamed again.

"We got room," grinned Vic looking at the 7ft tall, 300lb creature, as Auk slowly stood up, looming under the stars like a living statue…

Robby and Michelle were hovering over Mt. Everest in the dolphin-copter.

"I thought you were kidding," said Michelle, as she looked open-mouthed at the endless snow-covered pyramids below them.

"I was kidding," said Robby. "I said 'climb Mt. Everest.' We're only going to land on it!"

"Why?" asked Michelle.

"To meet 'The King to the Snowmen'."

"The King of the Snowmen?"

"The abominable snowman! He has climbed all the way up here to talk to us. He has been meditating up here for days like hermit, waiting for us.

"We have to referee a meeting between him and the lone mountain climber who is right now making his way up the North Face of Everest—without oxygen—up the final ascent. He'll make the summit this morning. He doesn't know it yet, but his solo climb of Everest will be memorable in more ways than one!"

"Who is the climber?" asked Michelle, looking down through the telescope Robby had handed her. She could see the tiny shape slowly, relentlessly, climbing toward the summit.

"The great Italian mountaineer Reinhold Messner." Robby had read all of Messner's books—about his first ever solo climb of Everest…without oxygen. About how he was the first to climb all the world's highest peaks. About his conquest of the killer mountain K2, second highest in the world, just down the range a ways. The enigmatic, mystical climber was the perfect link to meet the snowman, and lead him back down to the Tibetan priest waiting in the lonely hermitage in the peaceful but bleak valley at the base of the mountain, for the first "official" contact between the two races.

"I see the Snowman!" Michele suddenly said. "He's almost invisible against the snow, but he's jumping up and down right below us."

Robby took the telescope. "Yes. It's King Rok, the king of the yeti."

"The yeti?"

"Yes," said Robby. "They dispersed into the mountain regions of the earth to elude the homosapiens. They evolved mysterious 'extra senses' which helped them evade their civilized smaller cousins, which also made them easy for the Star Dolphins to contact. The Star Dolphins have helped protect their species over the centuries."

The white furred hominid was gesturing up at the whirling dolphin-copter. It scurried away as the "flying fish" slowly settled down on the summit.

"Here. Put these on. Quick," said Robby, handing an arctic suit to Michelle. "We have an appointment—with destiny—to keep."

"We? Why 'we'?" asked Michelle. "I'm shivering just looking out there."

"C'mon!" said Robby, as he put his glistening suit on. "It'll be fun. And then you can say you've stood on the top of Mt. Everest."

Robby and Michelle jumped out of the dolphin-copter. Like Reinhold Messner and the abominable snowman, they too could breathe up here.

"Wow! Look at this view," gasped Michelle. The rising sun made a streamlined swath of light across the sparkling snow covered Himalayan peaks.

The white-furred snowman slowly approached them. Robby put his "hearing-aide" on, the very one Heaven had first used to hear the dolphins talking. With a little reprogramming, it could now translate the grunting "language" of the snow man.

"King Rok is here!" Robby heard the giant "apeman" say, his hominid face outlined by thick white fur.

Robby spoke into the reprogrammed "megaphone"—grunts came out instead of whistles.

"We too have come," Robby spoke.

"Where is the one who is to take me to the hermit-priest below?" King Rok asked.

"Right there!" said Robby, pointing.

They all looked to see the lone mountaineer slowly, very slowly, walking toward the strange group.

He must be wondering if he's having a high-altitude hallucination, thought Robby.

The figure stopped in his tracks. Robby called out to him.

"C'mon! It's all right. We're friends!"

"Who are you?" called the mountaineer, shaking his head.

"We come from the Star Dolphins," yelled back Robby, through the whispering wind, sometimes still, sometimes talking in gushes of rushing currents.

"And this is the King of the Snowmen," said Robby pointing to the great white-furred yeti.

"You mean—a yeti!?" the climber cried.

"Yes. A real authentic, live yeti!" answered Robby. "And I'm Robby and this is my sister Michelle."

"The ones of TV?" said the climber.

"Yep," said Michelle. "The very same!"

"Well, well, well," the climber said. "This is quite a day, now isn't it." He approached them.

"Meet King Rok," said Michelle, pointing to the yeti, who indeed looked like a giant snowman.

All Rok needs is a corn-cob pipe, thought Michelle to herself.

"I saw his tracks," the climber said. "I'd never seen them this high before, but I have seen them. I never told anyone—they all think I'm a nut-case anyway for climbing these peaks solo without oxygen."

He looked at the yeti. "Amazing. I wondered if I'd ever see one. I now meet the King!" He reached out his hand toward it. The yeti stepped back, and then—it smiled!!

The climber laughed and laughed and laughed, his laughter booming down the slope of the mountain.

The climber and the yeti made their way efficiently down the side of Everest, through the shifting ice fields, and finally they were at base camp 2, deserted and desolate except for the climber's small tent pitched precariously on the snow. They stayed there the night, the climber in his tent, the yeti in the snow, and in the morning the two walked down toward the base of the mountain.

The climber radioed down to his waiting girlfriend that he had a yeti in tow, and everyone was to take off.

"A yeti?!"

"Yes. He'll only come down if there is no one at the base, so you and the sherpas are going to have to get in the trucks and go back down to the village…Yes, I'm totally serious, dear…No I'm not kidding. Can't you understand Italian?…No this is not some kind of publicity stunt, though I have to admit it would be a good one! It's the real thing! I need a clear path to the old hermitage where the old monk is staying—so everyone clear out! Okay?"

"Okay. If you say so. But if this is just another one of your crazy stunts…"

"You mean like climbing Everest solo without oxygen," the climber replied.

"…I'll never talk to you again."

"Please, dear, believe me!"

"Okay, okay. We're all going, already!"

The two finally made it down to the base of the world's highest mountain, where the lonely camp had been deserted. Then they slowly walked down to the valley toward the ancient stone hermitage.

The climber knocked on the rough wooden door. It slowly came open, and the old monk looked out at the strange two. The monk smiled.

"Come in," he said in broken English, his voice ancient, far away, mysterious, "both of you. I've been waiting for you—a long, long time."

The climber entered and the yeti followed him into the dimly lit, stark room, like a trained elephant.

"We have come from the Star Dolphins," the climber said, "from the top of the world."

The monk nodded. Even up here the rumors had spread of the Star Dolphins. "Then they are real."

The climber turned to the yeti. "There is the proof. They have tamed the yeti!"

"Yes, I see," said the old monk, peering into the gentle hominid eyes of the smiling yeti.

The yeti grunted.

"And can you understand him? What does he say?" asked the hermit.

The climber took out the strange things the dolphin people had given him...exact replicas of the hearing-aide and megaphone...and the climber carefully listened as the yeti made his grunting sounds.

"He says, 'I am King Rok, the king of all the yetis of the Earth. We finally have made contact with you because of the magic starfish. We of the highest peaks have been in telepathic contact with them for centuries. They have been our friends. They have even guided us in eluding your capture. But now we are at last to join you! Our races are to live in peace together—side by side on this beautiful planet we all call home..."

486

Vic and Diana…and Auk. The bizarre trio drove down the highway in the dark of early morning, Auk stretched out in the back of the van, Diana huddled down against Vic in the front, Vic's headphones still on his head.

Now the sun's first pink rays were beginning to glide over the mountain tops. And soon, the white-pink slopes of Mt. Shasta came into view in the far distance.

Auk was sitting up in the back, now, looking out the windows.

"Where we go?" asked Auk.

"Where do you want to go, Auk," asked Vic.

Silence. Finally Auk laughed. "Over the rainbow!"

"What rainbow," said Vic.

"We are on the rainbow, and the mountain there is the end of rainbow. That is where Auk wishes to go."

"Mt. Shasta?" said Vic.

"Mt. Shasta," said Auk. "The end of the rainbow."

"Great!" said Vic.

Diana spoke up. "What does he want to do?"

"Go to Mt. Shasta."

Diana sat up. "Really?" Diana laughed. "Nick has some crazy hippie friends there in a commune at the base of the moun-tain. I'm sure they'd just love to meet…Auk. They're just crazy enough, they might even take him in."

"Auk will climb to the top of the mountain," said the sas-quatch.

"Great idea! Auk. That's usin' the 'ole bean!"

"What?"

"Nothin'. It's a good idea, is what I meant. I'll even come with you…"

"No! This is something I must do alone. The mountain is the end of the rainbow, and I must climb up by myself."

"Sure. Whatever you want," said Vic.

They finally arrived at the town of Mt. Shasta. "I think you had better lie down back there, Auk, stay outta sight until we get to the mountain. Okay?"

"Yes."

"What would we do if a cop should stop us," asked Diana, laughing slightly.

"Don't ask," said Vic.

They cruised through the bustling mountain town and then up the tree-lined road toward the base of Mt Shasta. Vic turned into the dirt road leading toward the commune, where Nick and Diane had spent the night on the way to Crater Lake. How much has happened since then! thought Diana.

Some people were standing around outside the quaint looking wood dwellings.

Diana said, "I think you should let me introduce them to Auk."

The van stopped and Diana got out.

"Hi! Remember me? Diana? Nick's friend?"

"Oh sure. How are ya? Is that Nick?"

Vic got out.

"Nick's up at Crater Lake. This is my husband, Vic. We just got married, and we're on our honeymoon. We're going back to Crater Lake and thought we would stop in and say hi…

"Hi," said Diane.

"Hi," said Vic.

"Hi!" said the smiling hippie. "You're welcome!"

"Who ya got in the back there," said another, as Auk rustled around.

"Big fella, whoever he is," the first said.

"Well…" said Diane. "You're probably not going to believe this, but you know about the Star Dolphins?"

"Sure! We saw one of their dolphin-ships go into their secret passage in the mountain just last night!"

"Well, they're in contact with the sasquatch and…"

"Y'don' mean…" the hippie said, pointing toward the van, which was jostling around some now as Auk sat up.

"Yeah," said Vic. "It's a sasquatch all right."

"No kiddin," said the second hippie.

"No kiddin," Diana said. "We were wondering if he could stay with you folks?"

"Auk wants to learn to read," added Vic.

Silence.

"And he wants to climb up to the top of Shasta, alone, like a pilgrimage, you know," continued Vic.

Vic walked over and opened Auk's door. Auk slowly got out, and stood before the group slowly forming around the van.

Somebody whistled.

"Yeah, that's what I thought," said Vic.

"Holy sasquatch!" someone said.

Everyone laughed.

"Sure he can stay here," the first hippie said.

"Auk, meet your new family," Diana smiled.

Auk pointed up toward the mountain. He began walking toward it.

"Where's Auk going?"

"I guess he's decided now's as good a time as any for his pilgrimage," Vic said.

They watched Auk until he had disappeared into the trees.

"Will he come back?"

"Only time will tell."

"What if Auk meets some other climbers up there?"

"I just hope they don't fall down the mountain," said Vic.

Auk easily clambored up the slope of the mountain, up Avalanche Gultch. Below him he could see the tiny community he had just left, and his home mountains of the Trinitys in the far, hazy distance.

Soon he reached the Shasta Glacier and scampered up the permanent snow field around the base of the cinder cone summit. He instinctively seem to find the most direct route to the top, as if some mysterious "homing" device was leading him on to his goal.

This was what Auk had wanted all of his life, to see what was at the end of the magic rainbow that led out of his home. When he found it was a beautiful mountain, he was happy for the first time in his life. And now, on the mountain itself, he felt a quiet kind of joy.

He passed some other mountain climbers, who looked aghast as he romped past them, leaving them far behind. No homosapien could climb like him.

He was panting as he finally reached the summit. This was the moment of truth! He would see the whole world from here!

The whole world, thought Auk.

The world stretched out before him in every direction. He saw endless forests, and other mystery highways, and lofty mountains, and the little towns of the homosapien people.

It was all there before him!

Auk spent the night on the summit. The climbers he passed had turned around and hurried back down the mountain! and luckily none other made it up. Truly, the mystery starfish were with him! The beautiful mountain was his this sparkling day.

Auk was king of the mountain!

He sat on a rock ledge, watching the twinkling lights of the towns below and of the night sky above. They seemed a little the same to Auk. Both were mysterious. Both represented the vast unknown.

Auk began to chant. The sounds came out of him as he sat on the top of his world between the sky and the earth—

Auk looked up at the stars again. One of the stars moved. Auk reached his arms out to it. It was just a falling star.

It was good.

Down below, at the crystal springed base of Mt. Shasta, Vic and Diana and their friends sat around the campfire, gazing up toward the distant summit of the magic mountain.

"What do you think Auk is doing up there?" one asked.

"Do you think he made it to the top?"

"I'd bet on it," said Vic. "He probably made it up in record time."

"Which is about two hours, now, I think. The caretaker of the Shasta hut is the current record holder."

"Not anymore, I bet," said Vic.

Everyone laughed.

"Do you think Auk'll come back down, or just stay up there."

"Who knows," said Vic. "Maybe he's already met a Lumerian," he said, knowing something of the myths of the region. The area around Mt. Shasta had become the world-wide center for people who believed in the lost Pacific continent of Lemuria, whose three-toed race was believed to have established their new home in the center of Mt. Shasta itself!

But now, with the appearance of the Star Dolphins...?

Everyone laughed again. "Maybe Auk is one!"

Jungle Jean stood in the audience, listening to (Ex) Pres Clark give his speech.

The trip running across America had been like a pilgrimage for the (now) long bearded "folksinger." As he stood in the audience, he suddenly started recalling vividly his other "pilgrimage," when he had, some years ago, trekked off to India and Tibet to try to find the answers to "the meaning of life." He had mingled with the musicians in Bombay, hoping to learn some of the mysteries of Indian music which he could use in his own music. He had listened entranced to the timeless "ragas."

Eventually, he had wandered off into the foothills of the Himalayas, up to where the Ganges flowed crystal pure from mountain springs, the ice-clad temples of the clouds seeming to hold up the sun-rent sky itself. There, he had come upon a hermit, a young Indian musician who had wandered up here from the Indus Valley to pray and meditate...and play his guitar! Not a sitar or a vena or the tabla or Indian flute, but a good old fashioned American classical guitar!

Jungle Jean was amazed.

Luckily the young musician spoke impeccable English, so they had long conversations in the shadow of the high peaks.

"I didn't think any musicians in India played the guitar," said Jean.

The musician smiled. "I'm about the only one," he admitted. "This is one reason I became a hermit. It was lonely down there. It's not lonely up here in these beautiful mountains, though."

"How come you chose the guitar?" Jean had asked.

"Well, once, I was in Bombay playing my sitar and I met an American musician, much like you Jungle Jean. He had a classical guitar with him, and was very good. He played a kind of 'classical folk' music, 'folk baroque,' I think he called it.

"He taught me how to play it. I liked the sound of the guitar. It was simple and, I thought, charming. I liked the harmonies you could get on the guitar, which you can't really do on the sitar. So I spent much time with him, learning the instrument and teaching the young man things about the sitar which he could use on his instrument.

"He stayed for some months. He left me his guitar!

"Before he left, he had composed a piece of music for the guitar, complete with lyrics, based on some of the raga scales I had taught him. It was quite charming...

"He called it 'Silk String Magic.'"

The young Indian musician picked up his old battered classic guitar and began to play the piece of music the young American had composed while staying with him. His fingers whirred over the strings, up and down the fingerboard, as he sang the words in a high, sweet voice, bringing out the melody and harmony of the strange song. "I've played for the tourists!" he smiled.

Jungle Jean had been entranced by the "song," an intriguing blend of Indian and American folk sounds in a piece of music about presenting a magic show in music. He sat and listened, amazed at wandering onto this young man who played the American guitar as well as anyone he had ever heard, but adding his own uniquely Indian ideas for a rich sound he had never heard. What a coincidence! he thought. (The young American had even brought a large supply of guitar strings with him on his pilgrimage, and left them with him.)

Jean stayed with the young man for some time, learning the song. Soon, he was able to play it perfectly.

An idea began to form in his mind now, about presenting a long "magic show in music," using "Silk String Magic" as the theme song, combining songs of his own he had already written, including some of the songs he had just played for the throng here—an elaborate, magical, musical show, but instead of emphasizing the Indian connection, he would base it on the old time "medicine show" of the "medicine wagons" which wandered the American West in the late 1800s, selling bottles of "Dr. Good."

It was an intriguing idea. With time, after he had returned to America, Jungle Jean had finished it. It was a tour de force of guitar pickin' and sung poetry.

He tried it out in some of the folk clubs of San Francisco. The reaction to it was decidedly mixed. In the first place, it lasted almost an hour, nonstop! going directly from song to song without pause, much like the Beatles' *Sgt Pepper's Lonely Hearts Club Band* album, which is some ways he was trying to emulate—the idea of a thematic unity to a long piece of music.

Some people had been intrigued by it, others had been overwhelmed. Some loved it, others did not. A mixed reaction.

So Jean had stopped playing it, and returned to doing individual songs—but not before he had recorded it.

At least he had gotten a reaction!

Someday, he thought, as he listened to the (Ex) President give his inspired speech, maybe I'll perform *The Silk String Magic Show* again. Maybe people will be ready for it, for something which challenges them, instead of stultifying them—the way music used to do, when the Beatles and Dylan were king of the mountain, before the days of decadence and cocaine and throw-away songs.

Someday…he thought.

A roar engulfed the crowd as (Ex) President Clark continued his address…

Meanwhile, back on Mars…

Heaven was suspended on the vertical wall of Olympos Mons. He felt indeed molecular in size as he inched his way up the red cliffs of the dormant volcano.

He had been "aide-climbing" now for days, the "mineralized mist" in his circulation tank his only sustenance. It was exhausting.

No wonder, he thought, as he climbed step by step up the rope ladder, over the overhanging ledge, the Martians had survived. The amount of strength and will power required for this climb was staggering.

If he made it, he would certainly remember this as one of the epochal moments of his life.

Heaven, now exhausted to a degree he had never before experienced, began seeing his life pass before him, almost as if he were a dying man. The mountain had become like a living, breathing, all-dominating presence to him. He recalled John Muir's writing of his encounter with the volcanic Mt. Ritter, an experience he called "A Near View of the High Sierra." Heaven knew the feeling. He was climbing up the wall of sky! Who could explain such a feeling? He was inching his way up the single highest mountain in the entire solar system!—by a long shot. No other mountains even approached the unbelievable grandeur of Mons—a volcano so large the base of this single mountain would stretch on planet Earth from San Francisco to LA!—virtually as long as the entire Sierra Nevada mountain range. Put that in your pipe and smoke it, thought an exhausted Heaven.

No wonder the Martians had looked up! from their citadel of the Great Face!

He looked down now, the distant rust red surface of Mars seeming to disappear as if some one had pulled the drain plug of the Martian plane, and it swirled away, down and down.

He recalled a strange little love song he had heard once:

"Don't look down!
Don't look down!
My baby tells me
My baby tells me

"We are free
You and me
Eternally!
Eternally!

"Don't look down!"

Heaven looked up now.   He was actually, finally, gaining the summit!

Suddenly he felt extremely light headed. Once again, his life seemed to pass before him.

What a life it had been!

He remembered his first swim in the incredible rippling sea with the laughing dolphins! his earliest memory. He remembered back to walking with his father as a young boy on the beach at Bermuda. He remembered the sky overhead. He remembered all the people coming to hear his father preach about love and dolphins. Then he remembered the day his father had flung him into the sea as the terrible helicopter had shot his father and Michael had floated in his own blood. And the dolphins had soared in and carried his body out and Heaven had dove down under, and his father's eyes had suddenly come open like light beams…

He remembered now playing with Rena as a child on the beach. The two had been inseparable right from the start…He remembered the crystal day he had found the magic conch shell, on which he could call the dolphins.

He remembered the wedding day of him and Rena. Then his friends, good friends, with whom he and Rena had sailed through the islands in eternal summer…and Michelle and Robby being born!

He recalled finding his father's journal and notes, which allowed him to finish Michael's work, and finally invent the computer devices for communicating with another extraterrestrial race—the dolphins.

Then there was the great treasure hunt, when with the help of the dolphins they had found the treasures of the sea, and used the wealth to build *The Dolphin* in which they had sailed around the world:

The encounter with the fishing seiner and meeting Capt. Jones and finding their island, Utopia II, in the Gulf of Mexico, the storm at Cape Horn, the meeting of the Indians of the tip of South America, up to Alaska and Sir Killer, who had disappeared finally, no one knew where. Had he returned to his own icy arctic waters? Storming the beach in northern Japan, and sailing to India and the Holy Land.

Returning to Bermuda and finding the lost Continent of Atlantis!

Then sailing home once again into the Gulf, and meeting Dr. Smith! the mad scientist who had performed the dolphin brain transplant on his father. Building their undersea Xanudu!

And finally, he and Rena meeting his father in the clouds and going to Planet Shine.

Now, after an eternity on the Mountain, he pulled himself over the final ledge. The summit of summits. Twenty miles high! He hauled himself up the final massive fissure system—and he was at the top of the universe!

The flat summit itself seemed endless…stretching to the horizon before him…and beyond the confines of the sky…

When Heaven awoke, the first thing he saw was flickering firelight on the walls of the cave. He slowly sat up, and looked around.

He was in a cavern with rainbow hued, glistening stalactites and stalagmites. A small fire burned nearby, seeming to come up out of the rock itself!

Then he saw the shadow of the antlers, dancing against the wall. He shifted his gaze, and saw the gazelle-like Martian watching him, sitting cross legged on the floor.

"I found you up there," he said quietly. Heaven and Rena had learned the difficult Martian language quickly with the help of White Dolphin.

"You were almost dead. I brought you down here."

"Who are you," asked Heaven.

"The mad-hermit of the Mountain, they call me," he said with a laugh, an eerie sound which seemed to ricochet off the walls.

"I watched you ascend the climb," he said. "You are to be congratulated. You are the first non-Martian to ever climb the Mountain."

Heaven hadn't even thought of this.

Then, from feeling elated, he felt somber.

"But I was to have no help. So the quest was a failure."

The old Martian sat in silence. Then he stood up. "Well, I think we can make an exception in your case. After all, you did have the disadvantage of not being from Mars. And, you made the top.

"So I think you did it!"

"So…your people will help mine in their struggle on Planet Earth?" asked Heaven.

"Well, the initiation is not yet over. First you have to learn the picture-stories and then you have to ride the wind! But I, the mad-hermit of the Magic Mountain, will be your guide."

Heaven tried to stand, but could not. He was too weak.

"You should rest for now," the Martian said. "And eat!"

He brought out a bowl filled with…seeweed!

"Where did you get this?" Heaven asked.

"One reason I moved up here was to try to establish contact with the Star Dolphins. My people on the Martian planes have rejected their offerings, preferring the simple but difficult life they have lived on Mars for ages.

"So I left my people and climbed up here to this cave I had discovered long ago, which has a natural spring of mineral water in it. I mediated for days. I thought I might die. But finally, the Star Dolphins came to me. They brought their 'seeweed.' They saved my life. I have lived up here ever since, learning the things they teach me.

"They told me of your climb. They told me I was to watch over you and teach you the ancient picture stories and guide you in riding the wind back down to the citadel.

"Nantook is here!" He extended a graceful hand, and Heaven took it, and the two smiled at each other.

The picture stories began to flash across the rainbow walls of the cave, the scrolls Nantook had lugged up here in his climbing pack to review the history of Mars in meditative silence.

Mars had once been a beautiful, almost surreal land of running rivers and trees and graceful cities…

There had been no time-period on Mars which coincided with the hundreds of millions of years of the dinosaurs and earlier life forms, before mankind appeared on planet Earth. The Martians themselves had been here for hundreds of millions of years!

The pictures told stories of their vast cities, where the Martians had lived since time beyond memory. In fact, unlike humans, the Martians had believed they had always been here—as old as the rocks themselves.

Over the hundreds of millions of years before the final great eruption of Olympos Mons and the other volcanoes in a chain reaction, Martian culture had evolved to a degree of refinement as to make the cities of Earth look almost stone age in comparison.

As Heaven watched, entranced, he thought of the *Martian Chronicles,* by the great fantasy writer Ray Bradbury.

There were some striking similarities between his fantastical depiction of Martian society and what he was seeing now— the playfulness of the Martians was evident in both—they were almost surreal creatures, more at home in fantasy than any science fiction an Earth writer could write.

This was because of the advanced nature of their technology, which had truly reached the realm of magic.

Their technology had become so refined over the endless—timeless—ages, they had achieved a true form of magic!

For instance, they never made doors in their homes, because, at will, they could glide through the walls! Their houses had no doors! Their houses had no windows! because they could see through walls, too…

Their homes were like marble mausoleums, structures only to keep out the howling Martian winds and dust storms, so the dwellers could live in refined elegance within…enjoy their sumptuous banquets of Martian delicacies…listen and watch their elaborate musicals as they materialized in the comfort of their houses, vast productions, which were surprisingly similar to the musicals of the golden age of Hollywood on Earth, complete with dancers and singers and opulent scenery. These though would just "show up" with the press of a button, and the "illusion" created in their darkened movie rooms were so real you could shake the hand of one of the performers.

Magic!

But it was based on a technology that was actually all too fragile, energy manipulators which could rearrange subatomic patterns of matter and energy to allow access to higher dimensional space-time.

Then, virtually anything was possible.

If one wanted to walk through walls, one must only change his (or her) dimension for a split second and he (or she) was through.

Etc, etc…the list was endless…

The pictures told the story of the first great breakthrough into higher dimensional space: the achievement of their greatest scientist, who observed the cosmos and finally deduced the obvious: in such a vast universe, virtually anything could be done if one had sufficient energy:

The energy of perfect love!

If society were perfect, if everything was flawless, then virtually anything you could imagine could be done. Perfection was the key...

Over the first couple of hundred million years, the Martians had finally achieved this perfection. Over the next couple of hundred million years, they had used it for a flowering of culture unbelievable by Earth's awkward, primitive standard.

...But the dark ones of the planet Voltomb around a neighbor star were displeased. They did not like perfection—had taken steps long ago to see to it that this did not occur on planet Earth.

These thrived off those energies produced by negativity—tap these energies for their own selfish ends.

Indeed, they had been attempting to overthrow the Martian Eden for eons, without success, until finally a small faction on Mars came to believe Olympos Mons belonged to them and them alone—all others were trespassers.

This was all it took.

The dark ones encouraged this single rebellious act until finally the negativity produced was sufficient to blow Olympos Mons—and the rest of the Martian volcanoes, too.

And when the windy season came...Here the story stopped.

Heaven was saddened by this tale of their fall.

How little it had taken to topple perfection!

Heaven looked at the lonely hermit Martian, who had come up here from his home on the plain below to commune with the Star Dolphins.

Was he trying to attain once again this lost state of grace from which his Martian ancestors had fallen so long ago? There was a sad, somber look on his gazelle-like face.

"Quite a story," Heaven said quietly.

The Martian hermit sighed. Outside the cave, the wind stirred.

"Yes. You see what can happen if a race strays from the straight path.

"Absolute destruction!"

"Yes," said Heaven. "It seems somewhat similar to Earth's story of Adam and Eve in the Garden of Eden, how one single mistake was enough to topple their perfection.

"How precarious perfection is!" sighed Heaven.

The Martian nodded.

"This is why I came up here. I am trying to find it once again.

"Please don't misunderstand me," he continued. "I do not think my people below are evil. But they are a war-like tribe. They have had to become so just to survive on the Martian planes. They had to revert to the ancient, ancient ways.

"But my people are not bad—they're just not perfect, that's all...

"I am hoping for a...miracle."

"Miracles happen," smiled Heaven.

"Mars could use one," said the hermit.

"So could Planet Earth."

CHAPTER FIVE
SHINE ON!

From the top of New Army Pass at the base of austere Mt. Langley, one could see the frozen statues of the army battalion which had been attempting to invade the Whitney fortress beginning to slowly thaw. Perceptible movement could now be seen, where before there had only been frozen statues, icy immobility—like a vast piece of modern snow sculpture zig-zagging up the steep mountainside.

Peter was carefully observing the "big thaw" through his binoculars, as the red sun was rising over the White Mountains.

He was also chuckling. The Star Dolphins, who loved practical jokes, had planned a good one on the movie-makers still filming at the base of Mt. Whitney.

He was also thinking of Michelle. Peter had not approved of the plan to send Michelle back to Washington D.C. with Hazel, but Michelle had insisted she wanted to try it. She had taken a liking to Hazel—but then Michelle seemed to like almost anyone.

Peter missed her greatly. In some ways, she was the most innocent of them. Robby had surprised him with the astuteness he had developed as he had become a young man. He was the youngest, but his intellect had developed rapidly after his stay on Planet Shine.

Michelle still seemed to Peter to be childlike in her naivete. She was the most gorgeous girl he had ever seen, her iridescent beauty seeming to radiate out from her very innocence. She had become his young bride in their wedding ceremony in the waves off Xanadu.

He thought back to just before the sub fleet showed up…

It was idyllic…

Peter and Michelle swam hand in hand through the living, sparkling coral. They wove in and out, around, about—

Peter had never seen the colors shine so, as if some great, inspired painter had dipped a magical paintbrush in living paints and to the time of idyllic, lilting music, lovingly and with infinite patience created a living masterpiece.

The water itself, lit aglow from above by the perfect, tropical sun, seemed ready to leap up to its brother sky, ready to exchange places with the water above the firmament—or perhaps already had? Perhaps, they were actually swimming through aqua sky. It could have easily been.

Michelle's smile from her mask seemed to highlight the scene with its own unearthly sheen. All was perfect.

The TV station was on now, shining the message all across the land.

Then the sub fleet had shown up over Xanadu.

Looking back on it, Peter could now see it was inevitable. "They," with the help of the Chinese who had already invaded their island citadel in their submarine and by tracing the calls between the dolphin people and (Ex) President Clark, had zeroed in on their location. It was no longer a secret, any way. Michelle's trip to the United Nations had all but ended their seclusion. It was only a matter of time before invasion. Capt. Jones and his men had left. (Loose lips sink ships…?) Oh well, thought Peter. It was time to leave, anyway.

The Star Dolphins had refused to erect any underwater force-field around Xanadu—no one had asked them to do so anyway. Such an energy would have seriously disrupted the ebb and flow of the watery world. Timeless migrations of fish and plankton would have been impaired in a matter which was offensive to the Star Dolphins, to who water was something holy. Even the very nature of the water itself would have been altered to an extent unexceptable to them.

They were hoping…hope against hope…the visitors had come in peace. But as they listened carefully to the radio communications they picked up on their microphones as the subs came ever closer, it became obvious this was no social call.

Invasion!

"This is not a friendly visit, I don't think!" Peter had said as he listened intently through the headphones.

"I'm afraid you're right, Peter. I keep hearing things like, 'Surround them!' and 'Sneak up on them!'" said Michelle, who had taken the headphones now.

All the pod quickly gathered their most precious belongings, and saying emotional goodbyes to their dolphin friends—Sir Killer had some time ago disappeared, presumably swimming the long, long trip back to his icy waters in Alaska—they hurried into the Star Dolphin's underwater sea saucer and had careened through the advancing sub fleet.

It had been like an underwater "Star Wars" as they had swerved in and out of the legion of submarines trying to close in, but the undersea saucer easily out maneuvered them and escaped.

Peter could now see the frozen statues of the soldiers beginning to look more and more like snowmen!

"Abominable snowmen!" thought Peter.

Now they were beginning to walk around...

Now they were beginning to salute each other!!

Now they started to form into marching units...

Now they began to slowly, stiffly march down the dirt road.

Hut, two, three, four!

Hut, two, three, four!

Sound off!

You're in the army now

You're not behind a plow

You'll never get rich

Don't fall in a ditch!

You're in the army now!"

Peter was almost rolling around laughing, as he watched the "Snowman Platoon" march down the road toward the base of Mt. Langley. They were marching, Peter knew, slowly toward the hapless movie-makers still filming "The Grinning Invaders" at the base of Mt. Whitney, just down the range. The Star Dolphins had planned a surprise for the director and his "stars"—one they would not likely forget.

Peter turned on his special eavesdropping gear as the snowmen finally began to approach the film-makers, so he could listen in on what happened. He could hardly wait for the director to notice the advancing "invasion." He focused his binoculars on the director sitting in his canvas chair—complete with "DIRECTOR" printed across the back. Suddenly one of the "go-fors" tapped him on the back and pointed at the advancing, snowmen.

The director's pipe fell out of his mouth as he gaped.

"Who the hell are you?!" he finally croaked.

"'The Abominable Snowmen of the Owen's Valley!'" the leader said.

"'The Abominable Snowmen of the Owen's Valley!'" yelled the director. "The name of my next movie. What a smash! It'll even be bigger than 'The Grinning Invaders,'" he said excitedly.

Then, the snowmen reached out their arms like frozen Frankensteins, advancing toward the director and his crew.

"What are you doing?" said the director.

"We're going to kill you!" the lead snowman said.

"Not a bad line!" said the director.

Suddenly it became obvious to the director they had all better get out of there!

"Grab the film—Let's get out of here!" He grabbed a handheld camera. "But keep shooting. Keep shooting!! What a movie this is going to make!" he said, as he focused in on the marauding snowmen.

They all dashed for the trucks, avoiding the frozen clutches of the "snowpeople."

All of a sudden, reinforcements showed up! Some of the snowmen had stayed behind to try to start the jeeps, and were now rolling rapidly over the sand toward the movie crew.

"Exit—stage right!" the director called out, as their movie trucks spun around in the sand. "But keep filming. Keep filming!" he yelled.

Some of the snowmen had leaped onto the trucks, holding onto the hood ornaments and sideboards, as the trucks spun around and around, trying to dislodge them.

Then the trucks took off toward the paved road down to Lone Pine at top speed, as the jeeps roared after them.

The last Peter saw of them, they were all speeding south on Highway 395, back down toward Los Angeles, from whence they had come…

Robby and Michelle were on their way back to the United States, the dolphin-copter taking off from the summit of Everest as the climber and the yeti had begun their long trek down the mountain.

"I'm beginning to understand the multi-dimensional beings a little better," said Robby, as they thawed out from their experience on the highest of Earth's mountains. "I think."

"You certainly surprised me when you appeared there in the prison cell," said Michelle.

"I had been wondering why they contacted me and prepared me for multi-dimensional vector travel. You saw what happens when someone's not prepared for it?"

"Yeah," said Michelle. "They turn into a fireworks display!"

"Uh huh," said Robby. "It all worked like their theory said it would."

"Theory?"

"Yes. You see, I'm the first person not of their own race they've ever initiated into vector travel. They live in a dimensional realm so remote from ours, like being at the other end of the galaxy, it had taken this long for them to figure out first if they could even initiate a human and then to work out the theory of how to do it.

"A bit like a human trainer working out how to best train a seal or dolphin to juggle a ball or blow a horn."

Michelle laughed. "So you're like a trained dolphin?"

"In some ways, yes. But just like a trained seal or dolphin, there are some things I can do in my own environment which no trainer could ever do. For instance—any seal, trained or not, can certainly get around a lot better in water than any trainer could ever do. You see? You know how a seal glides effortlessly under the water in a way no human could, holding its breath for long, long periods of time. No human could ever hope to emulate him in his own universe—water.

"In a way, the trainer, standing up there above the water is in a different dimension! from the seal. He or she can do all kinds of things in his or her dimension the seal could not even imagine—like the multi-dimensional beings can do all kinds of things we cannot even imagine.

"But once the trainer jumps into the pool with the seal, then—he or she enters the seal's dimension, and there are an infinite variety of things the seal can do which the trainer cannot."

"I think I'm beginning to understand," said Michelle.

"It's the same with the multi-dimensional beings. In comparison to the seal, the trainer is definitely multi-dimensional. Imagine a seal trying to imagine driving down the road in a car if it's never done so! Impossible! Or balance a checkbook!"

"Ridiculous," agreed Michelle.

"Ah, but in the water…

"Coming into our dimension in some ways the beings are at a definite disadvantage to us.

"What it comes down to—which is kinda scary if you think about it—they need me to help zap creeps into vector space. They really can't do so without me, because they're just not as good at getting around in this dimension as we are!"

"You're right," said Michelle. "It is scary."

"Very scary," Robby laughed, thinking back to the scene of the guards flashing off into vector infinity.

"You're saying, those guards could not have been zapped just by the beings themselves?"

"Exactly. I guess a good analogy is sending a trained dolphin underwater to attach a bomb on the hull of an enemy ship in a short amount of time, with no noise. Difficult for the trainer, but for the dolphin its easy—once they've been trained."

"And that's why the beings took so long to train—er, pre-pare—you, Robby?"

"Right, Michelle. First they had to work out the theory. Then just like good trainers, they had to take the amount of time required to subliminally train me for the task.

"I was the dolphin trained to attach the bomb to the enemy ship's hull."

Heaven sat in a cross-legged Martian meditational pose, look-ing out from the lip of the cavern over the vast distance before him on the red plains below Olympos.

He was meditating on the scrolls he had recently watched on the sparkling walls—more and more detailed accounts of the History of Mars.

The first moving scrolls had been an overview, and each suc-cessive one had portrayed in detail a specific chapter in the unbelievably immense field of time in Martian history.

…How the glaciers had grown and receded during the vari-ous ice ages and how the Martians had dealt with this in the differing stages of their development—in the ancient ancient days being forced to migrate like herds of elk to the Martian equator—in the sublime days of their golden age simply transferring into a different dimension which had taken them back in time...to when Mars had been a vast, lush garden planet. But a "different" time than actual Martian geologic time, because the dimensional change had actually changed time too, and so they had no worries of meeting themselves in the time- currents and what strange twists this could cause, because the time currents actually passed each other...like ships passing in the night—in other words they entered a parallel universe...

...So Martian "history," instead of being "linear" like human history—as least "white man's" history—was instead like a turbulent vortex, in some ways not at all unlike the myth cycles of Earth's American Indian tribes, who saw "history" as an intricate series of interlaced mythologies which ebbed and flowed outside the structures of so called "time"...

...Kings and Queens had come and gone, each generation outdoing the last in terms of opulence and wealth, flying their sailships across "the great gulf" to mine the asteroid belts, where unlimited quantities of precious stones were mined to build their wondrous King Solomon-like cities...the wonders of the cosmos!

...How the evil ones of the planet Voltomb from a nearby solar system had sent spies disguised as emissaries to see the great riches, but had been found out by the great king Rams II for what they were and had been invited to a feast in the King's doorless, mausoleum-like castle—and then lured into a dimensional accelerator where they had found themselves suddenly writhing on the beach of some ocean of fire somewhere as worms! Never again had the creatures of Voltomb come to Mars...until the final fall, when the "demon-seed" they had sowed so very long ago had, in imperceptible ways down through the millennia, produced its rotten, fatal, forbidden fruit...

Time seemed to go by in swirls for Heaven, as he learned more and more of the timeless history of Mars.

And of course, this was all in preparation for the final test of riding the wind like the Martians themselves did. First he had to ride the currents of Martian history, and then—and only then—could he ride the currents of the Martian wind…which had finally swept the planet clean of all traces of the fallen, fragile empire, finally even dispersing the elements off Mars and into the emptiness of space.

…For the wind of Mars was believed to be "alive", a living thing, with a will of its own…like God's breath itself!

…All these things and more he was learning during those seamless, Martian days and nights on the Mountian…

Up in Whitney Castle (a different place…a different time) Michael and Dr. Smith were observing a different scene. They were watching on the holo-screen the scene of all the runners around the Washington Monument listening to (Ex) Pres. Clark give his inspiring speech.

"If it weren't for the Star Dolphins," the (Ex) President was saying to the enthralled throng, "just think where a lot of you, us, would be…"

Suddenly, young Dr. Smith stood up, staring intently at the screen.

"What is it," inquired Michael, looking at him.

"Something's not right," said Dr. Smith. "There's something about the water in the pool at the base of the monument.

"Something's not right…!"

He dashed over to the computer and quickly inputed some data.

"That Hazel Macelroy…" he breathed

Ever since he had seen Hazel enter the Oval Office that day on TV, armed with a semi-automatic rifle, he had almost become "paranoid" of the evil girl genius—rather like Sherlock Holmes had become positively paranoid of arch rival Professor Moriarty. He had heard of Michelle's happy escape from the prison yard, but this had not diminished his paranoia of "Pres. Hazel."

Dr. Smith turned to Michael Hope. "We've got to fly to Washington D.C." he said. "There's not a minute to lose. We might already be too late…"

"What's wrong?" asked Dr. Hope, who was beginning to feel a little too much for his liking like Dr. Watson, off on some mysterious mystery about which he knew precious little in comparison to Holmes…

"I'll explain on the way. We've not a moment to lose." He busied himself at the computer.

"All right. I'll get the dolphin ship ready," said Michael, running for the dolphin-port.

Soon they were soaring over the sparkling tops of the White Mountains, shining in the sun.

"Hazel…" young Dr. Smith kept saying over and over again. "Hazel!"

"Now can you tell me what's wrong," implored Michael.

"Oh, I should never have trusted her for an instant!" cried Dr. Smith.

"We must hurry!

"We might already…"

Michael quickly grabbed Dr. Smith by his shoulders and shook him.

The young boy looked at him.

"I'm all right now," he finally said.

They were over the Rockies.

"There's a poisonous gas in the pool of water at the base of the Washington Monument," said Dr. Smith, "a 'sound-activated' substance, designed to 'go off', reach 'critical mass', right when the volume of all the folks around the pool reaches the level necessary to achieve 'sound saturation.'

"Whoever designed it was a genius, and I think Hazel Macelroy herself had no little part in its diabolical design…"

"You mean just when the people are cheering the loudest…?"

"Correct! If Hazel's noxious substance works they'll be gassed! We must hurry!"

"What should we do, Dr. Smith?" asked Michael.

"I'm still not exactly sure. We can't very well just hover over the pool, because I'm not sure what 'kind' of sound could bring the substance to 'sound saturation.' It's possible the vibrations of the dolphin ship itself could! So you see what a genius Hazel is!"

"Yes, I'm beginning to," said Michael. "What were you doing back there in the lab?"

"Synthisizing a highly concentrated substance which should neutralize and deactivate the gaseous compound—if we can get to the pool in time. But how are we going to get to the pool? We simply can't chance flying over it. I'm almost sure the vibrations from the engines of the dolphin-copter could cause the 'sound saturation' we're trying to avoid.

"The only thing we can do is land at the edge of the crowd and try to make our way through the people up to the pool!"

"Through all those people?" Michael said.

"I'm afraid it's our only chance. I was so busy with the formula I forgot about your flipper wings," Dr. Smith moaned. "It's all my fault! I should never have trusted Hazel…"

Soon they were hovering over the trees at the back of the crowd. No one seemed to notice them in the trees. Dr. Smith and Dr. Hope rode the camouflage energy ladder quickly down to the ground.

Dr. Smith gave Michael some of the substance.

"We're going to have to try to get through the throng up to the pool," Dr. Smith yelled to Michael over the incessant roar of the crowd.

He reached out his hand to Dr. Hope and the two shook.

"Good luck, Dr. Hope. If we never see each other again…"

"Keep the faith!" said Michael, as they dashed into the crowd.

Young Dr. Smith struggled through the surging sea of humanity like a young child in a stormy ocean, the waves buffeting him from all sides.

"I can't make it," he finally said. He started sobbing.

"Hey! What's wrong, little guy?" asked someone in the crowd.

"Professor Macelroy!" he said, as another roar went up over the crowd.

On Mars, the hermit and Heaven listened from the hermit's cave as the Martian wind began to roar again now down from the Mountain.

"It will soon be time," said the hermit Martian. "Have you remembered all I've taught you about 'riding the wind?'" he asked.

It had been like an extraterrestrial college course as the old hermit had patiently taught him all he knew necessary for successfully "riding the wind" down to the citadel.

"Yes. I believe so."

The old hermit had shown flashing charts on the cavern walls, detailing all the factors involved in becoming "kite Man" and soaring in the winds down to the citadel.

"It's a lot like a dolphin soaring through a raging sea," he said, remembering his studies of Earth. "…In a typhoon."

Little by little, the hermit had initiated him into the mysteries, like a bird teaching its young how to fly from the nest.

Heaven remembered how apprehensive but exhilarated he had felt the first time he had soared a little ways out from the cave and had ridden the wind back in.

But if only I had my flipper-wings, he thought. How easy it would be. Blast Martian tradition anyway! he thought.

Instead he had had to study and learn all the intricacies of Martian wind currents. The comparatively feeble force of gravity did strange, unexpected things with wind here. It had more of an "up-lift" than did wind on Earth (except of course hurricanes and tornadoes!), which made the enterprise risky but possible. In other words, Heaven had thought as the hermit had been going over some very technical details, the wind here on Mars makes it possible—with a little help—to be like a hang glider on Earth by just spreading out your arms and flapping like a big bird!

Big-bird can't fly, he laughed, as he thought about the primary hero of children's TV on Earth—before the Star Dolphins had arrived and "stolen the show."

Actually, Big-bird had not minded much being upstaged by the Star Dolphins, nor had a decidedly elderly benevolently smiling Mr. Rogers.

Big-bird would say, "Hey kids, how about those Star Dolphins!" And all the little kids would cheer.

"Ah shut-up!" the grump would grumble, sneering from his garbage can. "There's no such thing…"

"How do you know, Grump," Big-bird would say.

"Yeah," a little kid would say. "You don't believe in Santa Claus either!" and all the little kids would laugh at the grump.

Mr. Rogers, in his familiar cardigan sweater, made a field trip to Marineworld just to visit the dolphins.

"Do you know why the dolphins are all smiling," he would ask into the camera. "Because they love you," he would say. "Just the way you are!"

"Yep," Big-bird would say. "I believe in the Star Dolphins." He would flap his non-functional wings. "I bet they can fly right through the stars!"

The hermit had finally taught Heaven all he knew about the challenge before him. "And remember," he said. "I, the hermit of the Mountain, will be with you."

The pair stood on the edge of the cave, the wind tugging at them. Heaven "flapped" his arms in preparation. The hermit had a tether rope between the two (which the Star Dolphins had also given him), like a belay between two mountain climbers. This time Heaven would be ascending and descending the mountain of the wind!

"Now!" the Martian cried, as the wind reached just the right "lift." They jumped out…!

Icarus soars, thought Heaven.

He smoothly flapped his arms, the tether rope from the Martian giving him the extra "lift" he needed. He soared out away from the Mountain, riding the whirlwind as it roared out over the plains of Mars, looking up to see the Martian expertly sailing the currents.

I don't think I could do this alone, Heaven thought, still smoothly flapping his arms, even with the gravity of Mars. He was right. The Martians' bone structure was, as a result of eons of evolution on the small world, more like the hollow bones of birds.

Luckily, his experience with the flipper wings the Star Dolphins had personally designed for him had made him very sensitive to the variances of air currents, to the subtle but definite ways air flows could be indeed "ridden" to keep one afloat in the ocean of the sky.

But just flapping his arms! He would have thought it impossible, but here he was!

Look! I can fly! I can fly! he had thought the first time he had tried the flipper-wings successfully. He felt very much the same today. Below, through the swirl of wind rushing past him, he could see the Martian plain far beneath…

But he knew the extra tug from his mentor above him was necessary in keeping him "afloat." Just like a dolphin supporting another, he thought.

He was sure the Martians (and Rena) were watching him closely from their citadel at the underground Pyramids…

All at once there was a downdraft! He felt like the sky had been pulled out from under him as they quickly dropped. The elastic rope between them tugged on him as they both plummeted down. Something had gone wrong!

He looked up at the soaring Martian over him, but could see no expression of emotion behind his goggles.

Red plain was rushing up to them!

Well, thought Heaven, at least I tried…

He could now see more and more details of the rock strewn desert below him.

His last thoughts were of Rena…

Then they slammed into a cushion of rising air. Once again, his life had passed before him.

The Martian expertly soared beneath him and led them both down to the soft pile of sand he had told Heaven they were to land on—if they wished to live!

They bounced up from the sand a good long ways and then down again.

Finally they came to a rest.

Heaven simply lay on his back, gazing up through the air currents at the muted red sky. It was a glorious sight! Even if somewhat clouded by the rushing wind...

"What a great landing!" his Martian friend laughed. "It was a lot more fun than flying solo!" he said.

Silence.

"I'm glad you thought so," Heaven finally said.

Then they both started laughing.

The two were now in the giant pyramid beside the Great Face. Heaven and Rena embraced each other.

"I'm glad it's finally over," said Rena, laughing slightly.

Heaven nodded his head. "It was quite an experience...to say the least," he said.

"Where is White Dolphin," asked Heaven, who had hoped the dolphin sage would have been here to share in the triumph of his accomplishment—of his return.

"White Dolphin went to Earth after he had finished the translation of the scrolls. He said he knew you would make it, and he felt he should go to Earth to help prepare for the final, uh, 'transition' I think he called it."

"What's happening on Earth now, anyway, Rena," asked Heaven, who had been completely out of touch since he had flung his radio off the Mountain, a considerable amount of time, during which he had not only finished the long exhausting climb, but learned the picture scrolls and the secrets of riding the wind. When he had started his long, exhilarating, diminished-gravity lope across the plains of Mars, toward the base of Olympos Mons, the caissons advancing on Mt. Whitney had only just frozen on the steep zig-zag switch backs of Mt. Langley…!

Was it really late summer there now?

In some magical ways of which Heaven was still a bit confused, Martian time had stood still and accelerated at the very same time. He had, indeed lost all sense of standard time. Time had swirled like the wind he had just ridden! Time had seemed to be circular up there…up here!

So much time had seemed to go by during his epochal quest, as he had made the climb itself, and he had attended the hermit's "school", he could hardly believe it. As a matter of fact, one third of a Martian year had gone by. Mars had gone one third of "a circle 'round the sun," as the Martians called their year.

"It seems like such a long time since I was down here," said Heaven.

"To me it seems like ten Martian years since you left," answered Rena.

"Well, then, you had better tell me all the news from Earth."

She told him of recent happenings:

…Of the winter of the great snow in the west…

…Of the caissons and soldiers slowly advancing up the switch-backs, suddenly freezing into white statues in the blizzard, even as he had been loping across the Martian plain…

…Of the Star Dolphins rescuing the people in the floods of the lowlands…

…Of the final coming of summer and Nick's trek through the Sierra and his meeting Diane and going to Crater Lake and the Star Dolphins landing there in their greatest Starship…

("Wish I could have been there to see it," said Heaven. "Me too," said Rena.)

…Of Hazel Macelroy and her successful infiltration of the Whitney Castle with the "funny gas"…

("Are you serious?!" gasped Heaven. "Deadly serious," replied Rena. "She actually convinced Vic she was an injured climber and he took her inside.")

…Of bringing Dr. Smith out of the capsule in Mt. Shasta as a ten year old boy to deal with the situation at Star Castle…

…Of Michelle going back to Washington with Hazel and appearing on TV with Pres. Zak…

(Heaven had laughed when told of her letting out Young Dr. Smith's new and improved "happy gas" which was actually "truth serum", and (Ex) Pres Zak going zonkers on national television in front of millions of viewers.)

…Of Hazel rushing in with a semiautomatic rifle and taking over as President and putting Michelle in jail…

…Of Robby's encounter with the multi-dimensional beings—White Dolphin had explained them to Rena, who still didn't understand them—and Robby's dramatic rescue of Michelle from the prison…

…Of the mass of runners running across the country from San Francisco fortified with seeweed, slowly nearing the capitol city of Washington…

…Of Vic and Diana getting married and meeting Auk the sasquatch on their honeymoon in the Trinity Mountains…

("Holy cow!" Heaven had exclaimed out of lack of anything else to say.)

…Finally of Robby and Michelle flying to Mt. Everest to meet the king of the yetis…

"Whew!" finally gasped Heaven. "It seems almost like I've been away an eternity!"

The hermit Martian now approached him from where he had been conferring with the others.

"You have been away an eternity, Heaven," he said. "An eternity on the Mountain. It happens all the time."

The two laughed.

"What have the others decided?" said Heaven.

"They have told me to tell you, you have been adopted into the Martian tribe." Nantook reached out his hand to Heaven, which Heaven grasped. "Congratulations! You are the very first non-Martian to receive such an honor. Even the Star Dolphins were not accorded this honor."

Heaven slightly bowed.

"I am to be your 'Godfather,'" continued Nantook. "Since you, Heaven are the first from outside the tribe to be accepted like this, there is really no ceremony. We still cannot initiate you the way we do our young ones becoming full adult members, because there are secrets they have decided not even to show to you—ancient, ancient mysteries, which our ancestors made blood-oaths ages ago to never reveal to anyone not of the tribe.

"But, you are an honorary member…the first!"

"Well they help my people—and dolphins—on Earth?" asked Heaven.

"Yes! We will try to help."

"Great! When do we begin?"

"Even now, we are preparing the ancient space sailors, (the ones saved after the fall as holy relics), the ships our ancients used to fly to the asteroid belt for precious gems to build our cities. We have not used them, have not been able to use them, since the great fall, since the eruption of Olympos Mons—as you learned from studying the ancient scrolls up on the Mountain."

Heaven thought back again to this "lesson." The Martians, during their golden age, had regularly "sailed" to the asteroids to mine the precious gems needed for their cities. Their fantasy type ships, like everything else in their advanced society, had been propelled by entering higher dimensional space—similar to the beings of light who had contacted Robby. They could "sail" through the higher dimensions, using the energy of perfect love as the power source necessary for these transitions.

Nantook turned to the others now sitting in a quiet circle around an ancient shrine. They were beginning to chant.

"What are they doing?"

"They have begun to attempt to bring back the ways of the golden age," whispered Nantook. "Until now, they have felt they had little chance of returning to the perfect ways. The downfall had been so total, so complete, there seemed no hope of ever recovering from it. However, Heaven, you're quest up the Mountain, risking your own life, has inspired them. They are willing to try again—after all these eons! It is a momentous and miraculous time you are witnessing."

"I feel privileged," said Heaven.

"So do I," said Rena.

"So do I!" said Nantook. "But now we must leave. There are ancient ceremonies even I, who forsook my tribe to live on the Mountain, cannot witness.

"Come. We must leave now."

"Good news!" Nantook said, as he entered Heaven and Rena's living quarters one day, after a Martian week had gone by.

"What?" asked Heaven.

"The holy Martian monks, who have been meditating and praying, have also been fasting. They were all on the verge of death, for they had taken off their mineralized mist circulators, ready to lay down their lives, like you were, Heaven, on the Mountain, in their quest to achieve the old ways once again. Now, just in time, they have made a quantum leap! They no longer require their circulation tanks!! They have achieved the perfection of thought of the ancient ones of the golden age, but with a new difference! Instead of being almost epicurean in their delight of the sumptuous banquets of the first golden age, they have instead achieved a level of consciousness more like the ascetic sages of your own planet, Heaven. Instead of the sumptuous banquets...they can now live purely...on air! What a triumph!" said Nantook excitedly, "beyond their greatest hopes even. Don't you understand, Heaven and Rena? Mars has at last entered the Second Golden Age...! And I'll be able to get rid of my tank in time."

"Wow!!" Heaven said. "When I can get rid of my tank?" he laughed. ("And mine," Rena agreed.)

"That such a thing might happen was even prophesied by one of our prophets soon after the fall. He wrote, though no one believed him at the time, 'Some day, a messenger will come from our blue-green neighbor world of Earth. He will inspire our holy ones by his bravery and willingness to risk his life on the Mountain. This inspiration will give our holy ones the will necessary for the breakthrough into a new golden age, an age which will be quite different though from the first golden age, as it will see asceticism replace abundance, but the result will be the same—perfection! But 'perfection' of a different type. You will be perfect soldiers. You will go back with this messenger to his own planet Earth where an epic struggle will be underway between the forces of good and evil. You will be perfect soldiers in this war of the end!'

"You, Heaven, were the messenger from Earth! They hoped—no few dreaded—it might be you when you arrived here to ask for our help. Your successful quest up the Mountain convinced them it was true."

Heaven was now at a total loss for words.

"Whew…" he just whistled.

"We go now soon," continued Nantook. "The elders are even now rehabilitating the sailships to sail on the waters across the sea of the sky to the blue-green island Earth. Then as soon as we are prepared for multi-dimensional travel, and as soon as we are instructed in piloting the sailships, something of which you studied in preparation for riding the wind with me upon the Mountain, we leave."

"How long," asked Heaven, who was becoming increasingly anxious to reach his beleaguered home world.

"First the training must be completed, and you must partake of it. The training you began up on the Mountain you, and Rena, must now complete."

"Me?" said Rena.

"Your training will not be as demanding," assured Nantook.

"Travel through higher dimensions if very exacting. There is not room for even the slightest error…"

"What would happen," apprehensively asked Rena.

"Well, the fragile sailships would probably disintegrate." (Rena gasped.) "Although no one is really sure, because during the Golden Ages our perfection was achieved, well, perfectly! It evolved over such a vast spell of time, there was literally no error. Once our greatest scientist perceived the straight path we were to take, we did so, without error.

"But now…All this is so sudden and so new…We must be very careful…We must indeed be flawless.

"And, our ancient computers must be reprogrammed, indeed…reactivated."

Heaven recalled the lesson on the Mountain concerning the ancient computers of the Martians, computers so powerful they could manipulate ten different dimensions simultaneously, like juggling ten objects at once.

"What we learned from our greatest scientist," Nantook had taught, "was that the mathematics of higher dimensional space-time is actually much simpler than the equivalent mathematics of ordinary space-time. In other words, once we move from the fourth dimension of time into the fifth dimension, as if by magic, very complex mathematical structures become quite simple, even 'elegant'"

Heaven recalled something of this concept of mathematical "beauty" he had studied in college courses in higher math he had taken. Messy, "ugly" equations became nice and tidy when transformed to the 5th dimension.

The Martian computers had lain dormant in the underground pyramids for eons after "the fall."

"Can they be reactivated?" asked Heaven.

"Certainly," said Nantook. "The ancient scrolls contain all the necessary programming procedures to reactivate them. It will be rather like waking a sleeping giant," he said.

"The computers did not 'die,'" he continued. "They simply, you might say, 'passed out.'"

"You mean 'fainted'?" asked Heaven.

"Yes. They fainted at the sight of the eruption of Olympos Mons and with it the other volcanoes of Mars. Now we must..."

"Get out the smelling salts," said Rena, in English.

"What?" said Nantook.

Heaven only laughed...

They were in the Martian sailships! sailing beneath the sparkling, glittering stars. Heaven and Rena and Nantook along with the others had been prepared for multi-dimensional space travel and in piloting the sailships according to the instruction and rituals of the ancient scrolls. It was an exhaustive process, but primarily it consisted of freeing the mind from certain preconceived restrictions so as to allow one to enter a fantasy-like world—or universe. Perfect love was the prerequisite, which Nantook had been striving for virtually all his life up on the Mountain, which Heaven and Rena had already achieved to a remarkable extent.

There was also a course in the very nature of multi-dimensional space and of the essence of the tiniest of particles in space-time—ultimate physics...It was difficult stuff to grasp but with Nantook's help, they were able to come to at least an intuitive understanding of it, and an intuitive understanding was really all that was necessary.

"It's really all intuition, anyway," Nantook had explained.

...the ultimate mysteries of space and time had been revealed to them...

In the beginning there had been the One. There was no other. In the center of the universe. In the center of the Nothingness.

And then the One had begun to become the Infinite. The One had proceeded forth to become the Many. From the center of the Nothingness.

The One had gone out into the void. From the center of the Universe. It had abhorred a vacuum.

It had dispersed to fill the darkness with light. All the places of the Nothingness, of the Darkness, had been permeated by the light of the One.

The One had dispersed to become the many—had in essence sacrificed Itself to form the Many.

The Many included the different dimensions. The first dimension was time. Then there were the dimensions of distance— width, length and height.

And then the fifth dimension of—velocity!...distance/time.

Velocity was actually its very own dimension, they learned. Heaven had already learned something of this phenomenon on Shine—from the Star Dolphins.

Once you entered the dimension of velocity, you entered a dimension of space-time where speed was potentially infinite. You entered another realm—hyper-space.

One could learn of the very nature of space-time itself in the fifth dimension of velocity. This involved the extremely complex nature of "super-string" theory, which scientists on Earth had just begun puzzling over in the last part of the 20th century, the result of a "lucky accident" in which some pure, arcane mathematical structures from the 19th! century were found to have exact counterparts in the physical world. It had been called 21st century physics in the 20th century—the result of late19th century mathematics, evolved by a lonely hermit-like mathematician at a time when mystics had surely believed the end of the world was approaching, when spiritualism was everywhere, when scientists seriously discussed the nature of the "ether."

Finally, as physics caught up to pure math, came the search for the so-called "God-particle"…the ultimate building blocks of space-time.

Superstrings were the ultimate "particles" of structures of space-time, they learned. And it was the vibrational qualities of these structures which was proving to be the very key to the universe.

It seems the hippies had not been so wrong when talking about "good vibrations" after all!

And the velocity of the vibrations of the superstrings was as crucial in their qualities as the vibrations of the strings was to the sound of a priceless Stradivarius violin.

But the energy required to reach the dimension of velocity had been believed by Earth's scientists to be beyond anything they could ever hope to achieve. In some, oversimplified ways, it was like trying to build the ancient pyramids if you had only enough manpower, say, to build a simple hut. Theoretically imaginable, but practically speaking…

But with the energy and power of perfected, dolphin-like love, on a sufficient scale, then, it could be done!

If you programmed the computers correctly…

As they were about to plunge into the fifth dimension of velocity… Other ships approached!

It was the ships of the creatures of the Planet Voltomb!

"Oh no!" gasped Nantook, looking out on the bizarre, gothic-like ships approaching them. "They have returned."

"Who?" asked Heaven.

"The Voltombers."

Rena gasped. "Oh no!"

"Why?" asked Heaven, who felt he already knew why—to help the evil ones of Earth.

"They know why we can once again fly our sail ships. They too can fly through the dimension of velocity, but they use the powers of negative, dark energy to power their ships."

"The dark ones," said Heaven.

"I'm afraid so," said Nantook. "Now, we must fight. This must be why the nature of our new perfection is different from our former glory. The perfection of our Golden Age had developed during a time when the dark ones too were acquiring their own powers, and ours had been accomplished before they were able to effectively react. But now…"

"How do we fight them?" asked Heaven.

"We can't enter the fifth dimension, as they would follow us to Earth!"

"We have to evade them…somehow," said Heaven.

"But how?"

Nantook quickly conferred with his Martian comrades at the helm of the sailship.

They began erratic, evasive measures, going around and around in circles.

"This will get us nowhere!" Nantook finally said, as the ships of the dark ones followed them.

They flew in and out of the orbits of their twin moons.

All of a sudden, their sailships shook as a blast from an enemy ship hit them. There were other blasts.

"The shields held, but we're not prepared for this!" said Nantook.

The Martians were beginning to panic!

Heaven had learned how to pilot the ancient space sailors, partly from the extensive course he had taken on the Mountain, studying the scrolls which had even contained this instruction as a preliminary to riding the wind, and from the recent training he and Rena had received in the simulator brought out for the first time in eons and re-activated in the underground pyramids.

"Tell the others to follow our ship!" he yelled to Nantook.

He had leaped for the controls as the Martian at the helm had fainted. Nantook spoke into the radio to the other ships:

"This is Nantook! To all ships! Follow my ship! Repeat! Do not panic! Heaven will lead us to victory over the dark ones!"

"Tell them to quickly program their computers to link with ours, so when our ship enters the fifth dimension, theirs do too, with exactly the same coordinates. We all know there is no room for error."

Nantook gave the orders, as Heaven set the sailship's coordinates—for the moon! Planet Earth's own single lonely moon.

"Now!" said Heaven. He punched in the coordinates, and they entered the fifth dimension, aiming not for Earth, as the Voltombers had expected and for which they had programmed their computers, but for the Earth's solitary moon.

Suddenly, they were over the craters and mountains of the moon.

"Where are the Voltombers?" Nantook asked.

Their ships had blown to pieces! and scattered as far as the asteroid belt. They had taken a high stakes gamble, a suicide gamble, that the Martians would aim their sailships for Earth. The intricacies of entering the fifth dimension were such, no error could be allowed, down to the least subtlety, in the pre-entry programming. Once the enemy had set their coordinates for Earth, their course was preordained. Once they had taken into account the necessary variances of following, like a hound from hell following its prey, the Martians, down to Earth, the super-computers had expected the variances cause by the "time-wake" of the Martian sailships.

"When no 'time-wake' happened, as I led the sailships off toward Earth's moon instead of the Earth itself, the Voltomb ships slammed into a wall of vector time-space—partly caused by the moon's tidal wave pull on the Earth. It was a fatal one-two punch!" Heaven explained.

As the sailships sailed over the moon, congratulations were in order for Heaven. His quick thinking had saved them all.

He knew any of the Martians could have done the same. They had simply panicked was all.

"I guess we were so afraid of falling off the straight path, after all these eons, we couldn't do anything," said Nantook.

"We owe you our lives."

Heaven was once again at a loss for words.

"Believe it or not," said Heaven, as nonchalantly as he could, "I've never been to the moon. I've been to Planet Shine in the Milky Way and I've been to Mars—but I've never been to the moon."

"Neither have I," echoed Rena. "As long as were here, do you think we could look around a bit? The moon always looks so romantic from Earth."

"But what about Earth," said Nantook. "Don't they need our help?"

"I think we can best help them from here," said Heaven.

"I was thinking a stroll on the moon would be nice, too, Rena," said Heaven.

"A stroll?!" gasped Rena.

"Sure. Why not?"

"Well, for one reason," said Nantook, "we don't have any spacesuits!"

"A very minor technicality," said Heaven.

"What do you mean?" asked Nantook.

Heaven inputed some data into the computer. "Well, theoretically, I think it should be possible to walk around the moon without a spacesuit."

"Perhaps, but for how long," laughed Nantook.

"All we have to do, I think," said Heaven, who by now was becoming something of an expert in the intricacies of higher dimensional space, "is to change the dimensional coordinates of the moon just sufficiently to provide us with the best spacesuits of all. The space suit of an atmosphere!"

"Hmmmmn," said Nantook.

"All we have to do is change the dimension of time to a time in the future—I think—when the moon would have evolved its own atmosphere."

"But how?"

"And why?" asked Rena.

"Well how, is obvious—by 'tricking' the computer into thinking such a time would someday exist—even if it wouldn't—I think. Then we simply program the coordinates the computer itself gives us and—viola!

"And why? Well, I suddenly had this vision of the moon as a vast garden planet. There are too many people on Earth any-

535

more to feed them all, and you can't mess around with the time dimensions of Earth. Too many people. It would be impossible. If Earth had evolved perfectly, like Mars developed, there wouldn't be this problem in the first place.

"But, in a strange way, the moon is perfect. Perfectly desolate. So you see it might be possible here!"

"What does the computer say," asked Nantook.

"It's giving me coordinates! I think I was able to trick it into thinking such a time would someday exist—and then ask it for the dimensional coordinates. And who knows. Maybe such a time would exist in the future, no matter how far off." Heaven was beginning to feel like a professor of higher dimensions.

"If one goes far enough down eternity, if perfection is sufficiently present, like on the moon, then virtually anything is possible!"

"I don't get it," laughed Rena.

"I do get it!" said Nantook. "And I think you just might be right."

Nantook quickly conferred with the others.

"The consensus is, Heaven, since you saved us from the Voltombers and helped us to our new golden age, we would, we should, help you in this worthy goal—a garden planet for poor planet Earth.

"Our experts believe we must link all the computers together, all the way back to home planet Mars, in order to be absolutely sure of our results. Even the slightest error would never do."

"You're absolutely right, Nantook," said Heaven. "I was hoping you would agree to help, because I certainly couldn't attempt so vast a job without it."

"Even the slightest error and the moon might..."

"What?" asked Rena.

"Well, maybe turn into green cheese," said Heaven, with a laugh.

Meanwhile, back on Earth…

In the frozen tundra of northern Siberia, a strange, strange assembly was happening. It was occurring in the vast cratered area where all the trees had mysteriously been blown over in the early part of the 20th century. To this day, no one had figured out exactly what had happened there…

But to the sasquatch of Siberia, it had become something of a holy shrine. They often gathered there in the lonely moonlight to chant their ancient chants.

Now, there was a new reason to gather. They had been contacted by the Star Dolphins and told of the recent meetings between men and sasquatch in the American Northwest and with the yeti in the Himalayas.

They had gathered here to plan their march through the lonely isolated towns of northern Siberia!

They assembled themselves in columns and marched off for the nearest town, a joyful roar going up over the lonely, moonlit landscape of blown down trees.

When they arrived, the peasants, a superstitious lot, many of whom actually believed in lost sasquatch races as part of local folklore and superstition, gaped from out of their houses and hovels at the unbelievable parade going down the main street.

Nobody, however, attempted to stop them. Everyone was too stunned to do anything. One senile old man brought out his gun, but had it knocked from his hands by his son.

"Don't you see?" he said. "They come in peace!"

"It's the end of the world!" an old lady peasant cried.

"And not a moment too soon, either," another answered.

The sasquatch parade continued its long march toward Moscow.

Meanwhile, up in Lapland, home of St. Nicholas and the reindeer herders…

A lonely family of Laplanders, out in the wilderness with their herd of reindeer and dressed in their Santa Claus style festive red and white clothing, were sitting before their tepee, which like American plains Indians, was their ancestral dwelling.

Suddenly…they could hear faint sounds, like the sound of bells around the necks of reindeer.

They stepped outside their tepee and looked up into the sky.

There was a flying sleigh!! Pulled not by reindeer, but by strange gazelle-looking antlered creatures, running across the sky! It was the Eskimo Martians, who had flown to Earth in their own newly refurbished sailships and decided to have a little fun.

The Lapland family gazed up into the sky.

"Ho, Ho, Ho!" they heard.

Then, brightly wrapped packages floated on little parachutes down to the ground. The family quickly gathered them.

"From the Star Dolphins!" they heard, as the anti-gravity sled propelled across the sky in a semi-circle.

Even the isolated Laplanders had heard strange rumors of the "smiling space fish."

They gathered up the packages as the sled finally flew out of sight.

"To all a good night…!"

Robby and Michele were now approaching the East Coast in the dolphin copter.

"We must hurry!" the pilot Star Dolphin suddenly said.

"There's an emergency at the great monument!" said the co-pilot dolphin to them.

"What?" asked both Robby and Michelle.

Both Star Dolphins were closely observing the computer monitor.

"We just received a message from Dr. Hope, who is right now struggling to get through the great pod of humans to reach the pool at the base of the Washington Monument, that Dr. Smith has determined there is an evil substance in the pool which could release a poison gas if the 'sound saturation' of the substance is reached by the noise of the crowd. It could kill many, many people there!"

"Oh no!"

"I'm afraid so," said the worried Star Dolphin. "Dr. Hope said Dr. Smith was convinced the vibrations of a dolphin-copter hovering over the pool could itself activate the substance! So they can't just fly over the pool and pour in the stuff Dr. Smith has formulated to de-activate the noxious compound. The only hope seems to be to try to make it all the way through the crowd…"

"Why can't grandfather use his flipper wings?" asked Michelle.

"Dr. Hope said in all the confusion, they were left back at the compound!"

"Oh no!"

"Dr. Hope said they might not get there in time, and then…"

"What can we do?' said Robby.

The Star Dolphin was intent on his computer screen.

Michelle sat silently. Finally, she said, "And to think I trusted Hazel Macelroy. She's behind this herself!"

They were nearing Washington D.C. now.

"We better hover out here," said the Star Dolphin pilot.

Michelle sat in deep silence. Robby looked at her. He had never seen such an expression of concentration on his sister's angelic face.

"You all right, Michelle?" he said.

"I'm thinking, Robby," she said.

Her intense tone of voice told him not to disturb his older sister. Robby looked out on all the vast throng on the viewscreen.

"Look at all those people!" gasped Robby.

"Yes. Look at all those people…"

"Robby," suddenly said Michelle, "do you remember grandfather telling us his story about being carried across the water by a dolphin herd from the Florida Keys after he had attacked and almost killed the military officer demanding information about the language of the dolphins from him?"

"Sure, Michelle, but what…"

"And do you remember grandfather Michael telling of being washed up on the beach of an island like a stranded dolphin?"

"Yes…"

"Lying there…liked a beached dolphin?"

"Sure, Michelle…"

"And almost dying?"

"I remember, Michelle," said Robby.

"And then he had the vision. He saw dolphins flying in the sky, he said. Remember? And they were singing—or whistling—a piece of music. A song. Remember, Robby? Remember his telling us how this vision actually saved his life. Like a miracle."

"Yes..."

"Do you remember what the song was, Robby?"

"Sure, Michelle. It was the 'Ode to Joy' by Beethoven."

"Right," said Michelle. "'The Ode to Joy.' Of course. How could I forget," she mused, almost to herself. "I had forgotten the title, Robby," she admitted.

Robby was now becoming concerned about his sister. Was she losing her sense in the stress of the moment?

"I never listened too much to Beethoven, I'm afraid," she said. "I preferred Bach."

"Michelle..."

"Star Dolphins," she said.

"Yes, Michelle," said one of the Star Dolphins, who too was becoming concerned for the young girl.

"Do you remember the miracle?"

"Sure, Michelle."

"Do you think you could perform such a miracle now?"

"We had to pray, Michelle," the Star Dolphin said.

"Let's pray!" Michelle said.

They all prayed.

After a few moments, the Star Dolphin looked at the computer.

A great roar went up over the monument...

"It's working! Heaven," Nantook said, as he read the computer readouts.

They had been programming the computers now for some days. All agreed it was the most challenging question ever put to them.

"We can actually put an atmosphere of oxygen and nitrogen over the surface of the moon!"

"So," said Heaven, "the moon could be turned into a garden planet."

"Yes, indeed," smiled Nantook. "With the push of a button!"

"Let's do it!" said Heaven.

Nantook pushed the button on the computer which would activate the dimensional accelerator, which should propel the moon into a hypothetical time in the future when it would have evolved an atmosphere, according to the laws of infinity probability. Since there was no guarantee of such an event actually occurring on the moon, because of the extreme nature of its present lifelessness, Nantook and the other programmers had concluded positively that "actual" time, in distinction to "hypothetical" time, would actually remain exactly the same. Therefore, in relation to Earth, there would be no time change, no sudden disappearance into a future time universe, but only, a profound, total change in the physical nature of the moon. All this was so complex, only linking all the computers together could accomplish the task.

When Nantook pushed the button, as they watched from the Martian sailship hovering high over the lunar surface—the moon was suddenly transformed into a lush, green world!

"Wow!!" said Heaven and Rena simultaneously.

"It worked!"

"Indeed it did," said Nantook. "Our computers tell us you should soon have a virtual cornucopia of fruits and vegetables!"

"I can't wait until the first harvest," said Rena.

"Right," chimed Heaven.

"Shine on,

Shine on Harvest Moon

Up in the sky!"

Over the cheering throng around the Washington Monument, as the sun was beginning to disappear, people looked up to see the full moon suddenly change from it's normal yellow gleam to soft green.

Everyone was pointing up now at the "new" moon.

Then, simultaneously could be heard the whistling strains of the "Ode to Joy!" as the dolphin-copter flew in and hovered over the pool at the Washington Monument.

"It's working!" the pilot Star Dolphin said, viewing his computer monitor.

"Thank God!" said Michelle.

"It's a miracle!" said Robby. "You did it, sis!"

Everyone in the copter cheered.

The people now all looked up at the hovering dolphin-copter.

"And here are the Star Dolphins!" said (Ex) Pres. Clark, pointing up his finger.

The dolphin-copter settled down in the water of the pool!

In the White House, Hazel and her accomplices watched in amazement as the Star Dolphins dove out of the copter into the pool.

"I don't think it's working," said Hazel.

"Now what do we do?"

"It's time to activate plan B."

"Which is…?"

"We get out of here!" said Hazel. "There's a helicopter waiting out in the yard."

They all jumped up and ran outside to the waiting 'copter, which immediately lifted up and flew off for...?

Dr. Michael Hope had finally made his way up to the monument. He had been in touch with the Star Dolphins via radio and now knew Michelle's inspiration to deactivate Hazel's noxious substance had succeeded. He was so proud of her!

He yelled up at Pres. Clark.

"It's open house at the White House, President Clark," he said.

"You mean..." The roar of the crowd momentarily drowned out his words.

"Right," said Michael. "The Star Dolphins have informed me that Hazel and her cohorts have fled the scene of the crime."

"Ladies and gentlemen, boys and girls," said Pres. Clark into the microphone. "May I have your attention, please. I have just been informed that (Ex) Pres. Macelroy has abdicated the White House..."

A roar went up over the monument.

After the long rally was over, President Clark walked slowly up the walk to the front door of the White House, followed by Michael and Robby and Michelle, and a group of journalists, a throng on the outside of the fence cheering them on.

"It's been a long time," he said as he opened the door.

"What took you," said the woman smiling at him in the hall.

It was the President's wife!

"Surprise!" said everyone there.

"Dorothy!" he said. "I thought you had divorced me by now."

"I should have," she smiled. "But I figured you would come back someday."

They embraced as flash bulbs went off all over.

"But how did you get here?"

"The Star Dolphins…" she said, smiling mysteriously.

"Mr. President," one reporter said, "how does it feel to be back in the White House?"

"Mr. President, what's it like in the Star Dolphin's fortress on Mt. Whitney?"

"Mr. President, will you be in contact with the Russians soon now…"

"Mrs. President, did you miss your husband while he was away?"

"Mr. President, we've heard that the king of the lost race of sasquatch has asked for a private meeting with you. Is there any truth…"

"Mr. President, and what about the moon? Have the Star Dolphins really turned it into a garden planet for Earth?"

"I think I'll let Michael Hope answer that."

"No. The Martians have."

"The Martians…?"

"Mr. President…" More flash bulbs went off.

"Mr. President, what has happened to (Ex) President Macelroy?"

President Clark smiled at the reporter.

"Maybe I should let Dr. Smith, my new Sec. of State, answer that question."

Everybody looked at the young boy.

"(Ex) Pres. Macelroy and her partners were rescued at sea by a group of Eskimos after their helicopter went down over the Atlantic," he said.

Michael and Michelle and Robby all laughed.

"What…Eskimos?" said the reporters.

"Yes," he continued. "In a flying sleigh."

"You want to repeat that…"

The President chuckled.

He looked around at his friends.

"It's good to be home," he laughed.

Michael and Michelle and Robby smiled.

Then they all looked up at the harvest moon.

EPILOG

The lonely killer whale swam slowly through the oceans.

He was on his way back to his ancestral waters, his icy home of Alaska, home of totem poles and giant Kodiak bears and Indians and loggers and gold miners and oil men and snow covered glacial peaks and glacial bays and tundra and elk herds and moose and caribou and wolves and coyotes...all his realm, his domain, for he was Sir Killer, the once and future king of the Arctic.

He had rounded Cape Horn long days ago, swimming down the coast of South America, out of the tepid, blue waters of the Gulf of Mexico. He had left without goodbye. He hated sad farewells and preferred to mysteriously leave in the dead of night. He knew "they" would understand, for they understood so much. It seemed they knew all things about the universe. And perhaps they did. He was glad to have met these strange people of the sea—and the stars—but now it was time to return...

Sir Killer had passed the grey whales migrating north too from the warm waters of Baja. The greys were his usual prey... but instead he had been hunting large, voracious amounts of fish, with the help of some adventurous dolphin friends who had decided to follow him to Alaska. They would help him herd fish along the way.

The group had finally reached the coast of California, and were proceeding steadily north, past Hollywood, which had turned a killer whale into a big star recently, although Sir Killer knew little of this—just strange rumors of a brethren becoming a super-star—whatever a super-star was.

But he had heard that this killer had recently moved to the coast of "Oregon"—and was in a large whale tank there, performing tricks for all the wondering tourists, who were coming in throngs to see the "star."

As he neared the town of Newport Beach, Sir Killer picked up calls on his sonar from the direction of the town itself. This must be where the "star" was performing!

They swam slowly past. Sir Killer would have liked to see the "super-star" whale, but knew it was impossible…

He felt a little sad about it. But not for very long.

It would be soon now that he would complete his epic journey home, reach the crystalline waters which had spawned him long ago.

He wondered if he and his dolphin friends would run into his old pod. Had they established contact with the humans yet? He had let it be known when he had come upon any other killers that these dolphins were under his protection—Sir Killer—the once and future king of the Arctic!

Above, as they swam north under the starry starry sky, the moon was gleaming a strange green color. Sir Killer and the dolphins looked up at this wondrous new sight…the new moon…

On the moon…

The Martians were having a field day, wandering the lush valleys and climbing the steep, tree covered peaks, looking up at the blue-green spectacle of the Earth, hanging in the blue sky like an opal. The weak gravity of the moon made it like a vast play ground for the Martians…

In the craters, acres of fruits and vegetables were growing across the irrigated land…

Waterfalls soared from hanging lunar valleys, great trees, freed from the usual constraints of gravity, were reaching heights twice as tall as the Redwoods, geysers were sending plumes of sparkling water three times as high in the air as Old Faithful, rivers seemed to dance down their channels, song birds with wingspans larger than condors soared through the air, giant smiling Panda-like bears romped happily through the glens. The antlered Martians romped with them…

Up on Planet Shine…

It was another serene day. The watery world sparkled under its twin suns…

The Star Dolphins were observing the cosmos from their special underwater telescopes. They were right now preparing for a mission to the farthest reaches of the galaxy. They had only recently learned in the vast endlessness of the sparkling Milky Way there was another planet, not altogether unlike planet Earth, which needed a little help, so…

…Sharon, Dr. Smith's longtime friend, lay under the two suns on the beach, taking a sunbath. She had, of course, heard of the Star Dolphins rehabilitating him—he was now the ten year old "boy genius" who was President Clark's Sec of State back on home planet Earth. She would have to go there some time, but for now she would just lie here under the suns, by the sparkling, singing waves of the endless sea…where the gulls whistled like songbirds and little boys and girls played with giant Panda bears and glider horses flew over the water and dolphins held endless conversations as they romped through the pearl waves…

Suddenly, Sharon sat up. She gazed out over the vast sea. She had, without warning, just then recalled the golden, moonlit night on the beach at Key Largo so long ago when Dr. Michael Hope and her had swum out to sea to elude the authorities coming after Michael in the wake of his violent encounter with the military officer!

She felt little chills, wet from a recent dip, in the sweet sea-breeze, as she remembered…

That had been a long, long time ago and Earth was a long, long ways away…but at least Earth was a nicer place than it once was.

Thanks to Michael and Heaven and Rena and Michelle and Robby and Dr. Smith and Sharon and Johnny and Frankie and Peter and President Clark and Nick and Nancy and Vic and Diana and little Pearl and Auk and Sir Killer and Nantook…and the cast of millions.

And all the dolphins!

Appendix—Jungle Jean's "Silk String Magic Show"

Back on Earth, there was a command performance going on at the White House.

> Everyone was there.
> Ladies and Gentlemen!
> The Silk String Magic Show!
> De de de de de de de de de de de de de de de de
> Silk String Magic!
> Silk String Magic!
> Gonna cut the cards, no sleight of hand
> You'll see this ain't no jive!
> And deal to you aces four
> And to me jokers five!
> Gonna talk in circles, sing in tongues
> And make the muse appear
> Play the final, missing chord
> The sirens long to hear!
> Silk String Magic!

> Goin' 'cross the Universe, better grab your purse
> You might need it there!
> Don't forget your easy chair…uh huh!
> Say would you like to take a chance
> And baby you and I can dance
> Across the sky, way up high!
> Say would you like to go for a ride
> I caught a falling star last night
> And it can take us for a ride!

Can you see the galaxies
Go spinning off in space
Pin wheel spirals of silver and gold
They're floating there with grace
Floating out in space!

La la la!

High steppin'
High steppin'
We're goin', we're goin'
High steppin'
Tonight!
And I love you baby,
With every fiber of my soul
If I might get just a little sentimental
If you don't mind
I just might tell you all!
How you changed my life with a wave of your hand
And helped me to understand
Showed to me life's a dream
And everything's exactly like it seems!
We're goin' we're goin'
High steppin'
Tonight!

Streamline
I'm feeling fine
Streamline
I got some time
Streamline
On up the coast
Baby, you are the most!
Streamlined
Right out of my mind.
Streamline!

Now have you ever walked
Down-own-own
A country road?
Where the grasses grow right next to you?
Too good to be true, now
Too good to be true!
Now I was walking
Down-own-own
The country road…
When I saw her walking right ahead of me
She was picking flowers
Puttin' 'em in her hair
And I just had to tell her
How nice they look there!

Silk String Magic!

Bound for California!
Bound for California!
Come on brother, it's time to go
We're bound across the plains
Come on sister, see the wagons roll
There's so much to be gained!
Drinkin' water from the banks of a runnin' river
So you think maybe we could live there?
Sittin' 'round the campfire in the breeze
Listenin' to the wolves howl from the trees!
And we're bound for California!

Well we're marchin' to the sea
Yeah we're marchin' you and me!
Ah, we're marchin' to the sea.
And Peace
Hope
Truth
Love
Life
Will be our victory!

America!
You're still a dream
That's what you've always been
A hope and a prayer—
The figment of some men's imagination
But wishin' ain't a sin!
Now what are we gonna do?
We're gonna take one step and then another
We're gonna take one step and then another
Mother and father and sister and brother
We all just march on!
We're gonna take one step and make it right
We're gonna take one step and make it right.
Red and black and blue and white
We all just march on!
We're gonna sing the songs we once sung
Ring the bells we once rung!

Silk String Magic!
Gonna disappear
Right before your eyes!
Gonna make the smoke fall
Gonna make the water rise
Gonna pull a song
Right from my silk hat
And if you watch me closely now
You might see where I'm at!
Silk String Magic
I can make my fingers fly

Silk Strange Magic
I can take you to the sky!
Silk String Magic!
Gonna disappear
Right before your eyes!
(ping!)
(applause!)
The End

AFTERWORD
TO PROJECT LOVE

There are more things in heaven and earth, Horatio, than are dreamt of in your philosophy.—Hamlet

The quotation above from *Hamlet* is as true as it is obvious. There are more things in heaven and earth...And this, of course, is the reason for myths, for legends, to attempt an explanation of the unexplainable, to foster a feeling for things that cannot be rationally understood. In certain sense it may be that myth is closer to the absolute truth of the cosmos than science, simply because, unlike science, it, inherently and implicitly, recognizes, indeed glories in, those things which are beyond mere reason, which a good deal of the universe is. The scientist, if not buoyed by an unusual sense of mysticism, is "lost" when confronted with mysteries which do not fit "the facts", while the mythmaker, though is "found!" Indeed, where the scientist is faltering on the slippery turf of the unexplainable, the myth teller is on solid ground!

Of course, science fiction is a form of myth telling, and in the nebulous world of the ineffable, there is sometimes a crossover where fiction (myth) becomes truer than "fact."

Sometime after finishing the first draft of *Project Love* I happened upon a book entitled *The Sirius Mystery* by Robert Temple. In this curious (!) work is the thesis, supported by much anthropological and archaelogical research that at the time of the beginning of civilization—in contrast to an earlier, simpler state of mankind—Earth was visited by intelligent beings from a planet in the system of the star Sirius! The thesis states that the civilization of the Sumerians and Egyptians at about 3400 B.C. appeared abruptly, too abruptly to have evolved and was the result of instructions from emissaries from another star. Of course, being a writer of science fiction, I was intrigued by this novel idea, i.e. all civilization as we know it was the product of interstellar intervention.

But, as I read further, I became amazed at certain very interesting parallels to *Project Love* and these I would like to relate now.

First, though to begin where Mr. Temple begins. His interest in this matter came as a result of hearing of a "primitive" tribe in the Sudan area of northwestern Africa called the Dogon who had been studied for several years by the French anthropologists ("eminent," Temple calls them) M. Griaule and G. Dieterlen, who lived with the tribe from 1946-50 before publishing, in 1954, and article entitled "A Sudanese Sirius System," which dealt with extremely secret traditions of the Dogon, who had decided, after much discussion among the initiates, to impart this knowledge to the anthropologists. Their cosmology states that the focal point of creation was, not Sirius itself, very visible to the eye as the brightest star in the sky, but a star which revolves around Sirius, so faint it was not successfully photographed until 1970! In other words, the Sudanese tribe had a tradition based on an invisible star which was not discovered until rather late in the 20th century by modern astronomical methods. What's more, they knew the length of time it took for the star, a white dwarf (called by scientists Sirius B), to orbit Sirius—60 years. The Dogan said this star was "the smallest and heaviest star" in the universe (this is an apt description of a white dwarf star) and that it was invisible.

Through much schlorarly research, Mr. Temple imparts the thesis (as if the above were not extraordinary enough in and of itself) that the knowledge of and worship of this invisible star in the Sirius system is also the basis of ancient Sumerian and Egyptian mythology, the Dogon being descendants of the Egyptians. For instance, the Egyptian god Isis is identified with Sirius, and her companion, Osiris, once thought to be Orion, is in Temple's hypothesis, Sirius B. (Does "Osiris" mean, perchance, "around Sirius"?)

The obvious question is how did these people know of a star only discovered recently? The Dogon themselves give the "answer" in their myths: creatures called Nommo (the singular form representing the plural) descended in an "ark" from the sky and imparted this knowledge (and much other knowledge) before returning to their home planet, which revolved around, not Sirius, but its small, invisible (from Earth) companion.

One may view all this as one wishes. However what intrigued me was the nature of these creatures who came to Earth and imparted vast knowledge. A single picture is worth a thousand words and here I impart a (simplified) Dogon drawing of Nommo:

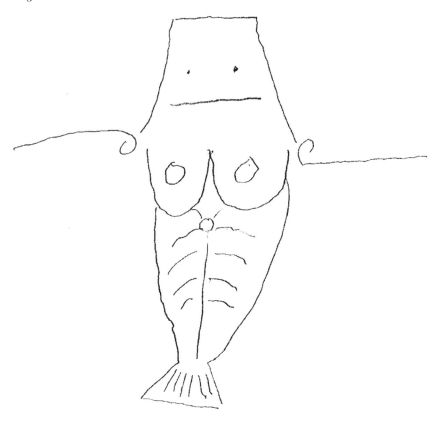

"Di tigi"—"master of the water!" A dolphin!

Nommo descended in an ark which the Dogon called a "star" (as I call the ships of my interstellar dolphins) and here is a Dogon drawing of the descent of the spaceship of Nommo, a swirling sphere:

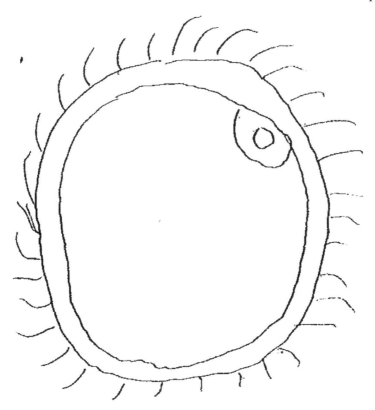

I was, as I said amazed by these parallels to *Project Love*. What's more, the descendents of the Nommo had stayed in Earth's waters—dolphins!—and the Nommo said they would someday return to Earth—the return of the Star Dolphins!

As is usually the case with the "simple" doctrines of "primitive" peoples, great depths were revealed. Consider: various elements of Judeo-Christian doctrine are related to various manifestations of Nommo, and one may read of these "weighty" matters on pp. 215-216 of Temples' book. Suffice it to say, the ideas are astounding.

The further information that these creatures had been teachers to the ancient Sumerians,* who describe them as coming from the seas in a "form between a man and a fish" (Dr. Michael Hope?!) whose teachings the Sumerians passed onto all mankind, put a new "light", as it were, on my novel. It now contained certain universal implications I myself had not seen—or even dreamed of...

Scott Campbell

*The beautiful story in the ancient Summerian epic *Gilgamish*, perhaps the earliest known story, was, in this hypothesis, inspired by this occurrence (the "heavy star," for instance). *Gilgamish*, of course, deals with the most absolute of themes, love, death and everlasting life, and probably influenced the Bible itself. Certainly the transformation of Gilgamesh from a tyrant to a compassionate seeker of the truth through love of and loss of his friend, is one the most poignant tales in all literature.

The Star Dolphins would be pleased!

"A true friend is like another me."

Made in the USA
San Bernardino, CA
30 March 2014